IN THE VALLEY
OF GHOSTS

Darith woke trembling in the dark and heard a gasping cry from Gonquin. Rolling up on one elbow he saw, gathered outside the circle of magic, a host of the ghosts of the valley. Their eyes were hungry, burning with desire. Their bloodless faces, blue in the doleful light of torches, pressed close on every side. Reeling, Darith sprang to his feet.

Then, from the distance, came a dreadful laugh.

The ranks of ghosts parted.

On the silver path of moonlight, a dark figure rode, mounted on a tall, grim beast.

Fearless, the rider advanced and Darith felt pain gnawing at his gut. Three eyes glowed, violet, cold, deadly...

Worlds of Fantasy from Avon Books

Blood of the Colyn Muir

Paul Edwin Zimmer
and Jon DeCles

AVON BOOKS ◆ NEW YORK

BLOOD OF THE COLYN MUIR is an original publication of Avon Books. This work has never before appeared in book form. This work is a novel. Any similarity to actual persons or events is purely coincidental.

AVON BOOKS
A division of
The Hearst Corporation
105 Madison Avenue
New York, New York 10016

First Avon Books Printing: October 1988

AVON TRADEMARK REG. U.S. PAT. OFF. AND IN OTHER COUNTRIES, MARCA REGISTRADA, HECHO EN U.S.A.

Printed in the U.S.A.

K–R 10 9 8 7 6 5 4 3 2 1

To Diana,
without whom this book
could not have been written . . .

Table of Contents

CHAPTER ONE
The Heir of Colyn

The Sword came nearer and nearer, swinging in great arcs, dripping with blood.

It was not like the other swords: it did not glisten bright metal. Its curved deadly blade was black as velvet: warm, filled with alien life...

There was something about it more horrible than the way it cut down the men around him, something his mind refused to focus on. He knew that he would rather draw his own dagger and plunge it into his heart than die by that Sword.

He reached for the dagger...

The sword arced down on him and he screamed with his shoulder's pain and everything vanished as—

...the ship swung wildly in the wind. Darith's hammock slammed against the wall, and he was suddenly awake. White-hot pain seared the arrow-wound in his shoulder. The violence of the *Maid of Tharda*'s motion told him that the wind had changed. Awareness trained by years at sea calculated the pressures of the myriad forces of air and water against hull and sail: the wind that had been hurrying them homeward under full sail was backing to southeastward now, as indecisive and undependable, Darith thought, as his own leadership had been.

A whistle shrilled above, like an echo of the wind, and bare feet pattered on the decking overhead as seamen turned out to trim the big sails. He could hear the familiar rattle of canvas, and a curse as someone lost his footing in the dark. They must be taking a reef in the mainsail to compensate for the freshening wind—in a moment the *Maid*'s smoother motion confirmed that guess, and Darith eased back with a sigh.

Roaring, the cold sea tossed mountainous waves against the distant shore. On a night like this, men would be bringing in their livestock and tightening the ropes that held down their thatch, shuttering their windows and barring their doors to keep the violence of the storm at bay. If only it were so easy to shut out memories! With his right hand, Darith clutched the ropes over his head and tried, vainly, to lift himself.

It was no use. He was too weak from loss of blood. He lay breathing heavily in the dark of the little cabin. A stray wind had blown out the oil lamp, and the hot reek mingled nauseatingly with the mixed scents of brine and damp wool. Where was Avlath? Asleep, no doubt: the battle had been long; no sense disturbing him just to make a light.

Nearly half his ships were gone and half his men dead. If the sleek black ships of the enemy had followed . . .

The wind howled, and the ship pitched. Darith reached out, hoping to keep the hammock from slamming into the wall again. As the rolling motion slowed, he felt another presence in the cabin with him.

"Who is there?" he called, his dry throat rasping. "Avlath? Would you get me some water, and make a light?"

No answer, and no sound of breathing. Darith listened intently—

A dry sound of laughter, like leaves in an autumn wind.

It was watching him, in the dark, *there,* in the corner . . .

"*Who's there?*" he demanded, suddenly afraid. This was how you felt Death coming. The towering black figure from his nightmare surged suddenly into his consciousness— "*Speak, whoever you are!*"

He felt it move toward him in the dark. Sudden, curling pain coiled and stirred in his abdomen.

"A light! I'll see who you are!" He grabbed the ropes and struggled to climb from his swaying hammock, but only tore the wound in his shoulder open again.

"*Avlath! Come here!*"

The dry leaf laughter came again, closer.

He reached out, groping for the peg where his sword-belt hung, and pulled the sword from the scabbard. It seemed too heavy to lift. Had he lost so much blood?

Awkwardly he stabbed out with his remaining strength. A chill went up his arm.

The sword fell from strengthless fingers. He shrank back,

knowing that if he reached out he would touch the thing. . . .

Footsteps. A faint light in the crack around the door . . .

"Avlath!"

The door flew open and streams of light flooded the compartment. The Chamberlain stood there, his sandy hair catching the lamplight from the passageway behind him in a straw-coloured halo as he balanced in the rocking doorway.

"Yes, Lord?"

"There is—there's been someone here." Darith fell back, panting. The pain in his middle was gone, but the arrow-wound still ached.

Avlath entered and checked the corners of the room, tossing aside piled clothing and battered armor.

"No one here now," he said.

Darith was suddenly glad for the man's unshakable stolidity.

"Light the lamp," he said. "It blew out while I slept."

"In *here?*" Avlath stared at him, eyebrows raised. "This far into the ship?" He felt the top of the bulkhead for the flint and steel and fumbled to spark the tinder. It glowed like a red eye in the shadow as he blew on it, then brightened to flame. In a moment the lamp swung from the bracket above the bulkhead once more.

"I didn't get up and put it out!"

"You should try to get some sleep," said Avlath, still staring oddly. "Do not let bad dreams—"

"If I was dreaming, why is my sword on the floor?" Darith snapped. Avlath stared at the fallen sword, then lifted it, frowning. Lamplight glimmered on steel and struck green fire from the gems in its hilt as he sheathed it and hung it on its peg again.

"Did you—hear someone?"

"No, but there was someone here! I drew my sword to protect myself. I stabbed at—whoever it was—but I couldn't hold the sword"—he shook his head—"and I've torn the wound open again."

Avlath got a small jar of salve from the chest in the corner, and tore clean bandages from a bolt of cloth.

"You've lost a great deal of blood."

"I've lost a great deal," said Darith, "not only blood."

Avlath did not answer, but went to work on the wound. The coppery tang of fresh blood mingled with the other odors in the small room.

"Tell me," said Darith after a long silence. "What about the men?"

Avlath was suddenly very still, as though caught at some improper act. His eyes fled his master's.

"Have I lost my command?"

"No, Lord."

"No? But perhaps they're no longer interested in following the man who led them to defeat?"

"Perhaps it—was not wise to go ashore," Avlath said hesitantly, his weathered face knotted in a frown. "We could have used fire-arrows to burn their ships, and then attacked. If we had divided their forces . . ." He fell silent, and bent to bind the clean bandage smoothly across the wound.

Darith winced as it tightened, seeing once more in memory the flotilla of enemy ships descending like a flock of crows upon the defenceless land. His own offensive strategy had seemed so obvious—to send boarding parties to overpower the minimal guards left on the black ships while the main force made a landing and marched to rescue the town.

But even a pirate feared to be caught between an enemy fleet and a hostile shore. At the first threat to their ships, the pirates had turned like a wave curling back from a breakwater, sweeping back over their pursuers with a disciplined effectiveness so different from the ragged fervor Darith was accustomed to in raiders that for one fatal moment he had not been sure how to respond, and in that moment—although it was only now that he understood how it had happened—the battle had been lost. Darith remembered how they had swarmed to box his men between blocks of bowmen. Arrows had scythed down half his force before they could close.

His memories of what had followed were a chaos of spattering blood and dying light on swinging swords, of the battle cries of his own men, harsh as squabbling gulls, fading into silence as the foe came silently after them.

That was what had taken the heart from them, Darith thought now. For how could you summon the fury to resist an enemy that came on with the passionless efficiency of a farmer scything grain, with no emotion at all?

Even then, he supposed, they could have tried to disable the black ships and fight their way back to their own, but his crews were frantic to reach their own vessels, and in that race for time the enemy proved faster than men plucked from their ploughlands and packed into the merchant caravels of Dalgir to fight upon the sea.

The warriors who were struggling to climb back aboard their ships had gotten in the way of the seamen who were striving to raise sail, and the Pirates had followed like shadows, overpowering some of the vessels still at anchor, and flowing in a dark tide across the water to ram others and send them to the bottom of the sea. And then for the first time he had seen the mocking flicker of their black flags against the fading sky, like the wings of ravens unfolding as they settled down to rend their prey.

"It is always easy to chart the right course *after* the event," Darith said bitterly.

"True, my Lord," said Avlath. "But *you* are the Colyn Muir. It is your part to see the right course *before* the event."

Darith closed his eyes, his lips pressing his teeth, remembering the days when he had been only the younger son of the Colyn Muir, when he had been free.

"And now they have have lost their confidence in me."

"My Lord, they—have lost many friends. They have no confidence in themselves. In the old times it was different. Peace has softened them. And these were only boys from Balcolyn and the valley. The hill clans were not with us. For many men, this was their first battle, and it has hurt—"

"Perhaps they think that *I* am free of pain?" Darith snarled.

"You are the Colyn Muir," Avlath repeated, finality in his voice. "They cannot believe in your pain."

Perhaps not, thought Darith then. Perhaps they saw their chieftain as he himself imagined Colyn the Great, his ancestor—a figure as much taller than they were as the clansfolk were above the stature of other men, with the thick, dark hair that Colyn had bequeathed to all his line. Did they see shoulders beginning to bow beneath the weight of a Lordship he had never desired, and sea-colored eyes forever haunted by what he had lost? Darith supposed that the grief in his eyes must be even greater now.

"And you, Avlath?"

"You are the Colyn Muir," Avlath said a third time, "but I am your Chamberlain. My father served your father. I have known your household all my life. I know you have blood, Lord."

"So you do," said Darith, considering him with a tired smile. "It covers your jerkin where you dressed my wound." The storm-wind whistled from the hatches, and blew skittering down the companionway. Darith shivered. "Bring your hammock in here, Avlath. Stay and see that the lamp is still lit at sunrise."

"My Lord?" Avlath's thick eyebrows lifted in surprise. "What is wrong?"

"Nothing," said Darith. "But indulge me. That wind, just now. The lights fluttered, and—and it brought—a feeling. Perhaps it *was* only a dream—but I'd rather not have it happen again. When will we make landfall?"

"Within two days. You've slept a great deal."

"That's just as well." Darith sank back in the hammock. "We will not stop long in Dalgir"—he snorted—"only long enough to leave news of our defeat! I must ride." He rubbed his eyes. "Back to Colyn Muir. You tell me we might not have lost if we had had the hill clans. I hope you're right, Avlath—for they are all that is left to us now." He frowned, counting them in memory—the fe Mavron, the fe Morulvu, the fe Varruk Clan of Caiplic, the fe Connuara of Ashir Fuaran, Clan fe Rogoin . . . and, of course, Scarriv.

Raonull fe Scarriv, with his angry eyes. The rivalry between fe Scarriv and Colyn Muir went back past the days of the Kingdom's founding. But now there was more at stake than pride.

"But, Lord," Avlath began, "a physician—"

"There is no time! I feel it! Did you not see the flag the Pirate flew? Black, with three white circles?"

After the battle, the raven flutter of those banners had only been part of the general horror, but now his awareness prickled at the memory, as if that symbol held some significance he should recognize.

"I—do not know its origin, my Lord."

"Nor I! But that flag—and something *was* here, tonight! The Council of chieftains must be summoned. We must return to Colyn Muir, and quickly!"

"My Lord?" There was fear on the Chamberlain's face. "It—it is not—the Curse?"

Darith sank back with a flutter in his belly that reminded him uneasily of the curling pain that he had felt when the Shadow neared.

He'd been a fool.

Once the Curse on his line had inspired awe in the people, proof of the blood of Colyn the Great, a link with the days of the War of Kings. But now it was only a sickness that left a man to die clawing at his gut. The Line of Colyn was long divorced from greatness: that men born of it died alike was only inconvenience—inconvenience leading to insurrection.

Darith had lost a battle, and now he'd asked for company

in the night. Whether or not the Curse had come to claim him made little difference. Raonull fe Scarriv would twist things in and about until war broke out among the clans, and the fisherfolk of the coast would be defenceless and helpless when the Pirate came again.

There was one way he could stem the flood of chaos. He could go to the City of the King and swear allegiance as his Fathers had done before him. That would silence fe Scarriv.

But if he did that, he would be breaking his own most solemn oath.

If he did that, any oath he swore would be meaningless.

"The Curse?" he said, forcing his voice to lightness. "I've not died! There's no great pain on me, except for the shoulder. But get your hammock, and keep the light. Anyone can be kept awake by bad dreams, and I need sleep, if this wound is to heal."

He lay back, and Avlath drew the heavy tartan over him once more, chequered with sea gray and black and a crimson dark as the blood that was drying on the discarded bandages on the floor.

Memories rushed over him . . .

Darith, you're a headstrong fool! his father's voice bellowed, far in the past. *Always talking of greatness! Always wanting to go elsewhere!*

And he *had* gone elsewhere.

He remembered the joy of his first ship, springing beneath him like a live thing as he headed her out to sea. He had hunted legends in those days, as a merchant seeks gold, and he had found them, too—uncharted islands, and strange creatures from the depths of the sea, and countries the men of Tondur believed to be no more than a Bard's bright tale.

He remembered Tharda, white towers tipped with gold rising from a golden, blue-flecked sea. Green meadows, hanging trees with yellow blossoms more sweetly scented than a spring dawn. Precious gems rolling in the surf on the white-sand beaches, polished by the waves of eons.

Tharda, the White Realm, the Magician's Resting-place . . .

And Lonarissa, seated on a white ivory dais: Lonarissa, daughter of the King; hair dark and deep as the night around the ever-white moon, gold-eyed as the corona of the sun in eclipse. The complexion of the lotus floating above a pool on a gentle breeze, pale pink, pearl-white blushed with a sunset brush. Like a woman fashioned by elves out of shells . . . or as if the winds, the sculptors of clouds, had deigned to show how woman ought to be made.

A gentler dreaming, this, than the demonic imaginings that had been haunting him. Darith clung to the vision of Lonarissa as if it were a talisman that could keep away the dark as the *Maid of Tharda* thrashed through the black waters toward dawn.

And as sleep took him, it seemed to him that her eyes glowed like twin suns, but her hair swirled out around her, shimmering with all the starry splendor of night. She reached out to him then, and words distilled like harp notes from the air:

"Oh, my Beloved, I will always be with you—only keep faith with me . . ."

Darith pulled his plaid more tightly around him and eased his weight against the rail as they rounded Wolf Point and moved into the quieter waters of the bay. The port city of Dalgir clung to the curve of the hills that sloped down to the bay. Beyond them, the mist-hazed ridges of the great mountains grew translucent with distance as they stretched southward toward the heartlands of Tondur.

The pale stone walls of the town were glowing bravely as the sun sank at last beneath banked clouds; slate roofs still glistened from the rain. Defying the damp, bright banners hung beneath the many-paned windows. Limp banners hung from the poles on the docks as well—white and azure and gold and the crimson of Colyn Muir—a fine display to welcome conquering heroes home. Bagpipes boomed and whined.

As the *Maid of Tharda* eased in toward the quay, Darith heard the bleating as the pipers faltered. For a moment drums continued to patter. Then they too ceased, and the only welcome song was the yammering of the scavenger gulls who followed the ships.

A word from the captain brought the foresail down in a rustle of canvas, and let the *Maid*'s own momentum bring her the rest of the way. Lines snaked toward them from the dock and skilled hands made them fast. The ship came to rest in silence.

To either side, other ships were sliding in to their moorings; sails drooping like the wings of wounded birds. In ones and twos and threes they tied up at docks where a dozen vessels could shelter, and had sheltered, two weeks ago. Storm and battle had tattered their banners and battered their carven bows. Those who waited on the docks did not need to see the bloodstains that storm had washed away to know that there had been no victory.

Clad soberly in black or maroon or indigo, the merchants watched on the waterfront as what remained of the army of Colyn Muir came ashore.

"Where are the rest of the ships?" asked one, hoping for good news despite the faces of Darith's warriors.

"Under the water." Darith's face felt stiff as he forced the words out. Leaning on his spear to spare his wounded leg, he limped across the weathered planks.

"We lost. You must close the harbour now, and prepare for siege. I go this day, without rest, to summon the hill clans to war. You must refit and repair the ships that remain, and ready any other vessel that will take the sea, and have them ready against our return. We still may win, but it will not be easy. This enemy is very strong."

The merchants stood looking out to sea, faces crumpling as if the lost ships sank before their eyes, while Darith waited for them to speak. *Curse me!* he cried silently. *My poor judgement cost my men their lives and you your livelihood! Why are you silent?*

But loyalty to the House of Colyn Muir still ruled them, or perhaps the disaster had simply been too great for any answer, for they said nothing. Avlath caught up with him then, and Darith was glad for the support of his arm as he continued up the hill toward the stables where his horses were boarded. And he was gladder still to leave the town whose dark windows all seemed to stare at him with accusing eyes, and take the road to the hills.

CHAPTER TWO
In the Bard's Tower

"Mannus!" Ylsa's voice cracked and subsided into an aggrieved mumbling. "Now where's the lad gone? A plague on him! I told my Lord there'd come no good of taking a Tanner's brat to serve him—it's against the right order of things! I told him—"

Mannus grinned, snatched up the grain sack, and slipped around a corner into the long shadow of the Bard's Tower. He had heard what Ylsa said to Lord Darith too many times to need to listen now. According to Ylsa, her advice could have prevented every calamity since the world's beginning: if Colyn the Great had taken her advice, he might have been King in Kaerbradan.

He wondered suddenly if the old crone thought that her advice could cure even the Curse that late or soon carried off every lord of Colyn's line, and his skin chilled as he realized that he had never once even heard her mention it. Chickens were clucking peaceably in the sunshine. Mannus stepped away from the shadow and began to scatter grain for them from the sack in his hand.

Maybe the Curse has died out—it's been so long! My Lord was well when he left us—it will not happen to him! Mannus's heart cried.

No one spoke of the Curse anymore. Only Mannus's father seemed to remember it, who had been castle-folk, though not noble-born, and served Lord Darith's father until the old lord died. It was afterward that he went to the village and married the Tanner's daughter and learned his trade and started a family.

And then one day a tall dark-haired man with the look of unshed tears behind his pale eyes had stopped to speak with the headman of the village just as Mannus dashed out of an alleyway, pursued by a carter whom the boy had tried to stop from beating his horse. Mannus knew only that the booted feet behind which he had taken refuge had not spurned him, and the threatened blows did not fall. He had not understood that this man was the Lord of the Clan, the Colyn Muir himself, until the Chamberlain Avlath had laughed and said that a lad with such a feeling for horses should be learning to tend them, not to make their hides into leather.

"Do you always pit yourself against enemies so much your superior?"

The Lord's voice had brought Mannus's gaze upward at last.

"Was *not* super—peror!" the boy had stammered, and remembering, wondered how he had dared. "*I* wouldn't've hurt the horse!"

For a moment, then, those sad eyes had warmed with the faintest of smiles.

"Well then," Darith of Colyn Muir had told him then, "perhaps you had better come up to the Castle and help protect *me!*"

And though Mannus's father had railed at him and promised that it did no good to serve great lords—that good or bad they had no care for common folk, and would break his heart one day—Mannus had gone, and had grown up in the castle, playing in the gloomy corridors, and learning to shoot the ancient crossbow—broken and useless now—that had hung on the castle wall.

It had been silly to think that a child's strength could aid the Lord of the Land; the wisdom of his seventeen years told Mannus that now. But those years had also given him a man's height and a man's burly shoulders, and there were more dangers in this world than the Curse of Colyn Muir.

Lord Darith should have let him go with them to the war.

"*There* you are!" Ylsa's fingers closed hard on his ear and he yelped with the unexpected pain.

"You *told* me to feed the chickens—"

"I told you to take the slops out to the pigs first, you dolt! You want to be a soldier and you can't follow a simple order! What kind of a warrior do you think you'd be?"

A great one! thought Mannus furiously. *But feeding pigs is not the way I'm going to learn how!* He wrenched free of her grasp and stood glaring down at her, breathing hard with the effort not to strike her down. The strength in him shouted for some worthy adversary.

And then the old woman's eyes, that were usually as sharp and self-absorbed as those of her own hogs, grew round and her gaze slid past him. Even the chickens had fallen silent. Mannus felt his anger vanish as he turned to see.

The Bard of Colyn Muir was standing in the doorway to his Tower.

Except when the old man came out in his snowy robes of office for some court function, Mannus could not recall when he had last seen the Bard in the light of day. And he was not robed now. A stained nightshirt showed every line of his gaunt form—had he always been so thin? They set his meals on the chest at the foot of the spiral stair at morn and at evening, but no man knew if he came down to fetch them himself or magicked them up to his chamber at the top of the Tower.

He did not look as if he had been eating them.

The Bard took a halting step forward, and the shadow seemed to flow with him. A little wind stirred the dust, and Mannus's nostrils flared at the aromatic scent of incense and something more familiar and less pleasant—the sharp-sweet odor of illness and old age.

"Help me!"

Mannus was not sure if he was hearing that appeal with his ears. Ylsa took an automatic step forward and focussed on the dark stains that spattered the chest of the old man's gown. Her fingers flickered in the Sign against Evil then, and she turned.

"It is the Curse of Colyn," she whispered. "Get away from him!"

Whether or not the Bard had called aloud, everyone in the Castle seemed to have heard. Suddenly the courtyard was full of people.

"What is it? What's wrong?"

"So close to the Lords all those years . . . their Curse has spread to the Bard." Ylsa pushed past them. "His spirits have turned against him!"

The Bard managed another step forward, then stopped, panting, holding to the stones. From behind him came a silvery shimmer of bells.

"The plague!"

"The Curse!"

"Demons! We'll all die!" Now everyone was backing away.

The powers of the Bard had been the wonder of Tondur, and its fear—especially in the Castle, where men could hear the strange sounds that sometimes came from the Tower, and see the odd light that flickered in its slitted windows. What safety could there be in the world, if such a wonder-worker could die?

And if the disease that killed the Lords could strike their servants, what safety could there be for anyone here?

Mannus found his voice suddenly: "We don't know what it is!" So Ylsa did know about the Curse—but it was impossible for it to have struck the Bard! "Will you believe a silly old woman's guess? Come back—we have to help him!"

"Fool! If it's only the plague, the danger will be ended when he dies!" said one of the stable hands. "But if the Curse is catching or his demons have betrayed him, we're all doomed!" He plucked at Mannus's sleeve, but the boy shrugged him away.

Slowly the Bard slid down until he seemed little more than a crumpled heap of rags against the wall. But his eyes were on Mannus, and his eyes were terrible. Held by that gaze, Mannus still sensed the silence around him and knew that everyone else was gone.

Come to me—my strength is gone! You must help me!

"What if I refuse you—will you force me to your will?"

I will die . . . came the desperate thought. *I must not die. You have to help me live, boy, until the Lord returns!*

"And if I do not?" Mannus fought to free his will.

"Then *he* will die," the Bard said aloud.

Abruptly the Bard's compulsion was gone, but it had been replaced by a greater one.

Mannus nodded. "What do you want me to do?"

The passage of the mountains took a week for Darith and what remained of his men.

As if the weather were in league with the Pirate, vicious winds stripped the new snow from the peaks in long white banners and flung it down the passes. Its icy fingers clawed through the thick wool of Darith's tartan as if it were gauze, and the wound in his shoulder ached fiercely.

The horses were out of condition from weeks of idleness; they staggered as the pathway steepened, and as they climbed, the morning sunlight failed to melt the ice that rimed the stones. Constant alertness was needed to keep them from falling. By the time the party reached the summit three animals had been lost, two from broken legs, and another whose slip sent it screaming into the gulfs below. That one had taken its rider with it. But the man had made no sound at all, only bounced from rock to rock, limp as an abandoned doll, until he disappeared.

The men's condition was a little better. They were hill-men—his own levy from the valley of Colyn Muir—but not equipped for wintry weather, and exhausted by weeks at sea. The nights were bitter, and frostbite was an added danger to men already weakened by wounds.

Darith rode muffled to the eyes in fur and tartan, but the wind that chilled his flesh was no colder than the fear that filled his soul.

Once, it was said, this road had linked all of Tondur, in the legendary days of the Sacred Kings of Old, before the invasion—before Colyn. Once the road had gone on to Kaerbradan, where the Sacred Kings had ruled, linking the warm lowlands with Dalgir and all the realm.

But now that road led through Haunted Valley, where no man went.

Snow already smothered the central peaks in white: a hard winter would block the passes. Then Dalgir would have to defend itself from attack without help from the highlands, and the treaties that supplied ships for the Colyn Muir would be broken.

Not that the treaties would matter then, Darith thought. The Merchants of Dalgir would not put up much of a fight. The city would fall with little resistance unless he could bring the hill clans to its aid.

But for years now, Raonull of Scarriv had waited for a chance to revolt, and now he had his excuse. Darith's fealty had not been conveyed to the King, and the Colyn Muir had proved a poor general. The battle had been lost. Darith could hear fe Scarriv now—and see him, as he had seen him last, black-haired and rangy, green eyes slitted with anger.

"*How can you speak* for *the King when you've never even spoken to him!*" Raonull had roared. "*You've got my fealty by a trick, under false pretences! If you're not the King's vassal—*"

"*I speak for Colyn Muir,*" Darith had answered, very softly. "*Who speaks for Colyn speaks for the King.*" Darith was willing to bear much from Raonull's sharp tongue for the sake of the precarious peace among the Clans, but this was dangerously close to treason.

"*Oh, aye, I know! Colyn Muir put the King upon his throne with his magic sword, or whatever mad tale it is they*

*tell, and so the King gave him power over all these hills. Aye,
but 'twas the King gave the Power, and he gave it to your
Fathers one after the other, but he's never given to you! If you
do not go to Kaerbradan, perhaps then I'll go to the City of
the King, and then when I come back, perhaps I will be the
one who speaks for Colyn!"*

"But you have none of the blood of Colyn!" the Bard's
rich voice had said, from near the fire where he sat tuning his
harp. *"Neither the blood nor the Curse! And do not think the
King will not know! The Eyes of the Crown are even now—"*

"Ah, mist and moonshine!" Raonull believed in nothing
he could not see. *"All these fables of the olden gods and the
sacred powers of the Crowns of the King and Queen: you
pious fools make me sick!"*

"If you do not believe in the Crown," asked the Bard,
*"why does it matter whether the Colyn Muir has taken your
fealty to the King or not?"*

"I believe in Power"—an elegant hand smoothed dark
hair as Raonull smiled—*"or you can call it Law. Some call it
crime. It's all the same. The Colyn Muir."*—his eyes raked
Darith insolently—*"represents the Power of the King. He has
no power of his own."*

"If you believe that, Lord Scarriv—"

"Oh yes, you've men enough," Raonull mocked, *"because
of their oaths to you. But can you lead them in battle? Well,
we shall see. If you can wield this Power, then it does not
matter whether it is the King's or your own. And if not"*—he
laughed—*"well, that won't matter either, will it? My Ancestors were wealthy before the War of Kings. Up and down this
coast they raided where they would. Until Colyn came. But
that was long ago. The line of Colyn is not what it was."*

And Darith had known then that he was in danger not
only from Scarriv's sneer but from his sword, and from the
sword of black-bearded Finn fe Scarriv of Rathnolawn, his
cousin, and those of their followers and kinsmen.

And now the failure that Scarriv had been waiting for had
come.

Why, Raonull would ask, defend Tondur from the Pirate?
Why not raid the coast, instead?

From the upper levels of the Bard's Tower, you could see
the whole valley.

To Mannus, who had never been beyond its borders, it
seemed suddenly smaller. From here, Colyn Muir was only a
green slash among a welter of blue-hazed hills. The snow-

capped summits of the tallest peaks seemed to float on the horizon, and the world fell away beyond them in dim folds that hid—what? Experience gave him nothing for imagination to build on. Perhaps it was the substances whose odors still lingered in the Bard's workroom that inspired his visions, or perhaps after so many years the magic worked there had seeped into the stones.

Not that Mannus had much time for musing, at least not at first, for the Bard had not been exaggerating his weakness, and for a time Mannus feared the old man would die before the Colyn Muir came home again whether he had help or no. But presently his condition grew, if not better, at least stable.

Mannus knew better than to do more than straighten the tottering piles of books and manuscripts that made a maze of the Bard's sleeping chamber, but at least he could sweep the paths between them, and open a window when the days were warmest to blow the dust away and let a little fresh air into the room.

And then there was nothing to do but wait, and gaze out of the window upon the world.

"Boy, you stare like a tethered gamecock," the Bard said. It was one of his better days.

Mannus shrugged. "When my lord left, I wanted to go along to protect him, as if he were going on a day's hunting after boar. I had not realized that there was so much world beyond our mountains."

"Do you fear it?"

Mannus nodded. "But I still want to go."

The old man made a sound, of satisfaction or perhaps amusement, deep in his throat.

"Leaving, you shall return; losing; you shall gain; serving, you shall be master."

"What?" Mannus turned to stare. "What do you mean?" he asked. But the Bard was asleep.

The gaunt moon swelled as if it were sucking the Bard's last strength away. Then came a bitter night when the old man seemed seized with some fever. The glitter in his eye silenced the boy's protests. Trembling, Mannus helped him to put on his robes.

"Go now to the gate and wait there," whispered the Bard. "The Colyn Muir is coming. You must bring him to me!"

"But you're ill!"

"I will live long enough!" A fit of coughing tore at his throat, and Mannus held the thin shoulders, feeling life flicker within the cage of the old man's chest like a frightened bird. "All the Kingdom is ill, boy! If Darith cannot aid the King, then the black—"

Coughing cut off his words again: blood flew from his lips.

"You have served me well," the Bard added when he could speak. "You will have your heart's desire, and whether that is a curse or a blessing depends on you!"

Mannus backed away and the old man began to laugh. As he started down the winding stair he saw that the Bard had taken a packet of colored powder and was painfully drawing patterns upon the stone floor.

It was dusk, with a round moon rising, when the last of the army caught sight of Castle Colyn, two miles below. Halfway there, smoke curled up from the chimneys of the village, and beyond the castle rose the twin peaks of the Devil's Jaws.

The village was the worst part of the journey. At the first sound of hoofbeats, doors flew open, and women came running out. Sometimes children in nightshirts were with them. Darith kept his eyes straight ahead, and clenched white-knuckled fists on his reins.

For some women there were returning husbands or sons: for more than half there would be only endless empty night.

When Darith passed the last houses of the village, only Avlath rode at his side. Tree-shapes grew indistinct as night closed in. Ghostly moonlight paled the fields. Recently mown stalks of wheat became an army of silver swords rising from the ground. *So fierce a land,* Darith thought, *with even the grain militant in moonlight.*

The Bard's Tower, shrouded in vines, rose above grey stone walls to obscure the moon as they approached. No light in the tower tonight, Darith noted. Perhaps the Bard was healing a sick child, or chanting a rhyme to comfort new widows—but no, the Bard was old, beyond such things now.

"No lights, my Lord," said Avlath, at his side.

Not only the Bard's Tower was dark. There was not a light to be seen in any of the dozen short, thick towers of the castle.

"Do you think that the Scarriv Clan could have seized the Castle while I was away?"

"Look there," said Avlath. "A light! At the gate—"

The gate was opening. Darith drew his sword from its sheath, and touched his horse lightly with his spurs.

"If this is an ambush," he growled, "fe Scarriv may learn that the Line of Colyn is not fallen so far as he thought!"

But there was only a single man in the gap as the great oaken gates swung wide: a brown-haired, brown-clad youth who held a torch high. Darith recognised him.

"Mannus," he said, reining up his horse. "Where is everyone? Why is the castle dark?"

"It is as the Bard said it would be," Mannus whispered as though to himself—then, straightening: "My Lord, the Bard —has need of you, in his Tower, now!"

"I asked why the castle is dark!" Darith snapped.

"It is the Bard!" exclaimed the boy. "He is ... ill! The other servants were frightened. They went to stay with their kin in the village."

"Then you are alone here?" asked Darith. Clearly, the boy was covering for the other cowards, but that did not matter now.

"Except for the Bard, my Lord," said Mannus. "The others—they fear that—that the Curse has spread from the Line of Colyn Muir, like a plague! That it has spread to the Bard, and will spread to them also, if they come near. And the Bard—I think he is near death. He is in pain—in delirium—just this moment he ordered me to come to the gates, and bring you to him."

"If he knew that you were coming, then the Bard has magic still!" said Avlath, drawing up his horse beside Darith's.

"So it would appear," Darith agreed, then, to Mannus, "Where is he?"

"In his Tower."

"You have been in the Tower?" Darith asked, startled. The Bard's Tower had been inviolate, forbidden even to the Colyn Muir himself, since the castle was first built.

"He called me there, to carry messages and tend to his needs," said Mannus. "My Lord, you *must* come quickly! He is near death. He says it is urgent. Something—something about the King."

Darith felt his face flush with anger. Even now, even dying, the Bard would try to force him to break his oath!

Sliding from his horse's back, he reached for the torch, and took it.

"Care for my horse," he said sharply. "I will have no more of this!" Mannus went white.

"My Lord, he is *dying!* Surely you will not—you would not be harsh with him on his deathbed?"

"He has been harsh with me," said Darith, "to make such

a demand. He knows my ways. He knows his death will not change them!"

As he strode through the gate, he remembered . . .

Remembered the scream from behind the doors of the bedchamber.

"*At least give me your word!*" the Bard had said.

"*I cannot!*" Darith cried in answer.

"*Then she may die! These are matters of ancient magic, bonds created long before we were born. We are powerless before such forces! Say it to me now, that you will go and swear allegiance to the King in the east.*"

Trembling with rage, Darith walked across the outer courtyard, while the light of his torch set gargoyles to dancing and snapping their stone jaws. This outer court sheltered the villagers in time of war. To his right, the entrance to the great hall yawned, black and empty.

The castle had been built as a circle, with the Bard's Tower at the center within its own inner courtyard. The rusted iron gates were ajar. Darith pulled them open and stepped through.

"*Darith, have you no mercy upon your wife?*" The Bard's voice shrieked in his memory. "*Or on your child?*"

Then the chill air filled with the mingled scents of fragrant herbs. The plants grew straight and tall and perfect. There was never any wind to disturb the unnatural silence here, never any frost.

Memories tore at him as he walked along the curious path, with its flagged pattern. The face of King Vastion of Tharda floated before him.

"*You have done well,*" said the King. "*By answering these riddling rhymes, by your bravery, the courage to compete in feats of magic of which you know nothing, for all these do I give into your keeping the hand of my daughter.*"

"*But Your Majesty, what have I done? I do not understand this wizardry. Have I slept through all my deeds?*"

"*No matter. It is not what you have done, but what you are. Now only one thing remains, a simple oath. You must swear allegiance to me.*"

"*That I will!*"

"*And you must give your solemn oath that you will never swear allegiance to any other than me, no matter how many years time takes from us both. I would not have my daughter's man torn apart by conflicting loyalties. You must swear, and if I die, still you must keep your oath never to swear otherwise. Think well, Darith, for this is the hardest thing.*"

And thus he had won Lonarissa, daughter of Vastion of Tharda, the White Realm: Lonarissa, hair dark as the blue night around the ever-changing moon, her eyes shifting fires from the sun's corona, her skin the waxen petal of the ivory moss rose.

And thus had he lost her.

He pulled open the heavy iron door of the Tower. A candle burned in a recess at the foot of the stairs.

He took the candle, and set his torch in the empty sconce in the wall.

"Where are you?" he called. His voice echoed lightly on stone walls, then there was silence. "The Colyn Muir has come!" Stone buzzed with echoes. Silence again. "I'm here! *Darith!*"

Still no answer. He raised the candle high above his head, to light more evenly the circular room and the stairs that wound around and up the wall, into a hole in the stone ceiling twenty feet above.

Darith hesitated a moment, then went up the stairs. The breeze from the opening made the candle flicker. On the floor above, the stair became a narrow tunnel between the outer wall and an inner wall of wood, with but a single door which he tried and found locked.

By the time Darith had passed a dozen levels with locked doors, carved dragons, and small, arrow-baffling windows, his heart pounded in his chest, and the wound in his shoulder ached. Out of breath, he stopped and leaned against the wall.

When he could breathe again he went on, and two levels up came to another great round room like the room at the base of the tower, with the stairs winding up to the ceiling. No mere breeze came down these stairs now, but a knife-cold wind that made the candlelight shiver.

Yet even such a wind could not drive the strange odours from the room, and it was not only its cold that chilled Darith as he looked around him.

Markings had been made on the floor with bright-coloured powders that shifted and danced in the blast from above. The open pages of books and scrolls crackled and rustled as chill air moved them.

Still the Bard was nowhere to be seen. Darith hesitated, looking up at the unlit opening to the roof, cupping his hand around the candle's hot flame, trying to shield it against the night wind. He did not want to go on.

But there was no choice: the Bard had called for him, and

Raonull fe Scarriv had already enough slanders to fill his quiver.

Like a razor through silk a single sudden blast from the roof left Darith blinking, stock-still, in darkness.

Curdled moonlight tumbled down the stairs. The room was like a tomb.

Step by step, he climbed on, and emerged on the roof.

Clouds scudded across the sky like drunken horsemen, racing the moon to hell. The land and the towers and parapets of the castle were hid in darkness, only vague shapes when the moon was free. A low wall ran around the tower's roof, and against it, opposite the stair, the Bard lay on a cot.

"You are here at last, Darith." The thin, reedy voice cut through the wind's roar, yet the Bard's lips barely moved. His face was a skull covered with dried white parchment, written with lines of care.

"I called from below," said Darith, crossing to the cot. "I would not have entered had—had the boy not told me you were ill."

"I am dying," said the Bard, "or I would never have summoned you here. There are things here which should not be seen by ordinary men. The boy bore it better than I expected. There is iron in him that should not be wasted. But that does not matter now—there is work to be done."

"If this is more of your talk about wedding, or about journeying to the King's City, then die quiet!" For all the compassion he felt, his voice was harsh. This was an old argument.

"It is talk of the King."

"Then I'll go," said Darith. "I would not make your death more painful by refusing your wish—but I will not take that vow!"

"I know that!" There was anger in the Bard's weak voice. "It is of *another* matter between you and the King that I must speak."

"Well, speak, then!" Darith muttered, suspicious. "What matter is this?"

"The Pirate, as you call him," said the Bard. The wind howled. The moon vanished behind a deep bank of cloud.

"Go on." Cold crept in Darith's veins.

"The King is a greater man than you, Darith of Colyn Muir. Though you refuse the fealty that was your ancestor's *only* concession to his power, he has *assumed* your loyalty, that loyalty which—"

"Speak only of the Pirate! I warn you, I am in no mood to be toyed with."

"The Pirate," said the Bard, "has only now begun to move around the tip of the Tondurn peninsula. But for years now, his forces have raided the domains of the King. He kills and plunders, but does not capture. He leaves such a wake of destruction as man has never seen. He is more than a Pirate, Darith, more than a warlord. His fleet is greater than the fleets of Dalgir and of the King combined. He is not human.

"Yet the King believes that this warlord may be stopped, and his home port found and destroyed. At this moment a messenger from the King is on the road, to bid you to assemble the hill clans to aid in this war."

Bitter laughter filled Darith's throat: tears stung his eyes. His head spun.

"Too late! You should have watched me with your magic, Bard! This call to arms is too late! The Pirate has already defeated me."

"Not so." The Bard's thin voice was firm. "He has one battle to his credit, but he has faced only a fragment of your strength. Call out the clans!"

"To what purpose? Not even my own men will follow me now! They have seen me lose a battle that could have easily been won! They think me a fool! They have seen me wounded, and by now they will have heard how I cried out in the night, frightened by a dream, and kept Avlath by me to watch the lamp! Worse, they think the Curse has come upon me. It no longer inspires them: it only makes them afraid. The castle servants have fled, for fear that it will spread, like a plague!

"The clans will not follow me to war: they will follow Raonull fe Scarriv. You are the last of your line, and I the last of mine. I am the last Colyn Muir, and worse than none!"

"I warned you, Darith," said the Bard, "that the power of Colyn Muir rested on an oath older than you could imagine. But you refused to swear, and now you cringe, not from an enemy, but from your own fear."

"*Enough!*" Darith shouted. "The power of Colyn Muir is ended! The men will not follow me! Nothing I can do do will win them back!"

"There is one thing you can do," said the Bard, raising himself painfully, slowly, onto his elbow; then, his face contorted with pain, to a sitting position; and last, to Darith's amazement, pushing himself to his feet.

Swaying, he raised an arm and pointed at the moon, low on the horizon in the west.

"I can sing strong runes tonight, Darith! As I have never sung before! You saw my spells written on the floor below?"

"Your magic has never been strong, Bard."

"Death is walking, Darith! Your weird is upon you. It has visited you once already, aboard your ship, at night. Tall and black, the stalking death with a sword in its hand, the death that comes for all the line of Colyn Muir."

"What . . . is . . . this . . . you . . . say?" Darith seized the old man's shoulder, but his voice was a whisper.

"Look there, Darith," the Bard lowered his arm. "See the path that the moon makes, across the silver fog out of the west, past our castle, straight into the Devil's Jaws, lighting your way to the Haunted Valley? You must go—"

"*No!*" Darith cried, leaping back.

"—into the Haunted Valley," said the Bard, "or die tonight, as the moon sinks into the sea."

Darith turned away from the old man, but still his eyes were drawn implacably to the Devil's Jaws.

His heart froze.

Between the twin peaks, on the shining path of moonlight, a dark figure was striding toward the castle out of the Haunted Valley, from which no man had returned in living memory.

CHAPTER THREE
The Haunted Valley

"I can bargain with Death," said the Bard. "I can buy you time, Darith."

Returning clouds swirled around the tower. Suddenly Darith felt the same hungry, gnawing pain that he had felt on the ship, like some small, sharp-toothed animal tearing at his intestines from the inside.

His head swam, and he caught at the low stone wall to keep himself from falling: in the thickened darkness he could see neither wall nor hand.

"Time for what?" he managed to gasp through the pain. "Time to lose my soul in the Haunted Valley? To join the damned that dwell there? Better to die than to be ensnared for eternity!"

"You have the blood of Colyn the Great in your veins," said the Bard, "and *he* faced those powers. You are proof against their evil—if you are brave, and face them, and ride without turning back."

"But those who enter that valley are trapped there for eternity!" Darith shouted, his voice shrill. "The people say no man has ever returned."

"None but Colyn," said the Bard, "and none since his time. *Listen, Darith!* If you ride to the valley, and destroy the evil there, then the hill clans will follow you. And that will open up the ancient pass to the City of the King."

"A pass to the City?" Darith cried. "And once again it comes back to the same thing! Do you think that will tempt me? To eliminate the long sea-passage, to make it an easy journey for me to take that oath that I *cannot* take?"

"Forget that oath!" the Bard half snarled. "You will not live long enough to take it, not even with my bargaining! All I can buy you is a year and a day, Darith! No more than that. But to buy that I must have your word that you will ride into that valley at dawn. If you do as I bid, you will have the chance to destroy that which awaits you. I can see no more than that, even in the Great Crystal. But I *can* see what will happen if you refuse. You will die tonight, and then all the world will fall."

"How will it help to risk my soul—"

"*Tondur was built on a lost soul!*" shrieked the Bard. "Yet Colyn did not shrink!"

"*Colyn?*" Darith was startled. "What—?"

"There is no more time!" the Bard cried. "Death is *here!* Can you not feel it?"

And he *did* feel it, there with them on the Tower's roof.

Footsteps, a dry, crackling tread on the stone stairs. The air trembled with a dry rattling, like leaves in an evil autumn.

"Swear to me you will go!" The Bard's voice was weak. Darith's tongue was dry, and something twisted and tugged at his gut.

"I swear it!" Darith wrenched the words painfully from his parched throat.

"The bargain is struck," the Bard said through darkness. "Death cares nothing for identity. A Bard is the price of a prince."

"What are you saying?"

He heard a body fall in the thick dark. Then the clouds thinned, sight returned with the moon, and he found himself alone, the Bard's dead body lying at his feet.

As Darith groped his way back down the black stairs, he searched his memory for the old songs and tales of Colyn the Great, that the Bard had sung long ago.

"*Tondur was built on a lost soul!*" he heard the Bard shriek . . .

Long ago, when he was a child, and Tichon his elder brother was the heir . . .

He remembered tales of great battles and victories, like scraps of faded banners, yet nothing . . . *Wait!*

Sudden memory of a winter's night, with bright fire roaring on the hearth, great logs cracking and popping, and the firelight rich in the room, and the Bard with his harp— younger then, hair bright in firelight—and echoes of the

Bard's fine strong voice humming on the stone hidden by the warm-woven arras.

"Time now to sing the song of Colyn the Great, and the Curse that—"

"No!" Darith's father had cried. *"Not that song!"*

"But, Lord—"

"No buts, Bard! Do you think yourself above my power, above my Law?"

"By custom, Lord—"

"By custom! Custom can be broken. So can your harp and your back! So can the bones of your fingers. Do not think to try your power with me! I am the heir of Colyn, not you."

"This boy is also the heir of Colyn!" the Bard had answered, gesturing toward Tichon. *"Does he not have a right...?"*

"I will tell him what he needs to know. Be still!"

Yet there had been other legends over the years, other tales of Colyn the Great he had heard . . . a fragment of old song.

> *"And when in triumph he returned,*
> *He found that all he touched, he burned."*

But only such fragmentary bits of lore remained to him. As he had grown older, he had come over the years to feel that Colyn was the symbol of everything he hated, and had refused to listen to the old tales, and banished them from his mind.

He knew that the Kings had once ruled from Haunted Valley, instead of from the City of Kaerbradan; that Colyn had been a companion of the royal heir whose brother had been corrupted by sorcery.

He remembered, vaguely, a nursery tale, that Colyn had entered Haunted Valley, and slain demons there with his great black sword.

And that he had put the King upon the Ancient Throne in Kaerbradan.

The people said that the demons or sorcerers that Colyn had slain had cursed him, and all his line, and that that was why each Lord of Colyn Muir, down through the centuries, had died screaming and clawing at his belly.

Groping to the torchlight at the stair's foot, he found the torch at last, still burning, and taking it, escaped into the Bard's courtyard.

Perhaps the Bard's magic had been real, after all.

The smell of herbs had changed: all the plants had died. Darith shivered in the cold; the plants were blackened as with frost, and thin lines of ice imprisoned the ripples on the Bard's pond. He ran to the gate. Raising the latch he threw the gate open, and Mannus and Avlath rushed to meet him.

"Lord! You are alive! We feared—" They fell silent.

"I am alive," said Darith. "The Bard is dead. Mannus, you must go to the village, and bring back men to bury him. Nor is that all. You must serve as a messenger—you must both serve as messengers, and find others to aid you, to call the Chiefs to Council, and their Clans to war. The Pirate is no mere Pirate, but a great Warlord, and even now he harries the Lowlands to the East."

"Yes, my Lord," said Mannus.

"I have one more task for you, Mannus," said Darith, his deep voice edged with an emotion he did not dare name to himself. "Go to the stables. Fetch me the oldest, most worthless horse you can find."

"My Lord?"

"This morn I ride into Haunted Valley." Darith kept his voice calm. "If I return, I shall lead you against the foe. If I do not, then the Chiefs must elect a new leader in Council—and at least"—his voice grew strained and bitter—"the horse will be no loss!"

"Lord?" Mannus stared at him.

"Go!" Darith snapped. "Dawn is near!"

And indeed already the sky was paling, and from somewhere in the distance came the raucous cries of hardy winter birds. Mannus scurried away, leaving Avlath staring at his master.

"My Lord, you look pale! Are you—well?"

Darith laughed. "I am *not* well! What you meant to ask, perhaps, was am I mad?" Avlath's face brought another laugh, but a real laugh this time.

"But, Lord, to go to the Haunted Valley—"

"To go into Haunted Valley is madness." While Darith spoke, Mannus returned, leading an old, dark brown mare, who looked as though she could barely support her saddle, much less the weight of a grown man in ring-mail. "Perhaps I am mad," Darith went on, "but that is no concern of yours." He looked up at the moon, and a fragment of old legend flashed through his mind . . . how the moon's son had insulted the Goddess. *Jesters shall be all your race, and lunatics, and clowns; and whatever they seek the gods shall deny.*

"My Lord," said Mannus, "I asked leave to accompany

you to the war, and you said I was needed at the castle. I was to guide you to the Bard, but you bade me care for your horse. I think I have earned a boon from you: let me ride with you now."

Darith looked at him, startled, then sighed, shaking his head.

"No, Mannus. Bravely spoken, but if it is madness for me to go to the valley, for you to go would be far worse. The Bard told me that my blood, the Blood of Colyn Muir, is proof against the evils there. But *you* have no such blood—and you should be thankful for it! No, stay, and do my bidding.

"Call the Chieftains to Council: tell them of this Warlord. If I do not return, they may elect a new leader, and do as they will." He turned to the horse, and climbed astride. "Go now, faithful vassals and friends. There is no time to spare. This may mean the end of Tondur."

The morning laid a long black shadow behind him. To his surprise, the mare did not balk at the Devil's Jaws—perhaps, he thought, in her age, she welcomed whatever lay beyond. He let her have her head up the gentle rise between the grim peaks.

At the top Darith reined her in, surprised. He had always imagined Haunted Valley as a place of black boulders and bleached skeletons, but all he saw was a pleasant, shallow, green valley.

A dry riverbed ran north and south. On its near bank a paved stone road ran past vine-covered ruins of white marble.

South, the mountains closed in, and the paving there was broken, but to the north the road ran smooth as far as Darith could see. There was nothing else to guide him, so when he reached the road, he turned north.

The valley was warm, as though summer lingered, mischievously. There was no sign of water, save the dusty bed of the empty river.

After several hours, he saw that the road and the riverbed curved east, and by noon he was sure he was going the right way. But still there was nothing but the road and the grass and the ivy-cloaked walls of long-fallen buildings.

The mare tired quickly. He had to dismount and lead her more and more frequently as the day wore on. She would have to have water soon, but the bed of the river was still dust. His wound itched under its bandage.

At last the sun sank into banks of purple and green and orange above the western peaks, and still there was no sign of water.

As the round moon reared up beyond the saw-jagged eastern mountains, Darith, sweating and thirsty, thought for a moment he saw moonlight gleam on ripples, but when he looked again, he saw only the dim grey of grassy fields. The air was still summer-warm.

Then, through the night, he saw moving sparks of blue and green. Darith stopped short, staring.

Where the empty riverbed had been, a wide lake lay.

On shallow boats on its surface, young men and young women waved torches of coloured flame, and sang strange, half-whispered songs in some ancient tongue.

He took up the mare's reins and pulled her toward its shore. Reaching the edge of the lake, Darith pulled the horse's muzzle down to the water, but she would not drink.

The young people in the boats were dressed lightly for autumn, in filmy pastel garments that drifted in the slight breeze. But then, the valley was warm. Much too warm for his mail and padding.

From the opposite side of the lake, a great conflagration moved across the water, as a barge lit with hundreds of torches of all colours slowly approached.

As it drew near, Darith saw a throne upon it, and seated on the throne, a huge, horned black shape with three, blue, glowing eyes. As he stared, the barge came close to one of the little barks, and men leaped from behind the throne, and, reaching down, seized the young man in the bark. They dragged him before the throne, and drew small daggers tipped with flame.

Screams echoed across the water. Sickened, Darith tried to turn away, but could not.

It was not a quick end, and the screaming went on for a long time. Darith wanted to set flames under the horned idol, and cut through the flesh of its ministers with cold steel.

Then, as his fingers clenched on the hilt of his sword, the black, horned figure stood, glaring at him with its three flaming eyes, and pointed a clawed hand.

The people on the lake all turned their pale faces toward him, and anticipation lit their glazed eyes. Daggers appeared in every bark, and each boat turned toward the shore where Darith stood.

He stumbled backward. There were so many of them! Once they swarmed ashore he would be lost.

He turned to scramble onto the horse and flee back the way he had come, but saw that the villas along the road were no longer ruined, and from their gates figures bearing green torches swarmed onto the road.

No escape that way! He climbed into the saddle and turned the mare's head toward the east. If there were truly a passage through the mountains to the royal city he might be able to outrun the people of the lake.

He spurred the horse. She leaped forward. He turned, looked over his shoulder.

The valley was filled with people, running down the road and along the road after him. The dry riverbed was suddenly filled with water, its surface dotted with innumerable little boats.

And the black figure's barge slid majestically over the lake, parallel to the road, the three eyes malignant as it gained on him.

He spurred his horse savagely, knowing that the aged mare must fail at any moment, cursing the stupid pride that had asked for a worthless horse. Too late now to change his mind. He dug his spurs into her side, and shuddered at the shrill whinny she gave.

The lake curved north, and the road curved south, hugging its shore. His courage faltered as barks landed ahead of him, and young men with daggers blocked his path.

The horse was too weak to gallop past them; if he stopped to fight he would be caught. If he left the road, he would be in unknown country, and its dwellers would soon hunt him down. There was only one hope . . .

Unbuckling his sword belt, he fastened it to his saddle, and then leaned down from the saddle to let the short mail-shirt roll jingling off him, sending a throb of pain through his shoulder and plucking hairs from his head and beard as it fell to the ground.

The mare, lighter by thirty pounds, leaped ahead.

Young men, smiling, raised flaming daggers, and the mare shied and reared.

"*Back, you devils!*" Darith roared. "*Back from Colyn Muir!*"

His sword lashed out, and nearly pulled him from his saddle as it whipped *through* one smiling figure.

Phantoms! Fear chilled his spine. But if his blade flew harmless through them, perhaps his horse would do the same. He slapped the mare's hindquarters with the flat of his sword. The horse leaped forward: the young men fell back.

Then, not a hundred yards ahead, a white marble city sprang into being.

Golden light fell from its windows, and the road ran directly through wide, gaping gates.

Between the gates, dark against the golden light, a figure stood, beckoning.

Darith tried to slow the mare, but she plunged on toward the gates.

Then she stumbled, and Darith flew from the saddle. But he saw the beckoning dark figure clearly, tall and black and horned, with three glowing eyes.

His head hit hard stone.

CHAPTER FOUR
The Ancient Throne

The sun, too bright, burned his eyelids. Darith rolled over, shading his eyes.

"Not so quick, sleepyhead," said a lilting tenor voice. Something prodded Darith's ribs. "I've been waiting all morning for you to wake up!"

Darith felt his nose tweaked. He opened his eyes in outrage and saw a hand wiggling before his face.

"See? I'm human! Now, wake up and let us be off, away from here!"

Darith blinked, and found himself looking into black eyes that twinkled with immense amusement, set in a dark face above a small beard and neatly trimmed mustache; atop the head was a black slouch hat with a scarlet feather.

He sat up slowly, carefully. The pulse was pounding behind his eyes as if he had been drinking, and his still-healing shoulder protested with a pang as he moved. Had he landed on it when he fell? Tender skin and weakened muscle ached.

"Do you have any water?" Darith asked, his voice rasping as if his throat had been scraped raw.

The stranger lifted one dark eyebrow and slipped the strap of a leather bottle off his shoulder. The stuff was tepid and tasteless, but Darith felt life returning as it went down.

"I'm Gonquin." The man was young, not more than twenty-five, Darith thought, as he climbed to his feet. Still young enough to spend a night in the open and spring from his blankets in the morning as if he had slept on down. He glared at him.

He was a little consoled to find that, standing, he towered

over the stranger. This Gonquin, though well muscled and wiry, was thinner than the men Darith was used to. Raonull fe Scariv would make two of him. He wore a scarlet doublet over a black silk shirt; his hose, too, were black. *You'd best stop tweaking men's noses in these mountains, laddie.* With an effort he calmed himself. *If you want to live long!*

"I am Darith of—" he said aloud.

"Of Colyn Muir," said Gonquin. "Of course! No one else would be lying before the gates of this city alive."

Startled, Darith glanced up at the white stone gates.

The city was a ruin now, a confusion of roofless towers and shattered columns like the ruined villas he had seen as he rode through the valley, worn and pitted by wind and weather until they were white as bone. Yet it was the same city he had seen the night before.

This had to be the city in the old legend, the City of Sorcerers.

"You won't find any answers just staring," said Gonquin. "Ask questions.

"Who *are* you?"

"Gonquin!" The black eyes flashed merrily.

"I mean . . ." Darith felt annoyance.

"The King's Troubadour," Gonquin went on, with an elaborate bow. "And his messenger. The messenger that your Bard told you of, before he died." Darith started, and Gonquin laughed. "Why, you look surprised!" he said. "Did you not know the powers of Bards?"

"I knew the Bard could do magic," Darith answered reluctantly, "so I should not be surprised. And he told me a messenger was on the way. But I had thought you would come by sea."

"The safer path? But it is not, now. Not while the Black Fleet sails the Salmon Sea."

"The Black Fleet?" Darith asked.

"Their scouts have begun to raid your lands, also, I understand," said Gonquin, "but with only a few ships, as yet."

"A few ships?" A bark of bitter laughter escaped Darith's lips. "They had enough ships to outnumber the force I raised against them! We thought them but Pirates. They seized several Merchant ships bound for Dalgir. Men who saw the sea battle from the coast sent word, and when news came they had sacked a village on the coast, I sailed with only the men of Castle Colyn, and some few from the lowlands, and found myself facing both a greater and a more skilled force than I had expected. I lost half my ships, and more than half my men."

Gonquin nodded. "When the Black Fleet sails on the Sea of Salm, their black sails line the horizon like the black clouds of a storm. Even the Fleet of the King is no match for them in size."

Darith stared, trying to assimilate what the Bard had just said. If the enemy were so powerful, then his own failure to defeat them might be a lesser dishonor. But if the ships that had come close to destroying all his own were only a tithe of that strength, then what hope was there for Tondur?

"You see, then, why I chose to stay on land," Gonquin went on.

"Even so." Darith gathered his wits to answer, striving to control a sudden, unreasoning hostility that focused on the man because there was no way he could deny his news. "How could you dare this Valley? The Bard told me that the Blood of Colyn Muir was guarded from the Ghosts and Demons that haunt this place—but I saw no proof of it!"

"You are alive now, are you not?" said Gonquin.

"And wondering to find myself so! They pursued me until I fell from my horse, and I thought—"

"You thought they would take you while you slept?" Gonquin said, with a smile. "But they are only Ghosts; therefore they must prey upon your mind. Once you could no longer see them, they could not touch you, and in your sleep they could do no more than trouble your dreams. If their Master had been here, it might have been different."

"Their Master?" said Darith. "That three-eyed thing?" Gonquin nodded.

"Yes, the Demon who—" He stopped suddenly, and stared at Darith. "You *saw* it?"

"Tall and horned and black, with three glowing eyes."

"Then the Blood of Colyn has protected you indeed," said Gonquin, shivering. "I had intended to explore the city, but now I think not. Too many three-eyed idols in there. They have emeralds and aquamarines for eyes. Robbers used to come and try to steal them. The robbers are all *there* now, riding the barks." He gestured, and Darith turned away from the city, expecting the lake...

But there was no lake—only a deep, broad depression, with a small, black pool of stagnant water at its heart.

Halfway to the shore lay the white skeleton of a horse, and Darith recognised his own saddle among the bones.

He stared, while Gonquin went through the gates and returned, a few minutes later, leading a white stallion and two small pack mules, both heavily laden. The stallion's harness and saddle bore curious designs worked in silver that reminded Darith of the coloured-powder designs in the Bard's Tower room.

Darith looked from him to the skeleton, then back again.

"How did you survive?" he asked. "*You* are not of the Blood of Colyn!"

"By the Power of the Crown of the Ancient Kings," said Gonquin, with a curious gesture, and a bow to the east. "The same power that protected Colyn the Great when *first* he came here, before the Summoning. That, and my own magical knowledge," he added.

"Even so, if the Three-Eyed One has returned to this Valley we must hasten. We have a full day's ride before us, and only half a day before the sun sets, and the barks sail once more. And although my horse will carry two, he cannot go fast so loaded."

Gonquin mounted, then Darith scrambled up behind him. They rode in silence for a time; then, as they drew near the lake, Darith stirred.

"My mail-shirt should be along here, somewhere," he said. "I threw it off, trying to escape."

"There." Gonquin pointed. By the side of the road lay a heap of rust, in which the shapes of broken rings could still be seen. "It takes only a night. You saw what happened to your horse."

They were both silent as they rode past the baked clay lake-bottom.

"I still do not undersand how you survived," Darith said, when the Lake of Ghosts was safely behind them. "You said you were protected by the Power of the Ancient Crown. You—I mean—you don't have it *with* you, do you?"

Gonquin laughed.

"Oh, no, no indeed!" His laughter seemed to trouble the still land around them. "I am not *that* trusted a messenger! And in truth, if the Crown were to leave the City of the King it would lose all its Power—as it did in the days before the Wars of the Kings. But because I have sworn fealty to the King, the Power that the Seven put into the Crown and the City at the Dawn of Time is about me."

Darith gave Gonquin a sharp look at the mention of fealty. His final conversation with his own Bard was still too fresh in his memory. Were the whole line and order of Bardry dedicated to destroying his honor?

They passed a fallen wall that had once protected some-one's garden. He could see the fountain, cracked and clogged with dead weeds. The sight of it reminded him of the relative unimportance of his own problems, and he focused on what Gonquin was actually saying, once more.

"Surely you cannot have forgotten *that* tale, out here beyond the mountains?"

"We have forgotten much, I own it," said Darith. "I recall some strange stories about the ancient Kings, and I know that in days of Colyn the Ancient Crown was restored to its place, but—"

"After the Blessed Goddess had chosen among the sons that the Gods had begotten among men," said Gonquin, in that tone that Bards use when they are about to begin a song or a tale, "She lay with both the Son of the Storm God and with the War God's Son, the greatest of the Heroes of Old, and by each of them conceived a child, a boy and a girl, twin-born in one womb, who were the first King and the first Queen of Tondur. For their Marriage and Coronation the Seven Holy Ones met in Council, to decide what gifts to bestow upon the Race of Kings.

"Yet the Holy Ones knew well how weak men are—even these Children of the Gods—and how easily they become enslaved to *things,* if they come to depend upon them. So after much discussion of magical swords and armour, of fountains of healing and fertility, and many other such, the Lord of Wisdom, he who is both ancestor and patron to all Bards, bade them beware, lest the Kings become dependent on the Gods and their gifts. And thinking on this, they at last decided that there should be two gifts only, and that the blessing would only come when the two were together.

"And they called upon the Earth and the Sea, and at that spot where all the holy currents of the Land meet the bless-ings of the Sea, there rose out of the earth a great fountain of molten gold and silver, and the Lord of Wisdom then wrought there, by his art, the Throne, and the steps of the Throne, and the dais upon which the Throne sits, so that the holiness of the earth rises always in that spot.

"But a little of the gold he took, and each of the Seven blessed it, and the Lord of Wisdom by his skill wrought of it a simple crown for the King, and one for the Queen.

"The Queen's Crown was lost long ago, but the Crown of the King remains, and its power is great, as long as it remains near the throne, to heal all disease and hurt, and to drive away all powers of evil and darkness, and to bring plenty upon the land. But if it be taken away from the sacred spot, then it is only a piece of metal.

"When the King sits upon the throne with the crown upon his head, then the needs of any on whom he thinks will be known to him, so that he can heal them from afar, or—in my case—drive away the powers of Darkness."

He sighed. "Up to a point. The Demon that Colyn Muir summoned into the World is beyond the Power of the Crown. And that is the Three-Eyed Demon that you saw. Colyn drove him from this Valley once, but at times, it seems, he returns."

"The Bard told me," Darith said slowly, "that I had the Power to destroy the evil of this Valley. But he did not tell me how."

Gonquin was silent for a long time. They were moving more slowly now. The sun did not warm, but it glared from bleached marble. Darith closed his eyes, but he could still feel the menace of the Valley around him, quiescent now but dangerous as a serpent asleep in the sun.

"The evil of this place," Gonquin said at last, "is an evil of—of worship, as well as an evil of greed. The men who lived here wanted power, so they contrived spells and rituals to summon evil Powers into the World. As always happens when men become dependent upon things outside themselves they became enslaved to those they had summoned.

"Then Colyn came to save the people of Tondur from the destruction that the Magicians here had called down upon them. The Magicians died, but their souls, enslaved in life, remain here, enslaved in death. The evil spirits they summoned have gone elsewhere, to seek living men. But the ceremony remains, and the spirits of the dead Magicians still enact the ancient rites, fulfilling their part of the bargain, until the evil spirits are sent back to their own foul realm."

"How am I supposed to do that?" Darith asked dubiously.

"By mastering the talisman by whose power they are enabled to remain in this world," Gonquin responded.

"And where, oh wisest of Bards, can I find the talisman?"

Gonquin looked over his shoulder, and grinned at Darith sheepishly.

"I am not so wise, really, as I try to appear. It is my sister Edarissa who has completed the Bardic training. I am a Troubadour, and a student of Magic. All that I know of this matter I have put together from old tales, and from mouldering parchments that have come down from the time of the Wars of the Kings, that I have read in the Libraries in the

City. I do not know where the talisman is, or what it may
be."

Darith felt his anger dissolving before that grin, and realized that for a moment he had actually hoped that this little
man might know something. He licked dry lips and Gonquin
passed him the water bottle again.

"But Colyn, your ancestor, knew the secret of the talisman," Gonquin went on. "He used it to make a pact with the
Demons, and they gave him the black, curved sword, which
only a man of Colyn's Blood can use.

"And that is why the King has sent me to you, Darith.
For the realm is now in as great a danger as it was in the time
of Colyn the Great, and we need Colyn's sword if Tondur is
to survive. You must wield it against the foe."

"*This* is my sword!" Darith pulled the green-gemmed hilt
up so Gonquin could see it. "It has already faced the Pirate,
and it did not defend me from an arrow-wound, nor did it
win me the battle!"

"What do the traditions of your house say about Colyn's
Sword?"

"A thousand things," Darith said, with a bark of bitter
laughter. "But among them is the story that after he had
driven the enemy into the sea in the great battle on the plain,
he came back to the mountains and built Castle Colyn, and
gave *this* sword, which had been his father's sword, to his
son, and then sailed away into the north, taking the magic
Sword with him, and was never seen again." He shook his
head. "Some of the hill people say he will return in the time
of Tondur's need."

"Well, *this* is the time of Tondur's need," said Gonquin.
His mobile features were suddenly severe. "I do not think we
need hope for Colyn himself to come back, but we *must* find
his sword."

"Indeed!" Darith was suddenly angered. "And how will
we know where to look?" he asked. "Do *you* know where he
went?"

"No," Gonquin answered quietly. "But I have in one of
these packs a globe of black glass, that glows in the presence
of strong magic. If you will call the hill clans, we will sail
north, to search for the weapon."

"I sent out the summons to the Chieftains before I left
Colyn Muir for the Valley," said Darith. "But that was to
plan a new campaign against the Pirate, when I thought the
fleet that had defeated our first force was all they had. How
can I risk the whole strength of the hill clans on such an

expedition? If it fails, Tondur will be defenceless."

"With so large an army," said Gonquin, "it may be possible to hold off the enemy until the Sword is found. And if we fail—" He faltered. "If we fail, the whole realm of Tondur will be doomed, even though our whole strength should be arrayed before our walls."

It was almost dusk when Mannus came to the keep of the fe Scarriv, brooding above its narrow valley like some bird of prey. It must be even older, he thought, than Castle Colyn. The fe Scarriv were a proud and ancient line. Pride certainly showed in the height of those stone walls, already raised by the cliff they stood on two hundred feet above the valley floor. Lower slopes showed the ruins of an even more ancient dwelling, which had been partly cannibalized to build the outworks of the new castle and its great tower.

At its pinnacle a banner flapped as a shift in the wind caught its folds. For a moment Mannus saw the dark wings of a cormorant outstretched against a field of gold. Then the wind died, and the cormorant settled to rest once more.

Both the boy and his mount were weary, even though the horse he had chosen was a good one. Mannus bit his lip, remembering how the old brown mare his lord had insisted on taking had stumbled as he kicked her into motion up the road to the Devil's Jaws. Would he ever see the Colyn Muir ride back again?

The road to Rath Scarriv dipped and Mannus saw that a village had been hidden on the farther side. He splashed across a shallow stream and half-naked children ran screeching before him. Now adults were standing in the doorways, watching him suspiciously. Their clothing was little better than that of their offspring; the thatched roofs of their dwellings looked tattered, and whitewash was flaking from daub and wattle walls.

Clearly, the pride of the fe Scarriv did not extend to its dependents, thought Mannus, remembering the neat houses and prosperous people of Balcolyn. But the meager bottomland beside the river did not leave much room for tillage, and the hills were steep and barren with overgrazing. Food must be scarce here, he thought as he noted that. There would be crying children when winter came.

But if the clan scanted its peasants, it did provide for its warriors, Mannus saw, as he left the village behind him and set his horse at the steepening slope that led to the keep. A clansman whose faded plaid of black and yellow had made him almost invisible against the rough stones stood up suddenly.

Late sunlight glittered on the bronze rivets of his small round-shield and the hilt of his sword. His war-gear was in better condition than the rest of his outfit, but he looked well fed and well trained, and there was an aggressive jut to his rough black beard.

Mannus reined in.

"An' who may you be, that comes ridin' up the road t' Scarriv without leave?" The clansman looked him up and down.

"In Tondur the word of the Colyn Muir goes everywhere, and I am carrying it to your Lord!" said Mannus, a little more strongly than he had intended.

"You?" The warrior laughed and spat into the road.

Mannus realized abruptly that he was still wearing the old undyed tunic in which he had served the Bard—the same tunic in which he had been feeding the chickens so long ago. His plaid was no worse than the other's, but at his side he had only his eating knife—he didn't even *own* a sword. He felt hot color staining his cheeks.

"A messenger is protected by his office," he answered steadily. "Now you tell your Lord that I've come with urgent news!"

"Oh aye, I'll tell him!" The man began laughing. "I'll tell him the Colyn Muir has sent his kitchen lad for a herald—no doubt he'll like t' hear that just fine!"

Still laughing, he ambled toward the timber gate, and Mannus kicked the horse into a walk and followed.

Darith's flesh crept at the thought of spending another night in the Valley. But the Devil's Jaws were still distant, and the horse was tiring rapidly. Already the sun was low; they were still passing between ruined villas that leered at them like fragments of ancient, shattered skulls. They dismounted and plodded on foot, leading the tired horse and the two mules.

"That looks like a place we can camp, up there," said Gonquin, gesturing to a high, grassy knoll above the road, beyond one of the ivy-cloaked ruins.

"Camp? Here?" Darith shivered. "I thought we would press on until we were past the Devil's Jaws."

"Then we would have to follow the road, and then our protections would be tested indeed," said Gonquin. "But the Ghosts will keep mostly to their buildings and the road and the riverbed. They will not be hunting for us up there. My spells should make us invisible to them, and once we are asleep, we should be safe."

The sky was red above the Devil's Jaws as they climbed to the knoll. Darith slumped wearily. His shoulder seemed to hurt worse at the prospect of rest. Gonquin unsaddled his horse, and after a moment Darith got up and helped unload and tie the mules. Gonquin took crystals and incense and a flask of clear water from the packs.

There were four crystals, and he laid one in the north, another east, another south, and the last to the west. Beside each crystal he lit incense, and then walked around the camp, drawing a circle with the water, and with a powder that he crumbled on the ground.

Last he took from the pack a harp, tuned it swiftly, but carefully, and strode to the crystal in the east.

The red light faded from the sky. Green lights leaped in the ruin below them, and suddenly the building stood whole, bone-white and bright-lit.

The harp-strings rang. Gonquin sang:

> "By the Crown of Kings
> By the Wind's wan wings,
> Let this air in rings
> Ward and guard!"

He strode to the south, fingers still wringing the strings of the harp, and his voice rang out as he stood over the plume of smoke from the incense.

> "Starlight bright!
> Hide us from sight!
> By the gold Crown's right
> Watch and Ward!"

Sudden sparks shot from the incense and danced around him in a whirling cloud.

He strode to the west.

> "By Wave and Well
> By this water's Spell
> From all spectres fell
> Ward and guard!"

Now he turned to the north. Strange glows seemed to flicker in the crystals at his feet.

> *"By the Ancient Throne!*
> *By Man's flesh and bone!*
> *Let the strength of Stone*
> *Watch and Ward!"*

The harp strings rang with power, and were still. Gonquin turned back toward Darith.

"We should be safe enough now," he said, "but the sooner we sleep, the safer we will be." He began to unroll his blankets. Darith stood, looking down at the road, and saw ghostly figures rush out of the brightly lit house below.

Lights gleamed on the distant lake, and he saw water in the dry riverbed. He shivered, though the air was warm.

As he stretched out on his own bedding, he remembered, suddenly, the Thardan magics:

"Now the spell of defence. Blood flows in these tubes. Keep them tight, keep them flowing, and no enemy may pierce your skin.

"Thardan magics are the right of all who dwell in this land . . . Here is the spell that raised these towers: winding these threads through this amulet, over this charm. It spins, as you see, through ten degrees of the purple spectrum. Thus are held the Valences, and your villa is intact.

"Here the spell of waters rising. It must be kept always filled with living fish, that fountains in your courtyard may flow.

"Here the dream spell, by which you ward away all ill thought, both your own and others. You see that its balance is important. You will think well of others as long as it swings, and you will be well thought of, as long as it is well cared for.

"If the day grows too hot, or the fans atop your towers stop, open this carven chest but a crack and chant the spell written in the opals on its side, and a wind will spring to your summoning. Remember that the wind loves to be free. If you open the chest too wide, it will escape. Turned loose, this spell will sail a fleet of ships—but only once. Even magic has limits.

"By this spell, you will never hunger . . . this token, graven with the images of ten powerful demons, will stop the sun in his flight. It must not be used lightly.

"Here is a book of Compacts for summoning the creatures of the Lower Worlds. This next volume is for driving them

back. You can see it is thinner, and of less weight, for many of these, once freed, can never be driven back at all."

Memory drifted into dream, and once more young, Darith wandered with Lonarissa through the pleasant land of Thards, in the company of those long dead.

It seemed to him that they came out of the King's Palace into a garden, though some part of him knew that it was not any garden he had ever seen. He walked in the garden beneath a summer sun, and a woman walked with him. But as he turned to embrace her he saw that instead of black, her hair was flower-yellow. Her amber eyes were of Tharda, but he had never seen the girl before.

Cleanse Haunted Valley, in his dream she said. *Save Tondur . . . Renew the wounded land.*

Darith shook his head. *I am a barren branch. Others will have to bring healing. Death I bear and death I bring now.*

In his dream it seemed to him that the girl turned, and smiled. *Do not despair, Lord of Colyn Muir. Even out of death new life may come.*

The clansman had made Mannus angry.

Raonull fe Scarriv made him afraid.

The Lord of Rath Scarriv, black-haired and green-eyed, sat at ease beside his hearth with his warriors around him, reading the parchment Darith had given to Mannus in a dawning that now seemed very long ago. But the ease, thought the boy, was deceptive. He could see the faintest vibration running along the black-clad arm that held the message, like the tremor in a hound that waits for its master's word as it lies beside the fire. Only, from what he had seen so far, Mannus did not think that the eagerness was caused by any love.

"You know what is in this, boy?" His hazel eyes caught the firelight as if little flames were flickering inside.

Mannus nodded.

"He summons the clans to Council . . . and to war!" fe Scarriv grinned nastily. "Now, what I heard was that reivers were upsetting lowland shipping, and that Darith had taken his own men after them. And now he is back with his tail between his legs, whining for reinforcements!"

He took a long swallow of ale and set the pewter tankard down again. Then the fire in his eyes stabbed at Mannus suddenly.

"How many did he lose, boy? How much of the fighting strength of Colyn Muir is feeding the fishes now?"

Mannus licked dry lips and stared back at him.

"Stubborn? I could wring it out of you, you know." Fe Scarriv uncoiled from the chair and stood. He was a little taller than Mannus, but rangy, long-muscled rather than burly, and menace radiated from him like the heat off the fire.

Seeing their master's movement, the men moved in like wolves after their pack leader. Mannus glanced quickly around him. He saw no softness in any of the faces around him—there were almost a dozen, all warriors. He had not seen any women inside the Keep at all.

A show of concern might have surprised some admission from the boy, but as the fe Scarriv glared at him it came to Mannus suddenly just what Raonull was asking, and why. He felt a tremor go through him, and could not tell if it came from fury or fear. His fist clenched, but he fought back the compulsion to smash it into that sneering face. There were three messages still in his pouch, and the Colyn Muir had trusted him to carry them to all of the clans.

"I was at the castle, my Lord," he said finally. "The men were in a hurry to get to their homes. Then the Colyn Muir sent me off immediately with his messages. That is all I can say."

Which was true, as far as numbers were concerned. But Avlath had told him about the battle while they waited for Darith to come down from the Tower. Mannus knew that his clansmen would be no match for the fe Scarriv if their enemies attacked them now.

Raonull looked at him for a moment longer, and then laughed.

"No, *you* wouldn't know, would you! Very well. I have received your precious message. If the Colyn Muir comes back from Haunted Valley, I will be waiting!" Raonull fe Scarriv crumpled the parchment into a ball and snapped it into the fire.

Toward dawn Darith's dreams darkened: the horned dark figure moved, raising an arm, and twisted hordes came scuttling, weapons gleaming in their hands.

Dream shifted toward memory, and again he fled through Haunted Valley, while the barks kept pace. Ghostly waters filled the riverbed.

Then dream shifted to memory entire, into the memory he hated most of all . . .

"Take your ship and flee! The Jeweler's Apprentice has

played too wildly with the Astrolabe, and Tharda is no more!"

"Father, come with us!" Her voice was a cry of harps and doves.

"Would you see the King flee his drowning flock? Go, my daughter: sail with Darith to his homeland. He is a man of honour, tough and stubborn as his own northern hills. He will guard you well. Bear him children, and show something of Tharda's light to those who will live in the dusk of the world. You are all that will live of our land. All else we have conjured crumbles now into fine dust. Already the sea takes us. Go!"

The ship lifting on mountainous waves. Ears deafened by the roaring sea . . .

Gone, behind them, the towers tipped with gold.

And all beyond them, gone.

Gone, the red blossoms, the scarlet, the pomegranates, the weeping trees of gold and green, the fruit and grain . . . gone, the seashell faeryland . . . the gold-eyed, restful, mellow folk . . .

The white sand, swallowed by the surf.

All gone.

All swallowed by the blue-flaked, fire-flaked sea.

Darith woke trembling in the dark, and heard a gasping cry from Gonquin.

He saw the Troubadour leap to his feet in the moonlight, seizing his harp. Rolling up on one elbow, Darith saw, gathered outside the circle of magic, a host of the Ghosts of the valley.

Their eyes were hungry, burning with desire. Their bloodless faces, blue in the doleful light of torches flaring with uncanny fire, pressed close on every side.

Reeling, Darith sprang to his feet. They were entirely surrounded.

Gonquin's voice rose in song, fearless and sweet, as if he thought nothing wrong:

> *"Though Creatures of Night*
> *Surround the Ring:*
> *They must fear the might*
> *Of the Holy King!*
>
> *By Wind and wave*
> *By Flame and Stone!*
> *By the Gods that gave*
> *The ancient Throne—*

Shall this Circle hold,
This Spell stand true,
Like the Ring of Gold
When the World was new!

By Fire and Air,
By Water and Stone,
By the Silver Stair
Of the Ancient Throne!"

Ghosts milled and shook their torches, and danced angrily widdershins around the circle Gonquin had drawn. Darith drew a deep breath of relief. Gonquin's harp strings glinted in moonlight, shimmering as the plucked chords rang.

Then, from the distance, came a dreadful laugh.

Gonquin's fingers faltered on the strings.

The ranks of Ghosts parted.

On the silver path of moonlight, a dark figure rode, mounted on a tall grim beast, more like a gaunt, black elk than a horse—but its head was a horse's skull.

Three eyes glared down from the tall beast's back.

The harp strings rang out as Gonquin's fingers moved again, and again his sweet voice soared:

"Creatures of night
Around us moan!
Let them fear the might
Of the Ancient Throne!"

Ghosts shrank back.

Fearless, the horned rider advanced, and again Darith felt pain gnawing at his gut. Three eyes glowed, violet, cold.

Gonquin's voice rose, and the ringing strings thrummed:

"Beware the sting
Of defences sure:
The might of the King
and of Colyn Muir!"

The black mount reared, lashing with its hooves, backing from the barrier, while the violet-eyed rider glared down from its back, and strove to urge it on.

"In the dawning hour
 Let the Dark One fly,
 As the Sun God's power
 Climbs the sky!"

A thin line of red appeared on the paling horizon.

Wailing, the grey Ghosts began to back away.

Somewhere beyond the Devil's Jaws a cock crew.

The flaring torches faded. The Ghosts became insubstantial, wisps of mist. A wind began to blow, and they drifted back toward the ruined villas.

The three-eyed demon glared down from its rearing, plunging mount, then, wheeling, rode away.

The beast sprang from the ground, to gallop in the sky.

It faded, and was gone.

CHAPTER FIVE
The Council of Chiefs

The dark rider vanished; the sky turned blue as the bright sun reared up above the world's rim, filling that deceptive green valley with an illusory peace.

But Darith found even an illusion comforting after the struggles of the night.

He helped Gonquin break camp and pack the mules, then climbed onto the tall white horse behind him. Ahead, the Devil's Jaws opened against the horizon. The passage to freedom lay through those jagged cliffs, and the animals stepped out eagerly.

Darith's dream had troubled him, but in the sunlight some of his dark mood faded, though he was not sure whether this was due more to the sun or to the presence of Gonquin. Sometime during the night most of his exasperation with the younger man had dissipated. He knew now that beneath the velvet lay steel.

The arrow-wound in his shoulder still ached, and that new pain gnawed at his gut, yet somehow it seemed less important, and he found himself less afraid. His father and grandfather, he thought, and all their fathers back to Colyn's day, must have borne far greater pain than this.

Even if this was the Curse . . .

A year and a day the Bard had said? Darith wondered if the pain would last through all that time.

As they rode Gonquin chatted gaily about the King and his court. He spoke of the women, fair as elf maidens in their embroidered gowns; his own sister, golden-eyed Edarissa, who like him had studied magic and poetry, and splendid

48

Tarilain, who was betrothed to Prince Selvern. But Queen Serrenath had died some years ago, and now the King sat alone on the double throne of Kaerbradan.

"It is not well for the Land to be without a Lady," said Gonquin. "To perform the high magic requires a balancing of polarities. The Kingdom can endure without it, but King and Queen must preside together over the greater rituals of healing and renewal."

"Time enough to think of healing when the Demon is gone!" said Darith harshly. He knew only too well that the Troubadour had spoken truth—certainly nothing had truly prospered in his own lands after Lonarissa died.

"Indeed! For now we need the blessing of the War God— we will invoke the Goddess again when the battles are all done!" Gonquin laughed.

Today Darith found the sound of the young man's voice strangely comforting; and Gonquin, somehow sensing this, began to talk more and more freely.

Or was it simply that he liked to talk?

Of ancient wars he spoke, of Tondur's great battles against the Torians, the Erkalians, and the folk of far Stellastria; of legendary wars of gods and elves in the dawn of the world.

He sang a long ballad of Nahan the Wanderer, who sailed to the World's End, and of the marvellous Halls he had described, where sleep the banished Elf Hosts in an eternity of enchanted dreams.

Darith saw how Gonquin's gaze turned inward as he spoke of these things, saw the opaline glimmer that shone behind the Troubadour's eyes. *Here is one who has dreamed of those Halls,* thought Darith. *I wish we were seeking them,* and then, *Someday I will tell him about Tharda.*

And Gonquin told the old tale of the origin of the Bards, of how the Goddess tested the sons that the different Gods had begotten among men, and how in the form of a bent and withered crone She came to where the Son of the God of Wisdom sat, playing upon his Harp.

"O, Singer and Dreamer," she cried, "I crave a boon!"

And he looked upon her, and knew at once who she was, and why she had come.

"O Blessed Goddess," he said, "I can see indeed that it would be greatly for my good to grant any boon that you ask. But does that truly make me worthy of the reward?"

"You see clearly, and that shall prove both a blessing and a curse to those who come after you," she said. "And indeed, your wisdom would remove the point of this test, and so I would have to find another test for you."

'So be it," he answered. "But test my worthy brothers first. It may well be that they shall serve your purpose better than I."

"And if another fathers Kings, you shall father those who will guide those Kings," she said, and turned away, to where the Son of the Storm God wrestled in sport with the Son of the God of War...

But Gonquin told no tales of Colyn the Great, nor, with visions of the grim Valley still vivid in his memory, did Darith ask him to.

They reached the Castle of Colyn Muir before noon. Its towers rose like trees above a wooded hill, the crumbling stone walls green and brown with lichen, with the Bard's ivy-cloaked Tower rising in robed lordship above the lesser spires. Darith thought of other times he had come home to Colyn Muir—some of them after journeys from which he had not expected to return. The sight of it should have given him the comfort of long familiarity.

But this journey had been different, even though it had only been two nights long, and he saw his ancient home with new eyes. Old memories of childhood fancies came back to him, and of true tales, scarcely less strange, that the old Bard had chanted about the founding of those towers.

But remembering the Bard brought back the memory of their last meeting. Darith slumped behind Gonquin, shivering. The pain in his gut was more active now, as if that hidden animal were waking from its sleep. Now every jolting step of the horse brought new pain.

Then a sound struck his ears.

From somewhere in the mountain passes beyond the Castle came the wild skirl of a bagpipe, softened to a painful sweetness by distance, playing the ancient war-song of Colyn Muir.

Darith's flagging spirits soared above pain and despair, leaping wildly with the clear bell-like tones that lifted above the deep steady roaring of the drones. There was life and death in that song, the darkness of death and the undying brightness of honour.

He remembered suddenly an ancient tale of the Lady of Colyn Muir waiting in her tower for the return of the fleet from war, hearing over the waves the pipers of the returning ships playing at once a song of mourning and of Victory.

And she knew that her Lord was dead.

Feeling the first flicker of death stir in his belly, Darith wondered, *Will they play that lament for me?*

The Castle was empty: Avlath and Mannus were both still gone on their mission; and the other servants, Darith guessed, still too frightened to return. Gonquin only laughed, stabled his horse and mules himself, and lugged his own packs up to the guest chamber next to Darith's own.

"You see?" he said. "The old tales—and the gods—were right to warn us how easily man becomes dependent on forces outside himself!"

The skirling of the pipes grew louder. Looking down from a high window they saw bright red-and-gold plaids blowing in the wind as the nearest of the clans marched up the road, the great Clan Morulvu, with their young chief, Ruishiar, at their head.

With the swift, free-swinging stride of men who choose their own masters they marched toward the castle. What would they say when they learned why he had summoned them here?

"I should go down and greet them." Trying to hide his reluctance, Darith gave up the support of the sill.

"Have you looked at yourself in a mirror?" said Gonquin. "If they see you before you have rested, they will think you are dying! It may be as well, given what you have told me of the clans, to wait and watch before letting them know we are here."

"I do not understand," said Darith. Gonquin lifted an eyebrow.

"Before he performs, a Troubadour always tries to check out the house. I will be more persuasive if I know what these men are like before I make my presence known to them. And you may find that they speak their feelings more freely when you are not here."

Darith tried to match the other man's wry smile. "In the gallery above the hall there is a peephole."

"I thought there might be."

They watched the marching men. As they drew close enough to see details, it became clear that many shirts were patched and plaids were faded; men were shod in coarse brogues with leg wrappings instead of stockings or wore no shoes at all; the hide-covered round-shields they carried were hacked and scarred; even the cockades on their caps were tattered now.

Darith leaned against the wall again and shook his head.

"I suppose you must find this very—poor and—shabby."

"Well now," said Gonquin, "certainly it is a different thing from the richness and colour of the nobles of the court, gathered before the thousand steps of the High Throne of Kaerbradan, the City of the King. And yet—there is a sort of grim impressiveness here. A reminder that even the glory and splendour of the Ancient Kings rests on the earthly strength of these hillmen, barbarians though they be."

Avlath returned while Darith was asleep and bustled into his room. Darith woke to find him, bristling with suspicion, facing Gonquin across his bed like a mastiff over a bone.

"Lord, this stranger bids me keep your presence here a secret, when already the Clan Chiefs—"

"He is the King's Messenger," Darith said sleepily. Pain gnawed him, and he did not want to speak, and surely not to argue. "Let him have his way." It must be afternoon already. Amber light slanted through the shutters across the room.

"But already Raonull of Scarriv is gloating at your absence, and planning to make himself the new leader."

"And thus will throw himself bodily into the pit prepared for him!" Gonquin laughed. He crossed to the window and threw the shutters wide. Darith blinked at the sudden brightness.

"Not all your chieftains can be blind! Better to let him plot now, openly, than to have him breeding secret treasons on the open sea!"

Avlath looked at Gonquin searchingly, and passed his hand through his rumpled sandy hair.

"Well, maybe so," he admitted grudgingly. "But such traps care not who they catch. Watch your own step, Lord," he added to Darith.

Soon the chieftains of the wild mountain clans and the lesser lords of foothill and plateau began to arrive. At Gonquin's insistence Darith kept to his chambers until the Council was assembled.

Lesser leaders were seated far down the table, but the greatest chieftains took places near its head, where the great carven chair of the Lord of Colyn Muir sat empty. To Darith, that waiting seat was a mute accusation. He had accepted the necessity for Gonquin's strategy, but it still made him uncomfortable.

From his hiding place in the gallery the Lord of Colyn Muir saw grouped near his chair black-bearded Finn fe Scarriv of Rathnolawn, grim Goll of Caiplic, Bor of Ashir Fuarana, Niall of Lairog-nan-Cuivair, and the youngest chief, Ruishiar, a tall boy-warrior, kilted in the red-and-gold plaid of the great Clan Morulvu, of which he was now the head—for his father had been killed by the Pirate.

And greatest of all, Olegair of Clann Mavron, who sat at what would be the Colyn Muir's right hand. On the other side of the table sat his hereditary foeman, Raonull, war chief of the powerful Scarriv Clan.

Mannus stood beside Avlath, hands clasped behind him and face schooled to an unnatural immobility. From time to time one of the chieftains would glare at him, and some reference to village brats could be heard above the general roar. Darith understood that being summoned to this meeting by a tanner's son had not sweetened their tempers. But Mannus was doing a good job of pretending not to hear. If the boy could maintain that kind of steadiness in battle he might be useful on the campaign after all.

Darith grimaced. Of course Mannus was going. They were all going, for if the threat from the Black Fleet was half what Gonquin had said it was, they were going to need every hand that could hold a sword!

The chieftains sat in the great hall, arguing. Still the King's Messenger said no word.

"Gonquin, I hate this!" Darith said, letting the draperies that hid the peephole fall. Dust tickled the back of his throat, and he felt the pang in his belly as he suppressed a cough.

"Who is the big, yellow-haired man getting ready to speak now?" Gonquin parted the curtain again and peered through.

"Olegair fe Mavron. He will take my part. The fe Mavron are close kin to the fe Colyn, and have been our friends and supporters for generations."

Olegair was the largest man at the table, and the rather bright red and green of his tartan, shot through with yellow, did nothing to diminish his presence. Standing, he towered over the others, and one could see their awareness of it in the way they sat back as he arranged the twin ceremonial daggers in a cross before him.

When he spoke, it was with a voice so deep that it had become a joke in his family, though it was a terror to his enemies. Men called him the Bull Dragon—behind his back.

"Why we are in Council here," the deep voice rumbled, "seems a mystery. We are told that a Warlord harries the

King's eastern lands, and that our aid is required. Yet there is no messenger, and no news of one.

"Further, we are told that the Colyn Muir has ridden to the Haunted Valley, and that we must elect a new leader if he does not return. I would not wish to doubt the messenger, my Lords"—Olegair cast an amused glance at Mannus, who coloured, but stared back at him steadily—"but neither do I doubt the sanity of Lord Darith. Yet it seems to me that those are the choices."

A rangy man, black-haired and green-eyed, raised his dagger for recognition.

"Who is this one?" Gonquin whispered.

"Raonull fe Scarriv," Darith growled. It seemed to him that the eyes of the portraits on the wall had become fiercer as they looked on their enemy.

Olegair uncrossed his blades and sat. Scarriv rose, crossing his own.

"Fe Mavron," Raonull's piercing voice began, "we all know your loyalty to Lord Darith. We all feel"—he looked around the table briefly at each in turn—"a certain loyalty to the Colyn Muir."

A *certain* loyalty? The loyalty of the wolf who waits for his pack leader to miss his kill, thought Darith. There was strength in the way Raonull spoke, in the way he stood. But it was not a good strength.

"But I think the matter far simpler than you have put it. Messengers came to tell us that Lord Darith had called a Council: that a Warlord harries the King. They said that the Colyn Muir had ridden into Haunted Valley, and left instructions that if he did not return, we must elect a new leader. So our duty as loyal vassals is clear—he has not returned: we must elect a new leader."

And there came the dog wolf's spring. Darith realized he was holding his breath and let it out in a long sigh.

Fe Scarriv uncrossed his daggers and sat. Olegair was on his feet again.

"We are told the King needs our aid, but not how or where or when! An election is useless—no one here can answer those questions! And Lord Darith told his messengers that his blood is proof against the evil of the valley. We should wait one more day, and hope the Colyn Muir returns, while we think on what we may do!"

Gonquin tapped Darith's shoulder. Gut tightening, Darith turned.

"I think perhaps this is the moment for you to appear," Gonquin whispered.

"And you?"

"Soon."

Darith stepped softly from the balcony, went down a narrow stone stair, and paused before the great double doors to the Hall. He told himself that the ache in neck and shoulders was nothing—he had felt worse before battle, and these men were not his enemies. Not all of them, anyway. He took a deep breath, set his hand to the center of the doors and thrust them open. Raonull's raised voice met him:

"A *vote!*"

"On what?" Darith's voice, from the door, was calm and pleasant. Heads turned; men stared. The Lord of Colyn Muir strode into his Hall.

There was a long silence, then Olegair fe Mavron crossed his daggers and spoke.

"On your competence, old friend. Or so I would guess fe Scarriv's meaning through the twists of his words."

Darith walked the length of the Hall. He heard the familiar drumbeat of his footsteps on the worn boards, smelled the familiar odors of dogs and woodsmoke and leather, felt his own back straightening. Did fe Scarriv truly have the stupidity to challenge the Colyn Muir in his own Hall? When he came to the head of the table, he reached out and crossed his own daggers, carefully set ready by Avlath.

At his right, down the table, fe Scarriv remained standing, green eyes burning sullenly.

Other chieftains stirred uneasily.

"I was not aware the fe Scarriv feared words," said Darith mildly.

"I was about to propose a vote," said Raonull. "When the old chieftain has failed, it is time to choose a new. Since the old leader *has* failed—"

"*Enough!*" Olegair roared. "The Colyn Muir has not yet told us why we have been summoned. Before any decision can be made on his right to lead, he must be heard. The loss of one battle is *not* cause to depose a Chief!"

Fe Scarriv smiled coldly, and sat down, uncrossing the daggers. He had made his point: the subject of the Council, and the vote, was now Darith's competence to lead.

Olegair's face twitched as he realised the trap into which he had leaped.

"I said that if I returned from Haunted Valley I would lead you," said Darith coldly, "and that *if I did not return,* you should choose a new leader. I have returned." He let his eyes rove around the table, to meet the gaze of each man in turn.

"I have ridden to the ruined city at the end of Haunted Valley, and confronted the Devils there; I have faced the Ghosts that ride upon the lake. I have come back alive, after talking to the King's Messenger, and I know now how we may defeat this Warlord that we thought only a pirate."

"Tell us of Haunted Valley, Lord Darith." Raonull's voice was a sneer. "We know nothing of it. No man but yourself has ever returned, and we are eager to hear the tale—a good tale of the Colyn Muir is always stirring! So your cursed blood found some fellowship in that cursed place?" He leaned forward and threw all pretence aside. "Tell us of the beautiful princess you met in the valley. A good story always has a beautiful princess!"

Vision darkened, thought fled. Hands left the daggers, snatched the black cloth from the center of the table, grasped one of the duelling swords that rested there. Light glittered from the glass chips that powdered the steel as the blade came up, clenched in Darith's fist.

"*Stop!*"

Gonquin's voice trumpeted through the Hall. Chieftains jerked around as the curtain was hauled away from the gallery. For a moment there was silence as the chieftains in their bold plaids and ornaments of silver and bronze gazed up at the red and black flourishes and glinting golden chain of the man from the City of the Kings.

"What kind of foolish children do they raise here in these mountains?" Gonquin's voice dripped with haughty contempt. "The King Himself summons your aid, and you are so intent on debate that you do not give Lord Darith time to introduce me. And this—fe Scarriv, was it not?—is so mischievous that he would slow the King's campaign for a funeral?"

"Who is this man?" Raonull's voice was low and dangerous. "Do we allow him to interrupt our election?"

"The King's Messenger!" Gonquin again made that odd little bow. "Gonquin by name. And there will be no election: there is no time. We must move at once."

"Under this—under the Colyn Muir?" There was contempt in fe Scarriv's tone. Darith's grip tightened on the sword.

"Until your ships round the tip of the peninsula, and join with the fleet of Prince Selvern, the King's nephew and Heir to the Throne. He will command the combined fleet. You may, of course, refuse to serve him"—there was the slightest pause—"although that would be open treason."

"When the *King* calls, I am ready," Raonull said, deflating visibly. "I ask only a worthy general and a fighting chance."

"You have both, I assure you," said Gonquin. His pleasant baritone had grown richer, soothing as honeyed wine. "Selvern has fought the ships of the enemy on the Salmon Sea before, and he led the forces of the King into Toria, when their capital was besieged and our King sent aid. Now, Lord Darith, if you will place your blade back on its cloth and defer your blood feud until war is done, we can make plans."

Darith hesitated. He wanted Raonull's blood. He had had enough of veiled insults long ago, and now—a year and a day, the Bard had said. If the war ran beyond that time—

But to defy Gonquin now would destroy all authority.

He set the sword down, its point aimed at fe Scarriv's place, then uncrossed his daggers and sat.

Gonquin's voice filled the chamber. He did not mention the magical weapon waiting in the North, only that the fleet from Dalgir would sail under full armour, and receive further orders when they met Prince Selvern's fleet.

But he spoke in flashing words and a trumpet voice, and even Raonull stared at the Troubadour with attention, as the ardour of battle kindled in the chieftains' eyes.

Five thousand men gathered in the valley before the Castle, the full force of the hill clans. In each of them burned a flame that had long been dormant: they wanted blood on their newly sharpened swords and freshly burnished shields; blood soaking their garments and running under their feet.

It snowed as they marched through the passes; they had to force their way through deep, cold drifts. But these were men used to weather, and not weakened by battle as Darith's returning warriors had been. They were a fierce breed, the men born and raised in the inhospitable mountains, nourished more by hardship than by their scanty, stunted sheep.

Messengers went down to Dalgir before them.

If merchants who had already lost ships to the Pirate doubted Darith's wisdom, the royal message left them few choices. Even a careful merchant could understand when it was necessary to risk all. When the army arrived the largest

fleet in memory was ready, every vessel converted and armoured for war.

As the last ship left the harbour, the great chain was
stretched across its mouth, and the gates closed above the
wharves.

The fleet sailed north, coasting on the cold wind past
rocky beaches, past high, black granite cliffs. Days passed,
while icy winter winds swelled the great sails and tugged at
the tall masts and made the ropes of the rigging creak painfully.

Only charred ruins on the coast bore witness that the
Black Fleet had been there. On the day that they passed the
scene of his disastrous battle, Darith stayed belowdecks.

The wind stayed fair, but as the weeks passed with no sign
of the enemy, men grew restless. They'd been promised action. Nerves keyed up for battle, they wanted it. By the time
they reached the tip of the great peninsula, they had begun
to bicker among themselves.

As the fleet rounded the cape and tacked toward the entrance to the Sea of Salmon, men thronged the decks, hoping
to catch sight of the enemy, or least of Prince Selvern's great
fleet. But south of them they saw only the smooth, green
blank of the sheltered inland sea. It was a warm sea, this Sea
of Salmon, and once they had gotten safely south of this
opening to the great ocean, the sailing would be comfort-
able, even in winter: the peninsula sheltering against wild
western storm.

"Well, we are here," said Avlath. "But where is the
Prince?"

Only the creaking of lines and sails in the wind answered
as the ship glided on. Darith spread out charts on a carven
table built in from the prow, while Gonquin brought out of
his pack a long brass tube, with glass on either end.

"They make these on the continent," he explained, as
they stared at it. "Some interaction of spells placed on the
glass at the ends brings far things nearer."

"Then use it on the Prince's fleet," said Avlath, "for that
must indeed be a far thing!"

"That is what I am doing," said Gonquin, "but as yet I
have not been able to find what I seek. Here, Avlath, you
have good eyes. Why do you not look?"

"No!" Avlath made a warding sign in the air with his forefinger. "No, thank you! I've enough to fear without incurring
debts of magic!"

Gonquin laughed. "The folk from whom I bought it, in

Toria, said it was not true magic at all! But then, people on the Continent have such strange ideas, and so many marvels about them, that it is difficult to judge while one is among them. Magic or no, it does a wonderful thing, and that is magic enough for me!"

Darith smiled a little, but his gaze returned to the window. They had made good time to the meeting. Could they be early? But Gonquin had said that the Prince was already at sea.

"Tell me, Master Gonquin," said Avlath, "what were you doing on the Continent, so far away?"

Almost invisible in the dim haze of the horizon, something sparkled in the distance. Dark dots danced before Darith's eyes as he strove to see.

"Studying," said Gonquin. "Studying, and gathering stories about—"

Darith's sudden grip on his arm interrupted him.

"Your glass may be good," said Darith, "but you must still pay attention, and make constant use of it. There are ships there, to the south."

Gonquin put the brass tube to his eye.

"That's Prince Selvern's flagship!" Gonquin exclaimed. "And it's on fire!"

CHAPTER SIX
The Black Fleet

Soon all could see what had before been visible only through the glass: a tall galleon, its sails afire, beset by several lower, darker craft, that hung about it like wolves around an elk while battle raged on the deck. Struggling figures leaped into the water, or fell. Spears from the attacking ships kept them from clambering back aboard.

"There!" Gonquin shouted, pointing. "Prince Selvern! He fights almost alone, with only five of his men left against a hundred!"

Darith took the glass. On the galleon's high poop a tall figure in bright mail and tattered blue robes whirled a great sword against a horde of grey-shrouded foes, while a handful of ragged sailors, and one more richly dressed man who must have been an officer, struggled to guard his back—or perhaps, to hide behind him—for he fought with a tiger's energy, heavy blade lashing like a scythe.

But seen through the glass, the shapes he fought did not seem like men at all.

Darith shuddered, remembering where and when he had seen those loose grey robes before. They lent a ratlike shape to their wearers, or maybe something even less akin to humankind. But the other time had been at twilight, and at night, and then he had thought them only strangely dressed pirates.

Tension ran from ship to ship, leaping the sea like a mist of thin lightning. All around him, Darith heard men arming in frantic haste, those who had them pulling on mail-shirts, or thick coats of hard leather. But most of the clansmen were too poor for such protection. Their only defence lay in the swiftness with which they could raise battered target-shields and swing their lovingly sharpened swords.

The wind was freshening. The flagship's pennon still blew straight toward the southeast. A quick order to the sailing-master sent men aloft to furl the topsail and take a reef in the big mainsail. To meet the enemy at just the right moment would require careful sailing. Darith eyed the rapidly lessening expanse of water between him and his foe, calculating speed and distance.

This is always the worst time in a sea-battle, thought Darith, *when the enemy has been sighted, and you can only wait for the wind to bring you to grips with him.*

He felt the stiffness of tension in his neck and the back of his skull, and worked his head back and forth to ease it. The men would be chafing because nothing they could do would hasten the battle, while the captains and crews of the merchant vessels were probably trembling because everything in their training had taught them to react to the sight of an enemy not by attacking but by running away.

The other ships were following *Maid of Tharda* in a staggered vee to port and starboard, spaced carefully to keep from stealing one another's wind. Another order sent signal flags fluttering up the mast—*"Close formation. Encircle the enemy"*—and after a few moments the others acknowledged. Darith noted which ships responded most quickly, and which delayed the answer, or did not reply at all. He hoped that those who had forgotten their training under stress would be able to follow the example of the others.

The fleet had spent much of the voyage southward practicing communications. It was hard enough to convince his wild clansmen to follow orders in a land battle; the idea that ships at the mercy of wind and weather could follow any set battle plan had seemed laughable. Darith reminded himself to praise or reprimand the signalmen after the battle—assuming they survived.

At Darith's command, the steersman aimed the axe of the armoured ship's iron-beaked prow straight at the side of the nearer black vessel. Sails shuddered like the men's hoarse breath as Darith's flagship rolled down the waves, straight at the black ship's side.

Turning his glass on the enemy, he saw cloth-draped figures pointing. But no panic, no cowering. There was something strange about the way the dark shapes moved in the circle of glass; a unison and certainty in every action—like ants swarming over a piece of carrion.

He returned the glass to Gonquin and took the shield Avlath held out for him, while the horizon rocked and the sail hummed. His arrow-wound was nearly healed now; it itched under the bandage. He drew his sword, the gold hilt cold in his hand. A side glance showed him the other Tondurn ships coming around to close with their own enemies.

Waves lifted the dark ship's side to meet them, and Darith glimpsed muffled shapes clustered by the rail.

Both decks reeled as the *Maid of Tharda*'s sharp prow cut deep into fragile, splintering wood. Darith staggered, and pain shot through him like a sharp stake.

Like angry ants, the foe swarmed onto the deck of Darith's ship. He heard no spoken orders, yet they moved into line with obscene precision, swiftly linking their shields into a wall.

Rocking wood slapped Darith's feet as he sprang to meet them. Pain twisted in his gut, and he bit his lip to keep from screaming.

But no one among his own shouting men would have heard him; or if they did, they would have thought it another war cry, for their own shrieks rang shrill as the screams of the gulls that wheeled like vultures overhead.

Dark faceless heads stared at them, silent above the shield-wall.

What are we fighting? Mannus thought, as he saw the grey-robed, ratlike shapes scramble over the side, like a vision of the darkness of death.

His fingers tightened on the wooden shaft of the long spear he had taken, and something burned the back of his dry throat while his blood throbbed wildly.

Steel glittered ahead, swords rising all together above the wall of shields. Some of them were curved, as legend said Colyn's Magic Sword had been curved.

The ship's deck drummed as the shield-wall stepped forward in rhythmic unison. Mannus almost lost his footing as the ship heaved. But he got his feet under him somehow, running with the others, his eyes blinded for a moment by the light flashing off flying steel.

Then the rocking deck hurled a wave of swords against booming shields. Robed shapes fell in uncanny silence. A clansman went down, screaming, blood spurting.

This was Mannus's first battle. Old Avlath had made them

practice in shipboard, all the way up the coast, but this was not like pounding each other with sticks and laughing at the bruises.

But the spear was not too different from a hayfork.

The deck reeled, making Mannus dance from foot to foot on the unstable surface. He felt his spear's heavy iron head drag at his hand as he jabbed the point toward black robes and blank faces.

Panic clenched his eyes shut as he stabbed. He wrenched them open just in time. A shield lifted his point, and he had to jump back as sharp steel whistled past his eyes.

He reeled back, feeling the deck swaying underfoot, the frailty of hollow wood rolling on the waves. Now another shouting man fell, and a flood of blood-wet wood spread underfoot.

The undying brightness of honour seemed far from this fury of death and blood. Metal battered metal, clanging insistently; weapons beat on shields with a deafening hammering. Men died, screaming in pain and despair.

Half-blinded by flashing steel, he blinked for a moment at the tangle of battle, and saw that another in the plaid of Colyn Muir had taken his place in line.

Hot with shame, he rushed in stabbing.

He lifted his head, hearing the sudden moan of drones, the wild skirl of a bagpipe. Clear bell-like tones lifted above the drumming of battle.

The Clan's piper, in the stern, was playing the ancient war-song of Colyn Muir.

Mannus lunged, his spirits soaring. He dodged from under a sword, as he would have ducked old Ylsa's broom, and the spear in his hands stabbed up. He felt his spear-point pierce flesh.

Darith felt blood draining from his face, strength ebbing from his fingers. He faltered on the rolling deck and men rushed past him. He fought against waves of numbness that rolled up his skull, and staggered toward the waiting foe. The men must not know the Curse was on him.

If the Prince was killed, the fate of Tondur might well depend—

A silver line that trailed red lace, a sharp sword-edge lashed at his face. His shield thundered as he hurled it up, barely in time, the steel line quivering as it sank into the leather on his shield-rim, inches from his eyes.

Beyond, he saw blank darkness where a face should be.

Darith's arm was already whirling in the countercut, fist clenching the hilt to drive the edge through. The deck swinging under his feet added force to his stroke.

Grey cloth parted. He felt flesh and bone beneath.

All the enemy were masked in grey-black cloth. Darith shuddered. Were the hidden faces human? A heavy blow on his shield made him reel back, his feet unsteady on the surging deck.

The sharp-toothed thing in his gut woke to a sudden violent frenzy of claws. Why did this have to happen *now?* His shield lurched up, barely catching another whistling slash that would have split his skull; and then Avlath leaped past, his blade whirling in a silver wheel above his head, his shield battering down the enemy's arm.

Mannus's spear-point grated on the metal of a shield.

For a moment it stuck there, and a sword hacked at it. The heavy spear dragged at his hands as the blade drove it down. Mannus gripped the tough wood and, in his fury, twisted it around with a speed he had never had in practice. He whipped the iron point up, through cloth into flesh, as strength surged through him in his need.

What would he have done had that slash cut through the spear-shaft? That would have been the end.

Then Mannus remembered the short axe in his belt: he had cut enough firewood, pretending that it was an enemy warrior.

More and more of the shrouded men leaped from the broken ship, swarming over the rail. They fought in grim silence, while clansmen howled and shrieked. The reeling deck turned slippery red.

The newcomers took their places in line as swiftly and silently as ants coming out of a hole, while the clansmen leaped in and out, attacking as individuals.

Mannus wished desperately for a crossbow. He had always prided himself on that skill; from the first time he had picked up the old crossbow that had hung on the castle wall its use had come easily—a natural talent, it seemed. But that old bow was useless now, stringless and brittle from age. And he was too poor to buy one.

Then, suddenly, as the piper's song rose to a steady sweetness above the deep roar of the drones and the drumming of battle, Mannus remembered the ancient tale of the wrestling of the Son of the God of War with the Storm God's Son—how they wrestled on and on, and neither could prevail, for although the Son of the Storm God was far the stronger, the War God's Son had the more unconquerable Spirit.

Yet reality gripped hard as, beside him, a young man fell, his veins pouring out his life on the deck. Mannus's eyes warned him of falling steel blades, and as he twisted and ducked away from flashing death, stabbing at grey cloth, sweating, he saw that, although the enemy weapons moved as in a drill, the shrouded men fought as though they were asleep. On the ship's deck their unity was of little use.

"Knock them over the side!" Mannus shouted, whirling the wooden end of the spear shaft around in a butt-stroke. His tones lifted above the hammering of steel around him: the kilted men roared.

Soon the sheer ferocity of the mountain men had ripped great holes in the shield-wall, and their savage attacks hurled the enemy line staggering back, pushing muffled men into the water.

Once in the water they screamed; but on the deck they bled and died in eerie silence.

Darith reeled back. His shield's weight dragged down his arm. Death danced in flickering fire on sun-lit swords.

Darith remembered how, on land, the shrouded men had swarmed to box his men between blocks of bowmen.

Arrows had scythed down half his force before they could close. But here the enemy were not using bows. Had they not had time to seize them before the ship struck? Or had all their arrows already been used in battle with the King's fleet?

Still, many of Darith's men went down, pierced by mechanically thrusting swords, or hewn down by blades that rose and fell in rhythmic unison.

Darith staggered against the rail, and clung there, panting in pain. He glimpsed Avlath, laying about him with a heavy sword, and Mannus, lunging with a long spear in a thrust that drove two muffled rat grey shapes into the water, then whirling it around to sweep two more over the side with a butt-stroke. The weapons drill with which they had tried to fill the long hours of the journey had clearly given Mannus, at least, some much-needed skill.

Darith started to call out some encouragement, but he had no breath. Both sides reeled on their feet as the crushed black ship shuddered and began to tear free of the ram wedged in its side.

Other ships were closing on the remaining enemy vessel

as it cast itself loose from the Prince's flagship. Grappling irons flew. Black-bearded Finn fe Scarriv of Rathnolawn sprang from deck to rocking deck, grim teeth gleaming in the dark forest of his beard as his bright axe waved. His lord and cousin, Raonull fe Scarriv, sprang to his side, blade whirling as the two led the men of Clan Scarriv screaming across the enemy decks.

Darith knew he should be leading his own men, setting the example, taking the same risks as they. But the long sword in his hand seemed too heavy to lift, and he could barely breathe for the pain. He would not be able to get his shield up, and would die quickly. Then what?

With the Colyn Muir dead, the Warlord would conquer.

Bagpipes shrilled across the water. He looked across at the other ships. A second had joined the Scarriv Clan ship. Goll of Caiplic led his wild clansmen in a rush, sharp swords waving, and a clash of steel rose over the waves. Shrouded figures fell, grey cloth dyed scarlet.

Darith's ship shuddered as the splintered hull of the broken ship pulled free, and the black hulk reeled down through deep water.

The shield wall was broken in a dozen places now. There was no room for the grey-swathed men to maneuver: they could not bring their numbers to bear.

Darith stood gasping by the rail, while pain shot through him. But none among his men stopped to mark his weakness as they hurled themselves on their foes, broad blades whirling in glittering spirals.

The cloth-wrapped, grey-robed men—he was sure, now, that they were men, but under some evil spell—stood shoulder to shoulder, fighting in little groups, now that their line was broken. Their swords often swung in unison, and it was then they were most deadly.

Yet there was a stiffness to their movements, and they lacked the dynamism of the barbarians who fought them.

And they all fought the same way. It was as if, Darith thought, there was but a single warrior opposed to them, and although he had a hundred hands and a hundred swords, they all made the same moves, all fought with a single style, and Darith knew that each of his men had now had a chance to learn that style.

And now the outcome was no longer in doubt. Soon the last of their silent foes toppled, to scream in the water, and Darith's deck was clear. Fighting still continued on the other black vessel, but it too was surrounded by screaming, drowning robed shapes, and Darith saw Raonull's tall form leading a mass of bloody-handed warriors surging across the deck. At his side, Finn of Rathnolawn whirled his blood-wet axe, and robed shapes fell.

But the black ship was sinking under them as they fought. One of the robed men must have chopped a hole somewhere below the waterline. Darith felt his lips twitch in a grim smile. There would be no prize, no loot. Raonull would not like that.

He turned to look at the ship they had come to save.

Dead and dying men lay on the red deck of the Prince's ship; Prince Selvern stood to the tiller, steering the ship away from its sinking foe.

As Darith watched, the mast of the Prince's ship cracked and tumbled sideways. Fire leaped across the tilting deck, as the ship toppled and started to capsize.

"Get boats in the water!" Darith bellowed.

"Do they have a chance?" asked Mannus.

"If they swim quickly enough," snarled Avlath.

"And are not pulled down by the undertow when the ship sinks," Gonquin added.

They? Darith wondered, seeing the blue and silver figure leap from the tilting deck into the waves. It looked to him as though only the Prince was still on his feet.

Cautious boats edged into the whirlpool that was forming as the ship went down. They saw a hand grasp the gunwale of one, and saw the boat rock as a heavy figure heaved itself up from the sea, spitting water.

Darith swayed, and closed his eyes against the pain. His hand clenched on the ship's rail.

When he opened them, the blue and silver figure was climbing aboard, and then Prince Selvern stood on the aft deck, peacock blue clothes torn, smudged, and dripping. His eyes still burned with the fury of battle.

His face was strong, with bones showing through like chunks of rocks under his eyes. One cheek was cut, blood matting the golden beard, and his soot-smudged face was shiny with sweat. Around his brow, a golden band held long blond hair, still in place despite all he had been through.

There was a look of fierce pride about him, and his jaw was set grimly, as if he were even now about some bloody task.

Beyond the Prince, Darith scowled to see Raonull fe

Scarriv climbing over the side, his kinsman Finn beside him. He saw boats being lowered from other ships, and knew that all the chieftains would soon be here, to find out what had happened, and learn what would happen next.

"Get the Prince dry clothes," Darith said. Avlath looked the Prince over, judging his size, then went below.

"I am the Colyn Muir: I speak for Clan Colyn."

"I bring you no aid," said the Prince bitterly, "no fleet. We set sail with an hundred warships—you saw the last go down. As we made our way up the coast we met the enemy. He had perhaps two hundred warships then. We were outnumbered, but I had experienced captains, and I thought we could outfight them."

"Your Highness—" There was a horror in Gonquin's voice.

"Their ships are larger than ours and crammed with men," the Prince continued in a monotone. "They do not maneuver as well, nor do they seem as swift, but they are implacable in their pursuit. Each of my vessels accounted for one of her attackers, but only five ships out of my hundred survived that first fight.

"We fled north to join or at least warn you, but they followed. We pushed onward through each night, changing course to confuse pursuit, trusting to our charts to avoid hazards and using every breath of air. But each morning, we saw them close by, as though some night-spirit had kept them like hounds upon our track and filled their sails with wind. This morning there were but two of us left."

Other clansmen, wounded, were being pulled into the boats. The sea was red. Sharks' fins began to slice through the water, but Darith's men hurled grey-draped corpses at them to distract them from their living prey.

It was a curious thing. There seemed to be no enemy wounded. They pulled some of the bodies in to examine, and found that some had apparently died from wounds that should have been merely crippling.

"This enemy is stronger than Tondur," Darith muttered, shaking his head. "It is worse than I feared. But where is the rest of this fleet?"

"They followed my other ship after setting my sails afire," said Selvern. "We were trying to reach that chain of islands, north of here, the rocky archipelago men call the Islands of Grief."

"Those cursed islands?" Darith said. "Our folk avoid

them. They are surrounded by treacherous currents, and reefs just below the water's surface. I have sailed farther into those waters than I liked, but even the fishermen of the north coast avoid them."

"I know," said Selvern, "but in this I found hope, thinking that we might elude the enemy among the narrow channels. The commander of the enemy fleet seems intent on keeping the main body of his ships together. Among the islands, this would have lost him many. Then, I had hoped we could surprise the enemy in harbour or ashore, where I could set fire to his ships, and then hunt down his army at leisure."

The wounded men were being brought on board: their faces mirrored what the Prince had said, what Darith felt.

"A good plan," said Darith, gritting his teeth as he remembered the battle he had lost, the battle which he might have won if he had followed that very strategy.

Or would it have worked, after all?

Avlath returned from below, carrying a pile of plain warrior's homespun garments, brown or unbleached white.

"This is all that will fit you, Your Highness," he said.

Prince Selvern barely glanced at the clothing, then began to strip off his wet things. The men on deck stared openly at the heavy mail in which he had swum from his sinking ship. Under the fine silk tunic, his body was solid muscle. What puzzled Darith was how the circlet remained in place on his brow, even when he leaned forward to let the mail roll off.

Olegair fe Mavron, Goll of Caiplic, and other chieftains climbed over the side while he stripped.

"Tell me," Raonull fe Scarriv's mocking voice said, from where he had stood beside the rail since coming aboard, "do all the King's men turn and run at the first sign of a fight? Are they so prone to losing that it seems the most prudent course?"

The other chieftains who had come aboard only stared. They were not yet sure who this battered, blond-bearded stranger might be.

Selvern's face turned white; his lips slid back from clenched white teeth. His hand dropped to his sword-hilt.

"That man's blood is mine!" cried Darith sharply.

"Then he should be dead," said Selvern. His fist lashed out, and the back of his hand cracked across fe Scarriv's face, hurling him back against the bulwark.

"As you wish, Highness," fe Scarriv said, with a cruel

smile. Blood ran from the corner of his mouth.

"*Fools!*" Gonquin exclaimed. "*Kill each other another time! Look!*"

He pointed south. A wall of black sails stretched across the southern horizon, all bellied out, swollen with wind.

CHAPTER SEVEN
Accursed Islands

"There is no time for feuds," said Darith, "and no time for Council. We have wasted what time we had. For now we will turn to the north, there being no better plan. Later we can confer, and try to find another—if we live."

Turning, they stared at him, while unbearable pain twisted in his abdomen, and his blood boiled that this Prince, this Selvern, had *dared* to challenge a man whose blood the Colyn Muir had already claimed—as though the Colyn Muir were of lower rank than a Prince of the realm! That was an insult to the Colyn Muir, and a defiance to the ancient treaty.

But then, Darith reminded himself, he had never sworn fealty to the King, and thus the ancient treaty had never been ratified.

"You wish us to consider your order seriously?" asked Raonull contemptuously.

Darith drew a deep breath.

"I have not," he said, "conceded command of this fleet to any man. Until I do, all the men on all these ships, save Gonquin, the Prince, and those few from his ship who survived with him, are bound to me by solemn oath. Any man who attempts to break that oath now, in time of war, will be dealt with for the crime of treason."

"But suppose we merely leave your fleet to deal with private business, Lord Darith?" asked Olegair fe Mavron.

Darith was startled at the question coming from his friend and ally, then saw what Olegair intended.

"You will be declared Outlaw—on the plain of Colyn, in the hills, in the North, and in all the lands where the King

hold sway." Darith looked around the circle of chieftains as
he spoke, to make it clear that he meant all of them, not just
his friend fe Mavron; and he let his eyes linger on Raonull so
that no one could mistake his intent.

"Who speaks for Colyn Muir speaks for the King," Gonquin said. "Those are the terms of the treaty."

Sudden light dawned in Selvern's eyes and his mouth
moved in a curious half-smile. He looked at Darith sharply,
as if seeing him for the first time.

"So!" Raonull whispered harshly. "Very well. I shall
uphold your command as long as there is danger, and so long
as this voyage may last. I swear it! But I swear *this* also, and
mark me well, Prince Selvern, for you are called to bear
witness: I swear that when this battle and this war are done, I
will take for my own the blood of Colyn Muir. Further, I will
slay its House, and will take the title to myself. Then I will go
the King and swear the allegiance demanded by the treaty.
And then *I* will speak for Colyn Muir, and for the King!"

Blood pounded in Darith's head: pain twisted inside him.
Raonull had sworn the deadliest of oaths. To slay a man was
one thing. To slay his House was another, far deadlier thing.
To swear such an oath before the Prince meant that Raonull
was now obligated, no matter what changes time might
make, to carry it through or to die.

But then, Darith thought cynically, *to slay me is to slay my
House. I am all that is left.* Yet that oath could mean death to
Avlath and any other loyal retainers, as well.

His glance fell on Mannus, whose plaid had been dyed
redder by blood, though from the steadiness with which he
stood, most of it must be other men's, not his own. Not bad
for a boy in his first battle, thought Darith. But there was
something in Mannus's eyes as he looked at Raonull that was
not youthful at all. Darith thought, *The boy I brought with
me from Colyn Muir is already gone.*

Then Mannus seemed to sense his lord's gaze and turned.
Darith cleared his throat.

"Avlath, get the flags and signal the exact substance of fe
Scarriv's oath to all the ships in the fleet."

Raonull turned and stormed toward his boat. He would
have to keep his word: to break it would be greater humilia-
tion than to be hunted as an Outlaw.

Darith tried to relax, but the pain was still there. The men
must not see him weaken.

He had thought that once they found the Prince he could
relinquish command. But with the royal fleet destroyed, the

Prince was only a passenger. The fate of Tondur depended
on him now. He could feel pain growing within him as a wave
cast up by some violence at sea rushes, ever-rising, toward
the land. *Not now! Not so soon! There is too much still to do!*
Summoning his strength, he gestured for Gonquin and the
Prince to follow him.

Darith leaned against the door of his cabin until Gonquin
and Selvern were both inside, then slammed it shut. Pain
swirled up to engulf him.

"Trust Avlath!" He gasped. "Do not let any—of the rest
—know . . . Gonquin . . . Prince—you must—"

The world receded and darkened. The floor rushed up to
meet him.

Dimly, he heard voices in the darkness. He recognised
Gonquin's voice, crooning softly. He lay still.

That strange sweet taste in his mouth—had he ever tasted
it before?

He lay floating. The pain was still there, inside him, clawing and tearing, but it seemed further away somehow, and
did not matter as much. Waves rocked him. He lay in darkness, behind closed eyes.

After a while he decided to try to listen to the voices.
Gonquin was speaking now. Avlath's voice grumbled an answer, and then the singer spoke again. He strained to hear.

"You twist my words," Avlath said.

"Evil things can be done with magic, yes"—Gonquin's
voice was patient—"but good as well. You have just seen me
take away some of your Lord's pain. Was that evil? Will I
pay harshly for it? *Should* I?"

"You may," Avlath blustered. "Good is sometimes rewarded with evil, and—"

There was a sudden, sharp gasp from the minstrel.

"What is it?" Avlath asked.

There was a silence for a moment, then Darith heard
Gonquin's fine, high voice, chanting:

> "Glow with glory, globe of mage
> Show this Sorcery's source!
> Glassy Globe: magic gauge,
> Mark the Curse's course!"

Light began to glow through Darith's eyelids; after a moment, he forced his eyes open.

The light flooded from the glass globe in Gonquin's hands. The flames in it grew steadily brighter.

"It is no wonder their ships overtook you in the night, Prince Selvern," Gonquin said. "See where the fire gathers? The enemy fleet! And the power of their magic is far greater than anything this globe has ever been called upon to show —a dark, unholy power, like something out of old tales."

Darith stirred. What was happening? He tried to speak, to push himself up, but the cabin whirled around him, and the flaring magic light faded.

When he woke again only Avlath was in the cabin, and sunlight came through the port. They had survived the night, then. He sighed, and let his eyes drift shut.

Mannus stood up as the head of the King's Messenger appeared at the top of the hatchway, and reached down to help him onto the deck. They were thrashing along under full sail with the rest of the fleet strung out behind them. The brisk wind chased silver clouds across the sky ahead of them. It would have been a fine day for sailing if he had not known that the Black Fleet was still following.

And if the Colyn Muir had been at the helm.

"Thank you." Gonquin took his hand and let the swing of the ship help lift him the rest of the way.

"Is he better?"

"Who do you mean?" Gonquin's eyes flickered as he straightened.

"My Lord. He *is* ill, then," said Mannus. "I thought it must be so."

"Is that the gossip in the ship?" Gonquin asked sharply.

"No—maybe there's a little speculation—but mostly they think he's keeping to his cabin to help you and the Prince with your magic."

There was little humour in Gonquin's answering laugh. "You might put it that way."

Mannus eyed him narrowly, wondering how much he dared ask. This man seemed lighter of spirit than the old Bard had been, and of course he was much younger, but Mannus suspected he might have the same short way with unwelcome questions. Weeks at sea had taken the shine from courtly garments; there were marks like old bruises beneath his eyes; the beaky nose jutted more sharply. But as Gonquin met the boy's gaze the sardonic lift of his eyebrow was the same.

"I saw my Lord when he came down from the Bard's

Tower, and there was doom in his eyes," Mannus said simply.

"That doom was there before he went to Haunted Valley, before we found out how mighty the enemy is . . . and the look of it has only grown bleaker, and he has grown weaker, as the days have gone by. Sir, I kept silence when Raonull fe Scarriv questioned me, and I will not betray my Lord now, but you must tell me—has *it* come to him?"

The Messenger's eyes became opaque, though Mannus still felt the intensity of his attention. Desperation pressed him.

"Has the Curse of Colyn Muir come to my Lord at last?"

There was a silence.

"Mannus—is that not your name? I think the stern will be a better place for talking. You interest me."

Twice more Darith woke alone, and then Avlath was there, trying to spoon broth down his throat. The lit lantern, hanging from the ceiling, swayed from side to side. Darith swallowed weakly, and slept, and when he woke again, found himself with enough strength to speak.

"Avlath," he whispered weakly. "What is happening? Are *they* still following?"

The Chamberlain rushed to his side.

"They are still on our track," said Avlath. "It is just as the Prince said. Every day we draw ahead of them, for the ships of Dalgir are far faster: but each morning the Black Fleet is closer. They caught up with some of Clan Scarriv's ships and crushed them. Raonull is furious; he turned back to aid his kin, and Olegair turned back with him, and went to his aid. They sank one enemy ship—but three more of ours were lost in the fight. The entire fleet would have turned back, but Prince Selvern—in your name, Lord—ordered the rest to sail on, and he signaled to fe Scarriv and fe Mavron to rejoin us before too many of the Black Fleet were upon them. So Raonull has lost pride as well as kin.

"And now we are near the Accursed Islands. Some of the men mutter that we will be trapped there. No one knows these seas."

"*I* know them," said Darith. "But I cannot pilot the fleet from this cabin! Get me my clothes." He pushed himself up, and sharp pain ripped through his middle. The swaying lamp dimmed and faded as though the cabin had filled with mist, and he felt himself falling.

When he blinked his eyes open again, Gonquin and Selvern had joined Avlath beside the bed, and were staring down at him with troubled faces.

"What shall we do?" Selvern was saying.

"Magic," said Gonquin abstractedly. "If I can find a spell that will work. If Lord Darith had ever sworn fealty—or even been to the City of the King and seen the Crown—I could draw on the Power of the Ancient Throne. But this illness may even be beyond that! I have racked my brain to find a spell that will work. The best I can do will barely hold the . . . disease . . . at bay." He drew breath, thinking. The creak and roll of the ship seemed very loud as they waited for him to go on.

"I know one spell I have not tried, but even if it does work, if it works at all, it will only be for a little while—an hour or two, perhaps, so it is best that I wait until Darith is needed. And then we run the risk that he will faint in the sight of all, and the need for secrecy is real! But perhaps—do you know if there are any charts of the Islands?"

Avlath shook his head, but Darith drew a deep breath, and rasped out, in a choked whisper, "Only very bad ones. But perhaps . . . perhaps good enough to mark the main channel we must find . . . and show where I . . . where you can no longer do without me . . . when I *must* be brought on deck. Chart in . . . sea chest."

Avlath went away, and returned with an armful of mouldering parchments.

The charts were faded and much worn. Selvern helped Darith roll over on his side in the bed, and Gonquin brought a plank to serve as an improvised table. Darith scribbled weakly with a quill.

"Here is the place we must try to reach," said Darith weakly, before his head nodded, and he fell asleep.

"Why have you told me this?" Mannus looked up from his clasped hands and met Gonquin's dark eyes. They had fallen into the habit of meeting thus, here at the stern, when the Troubadour was not below. At least Mannus had thought it was by chance, until now.

"Perhaps it eases me to share the burden of knowledge with one who—if I may remind you—was only too eager to hear what he now wishes he did not know." Gonquin leaned back against the rail, gazing over the restless grey plains of the sea.

The Tondurn ships followed, all heeled over to the same sharp angle as they tacked across the wind, pennons blowing out to one side. Somewhere in the dim haze beyond them, the black ships were wallowing along before the same wind.

"I don't believe that," said Mannus. He picked up the scrap of wood he had been whittling and began to jab at it with his knife.

"No? Well, try another reason—perhaps I need someone who hears what the clansmen and the sailors are saying to tell me if any of Raonull fe Scarriv's nastier accusations take root."

The voice of the King's Messenger was even, pleasant, reasonable. Mannus shot him a quick glance, but could read nothing in those dark eyes.

"You know I won't spy, but fe Scarriv—" Mannus spat into the sea. "If any man of ours listened to that traitor I would knock his head in!"

"I won't ask you to inform on anyone," said Gonquin, "but I would appreciate it if you could squash the more exotic rumours. I would appreciate it even more if you could also discourage those that come too close to the truth!"

The wind fell off a little to the west, and the sailing master passed the order to trim the sails. Mannus shifted his feet to brace himself against the *Maid*'s changed motion, dug his knife into the wood, and drew it forward in a smooth curve.

"What are you making?"

Mannus shrugged. He wondered if he would ever finish the carving now. "It's supposed to be a copy of the figurehead at the *Maid of Tharda*'s prow."

"Do you know her name?" asked Gonquin, squinting toward the prow. "She looks like a Goddess to me."

"To Lord Darith, too, from all I have heard," said Mannus. "I believe she was modeled on the Lady Lonarissa, the Colyn Muir's wife, after whom the ship was named." He put down his knife.

"Oh," said Gonquin. "Finish the carving, lad," he added. "It might cheer him."

Mannus nodded, and let the knife's twist suggest the flowing line of a woman's hair. Old Ylsa had been at the Castle when Darith brought his Lady home from Tharda, and there when she died, and sometimes, when she had drunk enough mead to get sentimental, she would tell the tale.

The story had never meant much to Mannus, until now. But lately the image of a woman had haunted his dreams, a woman with glowing, bee-gold eyes. *If I had a woman like that, and lost her, I would mourn forever too.*

"Isn't it enough for my Lord to bear the Curse?" he said

finally. "Why must he spend what strength remains to him in this mad chase after a mythical sword?"

"I told you. Only the Sword can save us."

"By the time we find it Lord Darith won't have the strength to hold it in his hand!"

"Do you think that he will care, so long as the Sword saves Tondur?" Gonquin burst out suddenly.

"I care."

Mannus blinked quickly, hoping that the King's Troubadour would think the moisture in his eyes was from the wind.

When they woke Darith again, Gonquin stood over him, and Avlath and the Prince each gripped one of his hands. Gonqhin was chanting in his high fine voice:

> *"Strength! Avlath! Strength! Prince Selvern!*
> *By this potent sign, by the Grand Design*
> *By your true hearts and this Wizard's arts*
> *By the gifts of sweat and life-breath*
> *By hardy breed and hearty deed;*
> *By the strength you need—*
> *Life-power flows! Rise, Darith!"*

Darith felt fiery prickling in his palms, and warmth and strength pouring through his arms to his heart; felt his heartbeat matching time with theirs, felt their breath and blood, felt their power swelling, filling him, strengthening him.

> *"Life-power flows! Rise, Darith!*
> *Arise, now arise! Arise, Darith!*
> *Darith! Awake! Warm now with Power!*
> *Need shall be answered, nerves be kindled!*
> *A friend's strength, a lent strength—*
> *Rise now! Rise now! Rise, Life-power!*
> *Life-power pours! Rise, Darith!*

"I—I feel—better." Darith sat up, slowly. "Weak—but—" Pain receded. "What?"

Startled, he saw that Avlath was pale, aged, his face shrunk on his old bones, as though ill from wasting fever.

Prince Selvern, younger, looked less frail—but still bloodless, wasted, sick. Gonquin turned to them, handing them bread, lifting a goblet of wine to their lips. Darith stared. They were stuffing themselves as though they were starving.

As they ate and drank from the same goblet, their colour slowly returned. Darith slid out out of his hammock onto his feet, but the pitching deck moved out from under him, and he almost fell. Gonquin caught him and helped him wrap up in warm furs.

"What did you do?" Darith asked under his breath. "Did you steal their strength for me?"

Gonquin smiled at him, and supported him on his shoulder as they went out on deck.

"I did not *steal* it. They gave it freely. And in a moment, they will be as strong as before, for I have conjured strength into the bread for them, which will quickly replace what they have lost. You eat some too—it will help, although not as much. You are beyond such simple spells as that."

It was near sunset, and cold, when they came up on deck. The wind cut through Darith's furs. Islands lay ahead, great chunks of dark rock thrusting up from the frothing white hair of the grey-green sea.

The black galleons of the enemy loomed behind, closer than he liked; it would be a race to see whether the Tondurn fleet could reach the reefs and disperse before those black shapes could get into fire-arrow range.

Selvern took the tiller, with Darith, shivering, at his side. The sun touched the waves as Darith told him where to steer the ship, leading the fleet behind him into a narrow channel between two islands, the mouth of the complex maze of the archipelago.

White foam frothed on the shoals, but marked on Darith's maps there was a channel through the center, down which they could sail two ships abreast, while the white sea snarled on either hand.

But as the last ships sailed into the channel, a rain of fire-arrows flew from the enemy fleet, arching through blue dusk.

Only the last two ships were still in range, but their sails vanished in sheets of brilliant orange flame.

For a moment the burning ships would block the passage of the shoals, but it would not be long before the enemy was pushing into the channel again.

"What now?" asked Selvern, staring at the restless surface of the sea around them, broken by myriad rocky islands and white-furred hidden reefs. Spray lashed their faces like rain. "They will be on us in a few more minutes."

"North again, now," said Darith, "down that channel.

When it broadens, we can split up into the different channels beyond: the islands are further apart, and—"

"*Look!*" Gonquin exclaimed. He raised the black glass globe in his hands; its light flared about him. "Somewhere nearby must—*there!* See the other light in the globe? It is weak, but it is *there!*"

Red flame flared brilliant on one side of the globe, the side nearest the enemy fleet—but on the other side, a tiny spark glowed cold blue.

"But what does it mean?" asked Avlath, gnawing his lip. Red sunset dyed the sail. The sky was burnished copper above them, shading to pale green at the zenith. Only half a bloody sun remained above the sea.

Ahead, two great rocks thrust like blue-grey teeth from the surface of the water, rising higher than any of the ships, with just enough space between for a single ship to pass.

"We'll have to go through there!" Gonquin pointed to the narrow channel. Darith stared at him.

"There are shoals to either side of those rocks," he said. "But if we go through in single file, the enemy will have to go through the same way. If he wants to attack with numbers, more than one ship against one ship, he'll lose time assembling his fleet. But"—he paused, and pain washed through him while he stared between the rocks, trying to remember —"this is not one of the channels I explored when I brought my ships through here years ago." He frowned, remembering Tharda, and the voyage of his long-ago youth. "And I do not know where it leads, or what waits beyond. Still, there's a chance."

Suddenly, the wind from the south picked up. Selvern put the helm over and the ship shot ahead. But it was not the cool, fresh wind the sailors expected. A murmur went over the deck as they caught the foul odor on the wind.

"Witch-wind!" Avlath exclaimed.

Gonquin shook his head. "A Demon-wind."

Then the towering stone teeth reared up on either side, higher than the masts, and they felt the ship dip and pitch under their feet, as though the sea ahead were lower, as though they were being swept downhill.

Then they were through. Ahead was a broad stretch of open water, with broad channels, smoother, with no signs of hidden reefs. Darith turned, watching behind for the rest of the fleet.

They could see two ships following them through the narrow strait, but time passed before a third appeared. Sunset faded, and cold stars glowed in the turquoise sky.

Three more ships sped through the slot. Then fire-arrows flared in the sky beyond the stone pillars, where the enemy closed in for the kill. Battle sounds rang across the water.

"We must turn, and hold the passage," said Selvern. "One or two ships could do it, and keep the enemy away while the rest escape."

"But all of our fleet must pass through the gap before it can be held," said Darith.

Then a ship with flaming sails burst between the pillars of stone. And right behind came one of the black galleons, like a hound after a deer. Selvern's fist slammed on the railing.

"We *must* go back!" he cried. "None of them can get through now, with—"

"Wait!" screamed Gonquin. "Look at the enemy ship! The sails flap loose, the magic wind gone! What is wrong with it? The lines are going slack. It's losing— Look! *The ship is breaking up!"*

Eerily swift, the great black ship fell to pieces before their eyes.

The very planks broke: sails and cords fell from a splintered mast. In seconds, there was only a tangle of flotsam on the water, with screaming robed shapes floundering in the middle.

"What—?" Darith's voice turned to a shriek as sudden blue light blinded him: blue light that spilled from Gonquin's cupped hands and filled the deck.

The Demon-wind died: clean salt sea air returned.

Selvern caught Darith as he reeled, senses swimming. With the blue light the pain had returned, sharper and more terrible than before.

Gonquin snarled a harsh word of command. The blue light dimmed slowly, until he held only a black glass globe.

"Another night magic," said the Troubador. "Something that protects this place. Some magic stronger than that of the Lord of the Black Fleet."

"Why did it let *us* pass?" asked Selvern.

"Because Colyn Muir commands us?" suggested Gonquin with a shrug. "I can think of no other reason. And that can only mean that the Sword is here, the Sword of Colyn. That the weapon that we seek lies ahead."

Darith, fighting to breathe, said nothing; every breath was agony. The pain now was as though a thousand fishhooks had pierced his intestines—and every one was attached to a line that was being pulled in, slowly, inexorably, irresistibly.

"Land ahead!" the lookout shouted from the mast, and then, "A *peopled* land! Lights are being lit, there to the north!"

After a moment, they saw it against the blaze of white stars in the northern sky: the silhouette of a Castle atop a towering mass of rock. Lights burned in the windows.

Darith screamed. The tugging at his middle grew stronger, as though to drag him to that dark Castle. He fell.

CHAPTER EIGHT
The Velvet Scimitar

Dimly Darith was aware of Selvern and Avlath on each side supporting him, but there was no more room in his mind for anything but the pain. Pain came between him and his senses; he had lost his balance, and lurched like any landlubber as the ship lifted to the sea. He was aware that they were helping him to sit down. He sank into the softness of heaped furs.

Off beyond the pain, dim voices muttered . . .

"His father told me it was like having a lizard inside him, eating away his vitals." Was that Avlath's voice? *"Perhaps that is what it is. Look at the blood trickling from his mouth!"*

"No," said Gonquin's voice. *"An intolerable hunger is a better description."*

A lizard inside? No, it was worse than that now. It was hooks, it was pulling him, dragging him toward the island.

The island . . .

". . . take a boat and go ashore now," Gonquin was saying, *"by night. If any enemy rules the castle, we will surprise him."*

"But what of Lord Darith?" asked Avlath. *"You say only his Blood is proof against the weapon; but he is clearly not fit to fight for it."*

There was a booming sound. Someone knocking on a door?

"Who is it?" Selvern's voice bawled.

"Mannus, Your Highness."

Eyes clenched shut, Darith huddled inside himself, trying to hide from the pain. A year and a day, the Bard had said.

Must he live that long? He wanted to get it over with, die now!

"*. . . tower lights blinking in a signal from the Castle,*" Mannus was saying. "*There—to request that the Commander of the fleet come ashore at once, for some feast tonight. The ship can put in safely at a long stone wharf. You can see it if you look, there—see the torches? Yes, coming down to shore to light the wharf.*"

"*I see,*" came Selvern's reply. "*I think that we must go. Mannus—is it? You stay on guard here. Tell the men your Lord ate some bad meat, and we are taking him to that Castle for tending.*"

The deck echoed to Mannus's retreating footsteps. Darith lay very still, trying to breathe with the top of his chest only, but it gave him little ease.

"*Why are you frowning, Avlath? He won't betray us!*" came Gonquin's voice.

"*No. Mannus is a good lad, but a tanner's boy. Will the men obey him?*"

"*Are you willing to stay here instead?*" asked Gonquin. There was a disgruntled murmur from Avlath. "*Well then, don't complain. In any case, to the crew, Mannus is not your village lad, but a man who did more than his share in the battle of the Salmon Sea!*"

So the waves rolled under the ship, and relentless fangs gnawed at Darith's innards, while torchlight rose out of the cold darkness of the sea. He heard a confused thunder and felt the timbers of the ship tremble as sailors scrambled to take in sail.

Dim figures waited on the low stone wharf. One caught the rope, and the ship came to rest with a jerk that stabbed Darith with pain.

Cold bit through his furs, terrible cold. There was snow on the stone.

"*W—What—What are those people?*"

"*What's wrong with them?*" Darith heard another voice asking.

"*They walk like—they look—dead! Their faces are so white!*"

"*Is it human they are at all?*"

"*Their bodies, perhaps,*" Gonquin said, "*but I think they have no souls.*"

The pain went on. Darith felt himself lifted and moved, and laid in a closed chair: darkness rolled and pitched as he was carried from the ship, and suddenly the swaying changed, and the roll of the waves was replaced by the relentless steady jolt of striding men stamping on a stone street.

Darith stirred from stupour long enough to twitch a slit open between dark curtains; to glimpse first ancient eerie streets and grim stone walls; and later, long dim corridors with richly carven golden walls where jewels threw back the torches' light, while wood floors trembled under his bearers' tread.

Twice more he made the effort to part the curtains and peer through: once when a scent of flowers drew him from his pain to look out into a garden of pallid blooms open to the cold northern sky, where water from marble fountains froze and fell back as mists of crystal ice. *Like Tharda,* thought Darith painfully, but no—in Tharda all had been warmth and color. In Tharda there had been no pain.

Then, in his darkness, he felt the chair set down; and suddenly it was still—unnaturally so after long weeks swaying on the seas. It stirred him from his torpor. A sharp-edged voice rang out.

"Welcome! Welcome to my home, Prince Selvern! It is a great pleasure to meet you, a great pleasure indeed!"

"Baron Caranom?" As Darith twitched the curtain, he saw Selvern bowing beside another chair, and Gonquin and Avlath standing beside theirs, on the polished wooden floor of a huge tapestried hall.

He saw a small, plump man in green silk, standing at an immense table piled with food, who bobbed a pleased bow, smirking. An orange silk napkin was in his hand.

"You know me?" His eyes were small, his hands fat, his red cheeks dimpled; his curly short hair was as well kept as a lapdog's.

"Your servants, when I asked them to send for a physician," said Selvern, "told me I must consult you. One of my companions is gravely ill."

Darith was about to let the curtain's cloth slip from his fingers, and fall back to sleep in his chair, when something on the wall behind the dais caught his attention, and he held the slit open, staring.

On the wall behind the Baron, the Arms of Darith's Clan were worked in a mosaic of inlaid jewels: the eagle and dagger of Colyn the Great.

"Well now, my people are seldom ill." The Baron's brow wrinkled. "I have neither physician nor Bard. Yet perhaps"

—he rapped a small gong with his knuckles—"we do have an old woman who is skilled in treating injuries."

Darith let the curtain slip shut again. The lizard gnawed at his intestines.

"*Thank you,*" said Selvern. "*You are kind to unexpected guests. But how did you know who we were?*"

"*Did you think us cut off entirely from civilised converse here?*" The high tinkling laugh must be the Baron's. Darith's awareness of the conversation phased in and out with the pulses of pain.

"*There was a painter here a few years ago, one Cardilla, who sketched for me the notables of the court—you, my Lord Prince, and this young man—the King's Troubadour. And the Ladies!*" Once more Caranom giggled, and Darith thought he heard an indrawn breath from one of the other men. "*Tarilain, was that one of the names? A well-grown, lively armful for some man's bed, eh? But perhaps you do not wish to talk of women. Who is this other, the sick man whom my people must tend?*"

There was a moment's pause, as if the swift shift had taken even Gonquin by surprise. Selvern's voice was tight as he began to answer. "*He is the Lord of—*"

"*Of many ships in the southern lands!*" Gonquin cut in. "*Who seeks a legendary treasure. A myth, I am certain, my Lord, or surely we should have heard of it. But we needed his ships to deal with that fleet whose ships you saved us from with your magics. I hope your herb-woman has some skill. He will be little use to us as an ally if he is ill!*"

"*Indeed,*" said the Baron. "*Well, I suppose that after such a journey you have a noble hunger, eh? I shall order my servants to prepare more for you—and while you wait, perhaps you would like to wash and put on fresh clothes? We buy what we can when the merchants come by, and we have a great store!*" A breath of air stirred the box curtains as a door closed.

There was a short silence. Then, Avlath's gruff tones—

"*If you're willing to trust him with my master's life, why did you lie to him?*"

"*Perhaps the wisewife can ease him,*" Gonquin said bitterly. "*All my healing arts have failed! But I think that it is death he would get here if this Baron knew your Lord's true name. Man, look around you—there's the crest of Colyn the Great picked out in precious stones on that wall! Whoever Caranom may be, he is no rightful heir to Colyn Muir!*"

"*There's something else,*" said Selvern. "*I remember hear-*"

ing that the painter Cardilla was lost at sea—" His voice cut
off suddenly.

"*Now, gentlemen, my servants will take your friend, and
you must come with me!*"

Darith felt the chair lurch as it was lifted and carried from
the room. Rousing, he heard the Baron's voice again.

"Eat! The table is set."

The chair rocked, and he drifted back into pain-filled
sleep.

This time it seemed he dreamed in his torpor: the green
vale he had known as Haunted Valley lay before him.

He saw again the white villas, and then the white city at
whose gates he had stopped, and the broad lake bright with
barques.

But now the land glowed with sunlight: the city and the
villas were whole.

He watched deeds of horror in the white city, saw young
men and women of the hill clans and lowlands alike called
into the city and tortured, while Demons came from beyond
the world to enjoy their suffering and their blood.

And then it seemed that he walked through long corridors
at night, into a richly furnished room, where a very old, very
evil white-haired man lay sleeping in luxury.

Standing above the old man's bed, he opened an ancient
book. Flames burned in a white bowl beside the bed.

Drawing his dagger, he began to read aloud the words of
the book.

The white-haired man woke, terror in his eyes—but a
hand closed on the old throat, and kept him from screaming,
while the chant went on.

> *KREELATH, come from Ancient Dark*
> *From the Elder hells of Pain*
> *Drink this blood I offer you.*

The knife slashed, and blood fountained from the ancient
throat into the air.

And did not fall. It gathered above the white bowl in a
red cloud that darkened to black, and deepened as it took
form: a tall, lean, horned form, with three glowing eyes.

The Demon of Haunted Valley.

And the Demon called to him: *What is your desire?*

And it seemed to Darith that he answered: "*That first you
provide me with a weapon so potent that it will protect me*

*even against you—a weapon which will overcome any power
in this world or in your own, so mighty that it will prevail
against you yourself—and that you make me—and all my
seed after me—immune to the powers of this weapon.*

"Then, that you destroy all in this valley, except myself!"

And the Demon laughed: *So be it! I will give you my
sword! And of all the world, only the Blood of Colyn—you,
Colyn, and the children of your body—shall be proof against
the powers of this sword.*

And then, the Demon held out something long and black
and curved, that sang sweetly, moaning tones sweet as the
voice of a woman in her pleasure, a song of wonder and
desire that banished all pain, and the song was moving in his
blood.

He reached for the black sword's hilt . . .

Darith woke, feeling a cold, hard surface under him, feeling, too, that sweet song still in his blood, but hearing dim
voices, one of which was saying his name.

"Darith? I cannot reach him for these chains!" It was Avlath's voice, but curiously weak with pain. "Is he alive,
or—or dead?"

"Alive," Gonquin's voice said. "I see him breathing. And
the blood no longer runs from his lips, so he may be better
off than before—though that seems of little value now."

"Oh, I think it will be of *immense* value," purred a voice
from somewhere far above their heads. "If he wakes, he shall
provide me with some sport—or, at the very least, some
service."

"Caranom!" Selvern's voice was a snarl. "If I could get my
hands on you—"

"But you cannot," Baron Caranom answered sweetly.
"That is why you are down there, after all! Or part of the
reason. I'm sure you noticed what poor pork we had at dinner? That comes from keeping slaves too long before you eat
them! I am tired of tame meat, and hunger for wild game!

"Now you, Prince Selvern, are still young, and I'm sure
you'll taste better than the flabby things my servants have
become. Though you may be a little tough."

"You served us—human flesh?" gasped Avlath.

"Oh, not really," laughed Caranom. "After what happens
in the pit—well, you've seen my servants! You can't really
call them *human*, after all! Humans have souls!"

Darith heard the sound of retching, mixed with a mighty
noise of chain links ringing and rattling as they were shaken.

"*That* will do you no good," the cruel voice laughed. "There is a pin under my hand, and when I pull it, your chain will fall free from the wall—but until then, there is no force on earth that can free you."

Darith opened his eyes, and saw Selvern only a few feet away, leaning out, feet braced against the wall as he strained against the chains that held him.

Overhead, the cold white moon hung in a perfect circle of blue night sky, with blackness all around, except for where, near the edge of the circle, a window glowed, and Baron Caranom leaned over a little railing, looking down at them with malicious amusement.

In the darkness, there seemed to be other openings, as though the Baron's place was one of many such boxes—the others all dark and empty. Darith tried to sit up.

The pain that tore through his middle was worse than any he had felt: it curled him up like a spider, and he rolled back and forth on the hard metal floor. He heard low moans, and knew they came from his own lips, and did not care.

"Look here," the Baron's voice purred. "Your friend on the floor is waking up! I believe it's time to begin the first round of my little game!"

The floor under Darith began to vibrate with a deep, grinding sound.

"You won't like playing it," laughed the Baron. "But it amuses me. And soon, you will be interested *only* in what amuses me."

The grinding grew to a roar, booming through the floor under Darith as though he lay on a gigantic drum.

"We'll begin with that fellow. He should be able to walk, I think. I lied to you, you know," the Baron chuckled, "about a woman with healing powers. There have been no women on this island for—oh, for centuries! Since my wife died. They do not seem to survive the soulless state the way that men do. You know, Selvern, now that I look at you more closely, I can think of other things to do with you than fill my gullet."

A new sound began. The teeth that had been fixed in Darith's belly let go. Darith stiffened, almost more stunned by the pain's sudden cessation than he had been by its arrival.

The sound was low, but it cut through both Selvern's curses and the Baron's laughter.

Darith rolled up onto his hands and knees and looked toward the sound.

"That door you see opening," Caranom said, "the ancient people of this place made to release various animals into this arena, long ago. Animals so starved that they would eat any-thing—or anyone." He laughed. "Or sometimes, they trained the animals to do very—*special* things, to the people in this pit. Delightfully cruel, the old people! But that was all long ago. Now we are much more—refined. Do you hear its song? It is *hungry*." Again the Baron shook with laughter. "Hungry for the spirits, for the *souls* of men!"

Darith rose to his feet, pain gone as if it had never been. The faint sound grew, winding like a serpent from the door-way, striking poisonously at the ears.

But Darith recognized that call.

"Ah, he hears it. *Now* you shall see!" sang Baron Car-anom.

Darith strode toward the dark doorway that had opened in the pit's wall, and the floor drummed hollowly under his feet, as though it were only a thin metal shell.

It was a thin shell of iron, he knew, somehow, and there was a joint in the center, a junction that would open, and there was a deep well beneath.

He paused at the door. Avlath was shouting for him to come back, and now Selvern's voice joined in.

Darith looked through the door. Darkness, but in the darkness, white mounds: piles of bones everywhere.

And beyond them, a faint light and something moving. Something that sang.

He walked into the dark tunnel. Bones crunched under his feet. The light grew. He heard shouting behind, but paid no heed.

The tunnel ended at the mouth of a larger chamber, like a stone womb. Flame leaped purple and red from a tiny ala-baster bowl.

Behind the bowl, a figure stood, both hands raised, hold-ing above its head . . . *darkness*.

Darkness in the shape of a sword, a great curved sword.

The figure stepped toward him, and the light from the bowl showed its face.

The parchment skin was torn, and bone showed through. Bright eyes gleamed from far down, deep inside the caves of eye sockets. Rags of mouldered cloth hung in strips around withered, bony limbs, and a rib cage covered with shrunken parchment.

Fire glinted and sparkled from jewels still sewn to tattered cloth, and on the floor, fallen jewels lay unheeded.

Bearing the sword edge-up in its palms, the skeleton walked to meet him. Now the blade of the sword lifted from the left palm, and arced toward Darith's head.

Darith never moved.

There was a strange, grating shriek, and the sword twisted in the air, turning aside from Darith's body.

The sweet music stopped.

Darith's eyes met the sunken eyes inside the skull.

The ribs moved, for the first time, drawing a breath, like an ancient, wheezing bellows.

The leather that was stretched over the dried throat moved. The sounds that came out were not words, only dry scraping sounds, dust stirred by wind. Yet Darith understood them.

"Who—are—you?" the dried voice said.

"I am the Colyn Muir," Darith answered, his voice calm. "I am the heir of Colyn the Great."

"At last," sighed the dust-dry voice. *"Welcome, my Son. Take up, now, the burden of the Blood of Colyn Muir."*

And the bony arms stretched toward him, and across the fleshless palms stretched pulsing blackness in the shape of a sword: the velvet scimitar, the Magic Sword of Colyn.

Darith reached out. The blade was warm to the touch, more like flesh than metal, but the hilt was ice-cold.

As his fingers locked around the hilt, memories—*not his*—flooded him. Too many memories—more memories than a man should have in one lifetime.

His fingers touched the bony fingers of the other hand, and he felt the bones under the old leather move, slowly. Felt the leather crack and split as the hand opened.

Again the ancient bellows of the ribs filled.

"Atone for my Sin, boy!" Dry wind whistled in the throat's old dust.

The bony fingers let go the hilt, and the skeletal shape reeled back.

"Free!" the dry voice wheezed. *"Free at last!"*

The finger bones fell from its hands as ancient skin turned to dust, and the skeleton crumpled, to crash and shatter on the stone floor.

Darith stood in darkness, his head a whirl of memory, ancient brightly coloured scenes seen by eyes that were not his own.

He saw there the dream he had had, of the white-haired

old man whose blood had risen in a cloud to take the shape of the three-eyed Demon.

Memories of this crypt—far too many memories of this crypt, and memories of terrified, trembling men and women —even children—stumbling into the crypt, to kneel and touch the black blade of the sword, as the Sword—fed!

With a start he stared at the white bowl's flame, suddenly remembered what it was.

He reeled under the shock of remembered centuries, the mazes of memory. He sought to forget these long ages in this crypt, and the shameful horrors that haunted him, and strove instead to remember *before* . . .

Early memories, of herding sheep in the mountains, near the place where Castle Colyn now stood.

Memory of dripping, horrid shapes that came to seize him. Of others coming to his aid: two old men, Colyn's father and his Clan's Bard, and a young man in ragged, ill-fitting clothes.

That young man—*who?* Darith waited, and memory painted the face anew, older, and crowned by the Ancient Crown.

So! This, then, must be the exiled Prince, the heir to the throne of the lowland kings. That much of the story Darith remembered, at least: how—ages before—invaders had conquered the eastern plain, driving the Ancient Kings from the City of Kaerbradan, and the old people of the plains had fled into the hills to the west, to take refuge among the mountain clans. And the Crown of the Ancient Kings had been carried away in their flight, and all Power departed from it, and from the Throne in the ancient City of Kaerbradan.

And he remembered how, after long years, the invaders had marched up the pass that led over the mountains, to build their new capital in the valley that was now Haunted Valley, controlling the pass, giving them a base from which to conquer the hill clans and slowly extend their rule through the mountains, until the ruler of that City was a great King, ruling even the defiant clans of the hills.

But one day a Magician had come into that City, and offered the King great power, and that King was tempted and fell under the Magician's spell. And more Magicians gathered to the City, and many who lived there studied under them, and those who did not they sacrificed to the Demons that they called up to serve them.

But the younger brother of the King had fled, and found

refuge among the hill clans—and, hiding in the hills, had come to the aid of the simple shepherd boy.

A simple shepherd boy who never forgot.

Memories of years then, to which the confused tales he remembered were a key. He saw the girl that the Royal Heir loved pulling from its chest the secret, hidden crown, the Ancient Crown. For the line of the Children of the Twin-Born King and Queen had not died out, though they were few; and they hid still their one great treasure, the Crown of the Ancient Kings—although its power had gone from it, and it was only a relic from old times, and its mate, the Crown of Queens, had been lost forever. And to this clan by chance, the Prince Royal had come for refuge, and had fallen in love with a daughter of the ancient line.

He saw the Royal Heir and his beloved going to the deserted city of Kaerbradan, to reunite the Ancient Crown with the Ancient Throne.

And always with them, their faithful servant, the boy Colyn.

Darith remembered the struggle between the Power of the Ancient Crown and the Demons who served the Sorcerer-King of Haunted Valley. Darith had not known how Colyn had destroyed the Sorcerers, but now he saw—and it was in his dream before waking here. The old white-haired man who had stared up at him in shock, the shock of betrayal. And suddenly Darith knew that it had been by treachery and deceit that Colyn had destroyed the Sorcerers.

He remembered, now, Colyn guarding himself with magic he had learned from the Bards, as he entered the fearful Valley. How he had strode then into the very Palace of the Sorcerer-King, and declared himself an apprentice Sorcerer, seeking a Master.

And as he had hoped, the Ruler of the Magicians—not the former King, but the Sorcerer who had corrupted that King—had accepted him as a pupil, and trained him in Sorcerous Arts far beyond the simple magics of the Bards.

And the old man whom Colyn had sacrificed to the three-eyed Demon had been Colyn's teacher. The old man had trusted him, and he now writhed in the torment of the Demon's home.

He saw Colyn walk out of the hills, with the Black Sword singing in his hand, to slaughter an army.

He turned away from those memories with a shudder. The Sword was silent now, and in that silence he heard,

warped by echoes, the whining, petulant voice of Baron Caranom.

"*No,*" the Baron snapped irritably as though in answer to
some question. "*Nothing is wrong. It is only—the scream.*"

"*I heard no scream,*" a voice answered—too deep for
Gonquin's voice, Selvern perhaps, or Avlath.

"*That is the point!*" the Baron snapped. "*There is usually a
scream!*"

Darith turned his mind back to the bewildering swarm of
memories. Suddenly, among thousands of bright-coloured
pictures, he saw a memory of Tharda.

"*No,*" *the old man was saying,* "*we know no spell to drive
Kreelath from the world, save for that which now rests upon
your shoulder. That is why we never summoned him, and why
we placed that warning in the book that you stole. We had
hoped that the warning would be heeded.*"

"*Why give the spell for his summoning at all, then?*" Colyn
shouted. *The sword writhed on his shoulder, but he gripped it,
and held it back. The old man shook his head.*

"*The Book would have been incomplete without it. Knowledge must grow, for its own sake, whatever the danger. And,
indeed, good came of your summoning, did it not?*"

"*So I thought at the time.*"

"*So the Bards still think who sing of Colyn Muir.*"

"*Yet Kreelath still walks loose, and compared to his evil,
the Sorcerers he destroyed were mischievous children.*"

"*But he has had no chance to do great evil, because you
pursue him around the world, and he flees.*"

"*But always he has time to do evil before he flees. For I am
still a living man, still bound by the speed of horses and ships.
He can fly! It is always a long journey for me to reach him—
and he has done his evil, and is gone, and begun again in
another place. But that is not the worst.*"

"*I sought, and thought I had gained, the power to destroy
evil. Instead, I find that I am myself becoming evil.*"

Caught in the maze of memories, Darith let the point of
the Black Sword drift to the floor.

He started, as flames flared from bright-glowing stone.

Memory warned him then, and he jerked the point free.
Still the stone glowed, and a terrible heat and choking stench
began invading the room.

In his mind the memories of the thousands of times in
hundreds of years that the blade had slipped told him what
he had to do—but he could not believe it. He stared at the
glow, then, kneeling down, spat on the bright spot.

Flame dimmed, but did not go out. Then, drawing a deep breath, he reached down with his left hand, and laid his cringing bare flesh over the spot of hell-flame.

He felt a surge of power from the Sword.

The heat did not burn. He stared down, trying to interpret this tangled mass of memory.

The distorted echoes of voices came from outside.

Darith took the bowl of flames from its place with a little shudder, then, with that weird hell-fire to light his way, began to move quickly down the tunnel.

"Your Highness," Gonquin's voice came ringing clearly down the tunnel, *"I am truly sorry that a Prince of the Realm should have to die at the hands of such an incompetent boorish, small-minded..."*

The voice went on for a while, and Darith could not help smiling as he hurried down the tunnel, although he knew that reaching the Baron would be difficult.

Colyn the Great had entered this tunnel of his own free will, in order to keep his own men safe from him, choosing this place because it would be difficult to escape.

But with help, it could be done. When the Baron released his friends to come to the cave—

Bleak memories arose. If his friends were sent into the cave, could he keep them safe from the Sword? Colyn had been mastered by it.

The mouth of the tunnel opened before him, and the moonlit arena. He set down the bowl of flames, lest its light betray him, hoping in the moonlight dimness of the pit to run around the shadowy rim to the door at the side. The Sword would burn through door and lock in an instant, and he would be in the maze of tunnels by which the prisoners had been brought down.

Then he would hunt down Caranom. But first he had to get across the arena unseen.

Gonquin's skilled tongue was still flaying the Baron with epithets.

"Enough!" Caranom shouted shrilly, and the floor of the pit dropped away, leaving captives hanging by their wrists, their arms almost wrenched from their sockets. Darith stood on the edge of the cliff, with a sheer drop into endless darkness at his feet.

CHAPTER NINE
Loyalty and Legacy

Mannus jerked as *Maid of Tharda* was brought up short by the cable that moored her to the dock. Then the swell swung her in again, and he leaned back against the cabin wall. The motion of the tethered ship seemed unnatural after so long at sea, but then, everything else about this anchorage was strange, so why should he expect to feel at ease?

Above him, Darith's empty hammock swung listlessly. Light from the hanging lamp glinted from the gems in the hilt of the sword on the wall.

When Darith had been out of this cabin before, that sword had always been at his side. His Lord's absence without it, thought Mannus, was the most unnatural thing of all. What were they doing to him on that island?

Perhaps if Mannus had been swinging in his own hammock in the crowded warmth of the seamen's berth, the waiting would have been easier. But Prince Selvern had told him to keep watch, and like a good dog set to guard his master's door, here he would stay.

It was a role more suited to Avlath, thought Mannus as he drew up his legs and wrapped his arms around his knees. But the Chamberlain had gone with the others. Mannus had received his share of cuffs from Avlath when he was serving as a page in the Castle of Colyn Muir, but he knew the older man would never desert his Lord. He could be tricked, though—Mannus's lips twitched as he remembered some of the things he had gotten away with in the past. Still, Gonquin was there; it would take a master of magic to deceive *him*.

And for physical protection they had Prince Selvern's strong right arm.

So what do you suppose they would need you for, tanner's brat? You've been left behind again, but at least you're in a post of honour this time. Mannus tried to defuse bitterness with self-mockery. But through the porthole he could see lights like slitted eyes in the dark bulk of the Castle, and he could not stifle his conviction that something was badly wrong.

Mannus stretched his legs straight before him and considered the boots that Gonquin had found for him somewhere. *Wearing boots like a gentleman!* he thought, and bundled up in trews with a sheepskin bound around his body and a good beard started to help ward off the cold—Ylsa would hardly recognize the lad she had ordered about for so long.

And do I recognize myself, even? he wondered then. Surely journeying, and facing death in battle, and even those conversations with the King's Troubadour that seemed so rambling until some chance phrase would suddenly revise Mannus's view of the world—surely those things must make him different somehow.

He tried to visualize the hills around Colyn Muir, the ivy-clad silhouette of the Bard's Tower against the sky, and found their images appearing to memory with the distant clarity of a dream. The Colyn Muir strode through the dream like a hero out of legend—with the bronzing of long voyages on his skin and the ghost of ancient sorrows in his eyes. A far cry, that, from the gaunt, half-conscious wreck they had carried ashore.

We have both changed, these past weeks, both Lord Darith and I.

The ship dipped and lifted; through the distorted glass of the porthole, the little lights in the Castle seemed to rise and fall. No—it was the lights that were moving—points of light were bobbing down the causeway from the Castle to the shore. Were they returning already? Was Lord Darith dead, or cured? In a single, swift motion Mannus came to his knees before the porthole, fumbling the window open to see more clearly, despite the icy air.

Men were coming. They were carrying something, but not a stretcher, and none of them moved with Gonquin's light grace or Selvern's purposeful stride. As they reached the dock he realized that they were more of those strange servants from the Castle.

"Well, I dunno about that," he heard the seaman who was

on watch replying to some question. "Ye'll have to speak with Master Mannus about it. He's in the captain's cabin, below."

Mannus twitched uncomfortably at the title, but he was on his feet, trying to look as if he deserved it, when the Baron's servants filed in.

As the door was closed his nostrils flared, for the air in the close space was already filling with wonderful odors—the spicy scent of mulled wine, the rich, heavy smell of roasted meat and the warm seduction of pastry.

"By Baron Caranom's order—food from the feast for you and your men."

Mannus's gaze jerked from the covered basket of food back to the face of the man who held it. He had only seen the Castle folk from a distance, before.

These pale faces might have been carved out of wood: their eyes were dull stones. Unease tickled his nerves.

"That's very kind of him. It's unusual to give the same food to the masters and the men."

He had carried the festival dishes to the High Table when the chieftains visited Colyn Muir, and joked with their retainers in the kitchens while they ate it. There should be some hint of appreciation, of amusement, even of complicity in the man's eyes.

But there was no expression at all.

"Food from the feast. For you—"

"No, I don't think so." Mannus swallowed, the rumbling of his belly giving him the lie even as he said the words. "We are not used to such fancy fare."

"The Baron's order. You will eat the food." The other three servants stepped forward. One pulled the cloth from his basket and Mannus saw a whole roast fowl, skin golden with basting and crusted with herbs. His mouth watered as the delectable aroma filled the air.

"No." Mannus eased to one side, getting his back to the wall.

"Eat—"

Swallowing, Mannus shook his head. As if at some unspoken order, the four men set their burdens down.

Knives flickered into their hands. They moved in.

Mannus's own knife was useless at his waist, hidden under his swathing of sheep's wool.

Goddess, help me! As he dodged, a gleam caught his eye; in the same movement he reached up and ripped Lord Darith's sword from its hooks on the wall.

The sheath clattered against the bulkhead as he jerked the blade free.

The servants' daggers came up to guard with mechanical perfection, but as it had in the battle, fury surged through Mannus's veins and doubled his speed. He whipped the sword down in a slash that sheared one arm fully off at the shoulder: a hot wet splash spurted on the deck.

The man crumpled, bleeding to death in eerie silence.

The other three moved in, sharp steel bright in their hands. Their daggers were more deadly in this small cabin than the sword.

A knife-blade glinted in the trembling light—*too close!*

Mannus danced back, with no space to swing his sword, and fear that he should be trapped against the wall surged through him. That would be the end!

He swung up the gem-hilted sword, but the pale faces did not flinch. Like the shrouded men, the three seemed not to care whether they lived or died.

He never knew how he scrambled away from the swaying, leaping blades. One scratched his shoulder, smearing red blood across the wool, as he backed away, sweating from his narrow escape. They followed, silent, arms held out to grip him. Mannus jerked Darith's sword back behind him, knowing that if they could seize and hold that arm, he was done.

Steel struck the swinging lamp and rang like a clear bell. And still the servants moved in, as though asleep.

Mannus sprang with a speed he never had in practice. Darith's blade ripped a servant's throat out, and went on. A turn of Mannus's wrist flattened the blade as he struck out for the face of the man behind. A flood of blood hid the still face. Fingers rolled the green-gemmed hilt in his hand, as he lunged to drive his fleet sword's point into the last man's heart.

Yet no death cries rose.

The breath rasped his throat in harsh gasps. Mannus looked down at the men he had slain, and saw no rictus of fear or grimace of agony. Their still faces had not changed. Like the shrouded men, they had bled and died in silence.

These men had died to make him eat—what? Food doctored with sleeping stuff, or more likely, poisoned? Was this how Baron Caranom feasted his guests? Realization turned the fire in Mannus's belly to ice.

Bloody sword still in his hand, he burst through the cabin door and scrambled up the ladder.

He glimpsed the cloaked shape of Darith's sailing-master

with the sailor on watch and thanked the Gods—the man must have come on deck to see about the disturbance. His boots slid on the slick boards as he hurried toward them.

"There's something wrong at the Castle—those servants attacked me and I had to kill them. The bodies are in my Lord's cabin. Get rid of them, and the food too—I think it's poisoned—if you can, without alarming the men!"

"But what about you—"

Mannus was already turning away. He forced himself to stop, to think what must be done.

"I'm going up there to see what's happened. But there may be danger for all of you. If I don't return by daylight, cast off and get the *Maid* out to sea!"

"But Master Mannus, who will take command?"

Mannus trembled with the need to be gone, but some other part of his mind was working with unaccustomed clarity. The faces of Darith's chieftains flickered through his awareness.

"Signal to the fleet...to follow you out, and then... summon Olegair fe Mavron and tell him His Lord is lost."

Mannus did not wait for an answer. The gangplank by which the Baron's men had entered was still in place. He sprang over it and started up the hill. *Lost!* His own words echoed in his ears. What was happening to Darith and the others now? It was only as his bootheels echoed on the worn stone of the causeway that Mannus realized that the sword he still gripped so desperately was his Lord's.

"...and unable to control his temper, as well," finished Gonquin.

"You think," said Caranom, leaning out over the edge of the pit, "that because you are about to die, or something just as final, that you can insult me with impunity? You think there is nothing worse I can do you? Well, you are wrong! I put you down there because you amused me at dinner, and I thought you deserved an easy ending. Now I've changed my mind! After you watch your friends perish, we will play some of my more *elaborate* games. I have three hundred slaves, each of whom has all a man's ability except for a soul and free will—*but no! Better still!* Why use my old slaves? I shall have your friends to aid me. *They* shall do my bidding upon your body. I can wait for better meat for my table, with such amusing sport to keep me enthralled, I'm sure. And indeed, I will have meat as well!"

Darith gritted his teeth, looking down into the vast gaping

darkness. Had Colyn's memories not warned him of the arena's trick floor he would have tried to cross.

"Do you know, Troubadour," the Baron continued, "the variety of things that can be done to a man? Before I am half through, you will *beg* for the stillness and peace of which you have just robbed yourself."

Gonquin, dangling in chains, yawned.

"So you pulled a lever," he said. "I've seen that done before. You opened a trapdoor—a very large trapdoor, but not of *your* making. Where is the power of which you were boasting? Surely you can do card tricks, at least?"

"I could pull this pin and drop you all to the night creatures that dwell in the depths, this *instant!*" Caranom shrieked, a note of hysteria in his voice.

"Of course you can!" said Gonquin. "You *could* have poisoned us at dinner. What ´of it? So any man could do. It requires no special cleverness."

Darith, lurking in the darkness of the doorway, shook his head, astonished by the Troubadour's control. He knew that Gonquin must be in agony from the pain of his wrists and shoulder-sockets, yet the Troubadour kept the pain from his voice, with only the faintest edge to mar the illusion that he was talking over wine at dinner.

Caranom produced the black glass ball with a flourish.

He made a mystic pass with his hands, and weird blue light appeared, expanding until the ball was a globe of blue-white flame.

"You see this *toy* of yours?" the Baron snarled, his breath freezing in the icy air. "It is so small a gauge, that a thousandth part of the power of this island could not register in its blazing. Watch, and I will show you how insignificant it is, before *my* power."

He tossed the glowing ball into that great dark maw.

Darith watched it fall, a shrinking blue-white light, dwindling to a star, a vanishing spark, fading from sight.

He heard it splash as it hit the eternal darkness of the waters of the eternally lightless pool at the island's core.

Then he heard the echoes of water crashing like surf against the well's walls, as though huge bodies moved there.

A deep bestial moaning sounded far below, but whether it was a roaring of beasts or the sound of wind in the caverns he could not be sure.

The two halves of the floor slowly rose. Darith gave a sigh of relief.

The floor came up under the prisoners' feet, and at last

they were able to stand and lift the strain off their shoulder-joints. Darith heard barely stifled gasps.

"*You* are the small bright point," said Caranom smugly. "*I* am the great gaping darkness."

"An aptly poetic illustration," said Gonquin. "But an illustration is not the thing itself. If you are so powerful, Baron, where is the crashing of Chaos that so lately roared from yonder doorway? How long does it take your pet to eat a soul? You say there is usually a scream, but there has been none. Can it be that your power is ended? That the Blood of Colyn Muir is proof against whatever you keep in that room?"

Oh, Gonquin, you fool, Darith groaned to himself. *Why couldn't you keep your Troubadour's tongue between your teeth?*

"*What are you saying?*" asked Caranom, his voice rising an octave. "What is this about Colyn's Blood?"

"The man you just sent into that room," said Gonquin, "was the last living descendant of Colyn the Great."

"*No!*" shrieked Caranom. "*You're lying!* I'll have no more of this! I'll send a slave in, and see what really happened! *Here,* somebody, quickly!"

Darith saw Caranom turn from the pit, and poised himself to run for the door. If the Baron saw him before he could reach it—

"Quick!" the shrill voice shouted. "I need someone to run an errand *now!*"

Darith hesitated. Perhaps he should wait for the slave. Perhaps he could even disguise himself.

"*Who are you?*" the shrill voice cried. "What do you want?"

A lower voice answered, too soft to be heard.

"*No!*" the Baron's voice cried. "*No! It cannot be him!*"

Darith stiffened at the sound of steel.

Scuffling figures appeared at the edge of the pit. One reeled and fell; the voice that screamed was the Baron's voice.

The iron floor boomed as the Baron landed a few feet to Selvern's left.

Selvern lunged, but Caranom rolled away, and the Prince's chains caught him and pulled him back.

Caranom, squeaking like a rat, rolled further before scrambling to his feet. He looked around, crouching, frightened, eyes narrowed.

The sword moaned in Darith's hand, sweetly.

"*No!*" Caranom whimpered. "Oh, no! Not *me!*"

The strange music grew, sweet as the promise of peace—yet in it were the songs of unborn children, the voices of drowned sailors rising in the sea wind, the death-wails of a thousand women and their children, the screaming of all the men ever lost at sea. Like a serpent that strikes at the ears it moved through the still night air, poisonous and enticing as struggle's end.

Leaden steps bore Caranom toward the door where Darith waited.

"Please," he said softly, tears rolling down his fat, moon-whitened cheeks. "Oh please . . ."

Shaking and sobbing with terror, Caranom staggered the rest of the way to the door. He turned to look back at his prisoners, his eyes imploring aid.

He stumbled through the doorway, and his hopeless eyes met Darith's. Darith shuddered, pity stirring—

And then the sword moved of itself, dragging Darith's arm, and the Baron gave one long scream, a scream that should never have come from human lips.

Darith closed his eyes.

Distorted echoes called his name.

"*Lord Darith?*" a voice called in the distance. "*Prince Selvern? Avlath? Where are you?*"

It was the voice of Mannus, echoing weirdly from the walls of the Baron's hall.

"*Down here,*" Selvern shouted. "*In the pit!*"

Darith opened his eyes. He did not look at the Baron's body as he pulled the black sword free. A moment later Mannus's head appeared above the balcony's rail.

"My Lords!" Mannus exclaimed. "You are *chained!*"

"Why, so we are," laughed Gonquin, a little hysterically.

"There's a release up there somewhere," called Selvern, "but be careful what you pull—one of those levers will cause the bottom of this pit to fall away. The Baron spoke of pulling pins to free us. See if you can find them, but don't be too hasty—only the Gods know what you might loose if you touch the wrong device."

"No fear of that, Your Highness," said Mannus, and suddenly the chains rattled and clattered down. Selvern staggered as the chain he leaned against to peer up the wall suddenly fell free from the stone, nearly hitting him as it slithered to the ground.

Avlath and Gonquin dodged away as their chains, too, came ringing down the wall.

"The pins were no more than bolts put through an iron ring," said Mannus.

"We'll need a ladder to get out of here," Selvern called. "Or help from Caranom's—servants. They must know the entrance. Caranom didn't carry us down here himself, I'm sure."

"The—servants—will not be much help," Mannus said doubtfully. "They fight as though they were asleep, and don't seem to care whether they die or not. But—I will . . ."

"Do what you can," Selvern called up, "but be quick! We are still in danger here—"

"*Avlath!*" Gonquin shouted.

The Chamberlain was halfway to the dark door. Gonquin sprang after him, kicked his legs out from under him, and they both went down, scuffling, while Darith watched from the doorway.

"My Lord is still in there!" Avlath shouted.

Turning, Darith lifted the flaming bowl from the floor.

"You cannot help him by throwing your own life away!" Selvern exclaimed, while the struggling figures rolled back and forth.

Flickers of light and shadow hunted each other across the ground before him as Darith came out of the passageway, carrying the bowl and the Sword.

"You would have followed me, Avlath?" he said quietly. They looked up and saw him. "Even into that room?"

They stared. Gonquin released Avlath, and the Chamberlain climbed to his feet.

"I have served you all my life, Lord, in many places, against many enemies, and your father and brother before you. Should I deny you my service now, merely because you walk in a different land?" The Chamberlain swayed a little as he stood, but his voice was steady.

There was a long silence, as the two men looked into each other's eyes. Light and darkness painted Avlath's face with a dozen masks, but the meaning of all of them was the same.

How have I deserved such loyalty? And how can I possibly reward it . . . now? thought Darith, feeling the weight of the Sword in his hand.

"What is in that room?" Gonquin asked at last.

"Nothing—now," said Darith.

"What *was* in it?" Gonquin persisted. Darith considered a moment, then answered.

"Colyn the Great. Bones. Rags encrusted with precious gems. Dried flesh. This bowl and this sword— *No!*" he shouted, as Avlath reached out, as though to touch a finger to that soft, powdery black, like soot on finest velvet. "Do *not* touch it! It is worse than death!"

"What about—Caranom?" asked Gonquin. Darith raised the flaming alabaster bowl in his hand.

"Here, at the mercy of those whose bodies he kept as slaves."

The moon had left the mouth of the well above their heads: dawn's dusk dimmed the stars.

Suddenly a second door burst open in the arena's side, and Mannus ran in, red sword dripping in his hand.

"Come away quickly, my Lords! The servants are falling like flies in the halls! I fear some new evil is unleashed! Unless we—" He stopped suddenly, and his sweating face turned red, then white, as he saw their eyes all fix on the green-gemmed hilt of the sword in his hand . . . the sword of the Colyn Muir.

He fell on his knees before Darith.

"Forgive me, my Lord. I know I had no right, but it was the only blade at hand. We feared you lost. The—creatures —from the island came aboard with food and drink, and drew steel to try and force it on me. Prince Selvern had ordered me to stay on guard in your cabin—your sword was the only weapon—my Lord, take it back now!" Bowing his head he took the sword by its wet red blade and offered its green-gemmed gold hilt to Darith.

Darith stared at Mannus as if he had never seen him before. The demonlight was playing tricks with his features, too. Darith saw a man there now, a warrior; he saw the shadows that responsibility would grave in that face, and the noble sculpturing of power.

"Do not judge him too harshly," said Selvern. "I had ordered him to stay with the ships—he seemed the most loyal of your men, except for Avlath—and even if he has endangered the fleet by coming ashore—"

"I thought of that too, Your Highness," Mannus whispered. "I told the sailing-master to leave at sunrise if we didn't return."

"Well, you had been left in command," said Selvern, "and though part of my mind wondered what you were doing here, and how you dared disobey my order, I must admit I was never so glad to see any face as I was to see yours peeking over the edge of this pit. So I had resolved to say nothing. 'How dare you leave yor post?' would have been a most churlish greeting to one's saviour at that point—and that would have been the time to say it!"

"How many men did you bring with you?" asked Darith. His own voice sounded strange in his ears.

"None, my Lord—I had no right."

"That was foolish," said Darith, "but also brave."

Silence echoed around them, and the color that had come into Mannus's face at the praise faded once more. Suddenly he looked very young, but there was a vigor in that youth that was like the strength of a young tree unfurling its leaves to the spring sun. *As I am a blasted tree, with one last bitter fruit to bear,* thought Darith. *But perhaps there is a way for the House of Colyn Muir to flower once more.*

With sudden purpose he swung up the gem-hilted sword in his left hand. Round and lightless, Mannus's eyes followed it, but he did not flinch away.

A turn of Darith's wrist flattened the blade as it struck Mannus's shoulder, smearing red blood across the wool. The boy rocked to the blow, but the sword was already lifting to mark the other shoulder.

"Arise, Mannus, noble of the King's realm, tanist and heir of Clan Colyn," Darith's voice cracked across the arena. "Prince Selvern, do you bear witness to this deed?"

"I do," said the Prince. "Noble Mannus, arise."

"My Lords?" Mannus staggered to his feet, blinking. "What do you mean?"

"Now take back this sword," Darith continued. "It has served the Line of Colyn well. Remember that."

"But what will you—"

"I have another weapon," said Darith heavily. "It will serve as long as I need a sword. But I have no sons of the body, and no heir to lead the Clan when I am gone. Mannus of Colyn Muir, will you do this thing for me, for your people, and for the land where you were born?"

He was still holding out the sword. The gems on its hilt glittered like the tears that were sparkling in Mannus's eyes.

"My Lord, you did not need—" His voice failed, but Darith's gaze held his. At last Mannus nodded. His hand was trembling, but he managed to reach out and grip the blade.

"Oh, my Lord! I am your man in all things, even this." He brought the sword up in salute, then let it fall.

"Go now, and bid the ships wait," Darith added briskly. "Dawn already dyes the sky, and I have no wish to be trapped on this island. Hurry!" he added as Mannus hesitated. "Leave the door open behind you, and we will find our own way through these halls."

Mannus swallowed, bowed, and dashed from the room.

"My life will not be long," said Darith, turning to the others, "but I can reward loyalty, and provide for my people."

"It was well done," said Selvern, with an approving nod.

"Fe Scarriv will be furious," Gonquin observed wryly.

"Fe Scarriv," said Avlath, "is already sworn foe to Colyn Muir, and has sworn to slay our House."

"At least he now has a House to slay," said Darith grimly, "but we must hurry! Gonquin, do you know what you hold?"

The Bard looked down into the bowl of flames, and they saw his lips tighten against his teeth.

"I do indeed," he said. "It is a gateway into the Demon-World from which the Sword came—where the souls of its victims go. Do you wish me to sing the runes?"

"Can you?" asked Darith.

"I think so," said Gonquin. Turning, he carried the bowl of fire to the center of the arena, and laid it on the crack where the iron plates met.

He knelt beside it, and with his hands made passes over the hellfire flames.

> *"Demon-World's Death-Door*
> *Demon-Sword's War-Hoard*
> *Doom of Bard's words heed!"*

Amethyst-coloured flames swayed rhythmically, rising to lick at his fingers.

"I can learn from it," he said. "Stand well back, all of you!"

Selvern and Avlath moved to put their backs against the wall of the pit: Darith stepped back a pace, and kept the black Sword pointed at the flames. Strange sensations poured up the Sword into his arm.

Gonquin, standing, held his arms out above the swaying, leaping flames, and began a high, wailing chant.

> *"Dead Damned in Dire Fire:*
> *Sing now your Secrets!*
> *Wide gapes World Gate!"*

The red and purple flames reared up tall as a man. Gonquin stepped back, and continued to chant. The words seemed to twist as he spoke them, the vowels nasal and sharp, their jarring pattern suggesting damned shapes writhing just out of sight.

The flames grew higher, swirling and shaking like the colours in a devil's kaleidoscope.

> "Torture-tormented
> Demented Demon-toys
> Damned men. Doomed ones.
> Deem my Demands now
> Dominate Demon-dammed
> Dead men's doom!
> Dumb now no longer
> Linger no longer in anguish
> But answer my song!
> Turn to truth now.
> Torment-trapped traitor.
> Tyrant and trickster.
> Arise as the fire now
> Flares up to thrust you
> Through World-threshold:
> Flashes to carry now
> Crying now home—
> Caranom! Caranom!
> Baron Caranom!"

In the heart of flames that flickered and shimmered in a pillar thirty feet high, the naked figure of the Baron appeared.

His flesh was scorched and torn. Where his small, piggish eyes had been, two black, burned holes dripped red tears of blood down his ripped cheeks.

> "I charge and constrain you
> True tales to tell now:
> Truthful and Ruthful
> And Harmless to be!
> Malice toward me and mine
> Mirrors turn and return.
> Warding all harm
> From Friends of the Bard.
> From Flesh of the Bard.
> Harm not the Bard!
> Hurt returns to hater.
> Now, doomed one.
> New-damned one.
> Speak as I ask!"

Black smoke rolled up from the bowl and for a moment Caranom was obscured. Then the smoke cleared and he was visible again, covered with freshly bleeding wounds.

"How may we destroy the evil of Haunted Valley?" Gonquin asked.

"By destroying the Demon who rules it," Caranom answered.

"How may that be done?"

"By banishing him to his own world."

"And how may *that* be done?"

"With the Sword!"

Gonquin moved his arms in angular patterns. Weird shadows danced on the walls of the pit and the fire roared.

"Whence comes the Warlord who threatens Tondur?"

"From this Demon-World!"

"Is he then a Demon?" asked Gonquin in surprise.

"Yes," answered Caranom.

"How may he be overcome?"

"With the Sword."

The black, oily smoke swirled up again, and Caranom shrieked. Gonquin made frantic symbols in the air and the smoke cleared.

The Baron's abdomen had been torn open, and green and yellow fires licked at his viscera.

"Where may we find this Demon Warlord?" Gonquin asked.

"Far inland—on the Continent," moaned Caranom, "in the city of black clay, beside the river that was once called the Vley. The river too is black, and flows into the Sea of Salmon at the latitude of the tip of the Tondurn peninsula, in the land which was once called Ercalia."

"And by what name shall we call this Demon?"

"*Kreelath!*" screamed Caranom. "If you would lose your souls and join me here!"

Black smoke, shot through with green and yellow lightnings, engulfed the pillar of fire. Caranom's tortured screams were audible for a moment, then the entire apparition faded and there was only the alabaster bowl with its tiny red and purple flames. The air was filled with the smell of burning flesh.

"Quickly now," said Gonquin. "Back to the ship! From this moment time is our enemy. Kreelath will know what has transpired here, and he will call up his fleet to defend the mouth of that river. We must reach it first."

"What of that?" asked Darith, pointing to the bowl.

"Leave it where it is," said Gonquin. "It is a gateway to the Demon's world, and should never have been opened. Come, I will show you its proper disposition."

They ran out of the pit, made their way through the mazelike corridors to the castle, and, under Gonquin's leadership, emerged a few minutes later on the terrace from which Caranom had first shown them the pit. Gonquin found the partly concealed lever and jerked it downward.

Below, the floor of the pit dropped open and the bowl of fire fell into darkness.

There was a moment of silence, then a great explosion shook the stone under their feet.

A gout of white fire shot up from the hole and the walls of the pit crumbled inward.

"It will not stop until the fire is smothered by the sea," said Gonquin. "And all of this island and its contaminations are gone into the Demon-World. Let us flee!"

CHAPTER TEN
The Vampire

"Damn!" came Selvern's voice from above, on deck. "Gonquin, where's that seeing-tube of yours? I think fe Scarriv has decided to make his move."

There was long silence, punctuated now and then by someone walking overhead. The great black scimitar in Darith's hand seemed doubly heavy, like a lead weight, craving to be dropped. The sun fell in warm gold bars through the slits of the louvres, and dust motes danced in the brightness.

It was cool in the companionway, except for those radiant stripes, and restful. How long Darith had stood there, leaning against the wall, he did not know. The creaking of the lines as the sails strained before the wind made time a thing to be enjoyed and fought against.

The memories, the age-long, confused memories of Colyn the Great, drifted in bright-coloured, shifting clouds behind his eyes. All those centuries, all that turmoil of love and hate, of despair and grief and hunger, of betrayal and guilt, of loyalty and joy...

"Well, Prince." Raonull fe Scarriv's voice rang out above, a lazy drawl with an edge to it that made even courtesies sound insulting. "Do we follow the Colyn Muir, as we are bound to? So long as there is danger, so long as there is a voyage? So long as there is a Colyn Muir?"

Darith stiffened, remembering other times he had heard that voice. His own memories, now, flooded awareness, vivid as if he were reliving them. He and Raonull were of an age, but Raonull had always been his father's heir, while Darith's older brother was tanist of Colyn Muir. In Raonull's eyes that had made him of higher rank than Darith, and he had never quite stopped feeling that he ought to take precedence. They had had the usual scuffles as children, when Raonull's father visited Colyn Muir, but no serious contention until one day Darith had found Raonull beating one of the pages for some imagined inattention.

They had been matched equally, and after Avlath separated them, punished equally as well. Raonull had blamed Darith for that too.

Our first real battle, thought Darith. *But not the last.* The black Sword twitched in his hand.

"Lord Darith has no need of your counsel at this time," said Selvern coldly.

"Perhaps not," Raonull said silkily. "But I have need of his. My Clan's fealty to his gives me that privilege."

And where was your fealty when your wild men burned Lynn Du? thought Darith, listening. He remembered the blackened timbers where a snug village had been, and the blood of men of his own clan trodden into the mire. The tracks of the reivers had led toward Scarriv, but when Darith got there to charge Raonull with it, the other man had only laughed. By then, the stolen beeves were already butchered, and the survivors of the village too shocked to identify their assailants with any precision.

There had been no way to bring the fe Scarriv to justice, and Raonull had known it, for by then the Curse of Colyn Muir was already gnawing the life of Darith's father away.

But not me—Despite his weariness, Darith found his lips twisting in a sour grin. Whatever his other problems might be, that vicious animal in his belly had gone back to sleep the moment he took the velvet scimitar in his hand.

There was a hail from nearby and the *Maid* shivered as a boat bumped against her side.

"Raonull, are you at your insurrections again?" The deep voice of Olegair, the Bull Dragon, shook the timbers of the ship. "I thought I'd best join any party to which you invited yourself."

"I have come to request counsel concerning the course of my ship," said Raonull. "If we should become separated in a storm I must know our destination."

"I can tell you your destination," said Olegair.

"Now, now," said Gonquin. "We are not here to discuss Lord Raonull's place in the cosmic Journey."

Olegair roared with laughter, and the glass in the oil lamps rattled.

"If I cannot get counsel—" Raonull started, but Gonquin interrupted him.

"Look at this map, Lord Raonull. Here you will see a river, the River Vley. It is thence we go. And speed is all-important, for we must reach this spot before the enemy can gather his forces to stop us."

"Do you not mean to let me see the Colyn Muir?" asked Raonull.

"Can you not get it through your thick head that this is an emergency?" thundered Olegair.

"Fe Mavron," said Raonull, "I am only trying to establish the nature of the emergency. After all, how long has it been since we, since any of us, have seen the Colyn Muir? Over a week now, is it not?"

"It is," answered Olegair slowly.

"Since before we stopped at that strange island," said Raonull. "And in that time have we both not heard rumours of our Lord's failing health? Of strange events on that island? Has anyone told you, fe Mavron, why we stopped there, what happened; or even what destroyed the island as we fled?"

"No," Olegair muttered uneasily.

"I think we all know that the sinking of the enemy fleet was a work of magic," said Raonull. "And the destruction of the island most certainly was. Yet with all this magic, we are still told to sail south and east. At whose bidding, I ask? When last we spoke, Lord Darith had no plan for sailing south and east. At least, he gave no indication that there was any reason to do so. Perhaps he spoke to you?"

"No," said Olegair. "He did not."

"Then whose word have we that this is the plan of battle?" Raonull asked sharply. "That these are the orders of the Colyn Muir? Only these *spokesmen!*"

"Are we to doubt that word of a Prince?" Olegair asked.

"No," said Raonull. "But whose word have we that he *is* the Prince? What evidence? Only the men from his own ship and this so-called Troubadour—"

"I take issue, Lord Raonull!" cried Gonquin. "If your ear is so ill tuned that you can doubt me a Troubadour, then your mind too must be muddled!"

Darith shook his head. The cobwebs of drowsiness parted and flew away. Raonull would have to be crushed once again —and how many more times before this war ended?

"Enough of this," Raonull was saying. "I did not come here to argue esthetics."

Darith clenched his fist on the scimitar's hilt and headed up the stairs.

"Then you should have kept silent on the matter," snapped Gonquin.

"I came to ask counsel," Raonull continued. "Now it seems I am denied it. Take note of that, *Prince,* for you were called upon to witness my oath! Now I call upon you to witness that oath's invalidation."

"Your Highness," said Olegair. "If we could but speak a moment with Lord Darith."

"He has gone without sleep for a week," said Selvern. "He needs rest before we fight again."

Darith reached the top of the stairs and threw the door open. Full sunlight laved his face and he blinked, dazzled by the shimmer of sunlight on sapphire sea. A week's journeying with fair winds had brought them into warmer waters. A fresh breeze strained the *Maid's* white sails, and she ran on a broad reach before the wind. The sails of the rest of the fleet danced across the water behind her.

The chieftains turned to face him; Olegair's blunt features creasing in an anxious frown, Raonull's losing all expression except for the calculation in his green eyes. Prince Selvern took a step forward, his gaze dropping to the shadow sword in Darith's hand. But Gonquin stayed where he was, dark eyes darting from Darith to Raonull and back again.

"You are here again, Raonull fe Scarriv," said Darith coldly.

"To ask directions of my Liege Lord." Raonull had apparently made up his mind how to proceed. "According to the custom of war." He smiled, balancing easily as the *Maid of Tharda* rolled.

"You have asked," Darith nodded. "Now I direct you to speak further of the matter with those to whom I have delegated authority. *Prince* Selvern, Gonquin the *Troubadour,* and Avlath, my Chamberlain. If you have any questions they cannot answer, then ask them now; for I do not mean to play this game anymore before the battle."

"Lord Darith," said Raonull angrily, "I will *not* be treated as a troublesome child."

"Then stop behaving like one," said Darith.

Raonull's eyes blazed as if a fire had been lit within his skull. Darith stared at him for a moment, not even trying to mask his own contempt for the other man, then turned his back and started down the stairs.

"*Darith!*" Raonull began, but his sentence was cut off with a crash and a cry of rage.

Darith turned. Raonull was crumpled against the mast, clutching his broken right arm to his chest. Mannus, breathing hard, stood over him.

"He reached out for you, my Lord," said Mannus.

"Darith, I claim this churl!" hissed Raonull between clenched teeth.

"He is no longer my servant," said Darith.

"You will have to deal with Lord Mannus on your own," Selvern added, teeth showing in something that was not quite a smile.

"Deal with a *tanner?*" cried Raonull. "Whence came *his* title?"

"From the island," said Darith. "Where he came to offer his strength and his sword with a bravery it would do well for all my men to copy. For if all are as prone to questioning and fool's debate as you are, fe Scarriv, I have sore need of bravery." He tried to recover his calm, but he could feel fe Scarriv's fury like a fire that sparked from him an answering blaze.

Raonull's narrow features purpled, then went pale again. His eyes darted from side to side as he sought some way to vent his fury, like an animal, trapped, wounded, and ready to kill.

His eyes came to rest on the sword at Mannus's side.

"So!" he hissed. "This is what the Colyn Muir has come to. You must forgive me, Lord Darith, but events have been so confusing that my poor mind has not followed the progress of these relationships very clearly. A Prince comes to us in a burning ship. A Troubadour who deals in small magics comes from no one knows where. I find it very confusing! But not enough so that I cannot see corruption when it is flaunted before me!"

Mannus saw the direction of Raonull's gaze and his fist clenched on the hilt of the sword.

"Look you, Chieftains! The sword of Colyn Muir now hangs at the side of the tanner's brat. Is it not clear that Lord Darith is no longer in control of this ship? I ask you, *who* are we following now—now that the Colyn Muir is thrall to these strangers and the tanner stands in his place!"

Darith forced himself to speak softly: "Silence, Raonull fe Scarriv." The blood was pounding in his temples; he tried to blink away the shadow that seemed to flow from him toward his enemy.

"I will not be silent!" screamed Raonull. "There is some vile miscarriage of command here, and I want it disclosed. Now, before the Council!" He pulled himself upright, head weaving forward like some reptile.

The sword in Mannus's hand came halfway out of its sheath.

"Mannus is my heir," said Darith, stepping forward to get between them. "My son, as far as you are concerned."

Raonull looked from him to Mannus, and back again. Then he laughed, and the sound scraped Darith's ears like the cawing of some carrion bird.

"So—the love you once pledged to the Princess Lonarissa was not—"

Something stirred. An anger of the body, a feeling that Raonull's very existence was insufferable, set the muscles in Darith's arms to twitching. Perhaps the mention of Lonarissa set it off. Yet it was not wholly something native to Darith's nature.

It took only a second. Darith's right arm twitched, and the soft black scimitar leaped forward with an alien vitality of its own and split Raonull fe Scarriv from skull to breastbone.

A garnet mist swirled around Darith and engulfed him. It would be good, he thought, to let the scimitar continue. To bite into the flesh of all those around him and put an end to this silly war. And beyond that, to go ashore and continue, to bite and cleave and cut and drink up life by inflicting death.

His right arm tingled and throbbed with the inflowing, pulsating strength. He felt his chest swell as fresh, salt-filled, blood-smelling air was sucked deep into the caves of his lungs. He felt young again, new again!

Then the mist dispersed, and he saw Raonull fe Scarriv crumple to the deck before him.

As if from a dispassionate moral distance Darith watched himself draw the black scimitar out of Raonull's body. He watched as the soft, velvety blade *absorbed* the last of Raonull's blood. He looked down at Raonull's ash-grey face and limbs.

In his hand the scimitar moved, alive and seeking another victim. Silence pulsed in Darith's ears. They were all staring at him. Faces wavered as if he saw them through water.

"So this is what it does," said Gonquin softly. "The reason an army will fall before it."

With an effort of will Darith forced the blade down to his side. He shivered.

"Darith," said Olegair, looking up from the corpse. "What is this evil thing in your hand? It was never your way to kill a man without giving him a chance to defend himself." Olegair looked down at the body again. "What kind of magic is this for a *man* to practice?" he asked.

A wave of despair overcame Darith and he closed his eyes for a moment. When he opened them nothing had changed and the despair was complete. They were still watching him, friends and companions who would now never look at him without that flicker of doubt again.

Even Mannus.

And he had to say something before doubt turned to terror. He could not defeat Kreelath without their help, even with the sword.

"You ask me, old friend, what kind of magic?" Words came to him from the well of memory that he had inherited from Colyn Muir. "The only kind. The kind which wins in the face of defeat. The kind for which men give precious time and for which they pay even more bitterly with pain. It is desperate magic, the magic of last resort.

"This is a time of final confrontations, and the prices we pay now will be final payments. What we fight, Olegair, is not human—but do not let that strike fear in you, for what men usually fight is never human." Now the words came more freely—a bitter philosophy distilled from all his frustrated love and all the pain.

"Raonull lies dead of ambition; a man on that island was destroyed by arrogance. Pride, hatred, greed—all these take their toll. Many on these ships shall die of loyalty in the days to come, and others shall die of courage, of friendship—all the good reasons for which men die." Darith's gesture took in the ships that were bounding so gaily in their wake. The clean beauty of white sails and blue sea were a painful irony.

"But *always* our deaths, the battle we lose or win, are due to things inhuman, to ideas, oaths and loves. And so it shall be this time, as we die in battle against a Demon, against the inhuman given form."

Darith drew breath and looked around him. His sight had cleared, as if his passion gave him a measure of control over the thing he held. And his words were reaching them. The men who had come with Raonull still stared at him as if he were Kreelath in the flesh, but among the others, panic was transforming into a kind of grim resolve—they might still fear him, but he thought that they would follow him. He must finish it now, while this strength still throbbed in his veins.

"We must win this battle, and when we do, then this one thing, this demon at least, will be finished, and we can go back to our other battles. You ask what sort of magic, my friend—" His gaze fixed Olegair, and the man straightened to face him. "The magic of integrity, which can destroy, but which at least is something a man can choose!"

The jeweled night sky hardened the sea and turned it to a tossing blanket of diamond mail. Darith stared out over the glittering water, thinking of Raonull.

Would the fish, would even the sharks, eat that bloodless corpse, from which all the life force had been sucked by the Demon Sword? He supposed that Raonull had been an evil man—ambitious, proud, treacherous even—but he found it hard to hate him any longer, for now he knew the man's virtues too, as well as he did his own.

If he were to hate Raonull now, thought Darith, it would be because of what the man's death had taught him this afternoon.

"Lord Darith?"

He turned at the sound of his name and saw Gonquin and Avlath standing in the shadows with Mannus a half-step behind them.

"What is it?"

"It has been a week since you slept," said Gonquin quietly. "Today you did something that shocked all who know you. It will be hard enough to quell the rumours in any case, but when even *we* do not know the truth, it is impossible! Don't you think it is time you told us what happened to you on the island—what you saw in that room?"

Darith sighed. The scimitar again felt like lead in his hand. If only he could sleep!

"I suppose it is," he said at length. "But stand well back, away from me. Don't deceive yourselves that I am this Sword's master."

He sat down on the bench below the gunwale, resting the scimitar across his knees. For a moment he was silent, sending his mind back to the pit and the passageway, trying to find words.

"What did I see? Colyn the Great. What was left of him. Bones, dried skin, the eyes sunk in his head with time—but still alive, still moving! He still held this Sword in his hand. *He was still slave to it.*

"And now *I* am slave to it." Darith added in a terrible voice. "Watch!"

He lowered the curved blade and touched its point to the deck. Instantly a flame appeared and he pulled the sword back. With his bare foot he quenched the fire.

"The flesh of living things it cuts," he said. "But anything else it burns. Not only wood, but steel. I tried this morning to lay it across two pikes, hoping I could rest. But it burned through them both in seconds. Even the hilt sets fires!"

"Then you cannot put it down until the battle is won," said Avlath, horror shaking even his stolidity.

"Not even then!" Darith answered sharply. "Only one thing is proof against this weapon, Avlath. The Blood of Colyn. And all of the Blood of Colyn is in *me!*" He laughed bitterly.

"Don't you understand? The only way I can sleep is to lay the sword across my own body. As Colyn the Great must have done these many centuries. But *he* was on solid land, where there was no pitching, no rocking! There was no danger the sword would fall off and burn its way through the ship into the sea, and cause this whole world of ours to fall into the Demon-World, under Kreelath's sway! For that is what would happen if this scimitar went into the ocean. It is a talisman a hundred times as great as the bowl of fire with which we destroyed the island."

There was a long silence. In the darkness a fish leaped out of the water and sent a spray of silvery sparks aloft. The stars twinkled in the currents of warm air and the water lapped gently against the sides of the ship. Darith felt the black scimitar twitch, as if it knew it were the topic of discussion.

"Colyn the Great traveled by ship," said Gonquin. "He must have found a way. If he could do it, so can you. Darith, I sense that there is something troubling you that is more immediate than the threat to the world. Something—personal."

"That is a strange way to say it," said Darith. "But you are right. I told you I was slave to the blade, and that Colyn had been slave to the blade. Has it not occurred to you to wonder how it was that Colyn survived all these years, a pile of parchment and bones? Men do not normally live so long nor in such condition."

"That is true," said Gonquin.

"For each man I kill," said Darith starkly, "I am granted a measure of life. The sword drinks the blood and I drink the years, so long as I hold the sword.

"I did not wholly understand, until today. But when I slew Raonull, I felt all his vitality and strength flow into me. I have become a vampire, Gonquin! And I cannot deny myself this vampire existence, I cannot break free and cleanse myself of it, because this blade must neither fall upon the earth nor sink into the sea! I *must* go on living, as Colyn had to go on living, so that the blood of Colyn will always remain between this scimitar and the world of men." His voice caught, and he forced control.

"That is why he allowed himself to be put in that pit, where men would be sacrificed to him, but where he could not escape to wreak havoc on the rest of the world. For he knew that his will would eventually be broken, and that the bloodlust of the daemon sword would conquer him. As it must conquer me, unless I take the same path he took."

Thin clouds began to cover the sky, and the wind sharpened. The ship rolled gently and the sails creaked with strain.

"My Lord," said Avlath. "Perhaps there is nothing I can do to free you, but I *can* help you sleep. All that is necessary is that we raise your hammock near the ceiling, then tie the sword in your hand. You can roll and toss, or even sleep downward, and the sword will be well away from the floor."

"It would burn through the rope," said Darith.

"Not if we use a sailor's noose," said Avlath. "You clasp your hands about the hilt and lock your fingers around it with your arms to either side of your hammock rope, so that even the roughest seas won't pitch you out! Then we slip the noose around your wrists, and the rope doesn't even touch the sword!"

"It sounds reasonable," said Darith, considering. "We shall try it! At worst it may fail; and I certainly have no better suggestions!"

A few moments later Darith climbed into the raised hammock, clasped his hands so that his fingers locked around the soft, velvety hilt of the scimitar, and nodded.

"Slip the noose over carefully," he said. "It is useless if it touches."

Avlath tossed the large circle of rope under the vertical blade, then lifted one side as Gonquin lifted the other. A slight twitch at first, then a violent jerking, like an animal trying to escape from a trap.

Darith strained to hold it still, but the blade seemed to know what was happening, and fought him.

"Quickly, pull it tight!" he shouted.

The noose contracted like an iron band around his wrists.

The scimitar slashed out, reaching for the long cord whose end Avlath held. Then it was too late. The final knot fell into place and Darith's hands were bound.

"Get out of here quickly!" he gasped. "It won't struggle if there's no blood at hand for it to drink. Station a man outside my door, and see that no one enters. I think I will be able to sleep now."

Avlath and Gonquin went out, shutting the door behind them. Darith felt the sword relax between his palms, and settled the weight of it along his breast, closer than ever lover to mistress, a companionship that would last as long as life endured.

"I do not think it such a good bargain," Avlath said. "He has been delivered from the pain that was the curse of all his ancestors. But now he is damned!"

The timbers overhead trembled as seamen ran to trim the sails. Darith's grip tightened as the *Maid of Tharda* came about and settled onto a new tack, but the vampire blade stayed secure.

Exhausted, Darith slept.

CHAPTER ELEVEN
Blood Feud and Mutiny

Mannus gripped the *Maid of Thorda*'s smooth rail, watching ships toil through a tarnished pewter ocean. Beyond, the other vessels of the Tondurn fleet were spread across the sea in rough formation.

But there was a gap in the pattern where the fe Scarriv ships should have been.

Not now! he thought desperately. *A night and a day of sleep are not enough, after what my Lord has been through!* He swallowed, aware that it was not only compassion that made him wish they could put off this confrontation—while the Colyn Muir slept, his Demon Sword slept too.

High clouds already obscured the sky, and the morning sun was only a diffuse glow. The ships of fe Scarriv pushed painfully through waves that rolled like molten metal, and even the wind seemed hampered, expiring and changing fitfully, as if infected by the uncertainties of men.

"Run up the signal to maintain formation," Prince Selvern said, behind him, "and mark it with the fe Scarriv pennon."

Mannus heard a low voice acknowledging the order, and then the squeal of tackle as a seaman hauled the signal flags up the mast. He turned to see as the Prince put the helm over a little, so that the flags would snap straight out in the wind.

Now they flew free, their meaning unmistakable. The sails of the first fe Scarriv warship shivered as she began to come about.

Mannus let go of the rail, then grabbed it again, as he

realized that the new tack was bringing the other ship toward them, not away.

A little raggedly, six more vessels followed, black mourning flags fluttering from their mastheads as they turned.

Abruptly the wind ceased to lift Mannus's hair. The big mainsail flapped loudly and the sailing-master shouted. Lines creaked as the seamen began to take in sail. Mannus could see the traitorous breeze ruffling the sea to starboard, filling the fe Scarriv sails while the *Maid of Tharda* wallowed through the troughs with just enough way on her to answer her helm.

The other ships drew closer, black flags flapping like the cormorants on the fe Scarriv arms.

Then they too outran their wind. Now they moved more slowly, but still they came.

Mannus watched that inexorable progress with a churning in his gut as if he had swallowed some small, unworthy cousin of the Curse of Colyn Muir. He did not think it was cowardice—he had not felt this way when they went into battle against the Black Fleet—perhaps it was because these were his own people, and he had seen the bloodless body of Raonull fe Scarriv given to the sea.

Peripheral vision showed him Gonquin standing nearby. There was sadness in the Troubadour's dark eyes. Mannus coughed, and the other man turned.

"What do you think will happen?" Mannus asked.

"Not the usual sort of treachery, at any rate, though the end may still be treason." Gonquin gave a bark of bitter laughter. "They are proud men, your clansfolk, and they have the most honourable motives for war."

"I understand how they must feel," Mannus said in a low voice. He felt a breath on his cheek as the deceitful wind picked up suddenly. The *Maid* let out sail to trap it, and began to forge away from her foe.

"Do you think that the men of fe Scarriv have a right to take vengeance?" Gonquin's eyes narrowed.

"They have a right to—desire it. If Raonull had killed my Lord, I would have wanted *his* blood—that was why I broke his arm, and why—" He broke off, shivering as he remembered how the scimitar had sucked the life from Raonull's skull. "Do you think they would accept my life in exchange for—*his?* He and Raonull quarrelled over me."

Gonquin was still watching him, judgement in his dark gaze.

"It was not Lord Darith's fault!" Mannus exclaimed, fist

clenching on the jeweled hilt of his sword. "You heard what he said last night! It was the work of that Devil's Sword!"

"Yes. I heard him," Gonquin said quietly. "Are you defending yourself, or him?"

Mannus straightened and faced the other man. "Before the gods, I do not know! I would die for Lord Darith, but now—" He half drew the gem-hilted sword at his side. "Oh, Gonquin, I would give my right hand if only he could bear *this* blade again!"

The wind freshened, filling the fe Scarriv sails. They darted toward the larger vessel like birds of prey. The *Maid* tilted a little, as everyone not otherwise occupied came to the rail to see.

Gonquin nodded. "I think we all feel that way. But Darith was right. We must use one evil to defeat a greater one. Kreelath can only be destroyed by Kreelath's blade."

"Are you telling me that a worthy goal justifies evil means?" Mannus stared at him.

"You should discuss philosophy with Edarissa—my sister—" Gonquin's mobile lips twisted in something that was not a smile. "Perhaps she could answer you. All I know is that only this evil can enable Darith to attain his goal. He has no choice now, but I doubt that he would have sought the Sword if he had known its nature—not even to evade the Curse of Colyn Muir!"

Mannus sighed. "Even I know that. I don't think Lord Darith has valued his own life very much since his lady died."

"Yes . . . and now this man whose life was already a sorrow to him faces an immortality of evil! Don't desert him, Mannus. We can't share his burden, but our—loyalty—may be all that keeps madness away!"

"I swore an oath, Troubadour. I am not going to break it now!" said Mannus steadily. "But what will happen to him? Was Avlath right? Is Lord Darith damned?"

"I don't know." Gonquin turned to face him, dark eyes luminous. "Sometimes the only way to deal with the unthinkable is to transform it into good. But to be honest, lad, at the moment I can't see how!"

The approaching ships shortened sail a little. New signal flags flared from their masts.

"Fe Scarriv to flagship," the signalman read off, *"meet with Commander."*

"I suppose that is one way of putting it," said Gonquin. "I do not think there is a code to signal mutiny!"

"Tell them permission is refused," Prince Selvern was replying. "Warn them not to approach!"

As the *Maid's* answer became visible, a flurry of new sig-
nals appeared at the first fe Scarriv ship's masthead. The
newcomers drew closer together and bore down upon the
flagship with increasing speed.

"Your Highness, shall I try to evade them?" asked the
helmsman.

"No, damn it!" exclaimed the Prince. "They're our allies!
If we run from them we will lose the others as well! Gonquin,
come here."

Gonquin touched Mannus's shoulder and strode quickly
down the deck.

"What are we going to do about this?" the Prince was
asking. "I will not wake Lord Darith, but—"

"I do not think we could outrun them even if we wanted
to," said the Troubadour. "We may as well wait for them.
Perhaps there will be some among them who are willing to—
talk . . ."

Mannus found it hard to believe that. He could see the
rage on the faces in the approaching vessels now, and hear
the fe Scarriv shouting. From the way Gonquin's words had
trailed off, Mannus did not think the Troubadour believed it
either.

The wind carried the hollow boom of sword blades
slapped against hide-covered shields.

"I'll signal to the other ships to come in for Council, then
—Goddess knows what rumours must be going around the
fleet by now." The Prince turned to give the orders to the
signalman.

"And what if the others mutiny too?" asked Avlath.

"It will not matter," said the Prince. "Without them we
are dead anyway. But we can hope that some of them will
remember their fealty!"

> *"Blood for blood! Man for man!*
> *Life for life of kin and Clan!"*

The clansmen's hoarse chanting came clearly now.

> *"Death for death! Lord for Lord!*
> *Justice from the Kinsman's Sword!"*

They are true to their first fealty, thought Mannus. *Am I?*
He had spoken bravely to Gonquin, but was one to keep an

oath to Evil? What if the Sword of Kreelath could not be controlled? If that happened, Darith, if he were still in his senses, would want his men to stop him.

Mannus heard Avlath bellow an order: feet drummed on the swaying deck. All around him men were running for their weapons. The boy stood staring at the shouting men, and wished he were still feeding chickens at Colyn Muir.

If Darith had never taken him out of the mountains he would never have had to worry about Good and Evil and the fate of the world.

But if the Colyn Muir had not made Mannus his heir, Raonull might not have said that last, unforgivable thing, might still be alive, and there would be no ships filled with furious men to force Mannus to make this impossible choice.

And what kind of choices is your Lord making, every waking moment he lives? Mannus asked himself then. *Do you not think he would rather cast the Sword into the sea?*

If he can choose to resist its Evil, then surely you can choose to live with your fear!

"*I swore an oath,*" he had said to the Troubadour. But Mannus understood now that no form of words could have given him the strength to keep it if he had not believed, ever since he was six years old, that if Lord Darith was not a good man, then there was no Good in the world anywhere.

Swiftly, the fe Scarriv ships swarmed around the *Maid of Tharda.*

"*Blood for blood! Slayers rend,*" came the clansmen's many-throated roar.

"*Colyn's sons your Lord defend!*" Avlath's battle cry rose above their shouting. On board the *Maid,* men grabbed weapons as Prince Selvern ordered them to battle stations.

Grapples bit into the rail like claws. Mannus almost lost his footing as the ship heaved. Men scrambled over the side, screaming.

For a moment doubled vision showed Mannus black robes and blank faces, but no! These were clansmen, like the folk he had left at home! How could he fight them?

Sun-sparked metal flared like webs of light on whirling blades, as Scarriv Clansmen, their black-and-yellow tartans crossed with white, swarmed over the ship's rail.

Suddenly Mannus wished he had used the time he had spent debating ethics with Gonquin in running for his shield.

Too late! A man came leaping over the rail, worn brown targe raised, and a sharp silver line flew at Mannus's eyes.

By instinct, Mannus's fingers found the green-gemmed hilt and ripped his weapon crying from the scabbard to cut at the sword-edge, driving the other blade down.

The shock of the crash rattled his arm bones: the moon-round brown buckler leaped, pressing his blade back. The sword-edge hissed, winging around him like an eagle, flying to kill.

It crashed loud on a shield; then an arm circled him, hurled him reeling against the rail . . .

Startled to find himself alive, he staggered up and looked around. A shield crashed, a sword flashed down on the brown targe.

Avlath stood there, bright sword flying, his white hair shining as the wind whipped it. Both shields boomed as bright steel lashed.

Then another sword whistled in the hands of another shouting man, and Mannus ducked, as he would have from under old Ylsa's broom, and stabbed up.

He felt his point pierce flesh, and a hot wet splash on his wrist: wrenching the sword free, he glimpsed black-and-yellow plaid as it reeled over the railing, into grey sea.

Mannus caught his breath, gasping. Loud he heard the sounds of battle all around him, steel beating leather with a grim drum's *boom!*

Behind him, he saw Avlath's blade, no longer gleaming, dyed suddenly red; and the man who had so nearly killed Mannus was staggering back, eyes pleading, while a red fountain rose from under his ear.

All across the rocking deck he saw men fight, battering their enemies with sharp steel swords. Garbled war cries roared above the hammering of battle: maimed men moaned like confused, bawling cattle.

"Where's the murderer got to?" came a yell from the stern.

"Skulking below—" The rest was lost in the drumming of steel on leather.

Darith! Mannus thought. In the press he had forgotten who he was fighting for!

He had gotten only one glimpse last night, before Avlath closed the cabin door, but now the image came to him vividly of his Lord tied, swaddled in his hammock, with the Demon Sword twitching vainly in his hands.

The ropes had kept the Sword from taking Avlath. Bound and helpless, Darith would be easy prey for anyone who could get through the cabin door.

Before the thought was finished Mannus's legs were in motion, lunging across the reeling deck, running through the confusion of lashing red swords to reach the door.

He slid through the hatchway and down the ladder, feet scarcely touching the rungs. His conscious mind had debated, but something deeper moved him now. And in that moment he did not reflect that it was to his own advantage to defend his Lord, because Darith's life was the only thing that kept the Sword of Colyn Muir from destroying the world.

Darith was awakened by shouts and the rasping clangour of steel. Stiff muscles spasmed as he tried to roll from the hammock, and for a moment he swung dizzily, straining against his bonds. Where was he? Who had imprisoned him?

Then the black sword pulsed in his grasp, and he remembered.

Through the deck overhead came fe Scarriv's battle cry. Darith took a deep breath, striving to control the pounding of his heart and the twitching of the sword between his bound hands.

Raonull's men, rabid for vengeance . . . I should have expected this. But exhaustion had dulled his wits. Fatigue still numbed him, but even these few hours of sleep had given him a measure of control.

A scream above him was abruptly cut short. *My own people are killing each other up there,* thought Darith, *because of me.*

I've got to get up there, stop it somehow!

"Guard! Get in here! *Guard!*" Darith did not know, with a battle raging above, if anyone was still in the passage. He tugged against the ropes that held him, but Avlath and Selvern had done their work too well—he would have to be cut free.

"Guard—" As he filled his lungs to shout again, the door flew open. But it was Mannus who leaped through it, bloodied sword in his hand.

The black scimitar, already awakened by the blood that was being spilled overhead, lunged toward the boy with a violence that jerked the ropes painfully against Darith's wrists.

"Back!" he screamed. "Mannus, get away!"

Mannus flattened himself against the far wall.

"I've got to get you free." His eyes were still fixed on the straining blade.

"Yes," rasped Darith. "But carefully!" He felt the

strength of the thing in his hands and bit his lip. In their desperation to help him sleep, none of them had thought how he was going to wake again.

"The rope goes under you and around a cleat in the bulkhead, my Lord," said Mannus. "If I can get behind you maybe I can sever it."

Darith nodded, and Mannus began to edge around the wall. The hungry quiver in the blade Darith held told him when the boy moved. Then he felt the rope jerk at his wrists as Mannus struck and dodged back, but several strands still held. The black sword twisted in Darith's grasp.

He gripped the hilt and whispered, "Again!"

He felt displaced air brush his cheek as Mannus's sword swept past. As it bit, the black blade's surge snapped the last fibers and carried Darith's arm up and back in a sharp arc as the hammock unbalanced and spilled him onto the deck. He felt the edge slice . . . something.

No—not Mannus! But he was still rolling, yanking the scimitar free and coming up into a half-crouch with it poised before him. He drew breath with a hoarse gasp.

Mannus was huddled in the far corner, carefully lifting the charred fabric of his left shirt sleeve away from his arm.

Next to him a gouge in the timbering flickered with tongues of flame.

"Didn't touch me." Mannus ripped off the ruined sleeve. "Had a lot of practice—evading Ylsa's broom!" He managed a crooked grin.

Thank the Gods for youth! thought Darith. *An older man would not have gotten away.*

"Thank you," he said aloud. Mannus flushed and made an awkward bow. Darith's eyes fixed on the fire. "Move around to the door. If the ship burns beneath us, it won't matter who wins.

"Who's leading them?" he added as he reached to rub out the flames.

"The subchiefs, by their pennons," answered Mannus, "The greater Lords are on their way, but the clansmen have gone blood-mad! They could carry the ship before their leaders arrive."

"I don't want this—*thing*—to eat their lives, too—" Darith began.

Then shouting reverberated in the passageway outside the door.

"Blood for blood, blow for blow!"

Mannus sprang aside as the door smashed open, his sword sweeping out in a slash. Blood leaped from the first man through the door: the wounded fe Scarriv stumbled onto Darith's blade.

A roaring mass of well-armed men surged from the mouth of the passage. Mannus struck again, and stumbled back as his steel edge belled on a shield.

Darith had to grip the scimitar hard to turn it from the boy's flesh, toward the attacker. Mannus, without a shield, could only reel back, guarding, as the enemy flooded into the room, but then Darith sprang past him, and the Sword of Colyn ate.

Death surged in Darith's hands, slashing down the first wave. Men hurtled as a body onto the whistling edge, and he felt the terrible drink of stolen life.

But the passageway was blocked with bristling steel. Darith realised he was in a trap: if he stayed where he was, all those men would pour into the room, in unknowing sacrifice to the hungry sword.

"Stay behind me, Mannus!" Darith shouted, and let the vampire blade drag him into the crowded corridor.

Swords waved, futilely, as Darith's terrible scimitar thrashed in his hands, burning through steel, splitting shields. Death ate the enemy, even as they dodged. Bloodless bodies littered the passage.

"*Back!*" Darith shouted, as the men before him died, sword and shield usless as they hurtled in. "*Back from Colyn Muir!*"

From wall to wall the cruel steel flew, whistling and carrying his hand. Still they did not run.

The vampire sword was able to scythe down a host of men! Why would they not run?

"*Darith!*" Avlath's voice answered, somewhere up in the continuing clatter. "*Lord!*"

Listening, Darith heard death-screams, and the tune of beaten shields echoing. A roar rose and grew louder: "*Colllyyyynnn!*"

Then sharp swords and axes came slashing down the corridor, splashing red, splitting shields, hewing legs and helmets. Dead and wounded men fell to the left and the right.

Avlath burst through the enemy ranks, sword dripping, and others of Clan Colyn followed, many wounded and bleeding.

Darith gripped the hilt tightly as the night-black blade twisted in his grasp, trying to escape, trying to kill this friend who had come to aid him in this wild fight under decks.

Avlath led them as they fought their way up the passage, while Darith held the deadly black sword back, aware that behind them a host of bloodless dead men lay. Some might have run away.

Sunlight dazzled Darith as he scrambled through the hatch. Death lashed at him and he loosed the hunting hunger in his hands.

Mannus slipped on the red deck, slicing at a man. He heard cloth and skin rip, felt a sharp prick and the blush of rushing blood. Then steel flexed in his hand: he saw a body fall, and a raw wound spouting red.

He looked down and saw blood staining his torn tunic. The confusion of the battle had parted Mannus from his Lord, but the fighting had passed him: he looked around.

> "Death for death! Lord for Lord!
> Justice from the Kinsman's Sword!"

Rage was all around him on the pitching, slippery deck. Swordsmen battered bucklers with their heavy swords of steel; shrieking, bleeding, reeling as the wet deck reeled.

Selvern and Gonquin stood back to back on the poop, tempered lightning flaring above their shields. Selvern's shield was a struck dome, booming again and again as Scarriv men tried to kill him.

Darith strode toward them, over rent shields and falling corpses, Avlath at his back. Men screamed and fled as the Black Blade of Colyn cleared a path.

Mannus tried to rejoin his master but in the middle of this grim fight it was hard to be without a shield; and they would all be on him in a few moments. That would be the end.

The enemy closed in around him. It was not like his first battle: these men had faces.

Men on high aided the others to slay; a pale man lay writhing, a cruel arrow jutting from his breast. Mannus looked up, strained his neck to see.

Several Scarriv bowmen were shooting from the rigging: one with a crossbow.

Mannus ran over the blood-wet deck to the mast, keeping to cover. There was somewhere he could fight even without a shield—where a shield would do no good at all.

He sheathed his sword and jerked the long dirk from his belt. His fingers found rough rope, and he climbed, thews straining his wounded side. He had always been good at climbing and quick on a rope, but it was all he could do to clasp it with his left hand.

Around him winds howled like grim ghosts. Twice they blew the rope against the hard wood of the mast, bruising his hurt side. Keen arrows sang out of the rigging, and he heard them whispering all about him. The bowmen could see him then, and more than one bow looked to find him, their arrows winging close behind him as he clung.

Behind him a shooting arrow hissed. Even as he dodged, he felt his tunic rip. His shirt sleeve jerked at his arm; though he felt no pain, the rope slipped away from his fingers, and he was spinning in the breeze, dangling from the rope by his right hand.

Ocean heaved dizzily below him; for a moment he swung with the sway of the ship, out, and back. How easy to let that motion fling him away from the reek of blood and the cries of the dying . . . into the cool grey bosom of the sea.

Then the weight of his body stabbed agony through his right shoulder, awareness narrowed to knowledge of his own danger. Time slowed. Mannus angled his body toward the spar, letting that momentum add to the speed with which the ship's motion was swinging him inward again.

Feet touched, strong calves scissored around rough canvas. Gasping, he let go of the rope and forced numb fingers to grasp the furled sail.

Where the spar crossed the mast was a crow's nest for the lookout. A fe Scarriv man was perched there now, arched over the rail as he shot into the battle below. The man with the crossbow.

Mannus's lips twisted in a grim smile. He gripped canvas and began to wriggle forward.

The bowmen in the rope ladder below the crow's nest looked up, startled, as Mannus flung himself onto the back of the man above them. He got his good arm around the man's neck, jerking him backward, to keep him from dropping the precious bow over the side. For a moment, only his hold on that hairy neck held him. Then a thrashing leg hooked the edge of the crow's nest; he heaved and resistance ceased as he heard the snap of breaking bone.

As the man sagged, Mannus grabbed for the bow and case of bolts the man had carried, then used his weight to thrust his enemy outward. For a moment the body hung on the edge, then the ship's sway tipped it over, to strike the bow-

men in the rigging and knock them, screaming, into empty
air.

One still, two flailing, the bodies hurtled down and struck
the railing in farewell before splashing into water like stones.

Mannus had his crossbow.

For a moment, then, he could catch his breath. As the
pounding in his chest eased he raised the crossbow, waiting
for a clear view of the struggle below.

His arm was beginning to ache dully. A look showed clear
the fighting on the ship's deck. He flexed the fingers of his
left hand, welcoming the pain as feeling returned.

The mass of fighters surged across the deck, blades flailing like hay in a high wind. For a moment, at this distance,
Mannus could not tell one side from another in that churning, swirling mob.

Then he glimpsed the black-and-yellow Scarriv tartan of a
figure on the deck below.

Mannus rested the crossbow on the rail of the crow's nest,
cranked the string back, and let the bolt fly.

In seeming slow motion he saw it strike, saw arms fling
wide as the impact spun the man around. He was glad he
could not see the man's face.

The body arched backward into the sea. Blood stained
the first wave to burst over it. Grimly he shoved another bolt
into the bow, braced it, and shot again.

Then, in the distance, Mannus heard a moan of drones,
the sound of a piper filling his bag.

Music began, and a mystic keening of war-pipes hummed
out of the sea.

A crossbow-shot struck another Scarriv man to the deck,
then Mannus looked up, across the heaving waste of tear-
grey water, to see other ships closing in around the *Maid of
Tharda.*

The pipes grew louder, but the tune was slower than the
battle-music that Mannus had heard. A lament for Raonull,
he supposed.

But no, he thought, he had heard that tune before! But
when? Where?

The mast seemed to sway in time to the long magical ca-
dences of sweet gold notes weaving through the thunder of
the drones. More than one piper made that blending of hollow booming with heartbreaking sweetness that rose from
every side, louder and louder as piper after piper wound in.

Mannus looked down and saw, on the deck below, fighters

falling back warily, lowering their weapons as they drew apart.

And, with a sudden quiver of awe, he remembered hearing old Rurith, who had been Piper to Darith's father, whistling that melody. "The White Peace of the Faery Women" it was called, and it was only heard when the clans met in ceremonial Council. It was the music for the proclamation of peace between the highland clans.

He stared at the infinite dim blur of the sea and on each of the towering ships, bodies appeared, plaids emerging moments before beards and faces showed.

A mass of men crowded each deck, but over and above them on each ship, Mannus saw, were two who stood high and apart. One figure clasped war-pipes to his chest, and at his side stood a figure kilted in the tartan of the same clan.

They were the chieftains of all the major clans, their pipers at their sides.

Mannus, his crossbow cocked, watched the caravels of the chieftains, graceful as swans, slowing as they neared the flagship, as if enchanted. Grapples smacked against the rail in odd rhythm with the wind-carried loveliness of the music.

After all of the blood and confusion of battle had the foe abandoned his vengeance?

Now the ships drew in and the water separating their rails darkened, as men scrambled from ship to ship. Mannus began to climb down. Below him the sound of the pipes died away.

The deck was crowded when he reached it. Chiefs had gathered from each of the clans, with black-bearded Finn fe Scarriv of Rathnolawn at their head. Although not Raonull's closest kin, he was now the leader of Clan Scarriv's forces on the heaving mountains of the sea.

But behind him, in a clear space by the rail, were the leaders of Tondur. Goll of the Clan fe Varruk out of Caiplic, with his dark plaid wrapped about him, and Bor of Ashir Fuaran, thin, with eyes that always seemed to see a little beyond the surface of things. Niall of Clan fe Rogoin glared around him, his tall son a step behind. There were others, a swirl of many-colored tartans blending as they pressed forward. Beards covered their chests, anger smouldered in their eyes.

Clansmen edged away to either side, for to face words can be harder than to face arrows.

Mannus felt the tension of those who stood face-to-face

there. The crowd of warriors resolved into two walls of men, still eyeing each other with snarls of hatred.

Between them, still bodies lying in a red pool made an impassable barrier.

Only Olegair and young Ruishar of Clan Morulvu stood with Darith's men. But they covered their eyes, and would not look on those who lay there.

"Holy Ones! What evil is this?" Lord Bor gasped as he saw the fallen clearly for the first time. Men called him a mystic, but he had the reputation of being a good fighter.

It was not the bodies that lay in their own blood that had shocked that oath from him, but those others, that lay drained and bloodless, eyes staring in mute accusation into the pale sky.

"Wizardry of the worst kind," Niall fe Rogoin answered him. "For it is the work of one of our own!"

"Kill him," came the mutter from the men behind him. "Kill the evil one before his wizardry kills again!"

"Hold!" Prince Selvern's deep voice cut across the babble. "That is the kind of talk that brought us to this pass. We are men of Tondur, not barbarians. We live by Law, not the passions of frightened men!"

"It is Law that I invoke!" Finn growled. "Let the Colyn Muir face trial for breaking his oath of protection, while Lord Raonull was still holding to his own.

"That Raonull is dead, were evil enough!" he said, and a low rumble of voices echoed him. "It is unjust that the men who came to serve the Colyn Muir become carrion."

"Worse than carrion," hissed another voice. "Look at them, bloodless as beef in the slaughtering shed!"

"It is the oath that Colyn himself had chosen, and his descendants kept, and it is just and fair," Finn went on, "and his heir should have been able to keep it, whatever his fate has brought to him."

Goll of Caiplic and Bor of Ashir Fuaran muttered agreement, but Niall of Lairog-nan-Cuivair was shaking his head.

"He has done worse than fail to keep it! He has turned against his own!"

The whispered sound of the crowd grew louder, like an approaching storm. Mannus tensed: they would be shouting in a moment—and what then would keep swords from leaping again from their sheaths?

Olegair and the young Ruishart of Clan Morulvu were still, but their faces showed their doubt. The Lord of Lairog-nan-Cuivair started to speak, then shut his mouth again. He was a good fighter, but no man of words—no way to tell which way he would go if it came to blows again.

"I believe in the good faith of the Colyn Muir, but I must question Lord Darith's sanity," Olegair said at last.

"So does Lord Darith himself!" said Avlath.

Avlath had spoken softly, but Darith heard. The words focused all his own pain.

Did they think he had no eyes? The bloodless bodies of the men he—no, this Demon Sword in his hand—had slain, cried out for justice. And he himself was their Lord, who ought to avenge them!

He stood here both as accuser and accused.

"I would stand trial willingly," Darith rasped painfully, appalled at the knowledge. "But this evil thing I bear would prevent that, as it prevented you from slaying me. Do you not yet understand? You may judge me, but judgement is useless with no power to sentence! And there is nothing you can do to harm this Sword!"

Had his voice revealed his pain and confusion? Perhaps it was so, for there were tears in Prince Selvern's eyes, and a bitter twist to Gonquin's mouth. But Finn's eyes flashed.

"So you would evade judgement by the just?" Face working, the Lord of Rathnolawn turned to the others. "It is for you to complete this heartbreaking task, and to sit in judgement upon our Lord, the Colyn Muir."

But even as he spoke Gonquin pushed forward.

"Listen to the words of the wise one," said the Troubadour sarcastically. "Dare you call yourselves just? Or wise? As though you were immune to the temptations of greater men! Is there one among you who could have borne what the Colyn Muir has borne, carried the burden he bears even now?"

Prince Selvern took a step forward, glaring around him.

"Blessed Goddess, what is all this argument? The Colyn Muir is your rightful Lord! He rules as Prince of an almost separate nation, even as agent for the King! Whatever Lord Darith has done has been done for the sake of all our world, from the direst necessity. Surely that is all you need to know! It is your own oaths that bind you to follow him. Is it necessary to negotiate between ethics and loyalty?"

"Even now he is weeping for the slain," said Niall of Lairog-nan-Cuivair, with doubt in his voice.

"What use are his tears?" young Ruishiar asked. "Or ours? A breast of stone would weep at the sight before us! I

would not choose to betray my Lord, but to help him, unsure
though I be—still, loyalty is of choice, not compulsion! They
have us all with tears, but how can we help him when he is as
dangerous to us as he is to the enemy?"

It was true, thought Darith, flinching from the boy's clear
gaze. All his own doubts came flooding back to torment him.
For a moment the Prince's words had silenced the men, but
now they were beginning to murmur once more.

They did not understand—they *could* not kill him, and if
he cast himself into the sea, the Black Sword would do
greater evil than they could even dream.

"Look," said Niall. "Unless my eyes deceive me, there in
his own eyes is all we need to know! Do you doubt his sorrow?"

"I'd rather be destroyed by the enemy than by friends!"
raged black-bearded Finn fe Scarriv.

"Destroyed!" shouted another. "Worse than death comes
from that black blade! Look at them—this was no natural
slaughter! Who knows what that Demon's Sword has done to
their souls?"

"Kill him!" And men surged shouting toward Darith.
"Kill the murdering traitor and smash the Sword!"

"Stay back, you fools!" Darith shouted, as the black blade
writhed in his hands. *"Back from Colyn Muir!"* All his own
grief focused into determination that the Sword would not
drink the blood of the clans again!

"Stay back, you fools!" shouted Gonquin. "That is the
Black Sword of Colyn! It can slay an army—whether its
Master wishes it or not!"

"The Black Blade of Colyn, eh?" someone sneered.
"Why, I saw that displayed at a fair once, or so they said!
Tales to frighten children!"

"Lay down your sword if you wish to talk peace!"

"Fool!" Gonquin spat. "He *cannot* lay it down. Do you
not remember the old song?

>*"And when in triumph he returned*
>*He found that all he touched he burned?*

"—show them, Darith!"

He snatched up a spear, held its point toward Darith.
Darith let the velvet blade touch the steel. For a moment
nothing happened, then the spear-point began to grow
cherry red.

Molten drops, shooting sparks, dripped. Darith lifted the

blade, brought it down on the wood. Flames erupted. Gonquin turned, and held the spitting, flaming spear out toward Finn.

"And did they show you *this* at the fair?" he asked.

They stared.

"It *is* the Sword of Colyn!" a voice exclaimed in awe.

"The Colyn Muir has come back into his own again!" exclaimed another. Rage and wonder warred in men's faces.

Darith blinked, daring to breathe again. As childhood tales assumed an awful reality, he could see the change in their eyes as clearly as if they had spoken.

But however terrible, this Demon was their own, their response to it conditioned by memories older even than the oaths they had given.

Suddenly ranks of men were kneeling in rows. Finn of Rathnolawn stood still, staring.

"Raonull always swore that the old legends meant nothing," he spoke at last. "And yet at the end, a legend he always scoffed at has killed him." He knelt awkwardly.

"You are truly the Colyn Muir," he said.

CHAPTER TWELVE
Blood Thirst

Fair winds drove the Tondurn fleet southward, as if the reconciliation of the chieftains had been a ritual to charm cooperation from the weather as well. The warm languor of the Salmon Sea lulled the warriors, and the sun baked generations of cold out of their bones.

At times when the winds slackened, fishing was easy. Once the men from the coast convinced the clansmen that fish was legitimate food, they ate it every day. Fresh mackerel or bass was certainly better than the dried beef from their stores, and as they moved into southern waters, even experienced Dalgir fishermen grew excited as the fighting totuava and bluefin began to hit their lines.

Mannus worked a strip of anchovy onto his hook and cast the line into the sea. The other end was already tied to the rail. The wind had fallen away to a light breeze as the sun reached its zenith, and the *Maid of Tharda* moved with barely a wake to mark her passing through a sea of gold.

Gonquin, beside him, inspected the tattered fragment that was all that remained on his hook with exasperation, then he dipped into the bait-pail for another try.

"Likely ye got flatfish down there," said the sailing-master, examining the discarded bait with an experienced eye. "Flatfish'll mouth your bait soft as a baby, and 'til ye bring up your line, ye'll never know! See the bitty marks there where the teeth went in? That's no crab's work," he finished triumphantly. "That's flatfish down there!"

"But do we want flatfish up here?" asked Gonquin practically. "Are they good eating?"

139

"Oh, aye," said the sailor. "They'll fry up nice. Put on a live bait and work it up and down a few feet from the bottom. If ye feel a tug, give her some line, and then haul 'er in!"

Gonquin lifted one mobile eyebrow, then flipped his line over the rail. It sank with scarcely a splash, and he leaned on the rail with the line held lightly between thumb and forefinger of his right hand.

"And people actually make a living doing this!" He shook his head in wonder.

Mannus laughed. "It might not seem such sport if we depended on it. People who have never had to herd them think sheep are pretty creatures, too!"

He felt a flicker of movement along his line and gave it a tentative tug, but there was no resistance, so he let it drop again. The sun was hot on his shoulders, and he felt tensions that had been building since the Bard summoned him to his Tower beginning to melt away.

"Do you remember those boating parties we used to have on Lake Elenath when the Queen was still alive?" Prince Selvern asked. "They would hang coloured lanterns from the rigging, and barges with food and drink were rowed from craft to craft."

"I remember the time Tarilain pushed you in." Gonquin grinned. Prince Selvern's handsome face grew red.

"We were still children," he said loftily.

"As I recall, she had reason—you had just put a small frog down the back of her gown!" replied the Troubadour. "It is amazing what changes may be produced by Time!" He turned to Mannus with a conspiratorial smile. "You have to understand that Princess Tarilain and His Highness are betrothed, now."

Mannus stared, not knowing quite how to respond. He found it hard to imagine a Princess, much less one with a frog down her back. Some things about his new status he had grown used to, but this talk of court festivals and ladies was still something from an alien world. *What will I do if we somehow win this war?* he wondered then. *The first word that comes out of my mouth will show me up, and they'll boot me all the way back to Ylsa's chicken pen!*

"I should have known better than to try anything against Tari." The Prince finally smiled. "She was always the canny one. I remember how she could always find a way to distract the cook when we wanted supplies for an expedition. And do you remember the time we stowed away with the gifts for the Lady's Shrine?"

Gonquin was nodding, and Mannus smiled as he remembered some of the things he and the other boys had done to Avlath.

But before he could speak, the line jerked against his fingers. Automatically they tightened, and he felt rope sear skin as something very strong tried to carry his hook out to sea.

"Careful, lad—get the line around this pin, now, to save your hands." The sailing-master hastened over to help him. A twist gave Mannus a kind of handle, and he hung on while his invisible opponent thrashed the waves into foam. Suddenly it leaped, and he glimpsed a glistening metallic dark blue body that changed to pearl as it twisted. Fins flashed gold in the sun.

"A yellowfin!" cried the sailing-master. "Fight him in, lad, fight him in!"

Mannus hauled back on his end of the line as the fish shook and jerked the other like a dog with a bone. After what seemed like an eternity of tugging, his opponent finally began to tire. Mannus hauled him in, hand over hand, until the sailing-master could finish the job with net and gaff. He swung the net over the side, and they all dodged as the flopping fish smacked the deck around them. Then the sailor brought down his hammer, and the yellowfin was still.

Mannus stood looking down at it, still breathing hard. A moment ago the fish had been energy incarnate, and now its iridescent colours were already fading.

"I thought he would be larger," he said finally.

The sailing-master laughed. "Fooled ye, didn't he! Fifteen pounds, I reckon, but the little ones will feel like a monster on the line. Never mind—he's big enough to be good eating, and that's what matters, after all!"

"Yes, of course," he managed to answer.

Still grinning, the sailing-master took the fish away. Mannus sat down with his back to the mast. They would have food this evening, and that was well, but he could no longer see any sport in killing beasts, now that he had had to kill men.

"There was a water festival one year with a song contest," the Prince was saying. "Your sister won it, Gonquin, did she not? I remember how her voice soared across the water—everyone was most impressed, for she had only just completed the first part of her training."

"Her training?" asked Mannus.

"My sister Edarissa is a Bard."

Mannus blinked. "I didn't know that women could—"

"Oh yes, but Edarissa is unusual in any case. We ran away once, too, Selvern—to the sacred spring of Ore. Everyone had been telling us the nymph of the fountain was only a legend, but when Edarissa sang, Something came . . . I suppose that is when we understood what her calling must be. I know the signs and the spells of Thaumaturgy, the words and ways. But Edarissa has the Deep Magic in her soul."

"What does she look—" Mannus realized that Gonquin was not listening to him.

He turned, and saw that Darith had come on deck. He was pale, thought Mannus, and thinner. Men backed away from him, so that he had the space between the mainmast and the stern platform free to pace up and down.

From time to time he paused, gazing out across the glittering sea, then resumed his pacing, and the black blade in his hand seemed to drink up all the brightness of the day.

They had been sailing thus for two weeks when the dream ended.

The signalman's hail brought Darith on deck before his usual time. One of the Morulvu ships had signaled landfall. Darith took Gonquin's spyglass in one hand and peered across the waves. He saw an irregular reddish blur on the horizon that grew steadily larger as they altered course to approach it.

"Gonquin, what do the charts say?"

"There are a few villages," answered the Troubadour. "Unless all our reckoning is off, we are still north of our goal, but when we see the smoke of their cook fires we will know more precisely."

Tall red cliffs knifed the blue-green ocean from north to south as far as the horizon and beyond. But there were no villages, only a few heaps of rubble, which could once have been habitations. In that arid climate it was impossible to tell how long ago they had been destroyed.

At last a river pierced the cliffs, spewing foul black water in a steady current, staining the water far out to sea. On either side of the river's mouth, atop the cliffs, a small fortress stood watch.

"This was all green land," said Gonquin, at Darith's side, "when I was here, years ago. There was a city here then, but there's no trace of it now—except for those forts."

Yes, thought Darith, *even if we destroy the Demon, this land will need healing.* The weight of the Sword had become like a part of his hand. *But I shall not be the one to do it. I can only destroy.*

Gonquin shook his head sadly. "I knew Ercalia had fallen, and then the first stories of the Black Fleet arrived, but—" He frowned, and bit his lip, then straightening, pointed across the water.

"We are in luck. Only one of Kreelath's warships is moored here. We can hope that means he has not had time to call up the rest of his fleet."

"He may not need the rest of his fleet," Darith growled. "There is no great distance between those cliffs. From the fortresses they could send down a rain of fire-arrows with little effort. Unless we can take or disable them we cannot make the passage."

"With this many ships and this many men we cannot help but take them!" said Mannus, who was sitting near the prow.

Darith smiled. The tanner's son had become a warrior indeed!

"Sound the battle alarm!" Darith called out to his piper. "We shall attack the fortress to the right with all our strength. If we can win to its walls we have won our passage, for if we sail along the right bank, the garrison on the opposite shore will not be able to reach us with its arrows."

As if to belie him there was a whistling sound in the air, then a splash that drenched the men to starboard.

"They have a catapult!" exclaimed Gonquin.

"One of great power." Darith felt his pulse quickening, and strove for control. "Its range is greater than that of our arrows. We may have to take both fortresses after all."

A second missile hit the water, slightly farther away than the first.

"If you can capture the catapult," said Gonquin, "I can rid you of the other fortress."

"More magic?" Darith asked, gazing at the Troubadour through narrowed eyes.

Gonquin only smiled in answer.

"My Lord," said Mannus. "From what I've heard, these catapults have a hard time hitting small targets."

"That depends," said Darith. "They can often be used with enough accuracy to hit a single man: but if men are spread out over a large area, they are limited. It depends upon what you mean by a *small target* and what you mean by *effective.* They are *not* very effective against a single warrior

—unless he happens to be commanding the army."

"I see," said Mannus, teeth flashing in a quick grin. "That's what I thought. We cannot take our ships in much closer, or they will sink us. But if we put the men in small boats and spread out over the water, their catapults will be nearly useless. The most they will be able to sink with a single shot will be ten men. We will make poor targets, hardly worth shooting at, and hard to hit if they try."

"Lord Mannus," said Selvern, who had come up during Mannus's brief speech. "You have a politic way of proposing a plan. Also very convincing. I am glad I shall have the privilege of seeing you at Court someday! Lord Darith, I think your heir has come up with a very good means of dealing with these infernal war machines! I advise you to follow his suggestion."

Darith looked at Mannus with new respect. The boy might be quick-tempered and a little too enthusiastic, but what he did, he did well. He thought now that the impulse that had led him to make Mannus his heir had been better-founded than he knew.

"Signal the fleet to hold back!" Darith called. "We shall attack in small boats. Keep the ships back out of range of the catapults!"

The plan worked. Most rocks fell between the little boats, splashing the men harmlessly. Only three boats were lost before the first of Darith's men swarmed ashore.

Only once did a missile splash close enough to Darith's boat to wet the rowers in the stern, and the men with him laughed gaily; but Darith went cold all over, seeing in his mind the little boat smashed, the sword sinking into the sea, and all these cheerful, laughing men drawn into the flames of the Demon-World, to scream beside Baron Caranom.

Instead, he came safe to shore, and the boom of battle where others fought the small contingent of robed men that had waited for them on stone wharves. Swords flashed and shields thundered above the keening of the war-pipes.

But then the enemy moved backward, uphill, and rocks started falling by the wharves, driving Darith's men to cover, and preventing further landings.

The strong river current kept them from land except at the wharves. For a moment it seemed to be stalemate.

Mannus took a boat filled with archers and rowed out toward the enemy ship. Fire-arrows flew. Black smoke rolled, creating a smoke screen. Though the enemy already had the range, and could continue to drop boulders as long as the supply held out, it was now impossible for them to tell *when* a group of boats was putting in.

There was a pause before rocks started falling again.

Ruishiar, the boy-chief of Clan Morulvu, rushed over the beach. *If Colyn Muir left a shadow,* Darith thought, *daring men yet live.*

Then a flying rock crushed bunched men.

Gonquin ran a little way uphill, and crouched behind the cover of a stone outcropping, to call warning whenever a missile came over the fortress walls. One more boat was lost, then the entire army was ashore.

They fought their way up the slope. War-pipes skirled, and the ragged warriors surged over the stiff, mechanically moving men in their rat grey robes. The resistance here seemed more to buy time than anything else.

An hour later Darith stood fifty yards from the gate of the fortress, sheltered by huge chunks of tumbled red sandstone, the scimitar hungry in his hand.

"Can you see up there, inside the gate?" asked Selvern, who had led the initial charge. "Your boy Mannus is a fine shot with a crossbow. He dropped a man right on top of that—that crazy, upside-down portcullis. It won't quite close with him there."

"What kind of madman built this place?" Gonquin wondered aloud. "One does not normally build a portcullis that raises from the bottom."

"It is strange," said Darith. "I suspect it was not meant as a fortress. As to who built it; look at the carving around the gate! At first you see only fruit and flowers. But look closely and you will see small, three-eyed creatures peering out from the blossoms."

"Well, they may have been Demons," said Selvern, "but they knew nothing about building a defensible fortress! The gate appears to be strong, but it is so well covered that five or ten men could stand before it and be unassailable from within."

"So I have noticed," said Darith. "I only hope there is no secret chamber above, where they may drench me with boiling oil or the like."

"There is no room for such a chamber," said Gonquin. "You plan to go against the gate yourself?"

"Yes," said Darith. "If this damned Sword will burn the decks of my ship, it will burn the timbers of that gate! Selvern, have the men ready for a charge the minute the gate falls. I would guess there are not many men here. But take care, nonetheless, for they may be reserving what strength they have."

"When you are ready to rush the gate, signal," said Selvern. "Mannus has his crossbow cocked and a good supply of bolts."

"It will take more than one man to keep the parapet clear," said Darith. "A crossbow is much slower than longbow. Is Avlath nearby? He was always good at quick-shot."

"I'll see if I can find him," Selvern said.

The Prince scurried away, keeping to cover, and a few minutes later Avlath appeared with his bow and a quiver full of arrows.

"His Highness told me what you plan to do," Avlath said. "There may be no room for boiling oil, but while you are cutting through the portcullis they could open the gates slightly and put an arrow through you."

"Burning wood makes smoke," said Darith. "I have the choice of taking the risk or staying here to starve them out. The latter is no option. Kreelath's fleet may be here at any moment. Is Selvern ready for the charge?"

"Yes," said Avlath.

Darith raised his hand in a signal, then ran for the gate. Immediately there were arrows in the air around him. A scream from the fortress, followed by a second, told him that Mannus and Avlath were at work.

"Darith! Go left!" came a cry from Gonquin.

Without thinking, Darith dodged left just as a small boulder hit the ground where he had been. The impact rocked the ground and made him stagger, but he retained his feet and ran on.

A moment later he slammed into the ancient wood-and-iron grating of the portcullis.

He looked up, his breath coming hard. No, there were no holes or traps in the arch from which he might be boiled alive: only the neat line of sockets into which the points of the portcullis would have slid had Mannus not blocked it with a dead man.

But more important: in the grooves to either side the chains from which the portcullis hung were exposed!

Quickly he climbed the right-hand side of the grating and set the edge of the scimitar against inch-thick iron links.

The metal glowed cherry red and melted like spring ice. Under him the portcullis slumped as the chain fell in half.

He climbed down, went to the left side and climbed up

again. This was the dangerous part, but it was much quicker than cutting *through*. But if he could not leap free as the chain broke, he might have a foot, or even a leg, mangled as the heavy portcullis fell into its pit.

And he might drop the Sword.

He set one foot against the grating, let the other dangle, and held on with his left hand. Then he cut the chain.

The stone gateway trembled. Darith sprang free as the portcullis crashed down. A volley of arrows fell all around him as he rolled into the protection of the arch. Seconds later an enemy archer, Mannus's crossbow bolt jutting from his smashed head, followed the arrows to the ground.

Darith leaped to his feet and drove the point of the scimitar against the dark wood planks of the gate: flame flared. He started two more fires this way, one at either side, then set the point to the centre of the gates and lunged. Like a sharp knife passing through cheese, the blade sank halfway to the hilt, then was through.

Slowly, Darith cut downward, through the heavy timber of the bar that held the gates shut. It took only seconds, then the gates moved, swinging open.

"Now," he whispered as the Demon Sword quivered in his hand. *"Drink your fill!"*

The blade leaped forward and Darith followed, insane bloodthirst filling him.

There were men around him, and flashing swords, but the scimitar danced in his hand, in a whirling wall of speed and damnation and death. Then it touched flesh, and through his arm, pouring into his veins like blazing lava and distilled mead, the glowing life of his victim passed.

He felt strength and youth renewed, he smelled the good sharp scent of death in the air. He gave himself up to the blind desire to kill, to cut down all living things that stood in his way.

The scimitar struck again and again. It did not wait to drink fully of each wound, for as men fell to the left and right there was blood in abundance—spilling, splashing red on grey stone, staining the walls of corridors and dyeing new colour into faded tapestries.

The fortress grew red in mottled, nightmare patterns, as Darith and the scimitar grew *strong*.

Robed men died as the black blade lashed around him. They kept coming, and he sensed dimly another will behind them: the same mind behind man after man. One will possessed them all, using all those bodies as its own.

Ragged clansmen came running, swords whirling in sunlit swirls above their heads before red stained the steel. They swarmed over the grey-robed army.

Then a man with a morgenstern blocked their path. He wore grey cloth robes and over his mouth and nose he wore a grey cloth mask, but he did not move in unison with the others; he whirled the cruel spiked ball about his head, and it broke skulls and hips and sent pieces of flesh flying.

Ruishiar, the boy-chief of Clan Morulvu, rushed the butcher. Heavy cold enemy metal lifted, whirring, as the boy charged, his wild hillmen following.

The cruel steel weight whirled to meet him: Ruishiar fell, skull shattered. His kinsmen shrieked.

Darith felt himself compelled toward that man. The scimitar wanted him more than any other in the fortress. Yet something about him troubled Darith.

Something more than the near-impossibility of getting in a killing blow before the spiked steel ball came crushing down.

Then the man was close, *before him,* and the morgenstern whirling in!

The scimitar shot up, stood up with all the muscle of Darith's arm and stance. The chain struck the blade and wrapped around it.

If Darith's weapon had been a mortal sword the man in grey would have ripped it from Darith's hand, killed Darith, and continued to fight.

But the chain melted. Darith had to shake droplets of molten steel off the blade before they dripped down on his hand. The spiked ball fell to the ground.

The eyes above the grey mask widened and Darith could see that this man knew what the scimitar was.

Then, before the thirsty blade could strike, the man in grey drew a dagger from his robes and plunged it into his own heart. The scimitar moved oddly as the man in grey fell to the ground, his eyes glazed, his lips curved in a strange, triumphant smile—dead, but free.

Darith felt terror, suddenly remembering the nightmare on the ship, so long ago. In that dream he had first seen the black scimitar.

This was the man he had been, and in his memory he knew what this man had felt. Not monstrous enough that he should have to wield the blade: now he must carry the burden of knowing what it was to be his own adversary, and defeated! A half-stifled cry erupted from his throat.

Then the enemy was about him again and the sword in his hand was in control. And he killed, cutting and rending, while the sword drank up life after life.

Darith grew stronger, quicker. His boots pounded on stone floors and sent back echoes until the blood that soaked his boots and his clothes and the walls of the fortress were so thick and clotted and black that all sound was deadened.

Running, strong and young with stolen life, he emerged on a parapet and stood, wet and red in full sunlight, chest heaving, mind spinning. Breathing was no longer a task, he thought. Not even hard breathing.

I am young again, a young man filled with young men's blood. I have a sword, I have ships, I have an army. The world shall lie at my feet.

No! Why am I thinking these things?

He looked down from the high parapet at the great Sea of Salmon, where waves like emerald fires threw flickering pearls against the shore. The sea seemed to stretch forever. A warm sea filled with life; a sea to be conquered. Beyond it there were lands, also to be conquered . . .

He shook his head, trying to clear it of the fabulous notions flooding and mushrooming there:

Lands with palaces of jewels, and tables set with rare viands, women . . .

With this sword I can take whatever I want! he thought.

His eyes blazed and the salt ocean air filled his lungs. This Sea of Salmon stretching before him was a warm body, not like the cold damp enemy that was the Great Ocean. On the southeastern shore of this sea there was a city. The City of the King.

Someone was coming toward him, along the parapet. The scimitar moved in his hand.

One more life, one more draught to add to the immortal liquor inside him. Didn't the approaching fool know? Hadn't he seen what happened to men touched by the Demon-Blade?

The scimitar leaped up in his hand, high over his head, ready to come down in a mighty slash and split this one last enemy to the breastbone.

Why didn't the man stop? Was he so enamoured of damnation? Closer, and yet closer now. The man was not tall, and his features were blurred, grey, formless, like a wraith.

Strike! the scimitar commanded.

Darith held his arm rigid. There was something wrong.

This was not a man to be killed. There was some reason he should be spared, some reason he should not die, whoever he was.

Kill! the scimitar screamed up his arm, into his blood and brain. *Strike, cut him down, rend him, drink his life!*

Before he comes close and puts a knife between your ribs! Don't be a fool!

He is your enemy, like all men!

Darith's arm flew back, poised to strike—

"*Darith!*"

A cry, a voice, tilting with destiny, flat and stony against the reeling power of tides. The hand gripped, the sword strained, the tearing tightening on the heart, then: the dream dissolved.

Only there was no sleep in which to dream, no dream to mask desire. It was all real, and terrible.

Avlath was standing there, his face pale under sunburn and dirt and sweat. Gonquin was running across the parapet with a bloody rapier in his hand.

Darith felt the scimitar quiver once, then grow cold and still. It had failed to master him.

"Avlath..." Darith began, but he could think of nothing to say. He had nearly killed his Chamberlain, his oldest friend.

"I understand, my Lord," said Avlath. "If you wish it, once the battle is done, I will put an arrow through your heart."

"That would solve nothing," Darith said after a moment's consideration. "But perhaps there is a way to bind me, as Colyn was bound, and keep my blood between the scimitar and the earth. I wonder if animals could grant me life? The prospect of men coming to me in sacrifice is not pleasing. I shall kill some creature soon and find out." Did his voice sound as dead in their ears as it did in his own?

Gonquin joined them, panting from his run.

"It is well you shouted my name, Troubadour," Darith said. "Save for your shout I would have—much grief."

"I sounded other things than your name," said Gonquin. "There are words one hears and words one feels. But let us speak no more of it. I followed your trail here on different business. This fortress is taken, with little effort beyond your own. It is time now to eliminate the fortress on the opposite cliff, and sail on."

"Then let us do it." Darith sighed. "The sooner it is done

the sooner this war will be ended. You said you could deal with the other fortress?"

"I can," said Gonquin. "Indeed, the catapult is ready and waits your signal."

They went back the way Gonquin had come; through a door at the end of the parapet, down the tower stairs, and through silent, necrotic corridors. As they approached a portal through which sunlight slanted, the walls rumbled.

"They've discovered our victory," Gonquin said. "They're trying to put a rock on the catapult we captured."

They hurried then, and emerged a moment later in the courtyard. The catapult was loaded with hay and rocks tied in a tight bundle, the arm bound tightly back, ready to launch.

Gonquin drew a small bottle of dark yellow fluid from his pouch, ran across to the catapult, and stuffed it into the hay.

"Go to the gate," he called. "And watch!"

Darith and Avlath did as they were bid. Gonquin set a torch to the hay, then pulled the huge lever that loosed the rocking arm.

The bundled rocks and hay shot up, arced flaming across the deep azure sky, and fell within the walls of the opposing fortress.

Minutes passed. Gonquin came to stand beside Avlath, and still nothing happened.

Then: with a crash like thunder in hell, the fortress exploded.

Yellow flame leaped above the walls, and black, oily smoke billowed forth.

The cliff beneath the fortress cracked, and with terrible slow finality, the cliff, and the remains of the fortress, crumbled into the sea.

"Our passage is clear," said Gonquin, bowing slightly.

CHAPTER THIRTEEN
The Haunted Land

Beyond the fortresses the river narrowed. The water was still deep enough to float the caravels, but there was not enough room to tack once the sun heated the clay hills and the land breeze blew against them, and in any case, the red cliffs cut off most of the wind. Before the Tondurn fleet had gone two miles, the wind failed them. The *Maid of Tharda*'s sails flapped helplessly and the sluggish current began to bear her slowly back again.

"Signal *'All ships anchor.'*" Darith gave the order and turned to look back down the line. The ships were strung out in an irregular line behind him, with the caravels of the chieftains towering like swans over their cygnets above the smaller craft that could both row and sail.

"Could we leave the great-ships here at anchor and transfer all our men into the longboats?" asked Gonquin.

Darith thought for a moment, then shook his head. "They could not hold us all, and I fear that when we come to our goal we will need every sword. Nor would they have room for our supplies, even if they could carry the men."

The life force that the black scimitar had stolen still sang in his veins, but he could see how the heavy heat was already wearing on the men around him. And the river water was brackish and foul. Perhaps higher up it would be drinkable, but he did not count on it, knowing where they were bound. They were going to need all the good water the ships' casks held.

"Could we march overland?" asked Mannus. "Leave the longboats only enough men to row them and use the extra space to carry supplies while the rest of us marched along the shore?"

"If there was a shore!" exclaimed Avlath. "Look at those cliffs, lad. Even if we went back to the forts to climb them, who knows when we could get down again, or what the terrain is like above?"

Mannus's face grew redder than the heat had already made it and he started to turn away.

"It was a good idea," Gonquin said, stopping him. "Better than mine! Don't shame the lad, Avlath, unless you can think of a better way!"

Now the Chamberlain was flushing as well. Darith felt tension building among them. It must be the same on the other vessels. If only his own determination could haul them —he grew very still...

Darith came back to the present, the idea that had been teasing at his awareness clear in his mind, and realized that all of the others were staring at him.

"There is another way," he said. "It will mean hard work for the men, but I think it will get us there. Someone get paper and pen and take down this message..."

Two hours later, they were moving again. Now each caravel was linked to a pair of longboats by towlines that thrummed with strain as the oars bit into the murky water. Progress was not easy, or even. The longboats would surge ahead, only to be brought up with a jerk as they came to the end of the line. Oars flailed as the tension was released and the transferred impetus brought the larger ships rushing forward, and the longboats would get under control again just in time to avoid being run down. At least they did not have the motion of the waves to contend with, as they would have at sea.

Every two hours one pair of longboats would be spelled by another, but it was punishing work. The *Maid of Tharda*'s timbers groaned at the unaccustomed motion, as if in sympathy with the labouring men. And the river wound on and on.

At night a miasma rose from the dark water, and troubled their sleep. The days of sport fishing became a fair dream. There were fish in the black river, but they were inedible, as tainted as the water in which they swam. Gonquin sang to cheer them—but his songs grew increasingly melancholy as the days passed.

The days were hot. By that alone they might have known they were in Kreelath's country, for even so far south, winter normally brought days of cool mist and rain. But where the black river ran, the weather was that of the Demon-World. Those who were not rowing tried to sleep through the heat, and woke to walk the decks at night, when the air was cold, yet too foul for sleep. Night would have been easier rowing, but in the dark the subtle riffling of the surface that warned them of hidden rocks and sandbars could not be seen.

But Darith found the merciless brilliance of daylight increasingly hard to bear. As the journey continued, he remained in his cabin until night fell. At least the scimitar stayed quiet in his hand. Perhaps it was still sated with all the blood it had drunk at the fortress. Or perhaps, thought Darith grimly, it knew that a still greater feast of life was in store.

The red cliffs held the heat between them like the walls of an oven. Belowdecks it was stifling, but at least in his cabin Darith was shielded from the merciless glare of the sun. He lay in his hammock with the black scimitar clasped to his breast, shallow breathing the only sign he lived. He tried to think of darkness—deep, cool darkness that would soothe all pain.

The night wind had been cool in Tharda . . . He tried to lose himself in a dream of moonlit waters lapping a white shore, and Lonarissa beside him, her hair dark as the night sky, her skin glowing as pale as the moon.

"It has been too long, my love—" She turned to smooth the hair back from his brow.

"Too long," he agreed. *"But the waiting is almost over now."* He looked down, and saw the velvet scimitar in his hand. He could feel the force of its stolen lives filling him until he too glowed with blue fire. *"I possess a power that will set all evil at naught—even you, my beloved, even you cannot be hidden from me now!"*

But already she was fading. He pursued her into darkness.

And then the scene seemed to change. He was striding through a burning city—there had been too many such cities for him to remember its name, and the Sword drank, and drank, until Darith towered above mortal men, and they fled from before him, screaming.

There was a palace—he knew that Lonarissa was inside, and he broke through its barriers, shouting her name. He pressed forward through velvet darkness, seeking her. Urgency compelled him: inward, downward he pushed—he was almost there now, almost—

*A great chamber opened before him. On the throne some-
one was waiting, wrapped in black draperies.*

*"Lonarissa! Lonarissa!" The shout ripped from Darith's
lungs.*

*The figure turned. In its forehead opened three glowing
eyes.*

Darith's scream brought Avlath running.

"Oh, my Lord, what have you done to yourself? You're
all tangled in the hammock here." Carefully the Chamberlain pulled at the netting. Full-fed, the scimitar was quiet as a
sated hound, but Avlath had learned how to serve his master
without touching the thing.

"It was a nightmare," said Darith when his breathing had
steadied. Sweat was pouring off him, and Avlath wiped his
brow. "Holy Goddess, how I wish this journey would end!"

At the end of three weeks the mountains opened onto a
vast plain of red clay, that seemed smoothed as by great
tides. There was life only where the turgid black river mean-
dered back and forth—and that life was only snakes and
spiked bushes that guarded the water's edge.

Mannus leaned to his oar and felt sweat curl between his
shoulder blades. The rag tied around his head kept some of
the moisture from his eyes, but sweat stung as he blinked;
every move wrung more perspiration from his labouring
body. His blistered palms wept, too—even the hard-handed
seamen were bleeding from the unaccustomed labour.

We are all dissolving beneath this dreadful sun, thought
Mannus. *Soon there will be only dry husks of men crawling
through an empty land.*

He could have pleaded rank and stayed on shipboard, but
his title did not yet seem real to him, and he was young and
strong. Here, his body was in agony, but it would have been
an agony of mind to him to stand and watch while his men
groaned and sweated. When they had attacked the fortress,
he had been first in the charge. It seemed to him that this
was the same.

Still, the river seemed endless. Heat shimmered above the
red plain and flowed in waves over the murky waters. Eyes
lost their focus as attention was drawn inward to the body's
strains, existence narrowed to the boat, the water, the pain.

And through that pulsing heat haze a figure came walking. Mannus saw it at first without surprise. They had become accustomed to mirages. But heat-visions stayed always
at the same distance, always approaching, never to arrive.

This image was coming nearer. Mannus straightened, and heard the man next to him curse as his stroke faltered.

"But don't you see her?" he whispered.

"Shut your eyes, lad," the man snarled. "You've had too much sun!"

But it was his lips that Mannus closed. He let the rhythm of the rowing take him again, but his eyes remained fixed on the figure, whose pale draperies seemed to flutter in the dry wind. Beneath that brilliant sun her hair was a nimbus of light—as she drew closer, Mannus was sure she was a woman.

And he had seen her before, in his dreams.

Mannus recognized now that his mental state was far from normal, but in that moment it seemed to him that the abnormality would have been to remain sane. And still she came onward, white feet not quite touching the oily surface of the stream. Her eyes blazed golden as the sun.

"Blessed Lady"—Mannus's whisper scarcely gave the words sound—"is it my death you are bringing to me?"

"It is life I will bring you, and more than life," she answered him, "if you will be true to the end."

"My Lord is leading us into the heart of Evil, and I am afraid." In that moment, he could name his fear. "If it conquers him, we will all be lost!"

"Even at the Gates of Darkness the Light may shine," said the Lady. "Even if your Lord abandons himself, you must not lose faith in him. Follow him not in fear, but in love." Her image began to waver. Now he could see the farther shore through her draperies.

Mannus nodded. "I always have. Will I see you again?"

"If you desire it." She had become a transparent brightness on the water. "Whenever danger threatens you, I will be near."

Sunlight sparkled blindingly as oars bit the water and lifted again. Mannus blinked. The Lady was gone.

The mountains dwindled behind, but there was no sign of Kreelath's city. Now nights as well as days were hot and fetid. The sun blazed on the clay desert from a bright ceramic sky, and the moon was the color of brick.

Then a mast was sighted, and another, to the rear, flying the black flag of Kreelath.

"They are rowing," said Gonquin, watching the enemy ships through his telescope. "And they have no caravels to tow. They will be upon us by nightfall."

"Let us anchor now and wait for them," said Avlath. "If we keep going, by the time they reach us our men will be too exhausted to fight."

"They may not have to," said Selvern. "I've been looking ahead of us, and the river seems to widen very soon. Gonquin, train your glass *there!*"

Gonquin did as he was bid.

"It widens, my Lord, but only into a marsh of some sort. No, wait . . . I see ruins. It would seem there was a city there at one time. The river ran through it. Now it is only rubble, partly submerged, with a central channel. And the channel is none too clear. There are pylons of fallen bridges here and there."

"Do you think we can get past it before the enemy catches us?" Selvern asked.

"Easily," said Gonquin.

Darith looked at the Prince and raised his eyebrows in question. "You have a plan?"

"I think so," said Selvern. "It worked at the battle of Sonaroy, four hundred years ago. Or so my instructors told me! I think for the sake of a battle we can afford to lose one ship."

"That is unfortunately true," said Gonquin. "For with each battle we have lost a few men, and some of the long-boats are already undermanned."

The passage was not easy: the ruins made a maze of the river channel. The foul black water hid fallen blocks of white stone that filled broad parts of the channel. They had to feel their way down the bile black stream with poles testing the waters in front of the keels.

By the time the last Tondurn ship was clear, the enemy fleet was already among the stones of the dead city.

Selvern ordered the last ship evacuated, then stripped the rest of the ships of anything that would both float and burn —extra canvas and clothing, wood-shafted weapons, quickly emptied casks—all soaked with oil, thrown overboard and lit with flaming arrows, when the enemy fleet was well into the ruins.

The river carried the burning debris directly to the enemy ships; it caught and piled up against their wooden hulls. Though the flames were not hot enough to ignite the wet wood, nor high enough to reach the rigging, the thick, dirty oil provided smoke enough to obscure the enemy's vision.

Under cover of the smoke, Selvern sent archers in long-boats close enough to shoot fire-arrows at the flagship. A dozen arrows were well placed before the archers were forced to withdraw, and by then the enemy ship was out of control due to panic. Flames gnawed her furled sails and snaked along her lines.

"Now, watch!" said Selvern. He raised his arm and dropped it. The empty ship moved downstream. "The ship I ordered abandoned is soaked with oil from stem to stern."

There was neither time nor room to maneuver in the narrow channel. The enemy had more than he could do trying to put out fires in the rigging.

With a ripping, snapping sound of timbers, the derelict rammed the flagship and burst into flames.

The two burning ships moved downstream and struck a third.

A fourth ship was spared by the ruins of an aqueduct. The channel was so narrow and littered where it had fallen in ages past that the triple wreckage was unable to pass. The three burning ships sank in the relatively shallow water, effectively blocking all transit.

The Tondurn fleet continued to row. Gonquin warned the men to keep their cloaks about them, but in the dry heat they paid little attention, and soon had blistered shoulders. But the riverbed was less treacherous, and now they were able to move at night and sleep by day, as Darith did.

Under the cycling red moon the water took on a green tinge. At first it was attributed to imagination, but as the nights passed it became apparent that some sort of phosphorescence was present.

By the end of the fifth night it was quite bright, shifting in pale green patches below the surface like ghosts. Some of the men said they saw faces in the water. Faces of women sometimes, or of little children.

One bright, moonlit night Darith found Gonquin staring sadly down into the water, and thought he looked troubled.

"What is it?" he asked at last.

"Can you not hear them?" the Troubadour asked, then shook his head. "No, of course you cannot. But you can see them." He pointed into the water. Darith looked down. At first he saw only the green phosphorescent glow he expected.

Then slowly, he saw faces forming in the dim light. He looked away, quickly.

"Who are they?" he asked. "And what is it that you hear?"

"They are the spirits of all those who lived here before Kreelath came," said Gonquin. "What I hear is their voices

—the voices of the thousands slaughtered here, mourning their land and their lives. Mostly women's voices," he said, "and children's. The men, I expect, are among the robed ones, the possessed who serve Kreelath." Darith shuddered.

"Most of them are not aware of us," said Gonquin, "or concerned with us. Only a very few. Those voices sing of vengeance."

"Do not speak of this," said Darith. It was bad enough for the men to know that they were going up against the Black Fleet; some already whispered of the demonic nature of the foe. It would not help them to know that the dead were watching through the waters of the river.

When dawn's bloodied fingers reached up to seize another day, Gonquin went forward, as had become his custom, to peer through the telescope at the land ahead. Darith stood by the forward gunwale, staring into the ominous dawn grey of the landscape.

"Good morning, my Lord," Gonquin said, his voice filled with false jollity. "Think'st thou this day we shall come to the Isles of Pleasure?"

Darith smiled tiredly.

"Not so, I fear, Troubadour. But one way or another, our labours must soon be rewarded. Water runs low, the food is nearly gone. Even if there were no enemy behind us, we could not recross this desert without fresh supplies."

Gonquin made no answer, but put the telescope to his eye.

Could it be a trap? Darith wondered. Was it possible that Gonquin's spells were not strong enough, and that Caranom had spoken as Kreelath wished? Perhaps there was no city of clay beside the river. Perhaps the ships now far behind had been sent to drive the Tondurn fleet ever deeper into an endless wasteland.

The greater part of his year-and-a-day of life was already gone.

The shimmering green ghosts in the water grew dim. The sky was coppery now, and already the landscape wavered in the heat of day. Something dead and bloated drifted near the right bank. It might once have been a dog, Darith thought, or a cat, or some large amphibian.

"It's there!" said Gonquin.

"What?" Darith asked, startled.

"The city. Just coming over the horizon. Black, as Caranom said! It is built on a low hillock next to the river. Perhaps on the ruins of previous cities, for there are no other hills in this desert. It is well walled, but arches pierce the walls, so that ships may sail in. The buildings seem, for the most part, to be shallow domes, and tall, thin towers—of—of clay!"

"For such a city to continue standing," Darith said, wondering, "the climate must be sorely lacking in rainfall."

"There is a huge dome in the centre of the city. No doubt that is where we will find Kreelath!"

Darith was quiet for a few moments. The oars creaked and sloshed in the murky black water. Soon the men would stop rowing and crawl into the shade of their cloaks or go below to sleep; at least, they were hoping to.

"We are too close to stop." Darith shook his head. "They will be able to see us now. We'll have to go on without rest. It's our only chance. I think perhaps the hour will aid us. Neither the night dwellers nor the day dwellers will be abroad just after dawn."

"I have one more trick left in my bag," Gonquin said. "It is a small one. Come with me."

The Troubadour led the way to the cabin he shared with Selvern, where there was an assortment of boxes, jars, instruments of music, and other paraphernalia. He moved things about for a minute, then unwrapped a small, carven casket. On one side opals were inlaid to form words.

"Open the chest but a crack," Gonquin read. "Then chant the spell written on its side. The wind will spring to your summoning. But remember that the wind loves to be free: if you open the chest too wide it will escape. Turned loose"—he paused significantly—"this spell is enough to sail a fleet of ships, but it will sail them only once. Even on magic."

"*That is a Thardan magic!*" Darith said, the words choking him and bringing back pictures of the lost realm. "How did it come into your hands?"

"I was born in Tharda." Gonquin's head rose, and a look of mixed pride and sorrow flashed in his eyes.

"My father was a man of Tondur who married a woman of the Thardan royal house. I take after my father, but my sister has our mother's golden eyes. When the King needed to send an emissary to Kaerbradan, he chose my mother, because she had already learned your language. My sister and I were still suckling. You know the rest."

Darith stared at the Troubadour for a long time, understanding finally the turns of phrase and outlook that had teased at his memory. *Tharda!* It should have lifted his heart to know that something of the White Realm had survived its destruction. But not here. The humped silhouette of the city on the horizon negated all other hopes or fears. After a while he closed his eyes, blinked away the tears that refused to run, and sighed.

"Take the chest to the rearmost ship, and prepare to use it. We'll let the men sleep a while before we attack."

Gonquin picked up the casket and prepared to do as he was bid, while Darith stood, lost in memories of Tharda, the White Land, the Magician's Resting Place . . .

But suddenly other memories came to him—Colyn's memories. Gonquin was at the door, but Darith's hand moved to his forearm and stopped him. Gonquin's dark brows lifted in question.

"It has just come into my mind—there is a flaw in our plan. Colyn my ancestor pursued the Demon even as we have, and at each confrontation the Demon fled. Fled far away, leaving his mortal foe plodding helplessly behind. That was what kept Colyn busy until the Sword gained the mastery, and he trapped himself on that island to protect his followers, and the world. If you have Thardan magics, Gonquin, have you among them a spell that will hold this horror to the spot while I spit him on this Sword?"

Gonquin paused and his brows furrowed, then he returned the casket to its place.

"There are no birds, but—we have seen serpents in the desert, have we not?"

"We have," Darith replied.

Gonquin sorted through more containers, untied boxes bound with silken cords of gold and green, considered various talismans and charms, then carefully rebound them, each time shaking his head in the negative.

"I may seem to have all these magics stored in my mind" —he smiled as Darith began to look doubtful—"but not as completely as I would wish. In each of the many jewels I carry there are thoughts, like written records. Much of learning the magic is knowing how to read the texts. It is like a song. One knows it, and yet one does not know it. One has almost all the words, then one has none of them. A single phrase of the tune is enough to bring it to the tongue, but one must find that phrase."

"And what book within a stone do you seek?" Darith asked as the Troubadour paused.

"A book that can be bound to a serpent's brow," said

Gonquin. "A book that will allow me to extend the spell of circles to bind an entire city. I remember two jewels, a chrysoprase and a piece of amber, both of which would be appropriate here, but which of the two would be better used will be a matter of the exact nature of the spells. I must see them to be sure. Will you have one of the men bring me two serpents from the desert? At this rate, I am sure he can catch them by the time I find my stones!"

Darith left him and went to the deck. He found Mannus, who was chafing for action, and happy to fulfill the Troubadour's request, no matter how strange it seemed. Then he ordered the men to rest.

Darith had an hour of waiting that seemed like more, while the men slept, not knowing that the city was ahead of them, and battle and death. In the stillness, it was as if they were dead already. And what about the city? Had they spotted the little fleet already, and if so, were they preparing their defences, or were they laughing at this sun-blistered, travel-weary enemy?

Then Mannus returned with a writhing sack, and strange stains on the thick leather gauntlets he had donned when he had heard what Gonquin needed.

"I had hoped there might be harmless snakes, my Lord," he said cheerfully. "But if there are, they stay well away from the river." Darith bit his lip, and shook his head in wonder.

"There is no end to your courage, it seems. I chose my heir wisely." Darith managed a smile. "Well, let us go and see whether Gonquin has fared as well as you."

Gonquin met them at the door and motioned them before him. He carried his harp and a small bag.

"I am glad you had the sense to wear a thick glove, Mannus!" he said. "I had truly not thought about what kind of creatures this Demon would allow to live in the land he ruled. But they will serve. Birds would be better, but alas, our foe has left no birds—not even vultures. The spell I had remembered would normally use birds—but that spell would not by itself be strong enough, in any case! So I must create a new spell, such a spell as has never been made before, a spell that calls not only upon the Wisdom of Tharda, but upon the Power of the Ancient Crown. And I may also need the aid of those who have watched us from under the water."

He paused, frowning in thought, while Mannus stared. After a moment the Troubadour straightened, and spoke:

"You may let the men rest fully, Darith, and sleep the day

and the night as well. This will take time, and I think it will
be better not to enter Kreelath's lair too near sunset. So we
will do this spell today, and I will release the winds at dawn.
But come, I will need your help!"

They went ashore. The men slept, except for the guards.
The sun glared down on the barren waste.

"Be careful, Lord!" exclaimed Mannus, as the Troubadour opened the sack of snakes. "They are poisonous!"

"They are deadly!" Gonquin laughed. "But I know them
better than you! Stand well back!"

Crooning softly, he reached gently into the bag.

> *"Come, scale-skinned kin*
> *Grass-rustling ground-stalker*
> *Eerie speckled Rib-walker,*
> *Come, hunter under stones!"*

After a long moment a dark, jewel-scaled shape began to
writhe up his arm. Darith's heart nearly stopped when the
viper, having crawled up to the Troubadour's shoulder,
began feeling his naked throat and face with its forked
tongue.

A second viper crawled up his arm, and curled beside the
first. Darith heard Mannus suck in his breath, and knew the
boy was trembling. But Gonquin only smiled.

From the small bag he had carried, Gonquin drew a drop
of golden light; with thread he bound it to the viper's head.
Stroking his harp with his free hand, he sang:

> *"Amber I name thee*
> *Tree-born, sap-born, life-born!*
> *The Throne's eyes see*
> *Ancient trees under the earth.*
> *Through this Jewel the Eyes*
> *Pour their power to our aid!*
> *Amber, tree-born ember,*
> *Sun-hearted Cinder,*
> *Life-fire flares from thee!*
> *Tree-born Amber Amulet,*
> *A line of Life's light leave:*
> *Evil-halting veil of light!"*

Now from the bag he drew a second stone, paler yellow, and bound it to the brow of the second snake, chanting softly:

> *"Praise the Crown Serene!*
> *Chrysoprase I call:*
> *Apple-green pale sheen*
> *Crystal, praised by all,*
> *Forged in earth's fire!*
> *By the Crown I call*
> *Earth's flaming blood!*
> *Earth's flame grows higher!*
> *Let Earth's power flood*
> *Where this serpent crawls,*
> *To lay a line of light no ill can pass."*

He laid both snakes on the ground, chanting,

> *"Long-fanged hunters: haunters of the sand,*
> *I send you now with power across the land!*
> *Crawl now, curling wide, around the domes,*
> *Carve a curving track across the dunes.*
> *Sun-Fire, Tree-Fire, Life-fire, Earth-fire—*
> *Ancient Powers, rise up now in holy ire—*
> *By the might of the Crown I call you here!*
> *Through these jewels the Crown's Eyes peer.*
> *Earth Power rides Rib-Walker, serving right.*
> *Life's Power Leaf-Stirrer bears for thee:*
> *Chrysoprase and Amber both burn bright*
> *To lay out long spell-linked lines of light*
> *To seal this Circle that no demon may flee."*

The snakes began to crawl slowly away, in a long curving circle into the sunlit desert. Gonquin shook his head.

"Too slow," he said. "As I thought."

He threw his arms wide; his voice soared.

> *"Ghosts of the long-dead, haunters of the waste!*
> *Gather here in haste; let our spell be sped!*
> *Speed from the east; speed from the west*
> *Rise from your rest in the river-bed!"*

A stillness filled the silence of the desert—a new *kind* of silence. Darith felt it hard to breathe: his lungs refused to fill. There was nothing to be seen, the desert looked no dif-

ferent; yet Darith *knew* that a great, invisible host of the
dead stood all around them.

Despite bright sunlight, he felt himself in darkness,
shrouded in a night the sunlight could not pierce, a night that
knew no dawn.

Gonquin lifted his harp, and his fingers shaped chords to
accompany his voice:

> *"Spirits unappeased—from east, south, west, and*
>   *north.*
> *Throng now forth, in anger unfed!*
> *Feed now your just need: speed this spell,*
> *Bind the Demon well in this Ring of Dread!"*

There was a sudden deepening of the silence, and suddenly Darith saw the serpents lifted from the ground, and
whirled away as though by a wild wind. Sand rose spinning,
and the city was hidden in a wall of flying sand.

"Sleep now," said Gonquin. "Even Kreelath cannot pass
the ward I have laid now about his city. We will attack at
dawn."

Darith went to his bed, and slept exhausted, dreamless
sleep until, at dawn, Gonquin opened the box and freed the
wind.

CHAPTER FOURTEEN
The City of Clay

The wind was delicious. It blew cold and fresh as they sped up the river, and sighed and creaked in the sails. It turned the gargoyle breath of the river back upon the evil city ahead. It moved the ships against the turbid current, up the river of darkness toward archways that opened like mouths to swallow them.

Silent as the tide, the Tondurn fleet sailed in. One after another the great ships of Dalgir slid under the city wall and into berths. Hands clenched hilts, arms felt the tightness of shield straps, but no one moved. Ten, fifteen ships were safely docked. Twenty. Thirty! Forty ships were now within the walls. Enough to hold the arches and let the rest through!

A cry went up. Darith's head snapped around: he felt the hungry sword in his hand.

Soldiers erupted from an alley between two warehouses, running in that uncanny unison that Darith remembered too well. They wore rat grey robes and carried glittering steel scimitars.

With an elation born only in part from the warm dark blade in his hand, Darith gripped a boarding line in his left hand and leaped to the gunwale. He waved the scimitar over his head.

Nearby, Selvern's voice rang out like a silver clarion.

"For Tondur!"

"For Tondur!" answered Mannus, suddenly at Darith's side. "And for Colyn Muir!"

Together they swung to the wharf, and the battle cry echoed back to them, torn with vengeance from the throat of the army that was spilling from the ships onto the packed earth of the shore.

"Colllyyyynnn!" Darith and Mannus ran shoulder to shoulder; Selvern and Gonquin joined them, and behind them Avlath led the men of Castle Colyn. The scimitar throbbed with thirst in Darith's hand. Harsh voices screamed themselves hoarse; sword-hilts hammered on thundering shields.

But the robed men rushed in eerie silence, and the lines met with a ringing of steel against steel.

Men died before Prince Selvern's shining broadsword. The circlet bound around his brow proclaimed his right to defend his people, and the hissing silver circle of his whistling sword, his ability and strength to do it.

At his side Gonquin cut and parried with an action that was light and efficient. Not only with words was he quick, but with steel.

From all sides muffled warriors pressed in, curved blades slashing. The hammering of battered metal filled the streets.

Steel rang: the warriors of Clan Colyn surged toward the great dome, bright swords whirling, rippling like sunlit water until red stains matted them.

Men died before Mannus; their blood ran in rivulets down the gleaming blade of his sword to scatter from the green gemstone in the hilt.

The velvet scimitar lived in Darith's hand, in the gutted and ruined bodies of a thousand men. It sucked up life, it condemned, it damned, and it grew in power.

But it was not alone in its bloodlust, for now Darith was with it.

From the right, a sharp edge lashed, ringing from velvet steel that parried and swung—now another to the left! Guarding with the back edge, whirling under, into the gut, and *twist!*

This was journey's end. The city of the Demon. If this battle were won, all would have been accomplished. Under a great dome Kreelath waited, and the men who rendered up their lives were only a wall to be surmounted or smashed. No need here to hold back from the scimitar's lust.

Two men's blades descended as one. The scimitar shot up to cross both, then its tip whipped under and slashed both throats.

A jerk that wrenched Darith's wrist lashed the blade right to cut off the head of a third man. The cloth mask slipped as the head fell to the ground, mouth open, tongue convulsing, open eyes rolling upward. The body collapsed.

More and more of the grey-wrapped foe swarmed from the buildings and down the street, but, pouring from their ships, the men of the clans rushed to meet them. Darith heard the humming of bagpipe drones as the clan pipers filled their bags with air.

The enemy went down like hay under a scythe before grim Goll of Caiplic, dismembered by his blood axe. Behind him the Clan fe Varruk howled like the wild winds of their rocky coasts.

There was death as the savage warriors of the fe Scarriv Clan swarmed from their ships behind black-bearded Finn of Rathnolawn, and their chiming blades ráng the knell for grey-robed men all down the street from the wharves into the city's heart.

Knives and swords flashed in brazen sunlight. Dust-dry streets grew wet with thick blood, the mingled blood of Tondur and the enemy. The harsh metal music of battle sounded in the street.

Bor of Ashir Fuaran led his clan ashore: gaunt fierce men from the icy northern highlands. The rat grey lines of robed men crumpled before them, their numbers crushed with sheer ferocity. Clan fe Rogoin with Niall of Lairog-nan-Cuivair at their head swarmed down the long street, exultant swords lashing.

Yet the sweeping united strokes of Kreelath's possessed minions, a thousand swords slashing at once, all at the same angle, like scythes, took their toll as well.

Darith heard the booming of beaten shields, and the death-screams of men echoing from clay walls. He knew the voices were those of his own men: Kreelath's possessed did not scream, but died as they had fought, in eerie silence.

The men of fe Mavron raged through the streets behind their Lord, into the heart of the enemy. For the first time in weeks the Bull Dragon was unleashed, as Olegair fe Mavron roared, with laughter and with rage, and killed joyously in the fierce manner of the hill people. He fought in a circle, and men died before him and behind him and to either side.

Now Darith's army was moving into streets choked with the foe, and clay buildings separated them as they followed different streets. Loud now the roars of the blood-mad chief of the fe Mavron sounded off to the left, echoing through hollow corridors. The exultant keening of the war-pipes sang above the screaming and the hammering of steel.

Clay houses collapsed, crumbling under stress, as reeling

masses of men and metal weapons crashed against their walls. Arrows hummed from the rooftops.

Finn fe Scarriv of Rathnolawn died at the head of his men, an arrow jutting out through the black beard. Voices cried. Men fell all around Darith, pierced by arrows.

"Our archers!" he shouted. "They have snipers on the roofs."

A flight of arrows, whirring like a flock of partridge, went over his head. Grey-robed men fell from the rooftops. Swords wheeled like silver lace. Darith's blade drank lives.

But all around him men were dying, free hillmen as well as the possessed armies of the Demon. From all sides the muffled warriors came, pressing closer with the mass of their numbers. He saw Clan Scarriv die to a man around Finn's body; saw Bor of Ashir Fuaran go down.

A sudden charge forced a wedge between himself and the others; he saw Mannus and Selvern swept back by the foe, pushed into a side street. The men of Clan Morulvu and of Lairog-nan-Cuivair fought and died all around him. Niall hacked his way to Darith's side, and they fought back to back. Another onslaught of the Demon's swordsmen, and the golden thrilling in his arm increased. The enemy died; the Sword, and Darith, lived. Lived strong, quick, moving ever toward the center of the city, and Kreelath.

Behind the wall of swords, Mannus glimpsed the Black Sword and the swarming men, but a solid wall of shields, bristling with curved blades, lay between. The shrouded enemy fought in silence, and their masked faces showed neither fear nor fury in battle.

At his side Selvern's great blade was lashing in circles, its whistling keen edge spattering blood as it flew: grim the windy sound of flying steel.

Avlath and Niall of Lairog-nan-Cuivair and his Clan fe Rogoin vanished into a chaos of flailing swords, and only echoes of a mystic deep sound from the drones, and a faint keening like the cry of birds over the boom of battle, told of their fight.

From all sides black-robed men swarmed into the street, scimitars swinging. Mannus could only reel back before the weight of the enslaved hordes that pressed him in, and he felt a softened clay wall give way behind. Clay dissolved; flashing steel flew; fighters surged all about him.

When things look black, advance! Mannus decided, fiercely fighting to keep his feet as their numbers rushed against him like a raging tide, and the falling blades of scimitars, dyed bright rose-red, hurtled in air around him, humming like birds.

Men held back, in fear of the sharp, curved swords above the shield-wall; some started screaming and backing away.

There was no surrender and no mercy in such a battle. His men might even run away in despair.

He must lead an attack! He was the heir of Colyn Muir!

"Colllyyyynnn!" Mannus shouted, and sprang forward, sword raised to charge.

He whipped the blade down as death flew at his face. The shield rang on his arm. He felt his edge slash flesh, and a ripped corpse fell.

Mannus sprang over his dead foe's body, into the rank behind. A mailed soldier turned to cut at him, but his shield had faced the men of Lairog-nan-Cuivair, and had not come all the way back across his body. Mannus launched his edge at the shoulder as the back of his own shield hid the foe from sight. His hand felt mail-rings part and bone snap; a sword fell away from his shield to the ground.

Another sword boomed on Mannus's lifted shield. But the shield-wall was broken now, and the man he fought fell. At his left, Selvern pressed in, bright blade lashing in deadly circles.

Booming shields were battered, the wall dissolved, and the shrouded men scattered, and died with no cries.

Then the air turned cold.

Thin, gauzy clouds appeared, and thickened over the city.

Mannus, shouting, rallied his running men, and they surged behind him, bloody weapons waving, their feet splashing red.

The green-gemmed hilt was hot in his hand; the blade hurtled on around him, steel winging easily, red from war. Selvern was bounding on and others behind him; their fleet swords bit. The Demon-possessed enemy slaves went down under the grim current of fury.

Now loud above the epic clatter of the battle Mannus heard the eerie keening of war-pipes.

And then, through the turmoil ahead he glimpsed kilted men reeling back from lashing swords, and saw that their tartan was the yellow-crossed red and green of Clan fe Mavron.

Was Olegair, then, nearby?

Then he heard the roaring of the Bull Dragon's voice, booming no longer with laughter, but with a terrible rage.

For here in the narrow streets Olegair and his men could only stagger back, almost falling, before blades numberless and mindless as wind-whipped hay.

Like ships before a rocky coast, the unled kilted men behind him had stopped at the sight of the street full of the black-robed slaves, with the force of their charge throwing down the soft clay walls.

Loud from the battle the humming bagpipe called. Selvern was shouting orders, but no man moved.

Mannus realized that he, the Lord's heir, must lead these men into action.

How had he gotten such a thought? Selvern was their rightful Prince! But he saw that in a fight they would never take orders from Selvern, or any man of the lowlands.

It had been only to their own chief or to the Colyn Muir that they had looked in battle, but now they had accepted *him* as their master.

He needed the fury that gave him his speed; to wait here before the advance chilled his heart and limbs, and made him tremble at the bone.

Then he saw Olegair fe Mavron, far in advance of his men, fighting alone against the armies of the possessed, as his men staggered back before advancing dull-robed ranks.

Mannus rushed with the vigor of youth into the turmoil of winging swords. His feet flew with a speed that only some threat to Darith had ever given him before. For this *was* a threat to his Lord—to Darith's friend!

Mannus heard more feet following his as he flew on a tide of sudden fury through black robes and blank faces.

The host surged behind him in a body, shields guarding chests, palms sweating on hilts, a fleet mass of flashing steel.

Through the keen scimitars of the slaves in their rat grey robes flew the blood-mad men, as the heir to the chief ran at their head: men of Colyn Muir, together with others in the red-and-yellow tartan of clan Morulvu. Grim swords hurtled, humming. Bloody from battle, the feet of the kilted men were splashing red.

Enemy scimitars, winging in air, flared brightly at Olegair fe Mavron as he fought alone against Kreelath's slaves. There among the swords, even a couple of his men, had they held to him in the fight, would have restored the order of battle.

But with each man guarding only his own back, no man had been able to hold his place. The fe Mavron clan had suffered major losses in the first encounters, and now most stepped back from the charge, or leaped away, stabbing with the point.

Mannus held to his fury as he crashed through the black-robed ranks that ringed fe Mavron's chief. His keen steel blade hurtled in a practiced slash. He glimpsed blank masked faces fighting him; flashing steel flew.

"Mannus!" Olegair shouted, as the blood-mad youth sped, leading his men in fury through shields of the silent enemy around him. "You young fool! This is death! Beware —but my thanks to you!"

Death had been close to the fe Mavron, but that grim fighter never backed down in battle. Not for rescue had the bagpipes called, not if he knew of it, not for himself. Grey-robed bodies in a circle on the earth showed how hard he'd fought, here where the grim swords flew.

But on the muffled enemy warriors came, pressing closer. Clansmen staggered, almost falling, forced back by more than twice their numbers toward the docks, flashing steel flailing against guarding shield-walls.

Like yellow-green oil, the blank river surged behind them, and over the horizon came . . .

"More ships than I've ever seen!" a voice shrieked in despair. "That fleet whose way we blocked, but reinforced a thousandfold."

The men knew it was magic, and memories of earlier battle showed in their faces as they held against their silent enemy. The city was crumbling about them as they fought, as softened black walls dissolved and fell apart from the fury of this clash.

And now red, terrible blades scythed down, and blank silence washed over cries of pain. Clenched air roared in the war-pipes as a dead piper crashed to the earth.

Together Mannus and Olegair fought against the keen blades of the silent, cloth-shrouded tide that rose about them, each guarding the other's back.

"Where is Darith?" Olegair roared as his own shield crashed, guarding his friend's flesh from the falling blades of the scimitars all about them. Mannus whipped his blade winging in a slash against rat grey cloth: red blood flew from full veins.

"There!" Mannus shouted, waving his point at Kreelath's black dome.

Niall of Lairog-nan-Cuivair went down before a mass of black robes and shrouded faces, his shield driven down at last by curved swords rising and falling all together.

The black blade whirled and danced, drinking the lives of the numbers that pressed about it.

Darith staggered, and discovered suddenly that he was alone in a street paved with corpses. The sun was at zenith and the heat was unbearable. He wiped sweat and blood from his eyes and took his bearings. Kreelath's dome would be . . . Yes! That way.

He ran up the street, staying close to one side in case there were archers above. The streets zigzagged back and forth, as if loath to approach the Demon's lair; and more than once he was forced to turn aside or retrace his path.

Footsteps pounded behind him. With a twist of his entire body he dodged inside a doorway and flattened himself against the wall. The footsteps grew close. He raised the scimitar.

Then, despite the blade's lust, he lowered it as Avlath stopped before the doorway. He must have made some sound then, for Avlath turned and saw him, eyes widening as he understood the meaning of Darith's movement.

"Do not worry," Darith said with bitter humour. "I can control it. It has fed well today."

Avlath nodded. "I couldn't find you—I was afraid you had gone to seek the Demon alone."

"Afraid? I should think you would be relieved! But if you insist on following me to an audience with Kreelath, very well. You seem intent on giving your life for me whether I will or no. Let us go and see if we can finish this battle before any more good men get killed."

Together they ran up the twisting streets, and emerged a few moments later on a stone-paved square before the huge bronze doors of Kreelath's black dome. Three white circles were painted above the doors, and three raised circles of bronze worked into their metal. Like three locked links to a chain across the crack. A strange, funereal odor pervaded the square, sharp contrast to the bright sunlight. Darith walked forward.

"Kreelath!" he cried. "I am here—Darith of Colyn Muir, come to challenge you!"

His voice echoed on the stone and clay walls of the buildings. The doors remained shut.

Then, from a street to the far left, a squadron of swordsmen boiled out and came at him. Some of these had naked faces, as though they had had no time to don the masks the Demon hid their humanity behind.

"Avlath, see if you can open the doors!" Darith called. "And stay back from me. You shall see why this Demon fears to let me enter his temple!"

Like dark lightning the scimitar flashed in a circle around him and the swordsmen fell. Yet before they had all perished another squadron emerged, then another. From all sides the Demon's warriors came, pressing closer with the mass of their numbers. Their plain steel scimitars licked at him like shiny silver tongues.

Even if the Sword is invincible, Darith thought, *they could smother me under their dead bodies!*

And then the Sword would burn its way into the earth, and drag everything into Kreelath's Demon-World.

"The doors will not open!" Avlath shouted above the tumult of battle.

"Then prepare to enter with drawn sword," Darith cried. "We are going in despite Kreelath's will!"

A single slash cut down four men as he turned and ran toward the doors. An inner certainty beyond reason flared through him, brought arm and blade up, balanced his entire body in one moment of readiness. Then he swung the velvet scimitar in a lashing arc that brought it against the three bronze circles with all his strength.

The doors burst inward.

CHAPTER FIFTEEN
The Black Dome

"My Lord, wait!" Avlath cried, twenty yards into the darkness. "They are not following. Perhaps even *they* fear to pass these portals."

Darith halted and looked back. A square of bright, sun-painted grey masks stared from the outer glare.

Clustering shadows, thick like falling drapes, darker than the wine of grapes, pressed Darith's skin with the sweetness of funeral flowers.

"It would seem the Demon has other defences than his possessed armies of men," Darith said.

He turned and walked on, Avlath guarding his back. The robed men in the doorway made no move, and as the dark grew deeper and deeper, the sun-painted face-masks vanished behind them.

Is it possible this place is so large? Darith wondered. *I would have thought that by now we'd have gone through, and on out into the streets beyond—but then, it would be strange indeed if Kreelath did not surround himself with spells and illusions.*

Blue sparks leaped from the scimitar's tip, and Darith felt his arm grow numb. His head swam, and he staggered backward.

"My Lord! Darith, are you all right?" He heard love and fear in Avlath's voice.

"Yes, yes," he answered. "Stand still. Touch nothing! Touch nothing!" He shook his head and drove away the buzzing, then flexed his arm. The feeling came back in a swift flood of hot needles. "Have you anything we can use as a torch, is there any way to light our way in this place?"

"A fire-arrow," Avlath said. "What happened? I saw sparks."

"I touched something, and some of the life my blade has soaked up was drawn out."

An orange glow erupted and Darith saw the Chamberlain's face outlined in the darkness.

A few steps ahead was a dull black wall made of some material very much like the blade of the scimitar.

"So!" Darith exclaimed. "The very walls of this place are evil. No wonder Kreelath will not bring his soldiers in!"

"There is an arch, there to the left," said Avlath. "I would advise that we try it, for this is my last arrow, and it will not burn long."

"Very well," said Darith. "Apply the flame to those curtains. I do not think we dare even touch them, so like black velvet are they."

Avlath did as he was directed and the curtains vanished in a sheet of yellow fire. Beyond the arch a stair led upwards.

Up they went, in a dimming circle of dying light, to a broad landing, up a second stair, up a third whose walls curved oddly and whose steps were of irregular height and spacing.

The fire died, and they were forced to feel their way with their feet. Up, into the enfolding darkness, into air that filled their lungs with the sweet smell of sepulchral spices.

Suddenly they were blinded by daylight.

The walls had disappeared, and they stood atop a thin tower, looking down on Kreelath's black clay city. Avlath clutched Darith's arm and pointed, mute with despair.

The men of Tondur were being forced back, their numbers shrunken to a tenth of what they had been.

Many of the Tondurn ships were burning, and up the river, rowed by slaves, a monstrous black fleet moved inexorably.

"This is illusion, a lie," Darith said. "Do not let it affect your courage, my friend."

"But if it is *true*—"

"If it is true it changes nothing! We are here to destroy Kreelath. Neither illusions nor despair will deter us."

"There, Darith—see!" Avlath choked. "Prince Selvern is struck down."

"Kreelath!" Darith shouted at the steel blue sky. "You cannot turn me back. I am the slave of this blade. It matters not whether Tondur falls: I will seek you out! I will banish you, drive you back into your own world!"

"They've captured Gonquin," Avlath began, but Darith would not let him continue. The velvet scimitar slashed out at the air beyond the tower's low parapet. Blue sparks showered and the darkness returned.

"Another draught of my stolen life gone," Darith said, shaking the circulation back into his arm. "He wishes to take it all. Well, let him try. Listen, my friend! If we should meet with more illusion, close your eyes tightly and stand still. I will deal with the magic."

Avlath sighed in the dark.

"My Lord, if there are many walls in this place, and we cannot see, it is left to chance whether we will find Kreelath or stumble to our deaths."

Darith thought for a moment.

"Did you keep the shaft of that arrow?" he asked.

"Yes, here," said Avlath, and Darith, bending, reached under his hauberk and ripped out a section of padding.

He touched it to the scimitar and it burst into flame. Avlath speared the burning cloth and for a few moments more they had light. When it was gone another section of padding was sacrificed, then another.

They came to the end of the stairs and emerged through an uncovered archway into a long, low hall. The scimitar began to quiver.

"Stand away, Avlath," Darith said softly. "There, at the other end of the hall—that's where Kreelath is. The sword knows."

The padding burned out, but even as the light failed, Avlath was ripping his sleeve away and igniting it. Darith strode forward. Fitful orange torchlight cast his shadow on walls and ceiling, and made him a giant, shape-changing and uncertain.

"*Kreelath!*" he called. "Kreelath, I am come to put an end to you!"

Two huge obsidian doors blocked his way, their polished surface gleaming balefully. At the top of each one was fashioned a circle, and at the bottom a circle joined them. Darith raised the scimitar.

"My Lord, take care," Avlath warned. "These doors may also suck the life from you!"

"Let them!" Darith said, a strange jubilation filling him. "Not even death will hold me from my purpose now!" All the lives the Black Sword had taken pulsed eagerly, pushing him toward that door; all Colyn the Great's frustration; all Darith's own despair.

A dry leaf-rustle of laughter mocked his words.

With all the force he could muster he struck the center of the doors, at the place where the third circle joined them.

Sparks leaped from the scimitar to the polished obsidian, and there was a ringing like a lead gong in a cave beneath the sea. Azure flames washed over the doors, and Darith felt strength flowing out of him.

He was suddenly old, decrepit beyond his years—and the scimitar he held was old, too; dull as unpolished pewter, and cold to the touch.

The obsidian doors parted slowly and swung inward.

Mannus ran down the corpse-littered street, searching for Darith. Olegair ran at his side, and behind them, fe Mavron's green-and-red tartan mixed with Colyn Muir's tartan of dark red and grey, black, and white, and with the red and yellow of clan Morulvu.

These few had been able to hack their way free from the carnage by the river, while all around them, helpless, bleeding men had died.

But here too had been a grim battle; here too was death. Their pace slowed.

A dismembered body writhed in a red pool. Men in the tartans of different clans lay in piles: yellow-crossed green and red fe Mavron tartan lay across the tartans of Rathno-lawn, of Clan Morulvu, of fe Rogoin...

Not far away, a bloody hand still gripped steel. Men's silent bodies lay all about.

"Many of these are from Lairog-nan-Cuivair," Mannus said harshly. "I think I saw Niall of fe Rogoin among them."

"He was a good fighter, for a mystic," Olegair muttered, gazing around him. "Though no more worthy than many other men—and too many lie here! But it is Lord Darith we should be looking for."

"The dead in this butcher's yard may tell us how to find my Lord," said Mannus. The tip of his blade lifted rat-colored wrappings, to show dark blood still seeping from a gash across the dead man's chest. "A clansman killed this one."

"And that one—with an axe," Olegair added with a grim smile.

Mannus moved past him. He turned another body with his foot and saw clay-cold, clay-pale flesh, blank eyes staring at the sky. A slash across its throat gaped like another mouth, empty, colorless.

Bloodless grey-clad bodies scattered all over the street showed Darith's road; abandoned shells of men twice-doomed, souls sucked dry by the Demon, veins drained to give Colyn's magic black blade power—the work of Darith's hand. Mannus shuddered.

"I see it! We must follow." Olegair eyed the road, then turned, gesturing. "Come!" More men had joined them, muttering as they saw the bodies. For the first time since the long voyage to save Tondur they walked solid land, but they stepped as if they trusted the blood-soaked clay less than the shifting surface of the sea.

"We've been fighting since dawn, Lord." said one man.

"Holy Twins!" another voice chimed in. "Who knows what's waiting for us up the road ahead?"

"Lord Darith is waiting for you!" growled Olegair. "Wondering what's keeping you, I dare say. Seven Holy Wise Ones! It's our battle he's fighting! Must he fight alone?"

"Let the Colyn Muir lead us, then!" came the reply from a man whose blood-spattered tartan was more red than grey now. It was not mutiny, thought Mannus, but weariness, and despair. He felt it himself as his blood cooled and he saw how many good men were already gone.

"*I'll* lead you!" Mannus faced them. "I am heir to Colyn Muir, and I call you to remember your fealty! Lord Darith serves Tondur through no constraint but our own need. Only he can fight this Demon, but we can kill these—slaves. If we cannot protect him, then Kreelath has won!" He paused for a deep breath, and held it until the distracting tension melted out of him. "Our work here is almost accomplished, and then, lads, it will be time to go home."

Suddenly he did not care whether they obeyed. He stepped over a body and pushed himself into motion; after a startled moment, he heard a grunt and the jingle of mail as Olegair came after him, and then others, following.

"Well done, boy—" Olegair began, but Mannus was not listening. He stared at the line of carnage that led to a blank wall of solid black clay that blocked the road. Where was the door into the Temple?

He stiffened, as awe and joy pulsed in his veins.

Looking up, he saw her, floating in beauty above those piled bodies, an ethereal form with flower yellow hair and amber brown eyes—the mysterious Lady of his Vision.

"Lady!" he gasped. *Goddess?* he thought. *Who is she?* "Aid me now!"

"Mannus!" she said, in his mind. *"Follow me!"*

She drifted straight toward that blank black wall—and vanished into it.

"Lady—" He drew a deep breath, then, resolute, strode toward the wall of clay.

He remembered then the way the clay houses had collapsed during the fighting in the streets, and lifting his shield hurled his full weight at the wall before him, hurling his sword down in a heavy blow—

The sword slashed empty air, and he lurched forward into darkness.

He sprang back in fright, into the light once more, and felt the hot sun baking on his skin. Olegair and the others with him were still gaping at him.

"It's an illusion!" he shouted. "Follow me!"

He leaped back through the wall, back into night.

Ahead he saw her, glowing brightly in the darkness, beckoning. She drifted toward a dim archway, floating ghostly backwards, facing him.

"Ha!" The Bull Dragon's voice boomed at his side. "More of this cursed magic, this trickery and deceit? So! Let us see if it can stand against honest men! Hamish!"

"Lord?" a muffled voice answered out of the dark.

"Have the men light their torches. It's dark in here." He chuckled, and turned back to Mannus. "Honest fire and steel," he said. "Fire is ever man's friend against the bugaboos of night."

Torches came through the wall. Olegair took one as he hastened to Mannus's side, while Mannus hastened after the Ghost who guided them.

"This way," she said, drifting insubstantial ahead. He stumbled on stone steps and crashed through age-old cobwebs up a stair that seemed to climb and twist forever, then they followed her down long corridors.

The space seemed strange: distances and perspectives did not add up. The torches seemed to illuminate walls of stone and walls of clay, yet at times Mannus was sure that a wall was clay and looked at it again and found it stone.

"Beware," she said, *"the Demon is aware of you. There is an ambush ahead."*

"I'll be careful," he answered.

"Who you talking to, boy?" asked Olegair.

"Don't you see her? The—the Lady?"

"Are you daft, lad? There's no one there!" Olegair roared. "And you could not see her if there was!"

"She says there's an ambush ahead."

"Ah, you loon! Why, you soft-headed, dafty! I—" A hissing rustle of dead leaves mocked him. "This is a trick of some kind. Divine Queen's Crown! Magic—you cannot fight magic with magic! This is some deceit, to lead us into the trap!"

Suddenly, torchlight flared from a thousand tiny eyes.

Then men screamed as rats and serpents writhed out of the walls: serpents like those Mannus had trapped on the desert, and serpents like tiny dragons with wings and tiny useless legs and heads like bulldogs.

"Defend yourselves, now!" Olegair roared.

A wall of solid stone blocked their way.

A voice whispered like a hissing rustle of dead leaves, mocking, laughing in the dark.

There was death, and terror beyond death. A sky the color of garnet hung like a canopy in which a shifting, watery blue-green sun swung back and forth like a pendulum . . .

"Lord Darith? Where are you?" Avlath's voice sounded as though from some great distance.

The black grass waved in a tidal wind. At the other end of the field a throne was raised. It was black as the grass, and covered with dark hangings that shifted uneasily in the wind.

Nothing was visible on the throne, but there was something there. The wind bore the smell of things rotting.

"Close your eyes tightly and stand still!" Darith said. "Do not be daunted by illusion! This sorcerous Sword will deal with the magic!"

Laughter frayed the silence like tearing fabric, rotten and immeasurably old.

There was death: conjured and raised and given form. An army of death. An army of the dead. Mindless, soulless men put back together from their decayed parts, glowing with the blue energy of stolen life. The rags of centuries too remote to imagine hung from their wasted flesh, and the rusting weapons of forgotten empires waited for blooding in their bony hands. They covered the field from side to side, waiting for—

Waiting for me, Darith thought.

He has plotted well, this King of Demons! I am old now, I am weak. The power of my Sword is gone. If I fight, I fight as a man, not as a magician. I have no chance whatever.

*Yet, I am a man of my word. I have said that death shall
not hold me from my purpose. If death will not deter me, then
I will surely not be stopped by fear!*

With a cry that tore his throat and brought the taste of
blood to his lips, Darith ran toward the army of dead men.

"Colllyyyyyynnn!"

Striking vipers coiled around men's ankles, and rats scurried through hay in a forest susurrous of mocking laughter
that bade them beware, lest the Demon come down among
them, laughing at them all.

Mannus thought, as he drew the sword that Darith had
given him, *What if she did lead us into this trap?*

He remembered, then, even as his blade whipped around
in a slash, how suddenly she had appeared, a maiden from
the holy Gods knew where: with lips and eyes of magical
loveliness, with clothing formed of clouds about her—but all
illusion! Not real!

Laughter behind him—Demon laugh. The glaring eyes of
rats glowed in the torchlight. He almost reeled about, as he
saw that more were on the walls above! Green gems glimmered as he struck and jerked back his blade.

He heard all around him the shouts and cries of these men
who had followed him down the long corridors, while her
swanlike loveliness had drawn him onward, into darkness
and danger.

He lashed the fleet sword down and his hand joyed in the
feel of steel in the air. His edge tore through some soft thing;
all about him rats and vipers bled, severed by his blade.

These terrors were too much for most of the men: they
scattered and fell back, and some fled, while Mannus and
Olegair fought back-to-back; their swords hurtled, humming
in torchlit dimness.

Except while rats ran leaping up their chests, paws plucking at their beards, fangs ripping at their lips, these were
brave men. But they had not been prepared for this hell, and
every one of them had been wounded. With physical pain
added to emotional, Mannus thought, how could they be expected to stand against evil?

They had to fight or flee, but some few, at least, held, and
met their foe as would any group of true-born highland men,
with steel in their hands.

Mannus laughed, to think how weak he had been—and
how nearly he had been captured by the superb face and
form of a young girl who had never even existed, that was

only an image in his head—but with beautiful gold eyes that seemed to seek his, to try to play on his feelings, to promise to become . . .

"*No!*" a voice chimed in his mind. "*I am good!*"

Mannus paused as she came suddenly out of the air before him.

His eyes blinked at torchlight, but she looked as though she stood in the summer sun, with sunlight dyeing vivid new gold in her yellow hair, and he stared, denial in his eyes, as he backed away from her.

"*No! This is—is not just!*" she cried. "*I came to help you through this illusion, when my brother needs me. No! Your men's blood is not on my hands! But you must go still deeper into danger.*" And she vanished. The darkness remained.

How weak men are, he thought.

Not a second time!

The Demon whispered far across the gulf, and laughing, destroyed his way through other dangers.

That was ended then, over and done, but . . . she had looked very apprehensive, whatever her intentions.

Rats scurried away into the hay behind him as he killed their leaders, and severed vipers jerked and bumped against the walls as their spilling veins drained, drowning them in a lake of their own blood.

The air was filled with the sound of iron. Now most of the men that remained moved in and out and back again, their blades leaping with the vigor of youth.

Yet each heard the long low cries of others who fled away. Racing feet, running from this place, echoed clashing in dark corridors, where men called or bleated, while rats gripped and bit.

Vipers writhed down fighters' blades. Only the ancient pride of the clans, that their own tartan should be the first in the battle, ruled their fear and kept any going forward.

Then mocking Demon-leaves rustled, and Mannus in fury sprang through dimness into a gulf that opened before him where a wall had been but a moment before, and found himself reeling, all alone, in blank, blind night.

He gripped the hilt of the sword he held. The darkness was all about him; even the eyes of the creeping things were gone. He gazed into a dark that seemed to have no features.

He heard a shout, then blinked at glaring torchlight, as Olegair came leaping from the air to stand alongside him.

The Bull Dragon's voice boomed; he wheeled away,

burning torch blazing in his hand, and vanished as he crossed back the way he had come.

But he returned in a bright blaze of torchlight, with other men following.

"More craft and illusion!" the fe Mavron roared. "But iron and fire can still drive away the powers of Darkness."

Not all of the men that Olegair had called had crossed. Only a handful of Clan Colyn and fe Mavron dared tread that road. For many thought that to leave now was very wise.

"By the Seven Holy Gods!" Olegair swore, adjusting his armour about half-ruined scraps of tartan, red from the wound in his shoulder. "Come, we have much to do, son of Colyn Muir! I know not where we are going or where Darith is, but I will do what I have pledged! Come!"

The fe Mavron turned and walked on, torch raised above his head to cast an irregular circle of orange light about his feet.

Not far away, an archway opened into a long, low hall, where shadows seemed to writhe and shift like black clouds.

Her face and her warning prodded gently in Mannus's mind.

"You must go still deeper into danger," she had said. The darkness ahead held danger, it seemed, though he could see no details of form or feature.

But *something* moved there.

Then, suddenly, eyes yellow and green blinked at him out of night-black air that thickened like soup in the torchlight, into a smoky darkness where evil things feasted on their prey.

Now he must be the shield that kept their fangs from his friend's flesh.

Cold glowed the eyes of the wolf's head when the beasts charged Olegair through the dimness.

Deeds of his hands were needed now; with speed Mannus sprang with the blade.

Eyes in the darkness roared as practiced hands drove the point home.

Now flashing eyes flew from behind. They were all about him. He could only reel back, guarding Olegair, and the other men behind him; his red blade whispered in the air, while doom came at him.

And he saw that some had the heads of wolves: many the heads of rats; one the head of a horse.

But they had the hands of men, and weapons in them.

One sprang forward, but steel moved in time to meet

flesh with the point. The red blood flew up the steel to his hilt as the iron blade pierced, and as they moved in about him he jerked his blade out, and away.

Only then was he aware of the falling blade he must block, and on the return take off the head from a grim foe.

He killed several, the clash of metal an irritation in his ears. Olegair and others were fighting all around, with their many blades clamouring as they mixed with an army of the foe.

Now it became a rout as more men ran through a darkness that was already filled with crying echoes.

It was knowledge of Darith's sorrows that kept Mannus going. How Olegair stood it, Mannus never knew. His steel whispered around him as grey wolves sprang.

Men fled—he and Olegair were the last: none other had kept fealty.

The beast-headed things now were falling back before their blades.

Only Mannus and Olegair, with wounds from battle, and with no army, continued forward.

Except, Mannus thought, that now they were as lost here as any of the wounded or dying men who still ran in terror through grim corridors, never knowing whether they fled toward freedom or deeper into danger.

"Still deeper into danger," she had said. Her face rose in his mind.

Unless she were deceiving us, he asked himself, *how could she know we would come to the trap?*

But he knew that this was nonsense: they had met no difficulty until after she had departed—and she *had* warned him. He could try now to make it right, but he had been unjust, he decided.

But would she understand?

Guided by her, he reasoned, this would be no difficult task. Would it be possible, he wondered, for once, to undo a mistake, instead of having that first wrong idea return over and over?

"Lady, where are you?" Mannus called. Olegair, in armour which hung in scraps of mail, looked at him sharply.

Before his eyes appeared the yellow of her fair hair, the vision indeed from that day on the river.

"Do you think you can trust me now? After what you thought of me earlier?" Her sharp answer shook him to the heart, but then she smiled. *"That was your answer. I need no more! I think, though, even if you had meant to deny me, I would have come when you called."*

"Lady!" he gasped. "After my—mistake—your forgiveness—"

"*King and Queen!*" exclaimed Olegair. "Are you talking to illusions again?"

"Illusions?" Mannus's lips quirked in something that was not quite a smile. "Perhaps. I begin to wonder now . . . Why does hope always seem to be illusion, and fear, reality?"

And why could none other see what his inner seeing saw?

He looked at her. She stared into darkness ahead, as if something she sensed there had disturbed her.

"At least I can choose what to—"

Three blue eyes opened like huge doors in darkness, and Mannus heard the grim sound of dead leaves laughing.

"*So, Little Moth!*" Words took shape out of the dry leaf-rustle. "*I thought I felt the flutter of your wings! I have been waiting for you.*"

Mannus could not move. There was no time.

Blackness reared before him—near enough to touch. He felt her fear, realized those words had not been addressed to him.

Blessed Goddess—what is this, that can make her afraid?

Her beautiful spirit-form flew up and back, but a night-black wall flowed after her while she turned and twisted, forward and back. Only a moment and it was done: past him, after her, upon her.

His eyes showed Olegair reaching to touch him.

But inner vision saw the fair spirit soul-form of the maiden strike the wall, saw her half-sunk in shadow as she fluttered helplessly.

"*Now, I have you trapped!*" the grim voice whispered. "*I will suck the life from you!*"

"Lady!" Mannus quoted a saying from long ago: "Take courage, spirit—none can harm the soul!"

"*Not harm the soul?*" dead leaves echoed mockingly. "*You shame me! After days of hunger, at last a trapped woman's soul! Harm has come for all I rule, for to destroy this will bring agony to put an end to you!*"

Her fair spirit flickered in the black wall.

"*Blessed Goddess! Save her!*" Mannus cried in inner agony, then shook his head; this was not some ancient legend! Perhaps long ago the Gods had aided men. Now defences did not come. "Spare her, Goddess!"

She changed.

Her fair hair's colour turned to flame. She bore the curve of the sacred breast, and lips to please: she threaded darkness, soundlessly. Queenly intensity of the Goddess supported a magical space over her, now so different. The binding blackness broke.

"Are you so wise, then?" she asked, seeing his thoughts by magical vision. *"Wait, and abide my judgement!"*

His flesh tingled, and he stared, for the light of Her presence cast shadows, as though the moon had risen.

Now, behind Her, darkness vanished in a sky of rainbow light: swans flew there, and singing flocks of birds.

Glory clothed Her as She lifted her arms. Mannus stared, filled with infinite, heartbreaking, mystic awe.

She, who had lain with the greatest of the Heroes of Old, both with the Son of the Storm God and with the War God's Son, and by each of them had conceived a child, a boy and a girl, twin-born in one womb, the first King and the first Queen of Tondur; She, the Goddess; Mother of Kings; Queen of the Gods, She spoke:

"Twin-born, the King and Queen came from My Womb, and so the Land is blessed! I guard Tondur for all time, and the Crown of the Children of the Gods, blessing the green land of Tondur with gifts.

"But if my sacred binding be broken, and if danger then come to one of My Chosen, harm has come for me too.

"Choose well, Kreelath! I bestow defences upon others than the Kings, and I protect My Own! I make good each bargain, too! Choose!"

From between her lifted palms stabbed a beam of white fire, burning into the heart of the darkness.

Now skulls grinned, and spears spiked at Darith from skeletal hands. Blue shadows danced in empty eye-sockets; age-encrusted blades fell on his helm and mail hauberk. They had no breath; their bodies reeked of death, yet they moved with uncanny vigor.

They were all about him. A lance drove in from the left, a halberd from the right. No longer invincible, the scimitar was only metal now.

But it could still kill.

First, slash the lance, break the dry-rotted shaft. Then dodge the heavy iron head of the halberd, go under, and cut off the arm of the lich wielding it.

Sparks, blue and shining as the scimitar bit into the mouldering flesh. But this time they moved *to* Darith, and the scimitar pulsed. The halberd bearer dissolved to dust.

The blade could still absorb vital energy, retrieve it from

the ensorcelled undead! There was still a chance!

A tall knight in plate came, whirling a double-handed broadsword. The long sword had an advantage in reach; but it glanced from pulsing steel and a single step brought Darith close to the knight. He lunged, and pushed the tip of the scimitar through the slit in the face plate, to suck up the knight's false life.

Soon the scimitar was black again, soft and warm. There was no blood in this battle, so it did not leap and twist on its own.

But leap and twist it did! For Darith was young again, strong and intent on his purpose. There was no feeling of defeat in his heart now. With each cut his strength grew. With each thrust and fall of man-dust a new confidence built.

The armies of the dead fell before his attack. The scimitar throbbed in his hand, alive, powerful.

And suddenly it was *his* scimitar. The life force with which Colyn had nourished it was gone, drained into the walls and doors of Kreelath's temple. That which now quickened it was of Darith's winning. And there was no shame, no guilt attached: for this was life forced through sorcery into those who had already won the sleep of death, recalled against their will to movement.

My sword! thought Darith. *My weapon, with which to win past this army and destroy the demon enemy. And once that is done...*

The name of Colyn Muir will ring again in song. Not in the death-chant of a bygone day, but in the glory and the praise of the living. For am I not living? Am I not a man? Do I not hunger for the ways of the flesh, even as do other men? No more to sit within my castle walls, brooding on a grey past!

With this sword, secure in my hand, I am the most powerful man in Tondur. I will not go to the City of the King to swear a hateful oath: I will go to rule! For is it not always the strongest who ascends the throne? There can be only one King in Tondur, and I shall be that King! One King, and...

One Queen.

Young and beautiful, dark-haired as the night, blue around the ever-changing moon, her eyes the shifting fires of the sun's corona. Her brow soft and sunset tinged by pink, the ivory petal of the moss rose. She shall be a princess, as was Lonarissa...

Lonarissa!

A flail fell on Darith's shoulder and drove unpadded mail into his flesh. Blood welled among the steel rings.

Forget Lonarissa! Forget everything but battle! Kreelath is only a little way ahead. When he is gone you have won . . . the world.

Out of the gulf beyond the fury of Her shifting fires, the dust-dry voice of the Demon spoke:

"But I am not of your world." A dry leaf-laughter rustled. *"You have no power over me, Mother of Kings! Not even all of the Seven together can thrust me from this world—or have you forgotten?"*

"Colyn's heir shall banish you, drive you back into your own world!"

"Is it so?" Laughter of darkness and of leaves. *"Colyn's heir shall give me back my sword—and, with it, your world."*

Her silver laughter rang among the stars.

"Do not trust to this prophecy in practice, or real fact! It is better than you would be able to do—for think you that these two before us, who could only be held for a moment, will abandon their Lord?"

"Do you put your trust in these?" Again, that whispered demon laugh. *"What of the children of the Gods? Where now are the sons that the Gods had begotten against evil? The Sacred Kings are dependent on the Gods and their gifts, and to save the World is beyond the power of the Crown. Indeed, even to save himself has proved beyond the power of the King!"*

Mannus straightened and looked up. Surely, he thought, Kreelath must be right: no mere mortal man could complete this task, in the face of such power.

And yet—if it was the Goddess who depended upon them . . .

"Earth and Sea!" Olegair, frowning in exasperation, muttered at his side— Olegair, who did not hold with spells and conjurings. "More trickery and illusion! Let me come within sword's reach of you, Demon, and we will see if mystic powers can stand up against steel and fire!"

Then see me! the Three-Eyed Demon whispered. *Perhaps, if you see how we deal with those who threaten, you will think once more! I will put your soul away, now, binding it into a thing to creep while others, deceived by—*

Mannus heard the sound of laughter bursting from his own mouth.

If he had put his hand across it, the strain would have stretched the skin. But he realized that he was putting himself, as was his way, between the Demon and the arguing highland Lord. In case Olegair came to harm then, he roared.

"What, again? Go on—show us more horrors!" His purpose would be complete if Kreelath's attention were distracted for just a little longer. "Are the Gods in Council all wrong? I am the tanist of Colyn Muir, Kreelath!—a son for the Colyn Muir!" He blinked, dizzied, a sobbing breath turned into a harsh laugh.

Something in the quality of the darkness around him changed. He felt the Demon's attention fix wholly upon him, but even that was funny now.

"But if you could frighten me to death, I'd be dead already! Bring on your horrors, Demon—or have you run out? Up to a point. No—talent for it, that's—" Mannus coughed and began to laugh again.

"Poor Kreelath—can't even scare a village boy."

"Oh, foolish—foolish! Do you not yet understand My power? Look, son of Colyn Muir, and see how we deal with those who would threaten us!"

Mannus gazed upon despair, and suddenly, none of it made sense anymore. He saw everything coming at once, tasted it, almost physically. He saw a burning stone melt down into a brook of green fire. To save his limbs, twenty years he strained but no muscle moved.

In black grass on a low hill, the dead lay still. Grim some find their dying: yet there they find rest from which none may return. He noted details of gear and swords and scabbard.

They moved. They rose. Niall and Bor and Goll of Caiplic, captured and destroyed, could rise. They did as Kreelath bade, sorrow in each set face as they admitted what harm they had done, and . . . they would not be able to end.

That was at times of war, for many were lost here and met with harm: stolen souls turned to wolf-shape mingled with what harm has been done to children.

"So shall you be enslaved, held: your name, Mannus, and your soul held in my spell with (Blessed Goddess not nightdark the thought of . . .) *Darith . . ."*

He had been seeking Darith. . . .

"He seeks his own," the Goddess cried. *"Enough illusion! Undo the spell!"*

A wind, no—a green fire, burning with molten bits of jewels, swirled them away, and his heels staggered on blank air; then sought and found blessed earth.

Her magic greater than good had countered the curse. In

thinking and feeling, the tale was driven away into scraps of vision that made him forget—but in memories no details would come to him and sometimes it seemed that such a thing was only some old tale, old as the green land, but at times images gemmed the fabric of magical vision.

Bitter cold this spot, as he saw black grass, a blue sun . . .

"Edarissa?" It was the voice of Gonquin. *"Edarissa?"*

He found two others. For there, beside the Troubadour, was Avlath, and all their beards were bright with ice.

He looked around then, searching for Darith. The black grass, the indigo sun had vanished. They stood in a square of sunlight between obsidian doors at one end of a huge circular chamber.

And Mannus suddenly realized that all this time they had been fighting among the twisted dark corridors of the Demon's brain.

At the other end of the chamber sat a night-cloaked shape like a King's throne in shadow.

"Ho, Darith!" Olegair's roaring bass voice. "By the nine hells of the cursed mother, where— Ah! There you are!"

The light of Olegair's torch glittered across a field of frost, where ice covered compacted black earth.

Only a single figure stood there: Darith, himself, turned away from them, to face the dark throne.

The sky grew dark and the air turned cold. The sun slowed its swinging and deepened to indigo. A wind sprang up behind Darith and blew toward the Demon's throne, ripping at black hangings.

Flakes of snow and of ice swirled and caught, clung to Darith's face and hands. A thick hoar frost formed on the ebon grass. Night gathered like flights of sable-winged angels.

The legion of dead warriors slowed, froze, stopped. For a moment they stood, grotesque statues in a gallery. Then the blue life-energy left them and they were resolved to component dust.

Darith stood alone, facing Kreelath.

There was a black cloak around the Demon. The shape beneath shifted continuously, as if a mountain of worms writhed there, waiting to pour out and down the steps of the dais on which the throne rested.

Three blue eyes peered out of hooded darkness.

Darith felt the cold that lies between the stars creep into

his body. It crystallized his blood and hardened his muscles into knots of ice. He willed himself forward, willed his legs to move through the chill quiet: but to no avail. With only yards to go he was halted, frozen to the frosted black turf.

"So the heir of my old ally has come to me," whispered Kreelath.

"Ho, Darith!" The roaring bass voice of the Bull Dragon distracted him. "By the nine hells of the cursed mother, where— Ah! There you are!"

There was silence. Then Darith heard footsteps, crunching brittle blades of grass, coming closer.

"Is my Lord alive, then?" That was Mannus's voice!

"So the Devil Sword was no use after all," Olegair's deep laughter answered.

He appeared at the edge of Darith's vision, bearing a bright torch. "Magic against magic! Spells and conjurings! Here, Demon, let us see how well you stand before *real* fire and steel!"

He started running forward, torch high in one hand, sword in the other.

"Olegair, don't!" Another voice—that of Gonquin.

"Darith is touched by frost," Olegair answered. "I'm going to thaw this beast's heart a little." He reached the dais and put his foot upon the first step.

Kreelath's mantle shifted slightly and the three blue eyes came to focus on Olegair.

The torch in Olegair's hand swelled, and the flames ran up his arm and over his body like a swarm of ravenous ants. In an instant all that was left of Olegair fe Mavron was a charred skeleton.

But in that instant the cold vanished from Darith's body. No time now to look at what had been one of the greatest fighting men of Tondur, nor even to order Mannus away. Darith ran toward the throne.

He was a yard closer to the throne when Kreelath's gaze again bound him with glacial chains.

"My child, why do you still oppose me? Do you not yet understand? I have been alone here all these centuries, bound to this world by your ancestor's spell. Only you can release me, Colyn Muir. Take back your binding, and I will return to my own realm."

Gonquin began to sing a high, wavering melody; the spell of safe conduct for the dead.

Though he could not move, his mind could form words.

"Creature of darkness, what do you want of me?"

"Release me from my oath in the name of Colyn Muir—"

"Why should I undo what my ancestor achieved with such pain?"

"What good did it do him, after all?" said Kreelath. *"Release me and I will give you your Lady back from the realm of Death. With my sword, you can conquer the world and lay it at her white feet."*

The Sword had already shown him that future. Once more Darith felt the lust for power throb in his veins. These were his own thoughts that the Demon was tempting him with. How could he not hear?

Then a warm, *human* hand touched his arm.

"There is only one way, my Lord," said Avlath. "I will mark the spot for you. Farewell!"

He had thought the Chamberlain still safe behind him in the other room.

Darith tried to cry out, to call Avlath back. But his lips were sealed, frozen by Kreelath's spell.

Darith watched helplessly as Avlath ran forward, a sword extended before him. Up the stairs of the dais he sped; the sword point pierced the Demon's cloak at a spot where a heart might be.

Three blue eyes focused on Avlath. Steel melted.

Avlath's hand, then his arm melted. His shoulder flowed like water. He screamed.

For a moment, as Avlath died, Darith was free. Rage fueled his lunge for Kreelath; he lifted the Sword . . .

And the Demon's gaze congealed the air around him.

Now only Mannus and Gonquin remained with him in the room. Darith struggled—he was so close now! A finger twitched; his friends had weakened the Thing!

Gonquin's eyes were shut, his features knotted in concentration. His mouth opened, but no words could be heard. The air pulsed around him, and Darith realized that Kreelath's spell had bound the Troubadour too. But only partially, for Gonquin's lips were moving—perhaps the effort to hold them both was dividing the Demon's will. Darith gathered his forces to try again.

"Do you still deny me?" The Demon's voice thundered through every level of Darith's awareness. "Take back the oath and I will release you from the Curse of Colyn Muir! You will breed untainted sons from your own body! You will set a new dynasty upon the throne."

And Mannus, face white as if he were a ghost already, started forward.

No! Anguish sent a spark of feeling along Darith's arm. *You are the future! You are the hope of Colyn Muir!*

Mannus stepped past him.

Gonquin whispered one tortured word.

For an instant Darith felt the will that bound him falter. He drew back his arm and hurled the velvet scimitar.

It sailed through the air above Mannus and pierced the Demon's body just where Avlath had marked it.

From a place beyond the measuring of light, Darith heard Kreelath's voice, a susurrus of dead leaves mocking, laughing.

"My own sword!"

Then pain struck with the force of a mace blow and Darith fell unconscious to the ground.

CHAPTER SIXTEEN
The Tears of the Goddess

"Darith! Wake up!" The rough voice shook his world.

Cool and green, as it was in Tharda, and the sun is friendly.

"Wake up! We've got to get out of here, quickly!"

Darith opened his eyes. Selvern stood over him, face streaked with grime and furrowed with concern. Beyond, the black dome was broken by a gaping hole, through which a light rain fell.

"Can you stand?" Selvern asked.

Thunder rumbled like a retreating army. Darith raised himself to one elbow, then fell back, intestines twisting in agony. He gasped.

"I'll get someone to carry you," said Selvern.

"No!" said Darith. He heaved himself up, fighting the pain. "I—it's no worse than—before. I just didn't expect—" Darith had never thought what would happen after Kreelath was destroyed. With a flicker of grim humour he realized that he had not expected to be alive to worry about it. He climbed to his feet, swaying. For a moment he thought the pain would snap his hold on consciousness, but then it subsided.

"Avlath!" he exclaimed, confused memories warring with his fears. "Where is he?"

"Dead," said Selvern. "Over there. But there's no need for you—"

Darith stepped toward the sable-draped throne, then stopped as his blurring gaze made sense of what he saw there. It was as he remembered. Not a dream, not some

195

perverted nightmare. It was all true. The charred skeleton of
Olegair fe Mavron lay next to . . . what remained of Avlath.

He looked up. There was no garnet depth of sky, no indigo blue sun swinging back and forth. Only the dull black of
a clay dome, darkening here and there as the rain began to
soak through. He looked down. No ebon grass grew beneath
his feet. Only compacted black earth. He looked around.
There was no field from which an army of dead could rise.
Only a circular chamber with double obsidian doors at one
end and the dark throne at the other. And the mocking whisper that had tempted him was still.

Illusions.

But Avlath was dead, and Olegair. That was real. They
were horribly dead. The remains he had seen, horribly real.
And Mannus had been there, too—in panic he looked
around, and saw Mannus arranging a sling for Gonquin's
arm. He had broken free in time to save the boy, then—that
much of all his hopes was true.

Truth?

Illusion?

How much of each? What part of the Demon's power
simply conjured fear, and what part spelled death? He knew
once more the shifting form, the triple eyes that saw in more
than three dimensions; the ancient voice that laughed with
autumnal emptiness down corridors centuries long. Had
there been victory or defeat in that laughter? And for whom?

"Darith, the rain—" Selvern started.

"Tell me what happened!"

The Prince looked at him through narrowed eyes, then
sighed.

"The enemy was winning," Selvern said. "Our men were
forced back toward the docks, and that fleet whose way we
had blocked came over the horizon, but reinforced a thousandfold. More ships than I've ever seen!"

Darith nodded. A breath of wind touched his cheek, cool,
damp. Rain fell on the dome with a dull patter, as thousands
of tiny drops soaked into the clay.

"Then clouds appeared over the city," Selvern went on.
"Thin, gauzy at first. But they thickened, and the air turned
cold. The men knew it was magic, and I nearly had a rout on
my hands!

"Then lightning struck this dome. But the enemy fell
apart, went down like hay under a scythe, and started
screaming and running and throwing down their weapons,
shouting for mercy. And suddenly—we'd won! The black

fleet was gone as if it had never existed, and the enemy was surrendering as fiercely as he'd fought."

"What about the Demon?" Darith asked. "When you got here, what did you find?"

"Nothing," said Selvern. "Just that cloak, crumpled up on the seat of the throne, with a hole burned in it."

"And the Sword?"

"Your sword—"

"Not *my* sword!" said Darith. He shuddered, pain clenching in his gut. He wondered how he could have forgotten what that agony was like.

"Whoever it belonged to—there was no sign of it!" said Selvern. "And good riddance, too. Now will you please come along? The rain is softening the clay, and this whole place may cave in at any moment. Gonquin already has a broken arm; when the lightning struck, that patch of ceiling fell on him."

"Very well," said Darith. "But we must take Avlath and Olegair with us, and bury them in clean ground."

"The rain will do that," said Selvern. "If we stay much longer it will bring down the dome and bury us as well!"

"*In clean ground!*" Darith repeated. "I will not leave their bones to mingle with Kreelath's dust. Now either help me, or save yourself and leave me to do what I can. Because they died, Tondur will live! I could not have destroyed the Demon without them. They deserve the proper rites—a hero's funeral, and I will not abandon them."

Selvern hesitated a moment, then smiled sadly.

"I'll get something on which to carry them," he said. "And a couple of men. You're right. After all we have survived, we can brave the danger a little longer."

A fine rain fell from a sky grey as tears. They used their swords to dig graves in the hard red clay of the plain, and the bodies were wrapped in silk banners for burial: Olegair in the war banner of his clan, and Avlath in the banner of Colyn Muir.

Darith sat on a chest with Mannus behind him. The younger man held his cloak out in an attempt to keep him dry. After the uncanny cold of Kreelath's illusions, there was a certain comfort in the chill of honest rain, but Darith did not tell Mannus there was no need to protect him—he knew that the boy felt guilty because his own flesh was still warm, and whole. He had not been able to die for his Lord—the least he could do was to shelter him from the rain.

And the least that Darith could do was to allow him his illusion. It was not Mannus—nor Avlath, nor Olegair—who ought to be lying in the cold clay with the fine rain soaking his shroud, but Darith himself.

A thin thread of pain coiled through his gut and faded again. *Soon enough,* he thought with what was almost a sense of release. *Soon enough it will be me.*

There were no rocks with which to build a cairn, so Selvern ordered that all of the weapons of the enemy, and all of the weapons left by the dead in the city's streets, be gathered and piled over the graves.

Then Gonquin came, his arm in a sling and his head bandaged with bloody cloth, and playing upon a harp with one hand, made a new spell:

> *"Now the gentle rain comes.*
> *Weeping of the Goddess.*
> *Enter into earth now.*
> *Leave thy love for mortals:*
> *You who walk in darkness now.*
> *For love of us, who live."*

The rain fell harder, but Gonquin continued to sing, weaving a history of the dead by which they might be remembered and recognized.

At odd intervals his music was punctuated by thunderclap sounds as, one by one, the domes and towers of the black city collapsed.

When he had finished, the city was gone. There was only a great pile of black mud, which even now the rain was washing into the river, to be expelled into the cleansing waters of the sea.

Those of Kreelath's men who still lived were only too glad to help uncover warehouses of food and other supplies, and to find the springs that had furnished the city with fresh water. Without the Tondurn ships they would be stranded in the desert.

But by the time a week had passed it was obvious that there was no need for them to seek passage anywhere. The normal winter rains had been restored, and the desert, under the influence of a week of water, was coming to life again. Seeds baked in clay since the building of Kreelath's city burst their shells and sent up tendrils of delicate green. The rain went on and the plain of the black river became fertile—except where the city had been.

At last, with the rain still falling and the ships refitted, the Tondurn fleet set back down the long river. The defeated soldiers were already building small huts on its banks, and planting some of the grain from the ruined warehouses. Most of them, it seemed, had no memories of the war. Selvern left them with a promise that a Tondurn garrison would soon be dispatched to help them with their reconstruction and, incidentally, to keep watch over them. And they left several ships, for there were no longer enough men to man them all.

By the time the fleet reached the stone ruins the plain was a green carpet; and as it approached the mountains there was a jungle sprouting where baked earth had been in an early, unseasonable spring.

It was still raining, and the water of the black river was running almost clear, when the fleet passed through the red cliffs and out onto the Salmon Sea. Two days from shore the rain stopped and the sun shone.

The fleet was now under Selvern's direction. Darith was too weak, and in too much pain most of the time, to exercise his rightful leadership. He spent his days lying on deck, letting the warm sunlight ease the constrictions of his bared stomach muscles.

This far south, it was hard to believe in winter, and the wind held fair. Men lowered their voices when they passed him as one does in the presence of the dying. At least now there was no need to maintain a pretence that nothing was wrong. With a kind of relief, Darith realized that his work was finished. As he lay in the warm sun, or swayed in his hammock below, he set himself to say good-bye to all the things he had loved, until he should be free.

"Lord Mannus, the men were wondering—"

It took a moment for Mannus to realize that the man was talking to him. He turned, flushing a little as he still did when someone used his new title. Except in battle—he had not noticed what men called him then.

Mannus struggled to remember the name of the fellow who was speaking.

"The fact is, sir, that the Demon is done for, and we were glad enough to be in at the kill—but now it's over. Could you be telling us when we will set a course for home?"

"Well, ah—Angus, is it not, from up by the high glen?"

The other man grinned and nodded, absurdly pleased to be recognized. Mannus cleared his throat. When the grey-veiled hordes were attacking them, he had known what to do, but what could he answer now?

"I'm not really the one you should be asking. Perhaps Lord Darith or the Prince—"

"Nay. The Prince is too high for us, and we would not bother the Colyn Muir now. He made you Lord over us, and you'll maybe not remember, but in the fighting at yon black city, you turned a sword blow that was meant for me. There's many another lad that was behind you then that minds how you led us. We're glad enough to follow you now."

Mannus felt himself flushing in earnest. He had been trying to prove himself worthy of Darith's trust, not of theirs.

"But what do you want me to do?"

"Well, you would never think it here, so far south, with the sun shining on the sea, but by now it'll be hard winter in the mountains, and I should be home. Thank the Gods we had most of the harvest in before the muster, and my woman's a hardy soul. But I don't like the thought of her tramping the snowy hills if a beast should stray. And soon enough 'twill be time for the lambing, and they'll surely need me then. It's the same for the other men. You understand."

"Yes." Mannus remembered the vale of Colyn Muir in the winter, when white peaks kept snow-laden clouds from crushing the land. He shivered, despite the sunlight, remembering how icy the wind from those peaks could be. But there was beauty there also, when ice made lacework of the barren trees. For a moment he too was seized by longing for his home.

And he knew well enough how hard life would be for the folk of glen and moor until the warriors came home again.

"You want me to talk to the Lords then, and find out—"

"Not talk, lad—tell them! The fighting is over. You're our chieftain—it's for you to get us home."

Angus gave a rough sort of bow and strode off to the bow, where a knot of others were waiting for him. Mannus recognized them now—all folk of hill or village. Some of them had known him from a baby. How could they look to him for leadership now? But from the grins with which they greeted their emissary, they all seemed to think that something had been accomplished.

Mannus stared out over the restless blue plain of the ocean. *Oh, my Lord. I wasn't born to be a leader! What am I going to do?* He could not even ask Avlath.

But if the Chamberlain was dead, Lord Darith was not—
and now that Kreelath was destroyed, surely he would recover and take back the burden Mannus felt so unready to
bear! With sudden determination, Mannus headed for the
hatchway.

It was dim below, smelling strongly of tallow and brine
and drying wool. Mannus hesitated in the passageway outside Darith's cabin. The door was ajar. He could see the
sway of Darith's hammock. Was his Lord asleep, or— Heart
pounding, Mannus pushed the door open.

"Gonquin, is that you?"

Mannus let out his pent breath. "No, my Lord. It's just
me, Mannus."

"Yes, of course."

For some reason, it seemed to Mannus that amusement
tinged that tone. Darith eased over on his side, and now the
boy could see that, indeed, he was smiling.

Mannus set his hand on the gemmed hilt of the Colyn
Muir sword in a gesture that had become habitual.

"My Lord, when you got that devil's weapon on the island
you told me to keep this blade. But now the thing is gone—
it's not right, my Lord, that you should go swordless. Take
your own blade back again!"

With a swift movement he drew the sword from its sheath
and offered it, hilt-first, to his Lord. Until the words came
pouring out, Mannus had not known what he was going to
say. Now he waited, pulse pounding, for the reply.

"No, lad—that is the chieftain's weapon, and you are the
chieftain now." Darith's lips twisted momentarily, then the
smile came back again.

"But Kreelath is gone, surely now you will heal." Mannus
heard his own voice thin as a child's, but could not control it.

Darith sighed. "Mannus, try to understand. When I gave
you that blade, I expected to buy Kreelath's destruction with
my own. I never thought I would survive the moment when I
touched him with his own Demon Sword. But you were
there, you saw: without meaning it, I tricked my life from
him. But his Curse remains. Even though the Sword no
longer exists—not in this world—my flesh hungers for it,
and the time the Bard bought me is almost gone."

For a little he was silent, and Mannus could no longer
deny the knowledge that Darith was fighting pain. His own
gut ached in sympathy.

"On the island, I asked you to care for my people. Your

fealty is to them, not only to me." The grey eyes narrowed, and Darith's voice grew harsh.

"You gave me your word, and I will hold you to it, Mannus. I would show you mercy if I could, but my first responsibility is to *them*. In the name of the Goddess, boy, do you think any man of us would have chosen the road we have travelled since that night when I went up to the Bard in his Tower? I have made my choices, and perhaps I will never know if there might have been a better way—but don't let me know failure in this one thing, Mannus! Don't make me regret my choice of *you!*"

Mannus fell to this knees, as he had in the arena when Darith made him his heir, and never knew whether it was from some impulse of reverence, or because the strength had left them.

He is asking me to let him die in peace, thought Mannus. His throat ached so that he could hardly reply.

"The men asked me . . . to find out where we are going. My Lord, they want to go home."

"We are on our way to Kaerbradan," answered Darith finally. His voice had become a thread of sound, as if he already spoke from the other world. "The King must be told the Demon is gone. So I will see the City of the Kings after all. But after that . . . after that, my son, you must lead your people back to Colyn Muir."

Mannus stared at him. Darith's eyes had closed. His face was like a deathmask already—so still, so still.

"My first responsibility is to them," the Colyn Muir had said. But his mind must be as weak as his body if he thought that Mannus was a fit leader for them as he was now. These past weeks, Mannus had learned to distinguish between panic and reasoned fear.

"My Lord"—he forced his voice to hardness—"your work is not yet done!"

The grey eyes opened, clouded by pain. Mannus flinched, but necessity drove him on.

"I would give my life for my people; I am willing to spend it for them. But all my willingness will be worth nothing without wisdom! You were bred up to rule—there is so much you grew up knowing that I must learn. Perhaps little time is left to you—but I beg you, my Lord—give me what teaching you can before you go!"

"Mannus," came the whisper, "do you understand what you are asking of me?"

The ache of unshed tears in Mannus's throat was too fierce for words, but he nodded.

"I believe you," said Darith. "I think you would be as brutal to yourself as you have been to me." Unaccountably, he smiled.

"Of all Clan Colyn, the poorest and the proudest are the folk of the high moor..." he began.

A new storm drenched them with warm rain, but it passed quickly, and the remnants of the Tondurn fleet thrashed southward beneath a new-washed sky. The sea was still lively, but the sun shone bright. Darith had himself carried on deck to get what good he could from the clean air.

Since his confrontation with Mannus, he had hoarded his strength. The pain was worse than it had been before he acquired the Sword, but he found himself able to distance it now. It was an odd perspective, like being on top of a mountain from which he could see the whole world spread out below.

"Darith?" Gonquin eased himself down on the deck beside him, pulling one-handed at the laces that closed the neck of his tunic. He stretched carefully, resting his splinted arm on the rail. "I have been wondering..."

"When were you not?" asked Darith. Sunlight slanting past the big sail brightened Gonquin's travel-stained garments. Now that the danger was passed, he could see in his friend the gaudy Troubadour he had met in Haunted Valley once more. Gonquin grinned, then shrugged.

"I was thinking about that city. It melted to the ground and washed away. There was nothing left but hinges and gates and woodwork. And a lot of cooking utensils."

Darith rolled his head on the pillow and looked squarely at the Troubadour. "What did you expect to find?" The patch of sunlight flowed across the deck as the *Maid of Tharda* lifted to the swell, then ran backward as she dipped into the trough again.

"A key," Gonquin said pensively. "Records, artifacts. Anything that might give us some clue to the nature of the people who lived before us. The ones who dealt with Kreelath and his kind. There should have been a wealth of information in that city, yet there was nothing! Why, we don't even know where his armies came from!"

"They were questioned," said Darith. "They told us they were captured and their homes burned. They must have been possessed by Kreelath and brought to his city. They have no memory of the war."

"Very plausible," said Gonquin. "But who did he use to capture the first town? You have to start somewhere. How did it all begin? How long ago?"

"It must have been after Colyn the Great was trapped on that island," said Darith. "When he failed to come after the Demon, Kreelath began to build his power anew. Further back than that—I would guess it began in Haunted Valley."

A whistle from the bows signaled a course change. Ropes creaked as seamen hauled the big sail around, and the *Maid* leaned into her new tack. Now the sunlight rippled over Darith's blankets, back and forth and back again.

"But *how?* What led men to worship Evil, to trade their souls for corruption? Were they even men? They looked like us, we can tell from the pictures. But willingly to give up their souls for an eternity of . . . of . . ."

The Troubadour stopped, uncharacteristically at a loss for words.

"Of life bought at the cost of other men's lives and souls?" asked Darith in a hard voice. "With the agony of all your descendants to the end of your line? Colyn made such a bargain in order to save Tondur. Ask what manner of man *he* must have been. The answer is that he was a patriot. He thought he could destroy Evil with Evil.

"*I* came close to making the same bargain," he went on. "I never told you how the Sword whispered to me, those last days. I saw myself leading a conquering army, setting right every wrong that had ever been since the beginning of the world. But it would not have ended that way." He paused and pondered. Colyn's long memories seemed to be fading from his mind, now that the Sword was gone, but his own struggles were still vivid in his mind.

"I was saved by a chance I could not have anticipated. The Sword vanished with the Demon. So what kind of man am I, Gonquin? For that matter, it was at your behest I set sail for the north to seek the Demon weapon. What kind of man are *you?* The only innocent among us is that boy, Mannus, and I have laid a burden upon him that he was not bred to bear. I have promised to teach him what I can in the time that is left to me, but who knows what compromises he will have to make as he strives to guard the trust I have given him?"

He stopped, drawing breath harshly; the hungry beast in

his gut stirred as if to say, *I am still with you, son of Colyn Muir!*

"If we have reasons for such dealings, it is only just to assume they also had reasons. Do not be too hasty in your condemnation of our predecessors, lest you find that we have faults as well. That they were men I have little doubt, for they seem to have behaved with characteristic human fallibility!" He lay back, met the Troubadour's astonished stare, and managed a smile. He had not known he could still speak so passionately himself.

"But tell me, what is it that troubles you so?" Darith added when he had got his breath back again. "You ask questions that even the planets in their wanderings might have difficulty answering."

"The existence of the planets does not depend on those answers," said Gonquin. "The future of Tondur may. I *must* ask, and I must come to some understanding. It was because there were no answers that the White Realm sank beneath the waves."

"Tharda!" exclaimed Darith, sitting up suddenly. "Tharda fell because the jeweler's apprentice played too wildly with the astrolabe! Was Kreelath there? Was it *his* doing?" His pulse raced painfully at the thought that the Evil that had destroyed his manhood might have poisoned his youth as well.

"I do not know," said Gonquin. "If I did, perhaps I could tell whether we are likely to wake Kreelath's Evil again, and what must be done to heal the wounds he has left in our land. I thought I might find some part of the answer in the ruins of Kreelath's city. But now—well, the ruins in Haunted Valley are stone, and there are still many chambers in the catacombs beneath the City of the King that have yet to be opened. Somewhere there must be records; and when I find them I shall have my answers!"

Wordless, Darith stared at him, and Gonquin shook his head, his mood changing like sunlight on the sea.

"I've tired you! I thought I was back in Kaerbradan, trading speculations with Edarissa! Ah well—we will see her soon, and perhaps she with her visions may find answers where all my reasoning fails. Rest now, my friend. Whatever befalls the world is not going to happen in the next half hour!"

He stood, shook himself as if to throw off accumulated sunbeams, and went to join some of the men who were shouting over a game of toss-stones in the stern.

Darith lay back, letting the sunshine lull his pain to somnolence. There was no cure for the wound Kreelath had given him, but there had to be some correction for the imbalance that had caused men to call the Demon into the land. He tried to picture this sister of Gonquin's. She had the eyes of Tharda, he had said. But it was Lonarissa's face that rose before him, and it seemed to him that she smiled. The bets and the laughter became part of the background as her image expanded, extending her hands in blessing above a world at peace and whole.

Gonquin lost first his fine red cloak, then his tunic, and then, as Darith's vision encompassed him, his silver-buckled belt.

CHAPTER SEVENTEEN
The Eyes
of the Ancient Throne

Above the azure of the Salmon Sea, the City of the King was white and silver and gold in the sunlight; a gem-glitter among green trees and scarlet blossoms under a sapphire sky. The ships of Dalgir seemed shabby before such beauty: yet, as a fresh wind bore them into the bay, their banners fluttered proudly. They were the King's fleet now, part of this magnificence.

"Something is wrong," said Gonquin with a frown. "There should be dancing in the streets, bells, pennants flying in festival. We signaled our news to the fortress at the point. The war is over."

But the banners sagged at half-mast; the bells were silent; the men waiting on the quay were still.

"Could the Demon have conquered here before we got to him?" Mannus asked, despair weighting his voice.

"I think not," said Selvern. He pointed. "Those are my uncle's ministers on the quay. They'd have been the first to die if Kreelath had won."

Licking blood from his lips, Darith looked numbly across the water, concentrating all his will in an effort to see the men, the ranks of delicate watchtowers, the streets that ran up the hill, the piled white masses of marble . . .

Such a beautiful city, he thought. *Here a man might grow comfortably old.* The air was warm all year round: no need for logs to feed the fire. No need to hoard grain and pumpkins here, where the trees bore soft fruit even in wintertime.

So different from the cold pine woodlands of Darith's home. Still, it was not Tharda.

The pain was worse when he stood; his vision blurred and he could taste his own blood. The beast in his belly was awake and ravening, as if the nearing power of the sacred Crown and Throne had enraged it. The others had been so joyful when they rounded the point and stood in toward the pleasant harbour of Kaerbradan. Darith had not wanted them to see how the agony ate toward his heart. Compelled by Mannus's need, he had held it off longer than he might have expected. There could not be much time left now.

But all the line of Colyn before me have seen this City of Kings, Darith thought stubbornly, *and I, who have paid the harshest price of all, will not be denied what I have earned— even though the bond of fealty must be withheld! I have no stake now in games of power: I have given all I can!* His gut twisted and he swayed with pain, but he managed to smile.

"Look!" Gonquin cried. "There is crepe and death-flower on all the doors!" Seabirds screamed around them, but none among them understood their cries.

Heavy losses in battle, Darith thought. *In time of war, none of us are alone in our sorrows.*

The ministers and soldiers on the quay stood silently as the ship put in. Sails rattled down and the sailing master let the *Maid of Tharda's* own momentum bring her the rest of the way. Sailors cast out the lines, and men on the dock warped her in. The plank was lowered.

As Selvern started down it, those who waited all dropped to one knee, and bowed their heads. The Prince stopped short, looking from one to another as he began to realize what their action must mean. He glanced back at the ship, but Darith could not read his expression.

"The King is dead," intoned the eldest minister. "Long live—"

"Silence!" Selvern barked. He lifted his hands as if to ward off the words. "Do not say it! I will hear no talk of King or Crown until I have seen where my uncle lies." The minister looked up at him in surprise; lines furrowed the ancient brow under the grey locks.

"He—is in the throne room."

Selvern beckoned. His face had gone very pale.

"My friends, please come with me."

Darith took a step, and colours mixed with sea smells in a

dizzy swirl. *Can I walk that far? It would be a joy I had not expected, to see my friend crowned.* Then there was a hand at his elbow, supporting him and helping him forward.

"If I may just take hold of your arm, my Lord," said Mannus quietly. "I do not wish to become lost in so large a city!"

Deep blue star sapphires were set in the gold of the Ancient Throne. The high seat of the Kings grew on its silver dais, as naturally and gracefully as a tree grows from the earth, at one end of a cathedrallike chamber whose vaulted ceiling was tiled the blue of summer skies.

It faced a great arch that opened out upon the sea, so that the King enthroned could look upon his city and his harbour and his ships, and upon the great, blue-tiled square where the people gathered in times of joy or of need.

The King lay now in the sunlight, just within the great arch, upon a bier of grey marble set with precious stones.

Selvern stared down for a long time into his uncle's face, so much like his own, save that the hair had turned flower-white above a face lined with care. One could see how he himself would look when he was old. The gnarled hands were folded on the gold hilt of a shining sword.

"How did this happen?" Selvern's voice was terrible, a King's voice.

"He was struck by a stone from one of the ballistae aboard the black fleet while the city was under siege," said the aged minister of state. "We tried to protect him, but His Majesty insisted on directing the defence in person . . ." His voice trailed off as he realized that Selvern was not listening.

Selvern stared down a long time at his uncle's body, then leaned over the bier to place the kiss of peace on the dead King's lips. Then, straightening, he squared his shoulders, his face calm, resolved.

"Gonquin, Mannus, Darith," he said, "come forward with me to the Ancient Throne."

The four men walked the length of the throne room in a silence that was like a held breath.

It must end soon, Darith thought, *or I will fall and ruin the ceremony and disgrace the Prince—no! Disgrace the King. Selvern is King now, or will be in a moment. He knows something of my pain. Perhaps once the Crown is his he will let me go.*

The golden Crown of the Ancient Kings, that the Lord of Wisdom had wrought from the same magic gold as the Ancient Throne, rested now upon that throne, pillowed on the blue and ermine mantle of state.

A single star sapphire sparkled blue-white like an eye in the tall spike that reared at the Crown's front. There was no other jewel, nor need of any: the divine craftsmanship that had produced the simple elegance of that Crown was beyond any work of man, an endless inspiration to artists.

Behind the eye in the Crown, the sapphire eyes set all around the Throne's back looked down upon them. Selvern sank to one knee at the foot of the dais, and inclined his head. The others followed suit, Darith swaying as he knelt, Mannus's hand strong upon his arm.

No! My vision is going again! Darith thought, his senses mingling with the force of the pain. He could feel the power that was in the Throne like a cool fire, but the agony in his gut recognized its opposite, and clawed to be free.

Selvern stood, and walked slowly up the waterfall of silver stairs. At the first step, a deep-throated bell rang, and then another, higher-pitched, jubilant.

I shall not see him crowned! Darith thought, sight blurring as pain knotted his intestines and tore and raged within him. *My vision turns to taste, and it is the taste of blood. Sounds hurl spears inside me!*

He clamped his mouth shut, to hold the war-agony sound within him. *Clench my fists on the burning bells until the fingers break! I smell death! The year and a day is almost gone! Why does death tarry? Is the bargain not fulfilled? Have I not paid enough?*

Suddenly there was no more pain.

The bells tolled. The air was cool. Darith felt a gentle pressure on his head. Something soft fell about his shoulders.

He opened his eyes.

Selvern stood before him.

"The King is dead," Selvern said quietly. "Long live the King."

Darith stared at him. Why was Selvern's head bare?

"Long live Darith, King of Tondur, Lord of Colyn Muir."

Darith climbed slowly to his feet, and looked into Selvern's calm sapphire eyes. He reached up and ran his callused hand over soft fur at his shoulder; reached higher, and touched the cool gold of the Crown on his head.

"You—give me the Crown?"

"I am heir to the Crown," said Selvern. "I may do with it as I will. You alone saved Tondur from Kreelath's power. Now Tondur will save you from his curse. The Gods that wrought the Ancient Crown put this power upon it, that so long as you wear it and sit upon the Ancient Throne, you are guarded against any sickness or pain inflicted by magic."

Darith stared. Was he dreaming? What had Selvern said? *No more pain?*

"Ascend the throne," said Selvern, "that the people may offer their tribute, and the nobles their allegiance. This day, this hour, you are the King."

King—And free from pain! Kreelath had promised him the Crown, but that had been an evil. And now it came to him as a gift freely given.

Darith set his foot upon the first of the silver steps, and a deep bell boomed. Darith closed his eyes, and insight flooded him, understanding, sadness, terror, a thousand different emotions.

Each time his foot touched silver, a bell rang; each tone higher than the last. The jubilant music soared as Darith reached the top of the silver stairs and turned to look down at Selvern. Could the Prince really have intended to do this? Their eyes met, and Selvern gave him an encouraging smile. Beyond him, Mannus's face was radiant, and Gonquin's thin features bore his usual sardonic grin.

The throne room below was filling with people in brightly coloured garments of rich fabric and elaborate cut. They came rushing, drawn by the bells that had rung with each step that Darith took.

Darith took a deep breath, and sat upon the Ancient Throne.

At once he felt the sacred power of the Earth flowing through him, and saw through the sapphire eyes of the Throne, as he saw through the eye in the spike of his crown.

Saw the Land of Tondur.

From this bright, warm southern city to the outermost frozen northern point of the peninsula, the King saw and felt his land. The sun glittered far away on the opal-shot green of the Sea of Salmon.

Through the eyes of the Throne, Darith watched the crowd below, and at a glance he knew their names, saw how the life force flowed through their bodies. He could see sickness or health, he could see love or hate, he could see loyalty, treachery, compassion, or fear.

He could see pity, and puzzlement, and it troubled him.

He saw Selvern reach out to draw a Lady in court dress to his side, and he saw love between them, love and a match of personalities like the complementary halves of a snapped coin.

He saw a woman in white come from out of the crowd to join Gonquin: her hair flower yellow, her eyes the brown-gold of a pheasant's wings. Then Darith knew her to be Edarissa, Gonquin's sister, for her eyes were the eyes of Tharda—Lonárissa's eyes.

But alone among all that multitude, she stared not at the King, but at Mannus, and through the eyes of the Throne Darith saw a sudden flame flare inside her—a flame that was answered, mirrored, as Mannus turned, and his eyes widened in astonishment as they met hers.

Through the eyes of the Throne he could see, far away, Castle Colyn beyond the mountains, and dimly sense the grumbling servants there, shivering in the cold. There was cold in the low stone houses nestled into the folds of the hills, too, where women's eyes avoided the empty places by the fires. He could see the great Castle of Clan Scarriv, where Raonull's widow waited, unknowing, for her Lord's return.

He could sense the nervous merchants in Dalgir, wondering if their ships would ever sail home again, or whether the black ships of the Pirate Fleet would swoop out of the frozen sea to burn their town.

He sensed the burgeoning life in the land where Kreelath had once reigned; grass already thigh-high, vines smothering the bare slopes in an attempt to make up for all the thwarted seasons when nothing had grown. Men were scratching out gardens; seed grain was already sprouting in the newly ploughed fields, and soon the red earth would be covered by a haze of tender green.

He could sense distant thoughts of plowmen and fishermen, watching the weather, caring nothing for King, for coronation or for war, so long as spring came again.

He felt the drowsy dreams of bears sleeping under the earth; the suffering of the wolf who wandered in the mountains; of a wolverine prowling hungry in the back country; of moose stripping the twigs in the deep snows. He watched the shoals of salmon that gave the Salmon Sea its name.

And beyond that, at a deeper level still, he felt the slow shifting of sap and stirring of seed in preparation for the coming of spring, and the humble spirits of the stones and the earth, working their slow changes, as warming sunlight thawed the frost.

A few moments ago he had been unable to see. Now,

through the eyes set in the back of the Ancient Throne, he
saw—everything.

He rested one arm upon the armrest at the side of the
Throne, aware suddenly of its size.

It had been made to hold not one sovereign, but two.

In the streets of Kaerbradan there was rejoicing for the
news of victory and for the coming of the King. If the people
were puzzled by the name of their new ruler, they gave little
sign of it. Prince Selvern had crowned him, after all, and the
Throne had accepted him.

From his chamber in the Palace, Darith could hear them
singing. The feeling of ease in his body was still a wonder to
him; it was not the stolen life that had burned within him
when he carried the Demon's Sword, but a sweet equilib-
rium.

The Curse had fled from the power of the Crown. But he
could not leave the city. He could sense the boundary, like a
deadness beyond the city walls. So far he could go, and no
farther, and then the spell that bound Throne and Crown
together would falter, his protection would be gone—the
Curse would strike.

He was still of the Blood of Colyn Muir: and the Blood of
Colyn still longed for the Sword of Kreelath.

But now he was King of Tondur. What could he do?

Mannus ran down the street after Gonquin, the beer-mug
sloshing in his hand. He had never imagined so many people,
such an explosion of rejoicing. Even Harvest Festival at Castle Colyn had never been like this. He came into an open
square. The fountain splashed pink with something more
than torchlight; men were dipping their mugs into the pool
around it; Mannus realized in wonder that tonight even the
fountains of Kaerbradan ran with wine.

On a platform at the other end of the square musicians
were playing. As he stared, a dark-haired girl grabbed his
arm and swung him into the dance. He did not know the
steps, but that didn't seem to matter. He was light on his
feet, and the other dancers pushed and pulled him through
the pattern, laughing.

When the dance finished, he staggered aside to catch his
breath. A hand closed on his arm. Mannus turned, half expecting another girl, but it was Gonquin, who had managed
to retain a certain elegance even with his hair rumpled and a
button from his tunic gone.

"Worse than battle, isn't it?" the Troubadour grinned. "Some friends of mine would like to meet you. Come on."

They went on to a party in somebody's town house, and then to another. It was well after midnight when Mannus found himself back in the Palace, in the lodging of one of the King's guard. Prince Selvern was telling the story of the battle of the Black City, and Mannus listened in wonder, blushing when the Prince's recital came to his own deeds.

His own part in that fighting had already grown dim in memory, but Mannus found it hard to believe that he had really done some of the things that Selvern was telling about now.

"Hey—we're out of wine!" somebody cried.

"Have to go get s'more."

"I'll come with you!" Mannus stood up, anxious to get out of there before somebody asked him to elaborate on Selvern's story.

But the twists and turnings of the Palace were not for the uninitiated, or perhaps Mannus had had more to drink than he thought. Soon he found himself alone in a small courtyard, breathing deeply of the clean air. As the wine fumes evaporated from his brain he became aware of the spicy scent of herbs released by night's coolness. The damp breath of the fountain soothed his hot cheeks and he felt his spirit still. Moonlight glistened on the falling water, and played with leaf-shadow to pattern the stones.

"Mannus . . ."

For a moment, he was not sure whether he had heard that calling with his heart or with his ears. Then he heard his name spoken again. It was a woman's voice, and a woman's form that he saw coming toward him, white-clad as if precipitated from the fountain's spray.

She came out from the shadows, and moonlight made a halo of her hair. He stiffened, for the face, like the voice, was one he knew.

"Mannus, I have been seeking you."

"Lady, are you real?" His voice sounded stupid in his ears.

"You saw me this afternoon, before the Throne. I am as real now as I was then." She laughed.

"I thought that was a vision, too. I have dreamed of you so many times." He blinked as she turned, and the moonlight lined the perfect line of cheek and brow.

"Those were not dreams." She was not laughing now. "I

have learned more than singing from the Bards. I used my skills to maintain contact with my brother."

He must have made some sound then, for he saw her smile.

"I am Gonquin's sister, Edarissa, did not you know? I saw you first through his eyes. And then I found that your spirit was open to me too. Will you forgive me for coming to you without your consent or will?"

"Lady, only your presence saved me from madness!" Mannus knelt and kissed the hem of Edarissa's gown. As he crouched before her, trembling, he felt her hand upon his head, her fingers tangling in his curly hair. Once more Edarissa laughed, but there was something breathless in her laughter now.

"Madness! It is a night for madness, for the Demon is gone, and beyond all hope you have come, alive and warm, to me!"

He looked up, seized her hand and brought it to his lips. "And beyond all hope, you are real," he whispered then.

"Oh yes, Mannus of Colyn Muir, I am real!" she repeated.

In one motion he was on his feet again, and Edarissa was in his arms.

Spring came, and Darith King of Tondur sat upon the Ancient Throne. Far in the north he could see the ice breaking: he felt the heavy flight of the geese and the swift darting of all the birds that filled the air, as the sapphire Eyes of the Throne followed them north, to the thawing lands, and eastward to Castle Colyn. He watched the salmon swarming, saw birds building nests, as they had in other years.

And yet all was less than it might have been, as if some vital force was still blocked that the land needed to come into full flower.

He felt the snow melt in the passes, and sent his men home—home, where Lonarissa slept in the hills above Castle Colyn.

Only Mannus refused to leave him, and made one excuse after another to delay setting off for Colyn Muir.

The green days of spring flowered into summer, and King Darith walked pensively in a garden where the sweet scent of roses was released by the life-giving radiance of the sun. But his heart remembered a woman's beauty, and a green grave below the crags of Colyn Muir.

He strove to drive such thoughts from his mind. There

was much to put in order, for the Kingdom had suffered greatly in the war.

"Lord King?"

His head snapped up, and his eyes widened—*his dream*...

But no—Lonarissa's hair had been black, and the woman who knelt before him now had hair golden as yellow wine filled with sunbeams. She wore white, and her eyes were the brown-gold of a pheasant's wings.

Still, there was something familiar. Something that reminded him of—who?

"I am Edarissa," she said, "sister to Gonquin, your Troubadour."

He remembered her then, and saw in her face Gonquin's face. But also saw much of Lonarissa as he remembered her —knew the face of Tharda. How closely, he wondered, had their parents been kin to the royal family—kin to his lost Lady?

Edarissa, Gonquin's sister, the woman he had first seen in the Throne Room, looking at Mannus...and with love's flame blooming in them both. He felt strangely abashed, like a small child brought suddenly face-to-face with a Queen. He tried to answer her curtsy with a clumsy bow, but the weight of the Crown on his head caught him, stopped him.

"Is there a message?" he asked. "Am I needed within?"

She shook her head, fair skin showing for a moment a faint blush of rose. He remembered just a colour in Lonarissa's cheeks at some sudden pleasure or surprise.

"I saw you from the terrace," she said softly. "You seemed...alone. If you wish it, I will go away again."

"No—you have seen truly." He tried to smile. There was no way he could explain to this child, poised at love's beginning, just how alone he had been, and for how long. "Walk with me."

Slowly, pausing often to consider the serene perfection of a lily or the delicate enfoldings of a rose, they moved down the path.

"I should have known you for Gonquin's sister even without an introduction. You are much alike. There is Thardan blood in your family, is it not so?" He stood still, his heart thudding painfully.

She nodded. "My grandmother was sister to Tharda's King."

Darith stared at her. *If Lonarissa had borne me a daughter, she might have looked like this!* Blurred vision showed him suddenly the girl's hair grown shadowy as night. And yet she was still the same.

But he had no daughter, nor any son, either—only Mannus, with his broad shoulders and steady eyes, to be his heir.

And when Mannus and Edarissa had looked upon each other, love had sparked to life within their eyes.

"Now that the war is done with, you will be looking for a husband, I suppose," he said. Again the faint colour came in her face, then disappeared.

"I may look, but others must say what I have found."

Darith looked at her sharply, then stifled a short bark of laughter. Did he indeed have so much power? He supposed it was so. No Lord could command love, but a King who was also Lord of Colyn Muir must approve the marriage of his heir. Abruptly he understood that more than pity for an old man's loneliness had led Edarissa to seek him here. Until Mannus had been formally invested with the Lands of Colyn Muir, he was still under Darith's governance.

"What do you think you have found?" he asked very gently.

"My destined love . . . the other portion of my soul."

"He is very young," said Darith, probing. Clearly Edarissa thought she loved the boy, but would this glamour stand the test of the times that must come? "Perhaps Mannus matches your years, but until this war began he knew only the valley of Colyn Muir."

"He has learned much in that short time. He will learn more," she answered him.

"He has learned war, perhaps too well, but what does he know of the courts and culture that bred you?" Darith watched her narrowly. He himself had been brought up as a great Lord's son, and travelled widely before he came to Tharda, and yet all he was and knew had seemed beggarly before Lonarissa's perfection.

"And what do I know of the cold land from which comes Mannus's strength, of the stony hearts of the hills which have given him their integrity? You would do better to ask, my Lord, if I will be worthy of him!"

Lonarissa chose me, and the land was too harsh for her.

Darith turned on her. "You are young, and in love, and you think that life will blossom for you like this garden! But you cannot know how you will be tested, and how dreadful the penalties for your choices may be! I know, for I made all the wrong decisions, and I killed what I most loved. If you could see the future, you would not speak this way!"

"But I can. I do," Edarissa said calmly. Darith felt the slightest of shivers, as if some knowledge beyond bearing were drawing near.

"My Lord, I saw you in the future and far away, for I am second-sighted, and Bard-trained, like my brother, and sometimes, too, it seems that some other being speaks through me." Her golden eyes studied him, her voice deepened.

"The woman you loved is dead, but because of you, the Land that you have loved even more greatly lives. You have driven Kreelath from the World, and atoned for Colyn's sin. You kept your oath to Tharda's King, and have sworn to no other."

He stared at her. *Have I?* Darith wondered suddenly. Was he not bound now to this Crown on his head? Did he not owe fealty to the people whom he ruled?

But how could she know of the oath he had sworn when she was still a babe?

Then, through the jeweled eye in his Crown, he saw that another Presence shone through her mortal flesh and bone, and the hair rose on his neck.

She spoke, and in Her voice was the singing of innumerable birds; he trembled in the Presence of a Majesty that dwarfed all the power of the Ancient Crown.

"To destroy Evil is not enough." The speckled honey eyes changed, like wood bursting into fire, like flaming chestnuts kindling, as a glory that outshone the sun poured through Her. "Health must be restored, good created."

He bowed to that glory, and now the weight of the Crown bowed with him before Her awesome power, that paled all the world and left them talking in a radiant void.

Trembling sweetness shot through him: the taste of oranges and the scent of roses and the orgasmic sweetness of love all rolled into one.

"Colyn tried to destroy Evil by setting bad against worse, and summoned up an Evil that was greater than he sought to destroy," She said, "and in the end he was himself corrupted by it." Stars flowed around them, and worlds were made and unmade.

"Twin-Born the King and Queen came from My Womb, and so twin crowns were made. But then the invaders came, Strangers out of the East, and overthrew the line of the Sacred Kings. When they fled the Ancient City of Kaerbradan, only one Crown was saved. The Queen's Crown was captured by the invaders, and melted down for its gold.

"Colyn restored the King's Crown to the Ancient Throne." Her voice was beautiful and terrible with power, beyond all glory. "It is for you, his heir, to complete that task he abandoned in his fight against Evil."

She ended, and for a moment he saw Lonarissa standing before him, but now there were stars in Her night-black hair.

Then suddenly the vision was gone: the world restored, and there was only a laughing girl with yellow hair and pheasant-brown speckled eyes kneeling before him in that quiet garden.

CHAPTER EIGHTEEN
The Magic
of Ancient Kings

He had never before been in the Throne Room when it was empty.

Darith motioned to the servant to close the great doors behind him, and looked around. *Not quite empty,* thought Darith, for it was filled with light. The golden illumination of late afternoon came slanting through the long windows, refracting in a soft glimmer from the polished marble of the floors, glinting from gilding.

But all the room's light seemed to gather in the shimmer of silver that led upward to the Throne.

It was not silent, either, he realized. The bare floors reflected sound as well as light, and the great chamber was murmurous with echoes, as if the memory of every word that had ever been spoken here remained.

And the focus of all sound was the Throne also.

He sought for the inner stillness to hear it, and realized that the Throne was calling him.

He did not try to resist it. That was what he was here for, after all.

Edarissa—or She Who had spoken through her—had hinted that Colyn's work was not yet completed, that the task for which he had already given so much was not yet done.

But Kreelath was gone, the land at peace, the work of restoration well begun, and the King upon the Throne to heal all disease and hurt and to bring plenty to the land. What then was lacking?

Darith understood too well what he himself lacked— youth, love, and health that did not depend on magic. Yet, except for the last, he had been without those things for half his lifetime. Selvern, when his time came, would sit with a woman of power beside him upon the double throne.

She would share his throne, but for her there was no Crown.

There was the imbalance, the thing lacking—for unless the Queen and King were empowered equally, how could the land thrive?

The stairs chimed softly as he mounted them, as if the magic understood there was no need, this time, to proclaim to the people that the King was approaching his Throne. He took a quick breath then, and sat down.

Living flesh linked Crown and Throne, power surged, amplified by the connection. Darith braced himself against the uprush of awareness. It was not knowledge of the present he sought now, but to draw forth awareness of the past. He forced his breathing to slow and deepen, let the swirl of impressions pass by.

The Crown . . . awareness pressed inward until Darith knew nothing but the weight of it on his brow; he hovered, dizzied, on the edge of understanding the maze of magics it contained. *Eyes of Power,* he thought, *through you I see . . . let me see now that other, your twin—show me the Crown of the Queen that was of old!*

At first dimly, then with greater clarity, he *saw* . . . bewildering in their changes, the faces and forms of the long-ago Queens who had sat on the other half of this Throne.

But one thing remained constant. He forced himself to look only at the blaze of light that crowned them.

Like a brighter eye above the brow, he saw a Jewel: the twin of the one that glowed above his own.

A memory of power flared between them, and he knew that even the mighty magic he now wielded was only part of the balanced wholeness whose lack he had sensed within the land.

Three Eyes—two of the flesh and one of the spirit—was this a human version of the divine model whose perversion he had seen in the three eyes of Kreelath?

Shaken, he thrust the memory from him. It was that sapphire splendour that he must memorize. Could such a thing have been destroyed? Knowing the power of the Jewel he wore, it seemed impossible, and yet if the Queen's Eye were still in the Kingdom, how could it be hid? Perhaps it lay in some shrine, or beneath the earth in a forgotten's reiver's hoard.

Eye of Wisdom, show me where the Jewel is now! Darith waited, striving to clear his mind of speculation.

Once more, images pulsed through his awareness. And then, for a moment he saw a woman who bore upon her breast a pendant set with a scintillating sapphire stone. Above her a half-broken Tower rose, where three golden crescents flickered on a pennon as blue as the Jewel.

Then the vision was gone. But however brief, it had been clear, something with which to begin.

But who could he send? Selvern? No—that would cause almost as much talk as if he set out himself in search of the Jewel. Someone must go who could pass unnoticed; someone whose knowledge would not shame him if he were wrong, if this whole gamble failed.

Still a little shaken by what he had seen, he sent a servant with a message to summon Mannus to him, then started toward his own chambers again.

"At home they would not know you in that gear," said Darith as Mannus came in.

Mannus bowed with an unexpected, fluid grace, then stood and brought up his hand in the old salute, grinning so that Darith recognized him once more.

It was evening in the City of the Kings, and light from hanging lamps of crystal silk lent velvet a richer glow.

In the elegant surcoat befitting his new rank, Mannus looked like the young nobleman he was becoming, and not like the sturdy clansman Darith had learned to value. He colored a little and eyed Darith, who was wrapped in a long gown of crimson silk brocade.

"Nor you, my Lord!" He grinned again. "This southern city has made peacocks of us all. But my plaid is where I can lay hand to it in a moment—is it time?"

Darith shook his head. In all the press of royal business, he had seen little of the boy; it seemed strange after having lived so closely all those painful months of the war against Kreelath. But now that he had met Edarissa, he thought he could make a good guess about how Mannus had been occupied.

"No." *Not yet,* Darith added silently. He tried to find words for what he needed to say.

"Let me tell you a story..."

Mannus looked a little surprised. Darith suppressed a smile, remembering that all the time the boy had known him he had been fighting pain, or the Sword. And before that, his grief for Lonarissa . . .

"In the Dawn of Time, they say, the Gods of Old made twin Crowns. But the Crown of the Queen was captured and broken long ago, and no mere craft of ours could make such a thing. But no reiver can destroy gold and jewels. It must have been fashioned of gold, that Crown, and jewels—or one jewel, like the Crown of the King. If they could be found . . ."

"Did the missing Crown also have an eye?" asked Mannus, becoming interested now.

Darith closed his eyes; once more he ascended the Throne of the Kings, and let his eyes open within his mind.

"When the King sits with the Crown upon his head, then the needs of any on whom he thinks will be known to him, so that he can heal them from afar," he said softly. "The power of the Crown remains great, as long as it remains near the Throne. Then, it can drive away all powers of evil and darkness. But men do not look upon the world as women do. The eye of the King is not the same as the eye of the Queen.

"I have reason to believe that the Crown of the Queen must have also been able to see." He opened the eyes of his body and looked at Mannus again.

"Before you return to Colyn Muir, I have a different journey for you. Somewhere in the west there lies a Castle." He smiled ruefully. "I cannot tell you its name, but an azure banner bearing three crescent moons of gold flies from a half-broken Tower. There is a woman there, who wears upon her breast a sapphire jewel. I will give you gold. You must find her, Mannus, and bring back the jewel to me."

"Is she fair?" Mannus blurted, and Darith smiled, remembering the beauty of Edarissa in the garden.

"Fair enough—but that should not matter to you. Perhaps that is why I am sending you on this quest, for the loveliness of your own lady should armour you against that of any other."

Mannus looked up suddenly. "You know?" Emotion flickered in Mannus's face—uncertainty, or fear? Then Darith thought he must have been wrong, for in a moment the boy was smiling.

Darith laughed aloud. "About Edarissa? Yes—did you think I would disapprove? When you have been installed as Lord of Colyn Muir you will come back and claim her as your bride. But first we must finish our work here." He grew serious again. "Someone I trust must act for me in this thing." Even if he had been physically able to leave the city, there was no secrecy in the journeyings of a King.

"This is no whim of mine, Mannus," he went on. "I believe that it is for the sake of the Kingdom that this Jewel must be found. Find this lady, Mannus, and win from her the Jewel."

If there had been any protest in the boy's eyes, there was now no sign of it. He saluted once more and then was gone.

Mannus had begun to wonder if harvest would come before he found the woman he sought.

Summer filled the land with long, slow days of vivid green. After a time, the life he had left in Kaerbradan began to seem the dream. He had begged leave from his captain, and his farewells to Edarissa had been constrained by the need for secrecy. Did she understand? Secure in her wisdom, did she understand all the things for which he had no words?

And yet, if she had such powers, how could she love an ignorant, jumped-up tanner's boy?

Wet he lay many short nights under the sky, when crystal rain ringed the moon. But although he questioned many, no man seemed to know of an azure banner bearing three crescent moons of gold, and his heart grew heavy in his breast. Mannus rode on a fleet, jet-black mare, west through lands where the people were descended from the invaders who had swarmed into the Kingdom ages ago, before Colyn and the War of the Kings. He wandered until past and future seemed equally illusory, and there was only this quest that seemed to have no end.

And yet one night, when he was still riding west through summer, Mannus looked up as the road curved around a hill and saw, black against the fading gold of sunset, far across the forest, a half-broken Tower.

He looked long and hard at the Castle as he rode up the hill, through the dimness under the apple trees of ancient orchards, and saw at last, in the brightness from the rising moon, an azure banner with three gold crescents.

The moon had begun to turn all the land to sapphire by the time Mannus came to the Castle. He dismounted and led his mare through the shadows of the open gate.

All was still in the courtyard, leaves a-spin in the night breeze on the one tree, on the tangle of bushes that came to the steps. But there was something—he turned, startled, to look into the garden. Someone was moving there. Mannus could see no details of form or feature, only the flutter of white cloth, until the moon rose suddenly above the parapet, and the sight took him by the throat with an almost mystic good.

A woman stood outlined in moonlight upon the white stairs, with a blue Jewel blazing from her ripe breast.

Darith had been right. The Eye of the Queen's Crown still existed. It was here.

The heavy oaken door behind her stood open. He came closer, noting now the plain gown, the curving lips that reminded him suddenly of his mother's smile. Had that magical loveliness been a trick of the moonlight? The Jewel nested between her breasts as if she had always worn it there. Did she know what she bore?

"I am Mannus, heir to the Colyn Muir."

"Then you have journeyed far."

He stared at the petal-soft beauty of her delicate face. "I have been seeking you," he said at last, as if that were sufficient answer.

"What are you?" she said then.

"I told you my name—"

The Lady shook her head and smiled. "You do not understand. But I must not question you on my doorstep. Come."

A servant appeared to lead the horse away. The Lady was already in the doorway when he reached her; he stared past her into a long hallway hung with faded tapestries, and before him, a sweeping scene of the Wise Crone beside the dancing maidens.

And at the sight of that tapestry his spine pricked and thrilled: this was the legend that told how in the Dawn of Time, before even the Ancient Throne and the twin Crowns were made, the Blessed Goddess had settled the quarrel of the Gods of Old. But the figures seemed to move.

The Son of the Horned God was dancing in a Circle with the maidens of the village. The Moon God's son was trying to join in the dance, while the Son of the Sun sat on a high rock, staring up into his father's face. The Son of the War God wrestled with the Storm God's Son, while the Son of the God of Wisdom sat nearby, tuning a harp.

"Holy Ones!" Mannus gasped, and felt a sudden prickle on his skin, and a lifting of his heart, as he strove to remember the full tale.

Long ages ago, in the Youth of the World, the first men in

Tondur dwelt in small squabbling clans, and the Gods looked upon them and said, "Let us make a King!"

So they sought through the land for the most worthy folk and bred them to each other, and then each of the Gods seduced a daughter of the new line. A few generations of such careful breeding produced a new and noble clan, and now the Gods were meeting to decide who among this select group should become the King.

But each God favoured his own son, and the quarrel between them grew ever more bitter. At last the Laughing Goddess, in the shape of an old and ugly crone, stood in the place where the young sons of all the Gods were playing . . .

"Welcome to my home."

Abruptly he was aware of the woman once more.

She came to stand behind him, and it seemed that the light of her presence cast shadows, as though a moon had risen above his shoulder. How could he have ever thought her motherly?

Her Jewel blazed out. As if another power were moving him, Mannus turned and knelt and closed his eyes. Words came from his lips, punctuated by silences, as though something were trying to express itself through him that was beyond the language at his command—as though there were things that could not be said.

"For too long the King of Tondur has reigned alone. In vision my Lord saw you and the stone you bear. This is his word to you; 'Give up the Jewel, and great will be your reward!' Give me the Jewel, my Lady, that the world may be made whole once more."

The words ended. Mannus looked up at her, afraid, but now she was only an ordinary woman again. What had he seen?

"Your Lord?" The Lady stood a time, and her hand went to her breast, and the bright power she bore, the blue Jewel with the living fire of a kingfisher's feather, that was the very mate of the one that shone from the Crown of the King. Finally she spoke again:

"I see now. You have touched a Mystery." Her voice was weirdly sweet, in her gentle tones an unquenchable joy, such music as no man can play. "And you have come all this way in search of a dream," she said. "Are you of the Moon's Clan?"

Perhaps he was—as crazed as any moonstruck wanderer! Mannus stared, his heart beating swiftly, and shot a quick glance at the tapestry.

The Moon's Son ran into the Crone as he raced around the edge of the ring of maidens, trying to find a hand that was free.

He helped her up courteously enough, and said, "How may I aid you, Mother?"

"I seek a man," she said, "and you seem amorous enough, from the way you ran! Will you lie with me this night?"

The Moon's Son laughed both long and hard.

"Such a jest!" he said. "And from one your age! Mother, you should not frighten a young man so!"

"I do not jest," said she. "But since you have answered so, let your answer stand."

Mannus felt his pulse tremble as his flesh stirred, felt all his body focusing on the Lady beside him. Without his noticing, the door had closed, and they had moved along the hall. The blaze of the torches behind the Lady made a halo of her hair. Mannus fought to remember Darith and why he had come.

He was crazed, yes, wanting this woman when Edarissa waited for him in Kaerbradan. And perhaps he was crazed even to think that Edarissa would still be waiting. Why should either of them look at him, when the mire of the tanner's yard still clung to his shoes?

"Stay with your own kind, boy," his father's voice spoke in memory, *"for the great ones will break your heart in the end."*

But music was sounding around him, seducing the senses. Desperate, he looked again at the tapestry.

The Crone stood then watching the dance until the maidens drooped and dropped from weariness, and still the son of the Horned God danced, until he saw her standing there. Then he bowed, politely enough.

"What is your desire, Mother?"

"I crave a boon," said she.

"And what boon is that?"

"That you lie with me this night."

"Ah," he said, and although his face did not change, and he did not laugh or shudder outwardly, she saw him recoil inwardly.

"Indeed, Mother, all women desire that boon of me, and I have already promised this night to another—to many others in fact. I would not promise a boon I could not fulfill. Choose another boon."

"I will take no other boon!" said she. "If you cannot lie with me tonight, then lie with me today! Here and now, upon this ground."

"Nay, Mother, that would be unfitting! Yet there are many other things I would do for you. Would you have this Golden Mantle? It is yours. Do you wish my milk white steed that my father gave me, that runs more swiftly than the wind, and can gallop upon the sunbeams? It is yours! I have a drawer full of rubies as large as pigeon's eggs, and emeralds great as mangoes, and pearls that are as round and white as the moon, and large as the eggs of parrots. They are yours. I have—"

"I will take no other boon!" she cried.

"Then, Mother, I fear I have no boon to give you," he said gravely. "For love given grudgingly is worse than no love at all."

"Because of your answer," she said, "you and your children shall toil to wrest from the soil the grudging love of the earth, upon which all men must live. You shall plow and sow, and struggle to please the earth, that you may reap. Yet you shall get value for value given, and honesty shall gain rewards for your children."

The Lady's hand touched his shoulder. Thrilled flesh swelled. Mannus felt his fast breath fixed by the throbbing rhythm of the music that pulsed around him. His heart was heavy in his breast. Unbearable longing was in that music, fountains of healing and fertility, and fast gasping sobs.

That was not the tenderness he felt for Edarissa, but something as simple and overwhelming as hunger—a hunger that must not be fed. His promise was given to Edarissa; why was this woman tempting him? He had come here for something else, for the sake of the Queen's Crown. He had come—

Fumbling fingers closed on the ridged hardness of the heavy pouch at his belt. He reached down to untie it, thrust it into her hand.

"Lady—give me the Jewel!"

She hefted the gold, then looked at Mannus again, and let the pouch fall.

"Are you a merchant, then?" she laughed, "Sun-Descended?" and stepped away down the corridor, leaving him staring openmouthed. He hurried after her. And the tapestry stirred—

And the Crone turned to where the Son of the Sun sat on a rock, staring up into his Father's great eye.

"Oh Bright Child!" She said. "I crave a boon!"

The Son of the Sun slowly took his eyes from his Father's great orb, and turning to her, poured out on the sand beside his rock a stream of bright gold.

"Take this for your boon," he said. *"With this much gold, surely you can buy whatever you need."*

"Not so," she said, *"for what I wish cannot be bought by gold."*

"If it cannot be bought by Gold," said he, eyeing her suspiciously, *"how do think I can, or will, provide it? What do you wish of me, Woman?"*

"I would ask that you lie with me this night, Bright Child of Light."

"It must be more than that you seek!"

"It is indeed," she said, *"but because of your suspicion, you will not be asked to provide it. Instead, since you think Gold can buy all things, Gold your descendants shall seek ever, and because of your suspicion, they shall always have to fear that it shall be taken from them."*

"No!" cried Mannus. "It is not like that. This is not my gold, but it is all I have to offer you!" His voice sounded stupid in his own ears.

"Is it?" she asked then. "Look within your own spirit and read the wisdom written there."

He stared at her. She had made him see himself as mad, and filled with lust, and greed. But wise? He thought of the Lord of Wisdom, he who is both ancestor and patron to all Bards, and turning, saw the God's features woven into the tapestry—

And the Goddess turned away, and strode to where the Son of the God of Wisdom sat, playing upon his harp.

"Oh Singer and Dreamer," she cried: *"I crave a boon!"*

And he looked upon her, and knew at once who She was, and why She had come.

"Oh Blessed Goddess," he said, *"I can see indeed that it would be greatly for my good to grant any boon that you ask. But does that truly make me worthy of the reward?"*

"You see clearly, and that shall prove both a blessing and a curse to those who come after you," she said. *"And indeed, your sight would remove the point of this test, and so I would have to find another test for you."*

"So be it," he answered. *"But test my worthy brothers first. It may well be that they shall serve your purpose better than I should."*

"And if another fathers Kings, you shall father those who will guide those Kings," she said, and turned away.

Mannus stared up at the Lady. From her breast, the Queen's Eye shone back at him. That was why Edarissa's eyes had reminded him of jewels—gems whose brilliance had been graven on his soul. The Lady's eyes still glowed in a glory that was not the reflection of the moon, and he saw then that it was Her beauty that he had seen in Edarissa, for now he saw his beloved in Her.

"It is not by chance that through me, images of another fly to thee, my Lord," She said. "It would seem that until I was like Edarissa, you could not see Me! But now you are wise. Do you understand now why gold cannot buy this stone?"

"The Son of the Lord of Wisdom could not grant the Lady's boon," he said slowly. "His heirs served the King, as I serve."

"Answer the question that I asked you before—*what are you?*"

Mannus blinked tears from his eyes. "A madman, and a man of the soil, and a merchant, and a counselor..."

"And a warrior," she finished for him. "And what must you be to rule Colyn Muir?"

"Lady, I do not understand. The Jewel is for the King, not for me, that he may make a Crown for the Queen to balance the one the King wears, and so heal the land."

"And have you no part in healing the land?"

Mannus felt his heartbeat shake his chest. Hard experience had made him accept the fact that the men of Colyn Muir would follow him. But knowing that he was an adequate war-leader had not made it any easier to imagine himself living in Castle Colyn. *The Lord is the land. The Colyn Muir is the land,* he thought. *Not me! Not me!*

The Lady's arm moved like a swan's wing lifting; a moment of beauty that divided past terrors from future uncertainties. In that moment of stillness, Mannus looked back at the tapestry.

Now the Crone stepped to where the Son of the Storm God wrestled in sport with the Son of the God of War. And they wrestled on and on. For although the Son of the Storm God was far the stronger, the Son of the God of War had the more unconquerable Spirit, and when it seemed that the greater strength of the other must pin him at last, he strove until he escaped the hold, and found some new attack to place upon the other. And at last, the Goddess saw that neither would ever win, for all the strength of the Storm's son was matched by the will of the War God's son, yet the Storm's son was too strong to ever be overcome. So she cried aloud:

"Oh Mighty Ones, I would ask a boon!" And the two sprang apart.

"Ask and it shall be given!" the two said with one voice.

"I had not looked for so quick a response," She answered, smiling upon them. *"Nor that you would both answer at once. But which of you will lie with me this night? For that is the boon that I crave."*

They both looked at her then, startled, and she could see in their faces that they liked this not.

"I have given my word," said the War God's Son. *"I will not break it. Come, Lady."*

"I too have given my Word," said the Storm God's Son. *"So you need not trouble yourself, my brother. I will—care for this Lady."* She laughed at them, as the other turned angrily.

"Indeed, Lady," said the War God's Son, with a bow, *"it seems that you may choose which of us you will have."*

"And how shall I choose between two such noble warriors?" she laughed. *"I can see no way to choose between you."*

"If you do not choose," said the Storm God's Son, *"then you must sleep with us both!"*

"So be it!" she said, and laughed at them more loudly still as they turned woeful eyes on each other.

When their eyes turned back, she had changed.

They fell to their knees in awe of Her beauty.

"Both of you, indeed," she said, *"will bring me joy, and in return, I shall bear a child by each of you, a boy and girl, twin-born in one womb, and from their marriage shall come the line of Kings."*

Light blazed from the Lady's eyes, blazed from the gem above her heart. Mannus took a quick breath, and it was as if he had drawn that brilliance inside him. He trembled, feeling fire flare through his veins.

Mortal flesh cannot bear this! came the memory of his fear. *I will burst into flame.* But the Lady's radiance was greater still—as she had looked when she stood against Kreelath.

"Nor gold, nor blood, may purchase this Jewel," she said then. *"My price . . . is of another kind. Remember—'The Colyn Muir speaks for the King.'* You are all Men, and as you serve me, I am served by the King. If the Lord of Tondur would restore the power of the Queen, then for your own sake as well as his, you must stand for him."

Somehow they had reached the end of the corridor. Another door stood open behind her. Within, a fire was flickering on a hearth of figured tiles. A quick breath brought

Mannus the spicy fragrance of burning sandalwood.

He saw a bed there, rich with pillars of cedar and hangings of blue velvet lined in crimson and worked with pomegranates in scarlet and gold. Lynx furs made a coverlet, but they were thrown back from sheets of moon-pale silk, soft as the breast of the woman who stood before him.

Mannus swallowed. "Lady, I am pledged already," he said. But she was looking at him with Edarissa's eyes. "But —But how can I face my beloved now I have seen . . ."

"Do you not yet understand?" Her whisper was the rustle of leaves in the woodland, the rush of waves on the seashore, the roaring of the storm. "I am All Women. In Me, you love Edarissa, and Edarissa in Me."

The Lady held out her hand.

The heavy mantle slid from his shoulders. He took a step toward her, suddenly aware of the weight of his weapons, and the cumbersome clothing that constrained his limbs.

With his shirt and breeches Mannus shook off his confusions; with his sword and dagger he abandoned his fears. Naked he came to her, and she received him clad in beauty. Joined in her bed they remade the world.

Mannus never knew what name he cried out as he was consumed by glory. But the Lady changed in his arms—her hair was burnished brown, then fair, fire-bright, and then dark as a night full of stars. At the end, it seemed that he was holding Edarissa, but her eyes shone like suns. . . .

They lay together in the early dawn, and Mannus, looking down, saw lying upon his own chest the golden chain and the Jewel.

"It was not bought, but given," came her whisper, "given freely, as you have given to me."

"And when I come to Kaerbradan, I will give it as freely to the King," he replied. The trees outside the window were mist-veiled, but the mist was beginning to flush with gold.

"Do you ask nothing for yourself, then?" Her smooth fingers traced the muscles of his shoulder, paused upon the ridged scar where the arrow had torn through.

"You have given me self-knowledge," he said in a low voice. "What could I ask more?"

"I will give you the future, man of the North, and the deeds that shall be done . . ." The mists of morning seemed to swirl around them, and as she spoke, Mannus *saw*. . .

"To the lands where only sheep grazed shall come commerce, and Castle Colyn shall be its hub. There will be build-

ing of roads and new travel on the waterways, for the river of
Haunted Valley shall run clean. It will be called the River
Darith, and its water will grow food for all your people. No
longer shall the hill clans war over stolen sheep or rights of
pasturage.

"Greatness shall return to Castle Colyn, now that the
road that passes through your lands from Kaerbradan to the
Western Ocean is clear. Tribes of the southern coast will
come north to sell their wares; workers of silver will cross the
Salmon Sea to sell their daggers and their jewels."

He nodded, seeing it all in a succession of bright images.

"All these shall pass through the lands of the Colyn Muir.
Its banner shall be renewed to bring pride and honor to the
children of your loins. The Bards who dwell in the Castle
Tower Colyn Muir will make new and noble songs of the
bravery and beauty dwelling in the land; and new songs of
the deeds of Darith, last and greatest of the Blood of Colyn
Muir."

Darith! Suddenly the image of the man who had been his
father in every sense of the word that had meaning came
clear. But the power of the Crown had healed him! Or had
it? The older man's time was nearly gone. With the eyes of
the spirit he saw Darith's face filled with light as once it had
been filled by pain, as if the magic of Crown and Throne
were transmuting the evil that gnawed him into something
nobler, but no easier for humanity to bear.

"You will lose one you have loved," said the Lady, "and
in that loss, find gain."

CHAPTER NINETEEN
Testament of Glory

Darith thought and meditated, putting his Kingdom in order, one land ruled from this one Throne.

This city had been the great womb of culture, until the Kings had been driven out, the Queen's Crown taken, and the folk of Tondur fled into the mountains. Most of the people of the lowlands were descended from the invaders who had swarmed into the Kingdom ages before, before Colyn and the War of the Kings.

Colyn and his descendants had kept the highland clans apart, almost a separate nation, ruled by the Colyn Muir as agent for the King. Now the Colyn Muir was upon the Ancient Throne, and the road through Haunted Valley was open. For the first time since long before Colyn's day, Tondur would become one land again.

But that was not the task with which the Goddess had charged him.

The Eye of the Queen's Crown still existed, and Mannus was seeking it. Where was the magic gold? It must have been melted again and again, mixed with other gold, scattered far and wide.

Once more Darith ascended the Throne of the Kings, and let its sapphire eyes open within his mind. The eyes found bits of the gold in coins. Though men might melt down stolen gold, none can harm the metal itself, which no reiver would destroy even if he could. Not all was still in the land—but much remained.

* * *

Mannus was still gone, and the vivid green of summer had begun to ripen into harvest gold when another woman came walking in the garden of the King. She wore robes of shot silk whose leaf green shimmer flickered with sparks of gold, and at her ears and neck great polished beads of amber like crystallized honey.

But her hair was dark—not the night black waves he had loved in Lonarissa, but the rich brown of fertile earth awaiting the plow, and her eyes were like clear water that can reflect the blue of the sky or the grey of the clouds with equal fidelity, but which at this moment picked up the colors of gown and garden to glow with the lucent green of a forest pool.

Darith saw Selvern take her arm as she stepped from the stone flags to the gravelled path, and noted the ease with which they fell into step as they came toward him—she was Selvern's woman, matched to him already as he had seen them first in the Royal Hall.

This was the woman, not his lost Lonarissa, nor yet Gonquin's sister, who would one day wear the Crown that he was laboring to restore.

Selvern drew her forward. Green silk rustled as she bent before him;

"My Lord King, may I present my bride-to-be, the Princess Tarilain?"

Darith nodded, reaching out to raise her to her feet again.

That she was fair he could see—deep-breasted and generous in build, and tall so that when she and Selvern stood together even Darith, who was himself a big man, felt himself in the presence of the line the Gods had made to rule the world.

And yet if the Crown of the Queen was all he hoped for, it would lend beauty to its wearer. He remembered how the touch of the King's Crown had shaken his soul. Tarilain would need something more than beauty to bear the weight and splendour of the other diadem, if, he thought, he could find the way to make the gold he was collecting obey his will—if he could recover the spell that would repattern the scattered parts into a thing of power.

"I have seen you, of course," said Darith. "But we have been so intent on healing the wounds of war, there has been little time for the things that we were fighting for."

A gallant speech, he thought as she straightened to face him, and perhaps she would even believe it, though Selvern would know quite well that there was no reason why the normal social rituals of the court could not have been resumed as soon as the healing power of the Crown had eased Darith's pain. The truth was that he had not cared whether or not he met Selvern's bride. With Lonarissa, his interest in all women had died.

Only Gonquin's sister Edarissa had shaken that detachment, and now, as Darith perceived the veiled humour in Tarilain's green gaze, he realized that this young woman might also be someone to be reckoned with.

"Were you fighting for *me?*" she asked sweetly. "I had thought there were more pressing reasons for the war."

Darith glanced quickly toward Selvern, who was laughing.

"In truth, it was to get away from you that I went warring," said the Prince. "But our enemies are all destroyed, and I am stuck with you after all!"

"This is no political pairing, I think. You two have known each other long enough to be at ease." Darith looked from one to the other.

"I was fostered at court after my own parents died," said Tarilain. "He used to threaten to cut off my braids for bowstrings, and I used to teach the other girls verses to sing at him when he rode by."

"She tagged after me everywhere," said Selvern. "Once I thought to scare her by letting her come along when we explored the tunnels beneath the Palace, but it was my cousin who started to weep when we lost our way and thought we would never come out again. Tari's eyes just got bigger and darker, but she never complained, and in the end she was the one who found the way out of there."

"And then she grew up," said Darith, beginning to smile.

Selvern laughed again. "One day she was making up limericks about me and the court ladies I thought I was in love with, and then suddenly I was making verses for her—very bad ones, I'm afraid. But until I came back from this fighting I could never get her to take me seriously."

"Do you think I take you seriously now?" She turned to him, eyes wide. "I wonder why?"

Selvern took her hand and pressed it to his lips. "Do you?" His voice had gone a little hoarse. She turned her hand so that his lips touched the sensitive skin of her palm, and the passion that leaped between them was an almost visible thing.

"No . . ." she said slowly, and smiled.

Their playfulness had relaxed something in Darith that he

had not known was still tensed against the heart's more subtle pain. But as the Queen needed more than beauty, more than playfulness or passion was also required.

As he had challenged Edarissa, Darith knew he must test Tarilain, and with even more reason, for the physical demands of the mountains were still less than the spiritual stresses of Crown and Throne. Selvern had been bred to bear their weight, but what about this girl?

"You do well to accept him," said Darith gravely. "He did not go to war for your sake, but I am sure that the knowledge that you were at risk lent strength to his arm. We fought a dreadful evil, and paid a great price. Do not take that lightly, Princess."

"I do not." Now her eyes were as grave as his own. "Nor was it easy to wait, wondering what was happening, knowing only that we who remained must seek the strength to resist that evil and to guard the city and the land. We had our own war here, you know—and the price *we* paid gave you the Crown that you now wear!"

Darith blinked. He *had* underestimated her. She was watching him a little warily, but she had only spoken the truth, and he valued her courage.

"Tarilain took charge and directed the defence when my uncle died," said Selvern. "If it had not been for her, there might have been no city to return to!"

Tarilain shrugged uncomfortably. "It was necessary. But I am glad that the only battles I will have to fight now will be to give life, not to take it away—to build, to heal, and to bring new lives into the world!"

In that moment it was Lonarissa who stood before him, Lonarissa's sweet voice speaking of the child to be.

Women risked death with every bearing, for the sake of love. . . .

Darith turned away with a stifled groan. Dimly he was aware of Selvern's hurried whisper, but he knew the girl stood unrelenting behind him. Selvern was wrong to try and hush her. She had the right to words no man would dare.

"You who are so wise, and know so much," he heard himself saying, "if I restore the Queen's Crown, if I can find the Spell, once again there will be a Crown for *you* to wear. Do *you* know how the pieces may be made whole again?" He turned to face her, startled by his own outburst.

Tarilain stepped forward, out of Selvern's arms.

"In the Temple they taught us that all women are dresses

of the Goddess. See Her in me, and perhaps She will speak
to you."

She held out her hands to Prince and King, standing between the two men like the Goddess between the Gods of
Storm and War.

"See me!" she repeated, and Darith remembered how that
bright Lady had looked out through Edarissa's eyes. He felt
that power now behind this witch's look.

She sang:

> *"For Aid out of Radiance*
> *We call Thee! Our Lady, awake!*
> *Guide us, Immortal Goddess!*
> *Speak through me your spell!*
> *When one are two but none are all*
> *Lady, restore to us Thy Golden Spell!"*

Power came. He saw the glory of the goddess descend
into mortal flesh and bone like a bee into a flower, and before Her High Majesty all things paled.

"Know, O Lord King," She said, and stars exploded from
Her eyes in infinite love, "that the power that lurks in song is
more ancient than the stars, and for your needs the Spell of
the Molten Gold shall rise, for the Lord of Wisdom, also,
dwells always in the Heart of the Arts of men."

Selvern too saw her, his bride-to-be, as the Goddess, and
now the likeness of the Goddess came to all women as She
spoke with the King.

"Bid his power arise through his Bard. For the magic gold
that flowed up from Earth's hot heart is alive."

It was high harvest, and the fields around the city were
the colour of the sacred gold with ripening grain, when
Mannus rode back through the gates of Kaerbradan. The
streets seemed oddly unfamiliar.

Even that first day, when they had put into the quay, the
City of the Kings had appeared as wondrous as a dream, but
not strange.

It is not the city that has changed, he thought then, *it is me.*
Above him the lacy towers of the Palace gleamed against the
pale azure of the sky. He swallowed nervously. In one of
those towers Edarissa was waiting for him.

He reined his black horse up the slope, and when he had
changed his dusty garments he sought the chambers of the
King.

Darith was sitting by the fire, more for cheer than warmth, for it was not yet needed in this southern land. *Or perhaps it only seems warm to me because for so many nights I have lain out under the open sky,* Mannus thought then.

For a moment he hardly recognized his Lord, for the air around Darith seemed to shimmer with the power of the Crown he wore. Mannus remembered the terrible splendour that had glowed in Darith's eyes when he bore the Demon Sword, and the wreck who had lain so still in his hammock when it was gone. *Which is the true man?* he wondered.

Then Darith looked up, and all those images flowed together into one.

"You have found it!" The King's words were quiet, but his eyes blazed with joy.

Mannus did not have to ask how he knew—the Jewel hidden at his breast pulsed in response to the blue stone in Darith's Crown. He stepped forward, knelt, and placed the eye of the Queen in Darith's open hand. Bright as a king-fisher's feather it flashed, and from the King's stone came an answering flare. Then Darith looked at Mannus again.

"Tell me . . ."

Mannus stared up at him. *How could I have thought he would not see?*

"I rode into the west as you bade me, Lord, and at last I found the azure banner with the three crescent moons of gold."

"And the Lady?" Darith prodded gently.

The Lady—how could he describe her? Mannus tried to remember how she had looked as she stood on the white stairs with the Jewel blazing from her breast, but no details of form or feature would come to him. He knew only that she had been beautiful.

"She was like Edarissa," he said at last, as if that were sufficient answer. "I told her my name, and finally, after she had feasted me, why I had come. I had the money ready—I did not see how she could be aware of the nature of the thing she wore. But she was, Lord—she *knew!*"

He reached down to untie the heavy pouch from his belt, and placed it in the King's other hand. For a moment Darith hefted the gold, then looked at Mannus again.

"She would not take the gold, and yet she gave you the Jewel?"

"Her price . . . was . . . different," Mannus answered with difficulty. His memories of that night still had the power to shake him, and yet the details were curiously unclear. "And I paid it, Lord. In that moment it did not seem to me I could do otherwise. But she changed in my arms—her hair was fair, and then dark as a night full of stars! And, my Lord, she spoke to me—" He closed his eyes.

"Greatness shall return to Castle Colyn." Words came from his lips that had been graven on his soul. And finally, the thing that had haunted him all the long ride home.

"Tell your Lord that his greatest enemy was not Kreelath, but himself, and that conquest has enabled him to gain this victory; but you, by surrendering to me, have won a prize that is greater than this Jewel. In time to come you will know its worth, and its meaning. But I think the King already understands."

Mannus looked up at the King, and saw a brightness in the older man's eyes that was not the reflection of the fire.

"At the end, it seemed to me that I was holding Edarissa, but her eyes shone like suns! My Lord, how can I face my beloved now? I do not understand!"

Darith nodded. "I think I have seen Her, this Lady of yours. Perhaps it is not by chance that She held the Jewel. Do not fear to tell Edarissa what you have done; I think that she will understand this better than you do, for you have touched a Mystery."

Mannus sat back on his heels, feeling the tension drain out of him.

"And what about the message?" he said then. "I must go back to Colyn Muir."

This time it was Darith who shook his head. "Wait just a little longer, my son. Our work here is almost accomplished, and then it will be time to go home."

Mannus stared at him, his heart beating slow and heavy in his breast. The Lady's prophecy still glowed in his memory in images of glory. But one thing that she had said he could not tell the King—

"You will lose one you have loved, and in that loss, find gain."

As the farmers gathered in the gold of the harvest, gold coins were found and brought to the King. They spread the hoard out upon a long table, and one-half of the weight of Divine Gold from the Queen's Crown Darith could see shining in glory through the common gold. More had been found in rings and brooches in the jeweler's quarter. He placed them in a heated brazier before the throne.

Goddess, aid me now! Silently he prayed.

Then Darith summoned Gonquin, and bade him sing the story of how the Lord of Wisdom had first wrought the ancient Crowns for the Goddess-born twins in the Dawn of Time.

> "From Earth the Gold Arose
> Flowing out of Earth's hot heart.
> Now the Lord of Wisdom's Art
> Shapes the Gold that molten flows
> Often men in vain imagining
> Dream of shapes and wish them real
> But the Ancient Sage's singing
> Sets the golden atoms ringing.
> Wrung with longing shape to feel;
> Like a seed that stirs in spring
> Reaching for its growth as tree;
> Seeking what it is to be.
> So the gold, while flowing free
> Writhes and rises, till full grown,
> It shapes itself into the throne.
> Blue and sapphire eyes appear
> Jewels to see both far and near
> Yet the Lord of Wisdom knows
> Well for whom the gold arose
> And out from Earth's Heart he calls
> Yet more gold, and bids it crawl
> Round and round two Circles small
> And bids it rise in graceful spires,
> And open eyes that are sapphires.
> In the Lord of Wisdom's mind
> Perfect patterns are enshrined
> Shaped by First of Poets singing
> Rings of golden fire spinning
> Wrapped around the heads appear.
> Of the Twin-Born King and Queen
> Twined by runes thick and queer,
> Golden runes with golden sheen
> Atoms whirl like hungry gulls.
> Like leaves wings rise from rings
> the Goddess's gift-gold grows
> Flowing from Earth's hot heart
> Out of Earth the Gold arose
> And the Lord of Wisdom's Art
> Molds the shape for all that grows.
> In the Lord of Wisdom's mind

Perfect patterns are enshrined
Into patterns atoms twined
Seek the Shape that they must find.
So was grown the magic strong
From the Lord of Wisdom's song."

And Darith fixed all the eyes of Throne and Crown upon the melting gold, and let the words of Gonquin's song work through him, and he told Mannus to place in the molten mass the Jewel called the Eye of the Queen.

Again he wondered at the power of the Crown. The gauzy fabric of space must be folded many times before its rich brocade grows thick enough to see. Through the eyes of the Throne he saw golden atoms whirling in a ring, as spires rose like flames.

And out of the spell of the molten gold, the form of a Crown arose, whole and new.

And he had thought his life such a barren thing!

And so it was done. Darith summoned Prince Selvern, Princess Tarilain and the people before the rising stair of the Ancient Throne.

The deep blue star sapphires set in the gold of the Ancient Throne gleamed watchfully as Gonquin and Mannus took their places to either side. With doubled vision, Darith saw the kaleidoscope of court robes before him and the multicolored tapestry that was the life of Tondur.

He felt the weight of the Crown upon his head and thought, *Now the time to fulfill this trust is come.*

He stood as Selvern and Tarilain ascended the silver stairs.

"This mantle is too heavy," King Darith said. He reached out, took the thin gold circlet gently from Selvern's brow, and handed it to Gonquin. "And I am too old to rightly serve the land."

With a single swift motion he pulled the mantle from his shoulders and swept it around the Prince.

Selvern's face flushed as he began to understand, but then he bit his lip, accepting, and Darith lifted the Crown from his head and settled it firmly on that of the rightful heir to the Ancient Throne.

Pain returned now, tearing, clawing, but he held his body's responses in check, compelled the muscles of his face not to give him away.

"The King is dead," he said strongly. "Long live the King."

And from all those he had gathered in the throne room rose the cry: *"Long live the King!"*

Darith staggered, his ears ringing, tasting blood in his mouth. *How well the Crown rides his head,* he thought, as he fell forward into King Selvern's arms.

Darith revived as the power of the Earth, the power of Throne and Crown, flowed through him.

This cannot be.

Selvern's strong hands supported him. He opened his eyes to see the sapphire eyes of Throne and Crown and King all focused on him.

"It is useless," he gasped. "I will not swear fealty. You cannot save me again!"

"What need is there for fealty," Selvern asked, "between friends?"

"I have sworn no fealty!"

"Between men who have fought together in war lies a deeper fealty than any between King and Vassal. What is fealty," asked King Selvern, "but a formal imitation of friendship?"

"Crown your Queen," said Darith, gesturing toward the Throne and the other Crown he had placed there. "There is—" But no! The Crown of the Queen was already on Tarilain's head—

Yet he beheld not the Queen, but the Goddess. As Her Eye beheld him, the Spell of Health brought ease to his body, and he knew at last the Judgement of the Gods.

Darith rode home through Haunted Valley, with Mannus, his heir, beside him.

But Haunted Valley was haunted no longer. The ghosts had fled, the shadows dispersed, gone with Kreelath back to their spawning place: exiled with the Sword of Colyn. A lapwing played and whistled high above the dry lake. A roebuck moved daintily across distant green hills grazing on sun-cured grasses. Groves of young trees had sprung up, to hide the crumbling ruins.

"Poor Gonquin!" said Mannus, stirring the small camp fire, and turning the grouse that roasted over it. "He was hoping to come here to dig up the secrets of this place. I don't think there will be much left for him to find."

Great winds blew through the valley. Darith glanced

around him at scattered stones from which ravens whirled upward, at powdery mounds where once the Dark Idols had stood. He shuddered.

"It will be as well if the secrets of this place are never dug out again," he said somberly, remembering what Colyn had seen here—what he himself had seen when he rode through. He remembered how he and Gonquin had talked on shipboard.

"The evil of the Sorcerers who lived here was so great that Colyn felt justified in the betrayal that called up Kreelath, and in opening the World to Kreelath's evil. It is Colyn's sin that we have been fighting all this time. Let us hope that it is ended now. With the evil cast out and the balanced power of King and Queen on the Ancient Throne, we may begin anew."

That you may begin again, he corrected himself. *It is already too late for me.* The Lady of the blue Jewel had been right. He understood her meaning only too well.

It would be a new beginning too for Clan Colyn, under a Lord with blood untainted by the Curse of the Blood of Colyn—the Sword and the need for the Sword. . . .

And the blood of Tharda will run in the Lords of Colyn Muir after all, he thought, thinking of Gonquin's sister Edarissa. The children they would have would be not cursed but blessed. He could anticipate the happiness that Mannus and Edarissa would know, as she bore her living heir to the lands of Clan Colyn.

With his heightened senses Darith could feel, still, death inside him. But the blessing of the Crowns had taken the pain away. After all that had passed, the Bard's promise was being fulfilled. When he rode into Castle Colyn once more, exactly a year and a day would have gone by. And then he would lie with Lonarissa in her quiet green grave in the hills.

The Blood of Colyn Muir would die with him, and the evil of its curse would be gone forever from the world, swept clean now, as wind and rain were washing its traces from Haunted Valley.

"We will need a new name for this place," he said aloud, "now that it is haunted no longer."

"Darith's Vale, perhaps, after the river?" Mannus looked at him across the fire, and Darith knew that he was remembering the Lady's prophecy.

"Perhaps." Darith smiled. "Without the name to frighten merchants away, you'll have many things coming to Castle Colyn that were always too expensive—dyes, spices, fabrics

—everything that had to be shipped all the way around the peninsula before."

"Well, that will certainly make life different," said Mannus, and went into an old joke about the chieftain whose son had made a pillow of snow. "Are ye so saft ye' need a pilla?"

Darith laughed appreciatively, but his thoughts continued to roam.

Fabrics, dyes, spice, all the things of the court—yes, perhaps the clans would soften.

But could any such luxuries alter the harsh grandeur of the mountain winter? The snow would still be as white, and as cold.

"Colyn Muir," he said at last, "rules an old and proud land, and a race of proud men. These highlands are not given to the breeding of weakness. When weakness creeps in, then the mountains give us harsh weather and storms, or drought and famine—and the weakness is gone. Sometimes we toughen from the ordeal—sometimes we die, and new blood replaces the old." He looked at Mannus and smiled. "Luxuries will not corrupt us. Not for long."

He slept peacefully in that nameless valley, while nightingales sang, and in the morning they rose and rode away.

Brown, red, and golden leaves flew from the trees, and the great winds of autumn scoured away the traces of sorcery and pain, cleansing the remnants of ancient evil from the land, as the Colyn Muir and his heir rode home.

PAUL EDWIN ZIMMER's first novel, the two-volume *Dark Border*, attracted an enthusiastic following. The knowledge of swordsmanship displayed in all his work comes from his many years of study of European and Oriental sword-forms. The richness and diversity of language with which he writes comes from an equally intense study of poetry—he has performed from Las Vegas to Rhode Island, and is well-known to the Berkeley, California, coffeehouse-reading scene. His poems have been published in a number of magazines.

JON DeCLES began publishing short stories in the sixties. His first novel, *The Particolored Unicorn*, was sold chapter by chapter to an enthusiastic fan club long before its publication in book form. Like all his work, it is characterized by a delicate sense of humor and a richly colored, at times almost baroque, sense of the fantastic. His flair for the dramatic derives from many years of experience in theater, in roles including Mark Twain, Edgar Allen Poe, and Charles Dickens.